THE LIFE YOU WANT

By Emily Barr

Backpack
Baggage
Cuban Heels
Atlantic Shift
Plan B
Out of my Depth
The Sisterhood
The Life You Want

The Life You Want

Emily Barr

WITHDRAWN FROM STOCK

headline
review

First published in 2009 by HEADLINE REVIEW
An imprint of HEADLINE PUBLISHING GROUP

1

Cataloguing in Publication Data is available from the British Library

Hardback 978 0 7553 3558 9
Trade paperback 978 0 7553 3559 6

Typeset in Garamond by Palimpsest Book Production Limited,
Grangemouth, Stirlingshire

Printed and bound in Great Britain by
CPI Mackays, Chatham ME5 8TD

HEADLINE PUBLISHING GROUP
An Hachette UK Company
338 Euston Road
London NW1 3BH

www.headline.co.uk
www.hachette.co.uk

For James, Gabe, Seb and Lottie with lots of love

First of all, thank you to Samantha Lloyd for coming on the best research trip ever, and to Laurie Keane for transportation advice. Many thanks to Michael Rosen. Thanks to Harriet Evans, Leah Woodburn and Jonny Geller for their patience; to my cousin Tansy Evans for letting me appropriate her name again, and my other cousin Jessica Barr for the word 'maggot'.

Finally, thank you, as ever, to James and the children, for everything.

chapter one

I think I am having a breakdown, and nobody has any idea.

It is preposterous. I am lucky; incredibly lucky. There is no reason for me to have a breakdown. I have the perfect life; I have it all. A strong marriage, two beautiful children, freelance work I do because I want to, not because I have to. Security of every sort. I am, therefore, happy. I remind myself of this, all the time.

There are times, however, when something overwhelms me. It happens without warning, in the most ordinary of situations. Today, for example, I am sitting on a tiny table, an ungainly giant in a world made for little people, and having an innocuous conversation with my son's teacher, when my vision starts to cloud over, and the ringing sounds in my ears.

I hear his words as if through a tunnel. '. . . not Beijing, though,' he is saying. 'I have a bit of a yen to spend some time in some of those places where you're days and days away from the nearest city, and it gets light at ten in the morning.'

It always starts this way. I don't say a word. I grip the edge of the table as hard as I can, with both hands. At home, I would slump down and close my eyes and surrender, but if I let that happen now, Mr Trelawney would call an ambulance.

So I screw my eyes tight shut, and listen to my heart pounding. It bounces around inside my chest like a dying fish. Then my throat constricts. I gasp for breath, as inconspicuously as I can. I open my eyes briefly, in an attempt to look normal. There are childish paintings of pirates all over the walls, and when they start rushing towards me waving their cutlasses, and shouting obscenities in Devon accents, I shut my eyes.

Then I realise that it has never been this bad before, and that I am going to die. I need him to call the ambulance. I am leaving my body, slipping away. I am vaguely aware that I am falling down, and choking on nothing, and having a heart attack. I am taking myself out of my life.

And it is exciting. At least something is happening. The world turns to stars and I give up trying to breathe, and drift away, grimly grateful, knowing that this is for the best.

'Tansy!' He is shaking me. 'Bloody hell! What happened?'

When I open my eyes, I expect, briefly, to find myself in hospital, being cared for. It seems, however, that I am on the floor of Toby's classroom. The wild heartbeat and the hysterical breathing have stopped. As soon as I was absent from myself, my body easily reverted to its usual automatic plodding.

'I'm OK,' I realise. 'Sorry. How long has it been?' As I speak, my eyes focus again, and I look from his beautiful, baffled face up to the clock on the wall. It is still twenty to four. I feel stupid.

'Don't move,' says Mr Trelawney, and he leans over me, his curly hair hanging down. I struggle to stand up, and he puts his hands on my shoulders and looks into my eyes. I look back. I am too weak even to make myself look away, as I normally do.

'I guess you fainted,' he says. 'Look, you shouldn't get up yet.'

I shake him off, more violently than is necessary. He pulls his hand back, as if I were on fire.

'No, I'm really fine,' I insist. 'Sorry. Happens occasionally. It's nothing. So, what were we talking about?'

He is full of wariness. 'China,' he says, looking furtively at me, waiting for more grand crazy behaviour. 'Look, at the very least, grab a seat. You can't go anywhere. Does this happen a lot? Have you seen a doctor?'

'Yeah,' I lie. 'It's nothing.' I try to think of a plausible diagnosis. 'Low blood pressure,' I add. It sounds convincing to me. I bustle about, pick up Toby's book bag, and push my hair behind my ears.

'Tansy! Let yourself recover.'

I sit gingerly on the edge of the table, and wait for my legs to solidify.

Toby saunters back into the room, and stands there, wholesome but scruffy in his green uniform. I am still shaking, so I ram my hands into my coat pockets, purse my lips to stop them trembling, and march over to my poor little firstborn.

'Hey, there,' I say, applying a big smile and making an effort to let it reach my eyes. I lean down and kiss his hair, keeping my hands in my pockets. 'Let's go fetch your brother.' The ringing has almost stopped. This will be all right.

Toby is skinny, lanky, six. He is wearing grey shorts, even though it is a chilly autumn day, because I keep him in shorts until the pavements turn icy, to avoid him standing on the backs of his trousers and making them ragged. Such are my concerns, these days. One of his socks is baggy around his ankle, and his green school sweatshirt is stained with splashes of lunchtime yogurt.

'Just a minute, Mum,' he says, full of enthusiasm. He pulls my sleeve, and drags me to the wall of pirates, all of whom are now behaving themselves, though I think I catch one winking in my peripheral vision. 'This is my pirate. Look, I put shiny foil on his sword!'

'I *love* him,' I say. I put all the excitement I can muster into my words. 'Well done, Tobes.' I turn to the teacher, who is now being ostentatiously busy. 'Why do you get them to do pirate pictures, Mr Trelawney?' I ask, though I meant to say *goodbye*. 'When everyone knows that pirates are bloodthirsty criminals?'

'*Does* everyone know that, though?' Mr Trelawney asks, looking up with the smile that makes me quiver. I wonder whether he knows what effect he has on me. 'I mean, they've been fetishised out of all recognition over the years, haven't they? It probably started with Stevenson. Arrr, Jim lad and all that.'

'Arr,' says Toby. 'Toby lad.' He laughs to himself.

'Captain Pugwash,' I say. 'Not to mention the horrors of those Johnny Depp films. Pirates have amazing PR.'

'What's amazing PR?' Toby demands, and I look at him, at his big dark eyes that remind me so much of his father's. Right now, I see Max watching me through Toby. He is guarded, wary, judging me. I often wonder whether Max has set up some kind of portal, whether he observes my failings through Toby's eyes, whether right now he is wondering what I am doing, hanging out after school with Mr Trelawney, flinging myself on to the classroom floor.

'Come on,' I say, and take my boy by the hand. My grip is almost firm.

Mr Trelawney smiles at us both. He has springy curly hair that reaches the nape of his neck, and a golden tan, and, unlike most of the teachers, he dresses like a surfer. I tear my eyes away from him.

'Bye, Toby and Toby's Mum,' he says.

'See you tomorrow,' Toby says seriously.

As I step out into the corridor, which smells of polish, and crayons, and eternal youth, it starts to happen again. I steady myself with a hand on Toby's head. There is a strange taste in my mouth. Black splodges appear before my eyes. Toby is saying something, but I can't hear him because of the blood swirling around in my ears. I can hear my heart pumping the blood around my body. It is not a 'boom-boom' heartbeat, not the sort of tidy beat you hear in the credits of medical programmes, but a great roaring swoosh.

I make the most enormous effort, stand still for a second, and nip it in the bud.

I try to talk about it, at the boys' bedtime.

'I thought I was going to die today,' I say to Max, from the table, as he gently closes their door.

He laughs, but in a whisper. 'Die of what?' he asks.

'Well, that's just the thing. Of nothing. Nothing at all.'

Max, the smooth, clean-shaven City man, looks quizzical. He walks across the room and puts his arms on my waist. I lean into him immediately, and we fit together the way we always do. He has sideburns, and an expensive haircut. I love it that he walks in from work and instantly, automatically, puts the boys to bed. I love it that he loves them so much.

'Right,' he says. 'But you didn't.'

I bury my face in his chest and try to find the words.

'That's right,' is all I manage to say. 'I didn't.'

*   *   *

At half past three in the morning, my eyes spring open. This has happened for the past four nights. Five days ago, I was living my life in a reasonably competent manner. The things that bothered me were mainly packed away into strong boxes, with lids nailed firmly down. One email has changed it all. A single, upbeat email, written with no intention of bringing my house of cards crashing down. I cannot believe it is happening: soon, I am certain, I will be sane again.

I look at the orangey light on the ceiling, from the street lamp outside. I can see the outline of the furniture, of my blameless husband.

When I met Max, when I realised that I loved him and that we would be together for ever, I was smugly amused by the fact that, in spite of my background, in spite of everything, I had ended up conforming to society's norms. I knew we would marry, that we would live in a monogamous nuclear unit, that I would accidentally be conventional. I should have known that my conventionality would be fragile.

I listen to the dull hum of traffic outside. My mother is right outside the window, taunting me for my failure.

'You're dead,' I say quietly, and she melts away. Max rolls over and mutters, but doesn't wake. The contours of his sleeping face are lit up in eery yellow. I sit up and look at him for a while. I hear his untroubled breathing, gaze at the bulk of his comatose body under the duvet. Part of me longs to pack a bag and tiptoe out of my life, to follow up Elly's idea. I will never do it. Instead, I lie down, roll up close to him. We are naked together, against each other, a picture of intimacy.

'Mm?' he says. 'What is it?'

I stare at him, at his smooth cheeks, the contours of his cheek-bones, the place where his hairline meets his face. I touch his cheek. Everything has been enchanted for us. That's what everybody thinks. It's what he thinks. I cannot bear to disappoint him.

'Nothing,' I mutter.

'Go back to sleep.'

I close my eyes, and try to think of nothing.

chapter two

At half past two, I have a bowl of clammy cold pasta and a drink. That is lunch. I eat it standing up, by the radiator, watching the feet go by, the phone held to my ear.

'. . . And we went to this wine bar,' Jessica is saying. 'And then Jasper came in, but he pretended not to see us, and Amelia says that's because I was sitting next to Conrad . . .'

'And do you think that's right?' I say, staring at the pavement that is at my eye level. A pair of clumpy boots goes by, with delicate female legs, clad in black tights, in them.

'Well, I'm not sure,' says my sister. I picture her, in her tiny hall-of-residence bedroom, with sensible bobbed hair, wearing black trousers and an ironed blouse. 'What do you think? I never thought Jasper would be one for playing games like that. But then he sent me a fish on Facebook, but he didn't write anything with it. I mean, what's that about? A fish? It was a pink one. I don't even like pink, and he knows that. In the wine bar he came over in the end to ask me about torts, but he didn't stay because some other friends of his came in . . .'

I look around, while her story continues. Our home is spacious for a two-bedroom flat, and small in every other way. It is reasonably tidy, because Max keeps it that way and because we have a cleaner, whose visit necessitates my weekly morning working in Starbucks; there is no way that I could sit around tapping randomly at my laptop while somebody's grandmother vacuums around my chair.

The windows are high in the walls, which Max always says gives a golden early evening light, but he is deliberately overstating the case. Occasionally a sunbeam comes in at exactly the right angle and gives us all gorgeous shadows and honeyed complexions, but it is like the place in Orkney where the light hits the altar once a year. Mostly we get no light at all. The living area is open-plan and L-shaped, with a kitchen area and a big, farmhouse-style dining table. Around the corner, we have two sofas, a chair and the television. The boys' bedroom is tucked into the square that is left by the L, and without bunk beds it could not possibly house two children. Our room, and the bathroom, are behind it. It is our burrow. We live half underground.

'. . . And she said, "You're not drinking the *house wine?*"' Jessica is saying. I pick up my own glass, and drain the dregs.

'Nothing wrong with house wine,' I tell her.

'Well, quite. So we said . . .'

I tune out again. The walls are so covered with stuff that their standard magnolia is barely visible. There are pictures by the children all over the place, and postcards, and, taking up more space than anything else, there is the map.

I go and stand in front of it, the phone tucked between ear and shoulder. It is next to the dining table, a part of the furniture for years and years. It shows the whole world.

'What are you doing in the holidays?' I ask, interrupting.

'Holidays? What, Christmas?'

'Next summer. Are you going away?' I stare and stare. I point to London, then fly my finger, as an aeroplane, all the way to the place I have long assumed I will never see. I imagine how easy it would actually be to do it.

'Oh, I've got no idea. Work experience, probably. In fact, I'll have to. I should start getting something sorted out.'

'Don't you want to go away? You could go anywhere.'

She is brisk. 'No, I have to work. That's the way it is, these days, you know. Holidays are for working.'

'You're making me feel very old.'

She laughs. 'Sorry. You're not very old.'

'Anyway, I have to go and fetch Toby and Joe.' I shift around, turn my back on the world, shiver. My stomach is contracted, and when I look down, I see that my hands are clenched into fists.

'OK. Look, we're doing a surprise party for Dad's seventieth.' She laughs. 'Now, *that's* old. Did Mum say? I'm coming down for it. In November, on his actual birthday. We're starting it in the afternoon so the boys can be there too.'

I imagine the scene. Family, stepfamily, friends, children. It will fill a day.

I hang up, and check my emails before leaving for school.

I have one new message, and I am rather nervous to see that it comes from GoThereNow!, an online travel agency I have been working for. Every week for over two years, I have tapped out a newsletter which has been sent to their mailing list. It is surprisingly time-consuming, and forms the basis of my tiny 'business'. I have not started this week's offering yet, and it is due tomorrow morning. But they should not be writing to me now: a girl called Azure has already given me all the information I need, and Bruce, the self-styled 'Head Honcho', never contacts me at all.

'Hey there, Tansy,' Bruce has written. 'Can I start off by saying you have done a more-than-amazing job of our humble newsletter over the past few years. And we really appreciate it. However . . .'

The chill starts. I don't really need to read beyond that 'however'. I have lost my job. I have failed in yet another way.

I force myself to look at the next few lines. It is all there: 'tough economic times', 'recession', 'making cutbacks wherever we can, just to keep our heads above water'. In short, Bruce is getting Azure to do the newsletter, to save himself a very small amount of cash.

I have no idea what I will do. I cannot bear not to do anything. I can't afford it, either. But I cannot bear to get a job. I blink hard. This is the thing I have been fearing for two years. I cannot possibly earn the money for Joe's childcare fees now.

Before I leave, I retrieve Elly's five-day-old message from the deleted folder, where I keep putting it. I know it by heart but I open it again anyway.

'Hi T, hope you're well etc. all fine here, heaps of people about, tourists everywhere, even some ozzies in the place at the mo. a rare treat to hear my accent. it's lovely and shady though pretty hot and stinky down in town.
anyway, i need some help. you know, every mail you've ever sent me, you say 'anything else we can do, just let me know'. well i'm going to call you on that one. i really need another pair of hands around the place for a month or so. we have a lot going on with the kids now the orphanage is up and running. stuff happening that i won't go into now but i'll tell all when i see you. the thing is, i know you, i trust you. and that's important for what we do here. i know you have your family etc, but would you come out for a month or so? am sure max can take care of things in london and it's about time we got you back to asia, don't you think? pondicherry and all that? let me know.
E xxx'

I shake my head. I know that I cannot go to India. My life is here. I made a conscious effort, years ago, and settled down to raise a family. Yet, for some reason, I have not been able to put the idea from my head. I imagine a tin can, deep in my psyche. The email has pierced the side of it, and the worms are slithering out. Elly's innocent words have opened the floodgates.

I met Elly in Vietnam, nearly a decade ago. She has lived in India for longer than Max and I have been parents. She lives in an ashram and does charity work with children; we send her money regularly, a pittance that makes me feel vaguely better about our comfortable, bland life. Now, apparently, she needs more than my money.

I snap the laptop shut, then grab my keys, belt my coat around my waist, and set off, on an excursion into the real world.

Unless I make an enormous effort and find another source of income that will pay the nursery bill while letting me work solely in school hours, I will no longer be able to justify sending Joe to childcare. Max could pay, but it would leave us short of cash, or Joe could stay at home and I could concentrate on being a mother.

I inhale deeply at the very idea. I wish I were the sort of woman who could happily spend all of every day with her three-year-old. Joe is the light of my life, but looking after him would drive me insane. I would not be good enough. He would grow to hate me, and at the moment he is the only person in the world who unreservedly loves me. That cannot happen. I must find a way to keep him in nursery, where he has a lovely time being looked after by patient people who have been trained for the job.

Max must have guessed that this was coming. This morning, he brought me a cup of tea in bed and sat down beside me while I was drinking it.

'Have you thought,' he asked mildly, 'about getting an office job?'

I swallowed and tried to concentrate. 'Erm,' I said. 'No. Why?'

He gave an undue amount of attention to the sock he was pulling on. Max dresses for work, every single day, in a very dark grey suit, a shirt which is either pale purple or white, a purple tie, and a pair of jaunty socks. He resolutely refuses to admit that the socks are a cliché. This morning he concentrated hard on the pulling-on of a Simpsons pair that Toby chose for his last birthday.

'Oh,' he said, not looking up. 'Get out of the house, make some new friends, broaden the old horizons. Don't you think?'

I could hear children's morning television, just outside our bedroom door. The *Bob the Builder* theme came on: Joe's turn to choose.

All I managed to say was, 'I don't think so.'

Our eyes met in the mirror, and I looked away. I wanted to cry.

Max and I were never about working in offices. We were always going to live our lives differently. We were going to work purely to save money for the next adventure. Eight years ago, we would have laughed long and loud at anyone who equated *broad horizons* with an office job.

For a few seconds, I allow myself to dwell, again, on Elly's breezy request. The only way I could help out at her orphanage would be if we all went there. And that is impossible.

As I turn to close the door, I see the picture, hung above the shelf where we pile the post. Max and me on our wedding day. Max grinning, tanned and far more relaxed than a bridegroom ought to be, an arm on my shoulder. Me smiling an uncompli-cated smile, my hair recently bleached by the American sun, wearing a tight cream dress that suited me in a way few other clothes have ever done, looking to the future in the absolute certainty of a life full of love and excitement and unimaginable new adventures.

That day, in the Peak District, I remember laughing at the way Max looked in a suit.

'It's *so* not you,' I told him. He laughed, and grabbed me round the waist.

'I wish you were in a frilly meringue,' he told me, 'so I could laugh at you too, but, Tansy, you are perfect.'

The pavement is wet and slippery. Rain hangs in the air, barely there, yet making things damp. A part of me thrills at being out in the city, the shifting, neurotic place that always manages to reflect my mood, where someone is always awake and nothing is completely quiet. I put my head down, pull my mac around myself, and stomp down the road. Out of habit, I cast my eyes down to the basement windows, hoping to see someone else looking out, the way I do.

The cars are already cruising away from school, their charges coddled within. As I get closer, I start passing children in uniform, dispersing around the area. I speed up my pace, almost breaking into a run. A boy who is a bit older than Toby brushes past and doesn't look round. He is talking to his mother with such inten-sity that he has no idea where he is going. I hear him say, 'And Mum? Then I got the goal, and everyone cheered for me, and that meant that we won, and Mum? That was the first time I had *ever* done that!'

I hang back, in spite of myself, to hear his mother's response.

As I look at the back of his downy blond head, I can imagine the eager expression on his face.

'Oh that's good,' she says vaguely. 'I've made meatballs.'

By the time I reach the school, the children, in their green sweatshirts, have left the building. There are just a few stragglers, and I hurry onwards, hoping that Toby might not be the last, that there might still be a few of them at the gates, waiting. Today, more than ever before, I cannot let myself be alone in a room with Mr Trelawney.

I rush past a skeletally thin woman called Olivia's Mum, who hurries by with the sainted Olivia grasped in one hand, and a violin case and an umbrella in the other. Olivia's Mum clearly doesn't eat, and her size-zero jeans are a reproach to my indulged curves every time I look at her. She throws her advantage away, however, by having rubbish hair, a home-cut greying Beatles pudding basin. She elaborately blanks me. I think it has something to do with a conversation we once had about the Gifted and Talented programme.

I have tried desperately hard to get on with the school mothers. I rehearse off-the-cuff remarks, and little jokes, but they never work. When I open my mouth, the wrong thing comes out. They have some sort of unspoken communication going on, and even when I say the exact words I have heard an accepted member of their clique use, I get wary looks and raised eyebrows. I know that my desperation must shine through, but I cannot ever manage to say the right thing. I have two friends: Sarah, and Mr Trelawney.

When Toby was in Reception, I stood at the school gates with a couple of other mothers, and laughed at what they were saying because I thought I was joining in with a joke.

'Tabby's actually reading at the level of an eight-year-old,' said Tabitha's Mum, back then. 'We had her IQ tested and she's almost off the scale. My husband's talking about *Mensa*.'

'That's *fabulous*,' I said. I completely believed she was messing around.

'Of course, girls are more advanced,' the woman added.

'They are,' said the woman on my other side, Olivia's Mum.

'Livvy's reading age is actually *nine*. She read the first Harry Potter book to herself this weekend. Finished it Sunday lunchtime!'

'Well, Toby's reading *War and Peace*,' I said, 'but he thinks the battle scenes are a bit facile. He preferred the Dostoevsky, I think.'

Olivia's Mum gave me an evil glare and has not addressed a word to me since. Tabitha's Mum looks at me in bafflement, and whispers about me. That was how I found out that they were not joking.

I sigh when I reach the gates. Toby has been taken back inside. I set off to the classroom, looking forward to seeing the gorgeous Mr Trelawney, in spite of myself.

Out-of-hours school automatically makes me nervous. There are displays stuck on boards everywhere, and as I pass down a corridor decorated entirely to a theme of Hinduism, I hear the clopping of my heels slow down. I take in the childish pictures of Shiva and Ganesh, Lakshmi and a couple of blue ones. I think of Elly's email, of India.

Toby is sitting on a little chair, drawing a picture of the Tardis, with a blue biro.

'Sorry I'm late,' I say from the doorway.

'Mum!' he says, his bottom lip jutting in petulance.

Mr Trelawney is sitting with his feet up, crossed at the ankles, on his desk, writing something on an A4 pad. I kiss the top of Toby's head, and make sure he has his book bag.

'Sorry,' I say. 'I'm really sorry, Tobes. Truly. I didn't mean to be late *at all*.' I say the last two words pointedly in the direction of his teacher, but without looking at him. My thing with Jim Trelawney is in danger of spiralling: I keep catching myself not mentioning to Max the wistful conversations we have had. I have saved his number under 'Olivia' on my phone, and I text him from time to time. The subterfuge is ridiculous, because if he were female, I would legitimately be friends with him. This is what I tell myself.

'Why *are* you, then?' Toby stands up, thin and wiry, staring into my face, demanding an answer.

'Jessica phoned,' I tell him briskly. 'I didn't notice the time. Sorry. Hey, Lola's having a surprise party for Grandpa's birthday. You know, he's going to be seventy. Don't tell him.'

Toby laughs. 'Doesn't Grandpa know how old he is?'

'Yes. But he doesn't know he's having a party.' I turn my attention to his teacher. 'Sorry, Mr Trelawney,' I say, swallowing hard. 'Sorry that you had to stay behind. I think I need some timekeeping lessons.'

I realise at once that this was a bad thing to say: inappropriately flirtatious, and impossible to retract.

Mr Trelawney shakes his head, and his curly hair springs around his narrow face. His cheeks are always a little bit rosy, permanently wind-blown from his hours on his surfboard. His features are casually perfect, as if he were a movie star, but he carries it lightly. His clothes – his loose cotton trousers and his Quiksilver T-shirt – are exactly right.

'Not a problem,' he says. 'I'd be here anyway. Though you can have private timekeeping tuition any time you want it.' He folds his piece of paper, puts it in an envelope, and hands it to Toby. 'Since you're here, Toby,' he says, 'could you just pop this down into Mrs Mellor's letter box?'

I take Toby's arm, to stop him.

'Give it to me,' I say, holding out my hand. 'We can drop it in on the way out.'

'No, let me, Mum.' Eager to be entrusted with a job, Toby takes the envelope and shakes me off.

'OK, then.' I capitulate. 'Go to the loo on your way back. We're going to the café and you can't wee in someone's garden on the way this time.'

I walk away, to the corner of the classroom, and I pretend to stare at the pirates. They do not rush at me shouting about 'scurvy knaves', this time. I notice that Mr Trelawney has added a note, in clear teacher's handwriting, explaining that 'Real pirates were bloodthirsty criminals, but today we enjoy treating them as amusing characters – me hearties!'

He follows me to the corner.

'So, how's Toby doing?' I ask, in a brisk voice.

'He's doing great,' he says.

I look at him. He is standing very close to me. I should step away, but I don't.

'I keep thinking about my friend's email. Elly's. I told you about it.'

Jim grins and pushes his hair behind his ear. 'Yeah. Does that mean you're going?'

I look away. 'I could only go if the whole family went. I couldn't leave them.'

'Take them, then. Great plan.'

I start to imagine it. I sit on a low table, and let Jim Trelawney's words wash over me. I imagine me and Max, backpackers again. I picture the boys, in little cotton trousers and T-shirts, with golden tans and sun-bleached hair. I see the four of us, living in a white-painted house, by a beach with golden sand. We eat fish curry (the boys miraculously enjoying it), and the boys play imaginative games with local children, using cardboard boxes and sticks rather than plastic Cartoon Network merchandise. The surf splashes my face, and the sun warms my limbs.

'Seven months in nineteen ninety-three . . .' Jim is saying. 'Three winters in Goa, over the years. Friend who stayed there. Just dropped out of everything and went to live on the beach. No idea what became of him.' Then he looks at me. 'Hey, Tansy,' he says, in a voice that makes me feel like a schoolgirl with an unrealistic crush. I try not to respond.

Then his hand is on the back of my neck. In spite of myself, in spite of everything, I lean forward, and our lips meet. For a moment, I relish it, lose myself in him. This is something I have imagined for months. I kiss him hard. He pulls me closer, puts his hands on my waist. I pull away just in time.

The door opens, and Toby is looking at us. Jim takes a hasty stride away from me, and I breathe deeply, and realise that nothing will ever be the same.

chapter three

In the café, I talk randomly and quickly in an attempt to block out the thing I have just done. I am making a concerted effort to be the best mother I can possibly be. There is no point fantasising. This is real.

The café is big, child-friendly, with high chairs aplenty, and jars of scabby crayons on the tables. The boys are tired, but eager.

'Can we have hot chocolate with marshmallows?' Toby asks, while Joe nods in support of this pitch. Joe is outrageously endearing. I am secretly offended that people manage to sit in the same room as us without coming over to exclaim over his gorgeousness. While Toby is as wiry as his father, Joe is chubbier, like me. He has big green eyes, and round rosy cheeks. Just being next to Joe makes me a better person.

'Sure,' I tell them, after a few seconds.

'Cake?' Joe pushes his luck.

'Why not? And then I thought we could bake some biscuits when we get home.' This is what good mothers do: they take children for treats, and they bake cookies.

'Oh, yummy.' They are happy, in unison. This is good.

I cannot help it: there is a manoeuvre I need to perform, and I must do it carefully. Today is an emergency, after all.

'Toby,' I say. 'Why don't you take Joe over to the corner there and choose a couple of colouring sheets.' The sheets are kept on a table, ready for all comers.

'I don't want to do colouring,' he says.

'But Joe will. Go on. You can hardly complain – I'll be buying hot chocolate and cake while you're at it.'

He smiles, nods, and takes Joe's hand.

I walk to the counter, and watch them across the room, Toby lanky in his uniform, Joe adorably haphazard in a pair of battered jeans and a blue sweatshirt.

A girl who can barely be out of her teens looks at me, the question on her face.

'Right,' I say. 'We'll have two hot chocolates with marshmallow. One large mug of tea. Two pieces of chocolate fudge cake.' I take my phone out and pretend to be reading a text. 'Oh,' I say, smiling. 'And a large glass of Sauvignon, apparently.'

'Sure. I'll bring it all over.'

'I'll take the adults' drinks now, if that's OK.'

There is a tall pot plant just past the till. I have pulled this stunt before, on occasion, and so far, it has worked. I check the boys, who are on their way back to the table with sheets of paper bearing the outlines of trains and rockets. I turn towards the plant. I tip the tea into the soil, hoping that I won't boil the plant's roots and give myself away, then pour the wine into the empty mug. I slip the wine glass on to the edge of the counter and walk to the table, cradling the still-warm mug, putting on a show. Nobody knows.

'So!' I say as I sit down. I sip my drink. 'This is fun, isn't it?'

My mother used to do this. I generally try not to remember, but, for a moment, I recall sitting in a café with her, after school, while she drank from a teacup and became gradually loud and abusive. But I am not loud and abusive. I push the thought away. But she is there, again, haunting me a decade after her death.

I talk, just to shut her out.

'What about a treasure hunt?' I say. 'At the weekend. We could have a treasure hunt, with Lucy and Ruby too?'

I have betrayed Max. A tiny, treacherous part of me is excited that I kissed Jim. Every mother in the school lusts after him; and he wanted me. But mostly, I am trying not to drown in the swampy blackness and the self-loathing that is creeping up, poised over my head like a tsunami.

* * *

17

At home, I throw flour and sugar, syrup, eggs, raisins and chocolate chips into the mixer, and make a huge number of biscuits. As I work, I sing 'The sun has got his hat on' and 'The wheels on the bus' and anything else I can think of. I sweep Joe into my arms and hug him until he wriggles, then sit him on the work surface. He watches me, and giggles.

'And can I have some mixture?' he asks. I put some on a teaspoon and hand it to him.

'Not too much,' I tell him, 'because it's got raw egg in it.'

I roll the dough into a log, and slice it, again and again, chop, chop, chop with a sharp knife. There is a glass of wine on the worktop, because it is half past five.

While the biscuits are cooking, I sit at the table with Joe on my lap, and I read to him for fourteen minutes, until the timer beeps.

'We're going on a bear hunt,' I recite. 'We're going to catch a big one.' I can tell from the shape of his cheek that he's smiling in contentment. This has always been one of his favourite books. He leans on me, completely secure.

'We're not scared,' he choruses, with me. I stroke his hair. He is, indeed, not scared. I, however, am terrified.

We end up with forty chocolate chip, and forty raisin cookies. It is insane, and when I survey my handiwork, cooling all over the dining table, I laugh with a decided edge of hysteria.

'You can have as many biscuits as you like in your lunchbox tomorrow,' I tell Toby.

'Can I have six?' he asks.

'Sure you can.'

'Can I have two right now?'

'Why not?'

He reaches for one, but pulls his fingers back.

'Ouch,' he says. 'You burned me!'

I know that I will not be able to keep up with this mania. Sure enough, there comes a moment when I am one of those cartoon characters who has run off the edge of a cliff. I know that when I look down, I will crash.

I might as well finish the bottle.

I call Max, on his way home from work.

'I lost my newsletter work,' I tell him, trying to be lucid. 'And I think I should apply for a proper job. You're right.' I do not say, 'And I kissed Toby's teacher, and this has been building for months and months, and I'm terribly afraid that I might do it again, and worse, just to distract myself.' I want to say those words, but I manage not to.

'Oh?' he says. 'What job?'

'There's one I saw online. A PA job, at Accenture. I won't get it.'

He inhales deeply. 'Well,' he says. 'You might.'

I don't even know why I said that. It is not the thing I meant to say at all.

chapter four

The next afternoon, I am struggling. I walk to the nursery to pick up Joe, with Toby, and concentrate very hard on thinking about nothing.

The clouds are lifting, and the sun is pushing through, lightening the grey pavements and the low walls that border the scrappy front gardens of the houses and apartments we pass. The air is fresh, for London, and as we enter the last hour of daylight, autumn seems to close in. Somewhere, there is a fire: the smoke tinges the air. Cars start driving with their lights on. Street lamps flicker on as we pass them.

This is London, and London has always been my home. I am chafing against it, every moment of every day.

When my mother died, I thought, with some triumph, that the worst years of my life were behind me. While she still lived, as soon as I was old enough, I indulged myself in the most flamboyant social life I could manage. I spent my life in bars and pubs, being loud and offensive, and using every method available to avoid reality. But at least I was living.

Everyone laughed at me. People I thought were my friends laughed at the fact that I would never say no to a drink, at the cocaine habit I flaunted. I was notorious: I went out every night, without exception. When she died and I was able to move out of the family house in Hampstead, I lived in a scummy flat in Soho, directly below some prostitutes. I never had the imagination to feel sorry for those poor, desperate women.

I flash on to a memory of myself, privileged, pissed, rude, shouting at them because their clients kept wandering into the flat I shared with Guy (Guy was one of my gang of pseudo-friends, most recently heard of being divorced by his second wife and moving to Paris). 'I am not a fucking whore,' I yell, in my mind's eye. I have no idea whether I really said that, but I have a bad feeling that I probably did, or something equally offensive. 'So do not send your fucking clients my way. Some of us have standards around here, you know.'

They cowered in front of me and apologised. I wish I could track them down now and make amends.

I was spectacularly rude to everyone. I had a horrible relationship with a man called Tom, whom I didn't even like, and we screamed and shouted at each other all the time and pretended that we were being Mediterranean and passionate, rather than miserable. Tom tracked me down on Friends Reunited when Joe was a baby, and tried to persuade me to meet him 'for old times' sake'. I happily ignored him, pleased with the knowledge that this would infuriate him. He tried to contact me again, on Facebook, last year, and I ignored him again.

All the same, a nagging internal voice is reminding me that, even though Tom and I were disastrous, I always let him know, usually loudly, how I felt. I never worried about disappointing him because I was ballsy, back then. And I never cheated on him.

I close my eyes and almost walk into a sad little urban tree. Toby is talking to me, but I am just saying 'Mmm'. I do not want to be this person.

The Mountview Nursery is a boxy building that must have been granted planning permission in the seventies. It lurks in a row of equally ugly buildings, at the bad end of a street that is otherwise lined with enormous Victorian houses. Hardly anyone at nursery gets picked up at half past three. When your children are tiny, the world accepts that you have work to do, that you don't get to drop everything and rush off to fetch your offspring halfway through the afternoon. Then they go to school, and everything changes: childcare becomes free, but short. It suits me, because I don't, in fact, have work to do any more.

I pay for Joe to stay until four. If it's five minutes past, I'm billed for an extra hour. I check my watch. It is quarter past. I shrug, internally. I won't be paying the bill this month anyway.

Inside, the nursery smells of wet nappies and poster paints. Everything is on a small scale, with tiny chairs dotted around the place. I feel ungainly in here, and the stuffiness of it, the tedium of a mass of small children contained snottily in one place, immediately overwhelms me to the point where I can barely move.

A girl who seems to be Joe's 'key worker' of the moment smiles at me with her mouth, while her eyes dart around, and alight on Joe, who is crouching by a tower of bricks, biting his lower lip in concentration.

'Hi, Alice,' I say to her, consciously using my best good-mother voice.

'Alison,' she says. She looks fifteen, although she might be as senior as twenty-three. 'You're Joe's Mum.'

'Sorry. Alison. Yes, I am Joe's Mum.'

''S all right. He's over there.'

Joe is frowning. The tower is nearly as tall as he is, and he has sensibly built it on a wide base. Slowly, he picks a yellow cube from the box, and stretches up to secure it on the top. The tower leans and wobbles. I watch my little Joe staring, helpless, as it falls away from him, in slow motion. He struggles to control himself, his lip wobbling. I walk to him and crouch down, and put a hand on his shoulder.

'It's all right,' Toby says briskly. 'I can build one *much* better.' He strides into the play area – the 'construction zone' – and starts piling bricks, working quickly and efficiently. A white-blonde girl, aged about eighteen months, toddles as close as she dares, to watch. Joe, as ever, is torn between resentment and awe at his brother's superior skills.

Alison looks impatient. She opens her mouth. I jump in first.

'Come on, Toby,' I say loudly. 'It's not your play place. This is Joe's place. And we need to go now. Can you both pick up the bricks and put them away in the box?' I look back to her, wondering why I am courting her approval.

But she could not be less interested.

'Daisy!' she says, looking at the tiny angelic toddler. 'Have you by any chance done a poo?'

Daisy turns and waddles off. Judging by her gait, and the aroma she leaves behind, I would say that Alison's hunch is correct.

'Oh, Mum!' says Toby. 'It wasn't me. It was Joe who got them out.'

I kneel on the floor. 'Come on,' I say, grabbing armloads of bricks and throwing them into a box. 'Let's just get out of here, shall we?'

'Don't worry about that,' Alison says, in a bored voice. She twists a strand of bleached hair around her finger. 'You off home, then, Joe?' she adds. Joe shakes his head.

'Going to the park,' he says gravely.

She has already turned to me. 'Joe's been a good boy today,' she says, with a patronising, sing-song intonation. 'He's enjoyed the book corner, and he had a lovely time playing in the kitchen zone, didn't you, sweetheart?'

Joe nods. I wonder whether he likes this teenager, in her Mountview Nursery sweatshirt, more than he likes me. I wonder whether she is closer to his age than she is to mine. Then I wonder why the nursery is called 'Mountview'. There is absolutely no chance of viewing a mountain of any sort from anywhere near it. The sections of window that aren't obscured by primary-coloured pictures provide luxurious views of the Spar over the road, and, today, a good collection of wheelie bins. I suppose they couldn't call it the Binview.

'This place should be called Spa-view,' I say mildly, pointing to the shop. 'It would be more accurate, yet still appealing.'

'Right, yeah,' she says.

The park is filled with little family groups. Even the grass looks tired. It is clumpy, scrubby, with patches of mud at regular intervals. The play equipment is the standard primary-coloured stuff that you see in every playground in the country; but it is ageing, battered by thousands of London children using it as their Great Outdoors.

Everyone here looks to me as if they are putting off the moment when they go home. A quick assessment of the adults in the play area suggests that nearly all of them are worried about cash. I can tell by their tight mouths, the hollow eyes that are focused elsewhere, the fact that they are doing something with their children that is free instead of the interminable faddish activities that the monied force upon their offspring.

I wonder, briefly, horribly, what infertility would have been like. I have a feeling that, for me, it would not have been a big deal. I am vile to have such a thought.

Sarah is next to the slide. Her cheeks are pink, and she looks every inch the obsessive London mother. Only the fact that her children are here rather than at Kumon maths or Junior Pilates suggests that she differs from the norm. That, and the smell of alcohol that hangs in the air around her.

She is holding her arms out, encouraging her daughter to let go of the bars at the top of the slide.

'Come on!' Sarah yells. Her hair bounces around as she jumps up and down to convey, rather too manically, the excitement and fun-ness of life at the bottom of the slide. 'Come on, Ruby! Down you come!'

I wonder whether I smell like Sarah. She cannot possibly have had just one glass. She has been drinking for half the day.

Little Ruby has Sarah's bouncy hair. They both have black curls, which reach past their shoulders. I always feel sorry for Ruby's elder daughter, Lucy, who has inherited her father's hair. It is mousy brown and ordinary. Sarah and Ruby have looks that stop traffic. Lucy and Gavin, her father, could lose themselves in a crowd of three.

'Rubbish,' Sarah says, whenever I mention it. 'I'm jealous of Lucy.' She pulls a hand through her curls, with difficulty. 'You have no idea what an arse this is. It's *pubic*.'

Lucy is on a swing, kicking higher and higher, soaring towards the branches of a nearby tree. Toby runs to grab the swing next to her from the grasp of a small girl. I look around for an outraged parent, see none, so leave him to it.

'Come *on*, Ruby!' Sarah's mask slips and her impatience shows. She notices me. 'Hello! Are you OK?' Without waiting for a reply, she turns to Joe. 'Joe? Darling? Climb up the ladder and give her a push, would you?'

Joe sets off on his mission. This involves inching past a small queue of children who are waiting, in a whingy, fidgety way, for Ruby to launch herself into the hands of gravity. I am impressed that he manages to do it, because Joe is normally shy and does not go in for pushing, particularly not of bigger children. He stomps up the ladder, calmly unhooks her fingers from the bars, says, 'Down you go,' and gives her a shove. She squeals with pleasure and lands in Sarah's arms. Sarah staggers backwards and sits down heavily in the mud, her daughter in her lap.

'More!' Ruby demands. 'Again, again!'

'Bollocks,' says Sarah.

'So, how are things?' I ask as she gets up and takes her coat off, putting on a brave face at the state of it. Joe follows Ruby down the slide, pleased with himself. 'Did I tell you, Elly wants us to go to India for a month to work with her? Well done, Joe.'

'You're jumpy. You're not going to *go*, are you?'

'No.' I look at her, and look quickly away. 'I might get a job, actually. A real one, I mean, where I leave the house.'

Her eyes are wide. 'No!'

'Probably not, but I feel I should. Do you want to come back with us?' I add quickly. 'Max's wine club box arrived yesterday. I put the white in the fridge.' Our eyes meet, briefly. I look down, and notice that I am standing in a centimetre of water. At least these stupid, expensive shoes aren't suede. I step hurriedly on to the grass, where my heels begin a slow descent into the boggy soil.

Sarah smiles, relief all over her face. 'Tabitha's Mum invited me and the girls for cat's piss tea and sugar-free carrot cake. You win, hands down.'

On the way home, Sarah tells me casually that Gav is going to be working in Singapore for a month, in the new year.

'They want to post him out there,' she complains. 'For a couple of years, at least. And make the rest of us bloody go too. Three weeks is just the start of it. And he wants to uproot us all and do it! He says he doesn't, but he does. He wants to swan around being the colonial master, having servants and drinking cold beer.'

I watch Toby and Lucy running on ahead. Toby scorns girls but makes an exception for Lucy. They are playing a version of 'it', chasing and pushing each other.

'Seriously?' I ask. 'They want you to move to Singapore?'

'I know. As if!' She is pushing Ruby's pushchair, her face set. I swallow hard.

'Singapore,' I say again. My head overflows with images of crowded streets and chaos, life, dust, humidity. Men in suits, women in silky Chinese dresses, me. I see myself in the middle of it all, wandering the streets, catching a bus to Malaysia, showing the boys a different way of living. Wearing flip-flops, going to travellers' cafés, being the antithesis of an ex-pat wife.

'If Max was sent to Singapore,' I say, as casually as I can, 'I'd be up for that.'

'Really?' She looks at me, and quickly looks away. 'But I thought you . . .'

'Long time ago,' I tell her, watching Lucy and Toby running from one lamp post to the next. 'I want to go back to Asia. I'm containing the impulse at the moment, but if I stopped concentrating, I'd run to the airport and get on a plane.'

'Have you been to Singapore?'

'Not really. I never even left the airport.'

Sarah becomes brisk. 'Well, not leaving the airport is closer than I'm going to get, I can tell you that.'

I keep hold of Joe's sweaty hand. The streets smell of exhaust and rain, and the sun lightens a patch of cloud, just to show us where it is. The encroaching night chills my nose and my fingertips. I am terribly afraid that I am going to be stuck here, for ever. That I will spiral into unwise behaviour with Jim. That everything will fall apart around me.

'Spare some change?' asks a smelly, bearded man on the corner. Sometimes I give him the coins from my purse. Today, I don't.

chapter five

As soon as I turn the key in the lock, Toby and Lucy push past and run to the television. The heating has come on. I notice an empty glass balanced on the radiator by the window, and I whisk it up and dump it into the sink. Its base is oddly warm, thanks to the central heating. I am slipping: I never, ever used to leave glasses standing around like that. My solo drinking, such as it is, has been carefully concealed.

'The children want to get a puppy,' Sarah is saying. 'Yeah, right. I'd have to walk it every day. I don't think.'

'You could carry it in your handbag,' I tell her. 'Like a Parisian lady.'

She nods. 'Except that they want a labrador. So while it's a nice image, I don't think I'll be toting it about.'

Joe sits as close to Toby and Lucy as he is allowed. Ruby, released from her pushchair, runs after him, and lies on the floor, chin in her hands, gazing at the screen. Joe and Ruby, as younger siblings, watch what the six-year-olds decree will be shown. I know I ought to ration television more than I do. It is on my list of issues to tackle.

Sarah looks at the glazed children, and closes her eyes briefly. Then she inhales sharply and claps her hands.

'Right!' she says, and I recognise the manic edge to her voice. 'Who's for juice? Who's for water? Shall we chop some fruit?'

'Erm,' I say quietly. I look at the fruit bowl. 'We're not actually very well plenished in that department. But we do have an amazing collection of slightly soggy cookies.'

She peers in. 'A mouldy satsuma and a squishy banana?' she asks, with a relieved laugh. 'This really is Pariahs Anonymous. I don't think I've got any either. Where are your biscuits?' Suddenly, she is standing in front of the map. 'And where's Singapore?' she adds. 'I actually don't have any idea.'

I show her. We stand together, and stare at Asia.

'Thanks,' Sarah says, putting her glass down, half empty already. 'I shouldn't, but I needed that.'

'What's up?'

She doesn't answer for a few seconds.

'I'll give you a clue,' she says, and now she is biting her lip. 'She is the bane of my life, and she smells worse than I do.'

'What's happened?'

'Arrested.'

'For?'

'Passing out behind the wheel. Of my fucking car. My lovely seven-seater. It's going to be in the paper.'

'Was she driving?'

'Not even trying. She was sitting there *pretending*, like the children do. You know, wobbling the wheel from side to side, saying "Brmm brrm", all excited to be going on an imaginary journey. Then she conked out in an alcoholic coma and jammed the horn down. Like the children *don't*. Cue every single voyeur in the neighbourhood immediately calling the police and getting off massively on the excitement.'

'If my mother was alive,' I tell her, 'I wouldn't let her within ten fucking miles of the boys. I'd get a restraining order. *And* I'd be on the next plane to Singapore.'

'You wouldn't. I can't. She's my mother and she would die on the street if I didn't look after her. One day I would open the front door and her corpse would be stiff and yellow on the pavement outside. She'd make sure she was right outside the house. If we went to Singapore she'd follow us just to spite me, and die there instead, and it would be worse because there'd be some cultural thing about looking after the older generation. And anyway, you wouldn't. You stuck with yours, too.'

'Yeah. It's impossible.'

We sit in silence for a while. I frantically push my drunk mother out of my head.

Then Sarah says, 'Mr Trelawney is fucking gorgeous. Don't you think?'

I look at her hard.

'Well of course,' I admit. I am scanning her features, trying to ascertain whether this is just an innocent remark. I wonder whether she can tell that everything contained by my skin has just turned to a stupid, infatuated jelly. 'Everyone knows that.'

'It's the ringlets I love. What's he doing in London? Do you know? He should be in Cornwall or something, being a surfer. Has he still got his girlfriend? The one Hector's Mum saw him with in Pizza Express?'

'I have no idea,' I say carefully. 'But I think he's earning some money to go away and have adventures. Footloose and fancy free, and all that.' I reach for the bottle. I'm going to say it. 'I like him because he reminds me of Max.'

Sarah frowns, an exaggerated, quizzical frown.

'Well, apart from the fact that he's absolutely nothing like Max – then yes, I can see what you mean.'

'That's what Max was like. When I met him. Mr Trelawney is how I thought Max would turn out.' I bite my lip. I should not have said that.

Sarah's face is a study in scepticism.

'Tans,' she says. 'You're remembering through a filter, aren't you, or something?'

'That's the hilarious thing,' I tell her, although it doesn't seem funny. 'You can't imagine it. But I'm not. I'm actually not.' I get up and hurry off to our bedroom, stepping over children and past the neon blare of CBBC. 'I'll show you,' I call back over my shoulder.

I pull the box out from under the bed, and grab a handful of photographs. For years, I have been intending to put these into albums. I should do an album of Asia, another of our more modest European travels, then one of Toby and one of Joe.

I pause, photographs in hand.

What will the album after Joe's baby photographs contain?

Toby and Joe growing up. I can picture them, ten and seven, and then fourteen and eleven, then pubescent, taller than me, embarrassed to have their photographs taken, looking away from the camera, shielding their adolescent faces. Then they will be adults, with jobs. I see Toby standing in front of the house (not this one, a bigger place we will have got by moving up or down the Northern Line), with his own backpack on, his face alight with excitement and nerves, off on an adventure without us. I see Joe, still sweet and solemn as a young man, packing the car, ready for university. I see myself as the mother in the background, quietly supporting them, waiting for them to telephone, my own adventures long since over.

Then I try to imagine an album filled with photographs of all of us at an ashram.

'This is Max.' I hand it over, indicating my husband with a finger. It is a shot from nine years ago, in Laos, taken sometime in the days immediately preceding our first kiss. There are five of us in the photograph, standing in a dusty lane, holding bikes. I am wearing a blue T-shirt and a baseball cap with 'Amazing Thailand' written on it, even though I hadn't been to Thailand at that point. My hair is loose over my shoulders, and I look happy in an uncomplicated way. Max is standing directly behind me.

Sarah leans over the photograph and squints at it.

'Which one is Max?' she says. 'Is that him, next to the guy with the bushy beard?'

This makes me laugh so hard that tears come to my eyes.

'No, Sarah,' I tell her. 'That's Greg. Max *is* the guy with the bushy beard.'

The Max she knows is a City worker in a suit. The man in the picture is a seasoned, carefree, and decidedly odd-looking traveller.

I carry on talking, my words falling over themselves.

'Greg was American,' I say quickly. 'Still is, but lives in Bangkok with his wife, Juliette. That's Anna. That's Marguerita. They were very wholesome and Dutch. I imagine they haven't changed. That's me – you can believe that, at least. And that really is Max. I made him shave, and I cut his hair, before I kissed him. A couple of days after this photo.' I grab another photo. 'And that's Elly – she's the one who wants me to go to India. She lives in Tamil Nadu. It's funny, she was a real "Australian on tour" back then, and now she does yoga and saves children. That's Eddy with her – he was her boyfriend but they split up soon after this. We were in Lhasa here.'

Sarah is barely listening; she is still holding the first photo, squinting at it. 'That is Max! That's the funniest thing I've ever seen in my whole life.' She is not laughing.

I pour us both another drink.

'You really would go back?' she says, an hour later. I am frying fish fingers, while Sarah boils frozen peas and mans the microwave and the potatoes within it. 'To Asia? I mean, you'd go to Singapore if you were me? It all looks really nice and everything in your photos, but . . . you know?'

'I know.'

She looks suddenly shy. 'I know you had a bit of trouble when you went before.'

I scrape a fish finger off the bottom of the frying pan. 'Yes, I did. In the past.'

'You want to go back?'

'Well. Yes. I keep thinking about Elly's email. We could all go. Max and I – we always said we would, when the children were older. We would go to Pondicherry. That would be the place. It's always been the place, and it's where Elly lives.'

I grab my glass and neck its contents back. Sarah instantly refills it.

'So what does Max say about that plan?'

'That he can't leave his job and we can't uproot the children and I'm being silly. I guess I need to talk to him some more. Make him see that I mean it.'

I turn the fish fingers again. They are black-ish, but probably acceptable.

Toby and Joe are fighting over the ketchup, watched with interest by Lucy and Ruby, when Max comes home.

Sarah grins. 'Hey!' she shouts. 'It's the beardy backpacker!'

As Max looks blank, Toby pulls Joe's fingers back, and Joe tightens his hold on the squeezy bottle. Ketchup flies into the air, and Max leaps out of the way as the red blobs begin their descent, but accidentally steps into, rather than out of, their path.

We all stare as the ketchup splatters down his pale purple shirt. His face – clean-shaven, handsome, unrecognisable as the hairy traveller's face in the photographs – looks suddenly mutilated. There are spots of ketchup running down his cheeks. There is a shiny red glob on his right ear. The children's faces are stricken, their eyes wide. Max freezes. I watch him, the banker assaulted by a condiment. I see him swallow his anger. His eyes are aflame with it. He is making an effort not to shout.

'You look like George Clooney,' I say quickly, because this is guaranteed to mollify him. 'In an action film. Where you've just been ambushed by the baddies. A superficial wound across your chest, um, nose and earlobe, which looks dashing and doesn't hinder you in your quest for justice.'

He nods at me, and then at Sarah, who is giggling. I see him make an effort.

'OK,' he agrees, at last. He kicks his shoes off, jumps on to a chair, and fires an imaginary gun around the room.

'That showed them,' he says.

The children laugh, relieved. Max climbs down, takes off his shirt and tie, wipes his face on his shirt then drops them on top of the washing machine.

'Hello, boys and girls,' he says, and heads off to change. I notice Sarah looking at his bare, and admittedly pleasing, torso.

'So are you going to ask him?' she says, in an ostentatious whisper.

'Ask him what?'

'About going to Pondywhatsit.'

I widen my eyes at her. 'Not *now*! Later!'

'Let's try my entrance again,' Max announces, returning to the table wearing a polo shirt and a pair of jeans. Even his casual clothes are corporate these days. I stare at him, trying to superimpose a springy-haired backpacker on to the City man, wondering if there is anything I could do to turn back time

32

and get the scruffy version back. 'So, how's everyone's day been?'

'Ruby did a big poo,' Joe informs his father. Ruby nods.

'Good to have the important news,' says Max. 'Well done, Ruby. So, Sarah, you're privy to the secrets of my bearded past?'

I hold up my face for a kiss. I hold my breath as I kiss him, in a futile attempt to hide the alcohol. Two empty bottles are lying down, beneath the milk cartons, in the recycling box.

'Tansy has something to ask you,' Sarah smirks, looking at Max. He turns to me.

'What?'

I kick her under the table. 'Nothing.'

'So I got an email today from some idiot over at Grahams,' Max says, when Sarah and the girls have gone and the boys are ready for bed. He pulls off his green and black spotted socks, wiggling his toes, and drops the socks on to the sofa. He does this every night. They stay there until I move them to the linen basket or the washing machine. 'Andrew Norton. He only signs himself "ampersand"' – Max draws the & symbol in the air – 'rew. I mean, what a moron. Anyone who can't spell their own name should be killed.'

'When he writes his full name, does he put "& rew 0-on"?' I ask, drawing a 'nought' in the air.

'I'd be amazed if he didn't. This is the guy who still bangs on about the absence of the letter "I" from the word "team".'

'Has he been on the receiving end of your famous ripostes?'

Max has honed two responses to 'there's no I in team': the first is 'and there's no "f" in "point"' and the second, when he's really riled, involves the presence of the letter 'u' in the c-word. I am beginning to think that, rather than focusing all his energies on hating people who talk in a way that annoys him, he might be better off looking at the bigger picture.

'He doesn't get it, so he ignores me.'

Max hands me a glass of wine. I accept it as if it were my first.

'He has no idea who he's dealing with, does he?'

'No idea with whom he is dealing. No.'

'That's just pedantry.'

'Sorry. But you're talking to the Bullshit Monitor, and some-times my brief takes me into pedantic territory. I almost strolled into the use of the "@" symbol, and called the guy in question a t-w-@. So, good day, all in all?'

'Fine,' I say. 'Everyone was entertained by the photos.' I nod to the shelf.

Max gets up, takes them, and flicks through, smiling to himself.

'I bet they were,' he says, with a chuckle. 'Those were the days. Everything seemed so straightforward.' He puts them down, and looks at me, suddenly serious. 'What were you going to ask?'

I look at the window. It is too dark to see the feet going past. I look at the map. There is a grey smear on it, where I have touched one word so many times that it is all but erased.

'Oh,' I say. 'It can wait.'

I am awake, again, in the middle of the night. Max has turned away from me. I stare at his back, listen to his breathing, feel the warm contentment radiating from him. I am as quiet as I can possibly be.

'Go to sleep,' he mutters, rolling on to his back.

'OK,' I agree, and I carry on watching him.

'Go on. Back to sleep.'

'All right.'

Twenty minutes pass. Then he flips over, on to his stomach, props himself up on his elbows, and looks at me. He smiles, in a wary manner, and I smile back. When it is just the two of us, things seem OK.

'Tansy?' he asks. 'Why do you never sleep? What's wrong? What *were* you going to ask me?'

I swallow and shake my head.

'Nothing,' I lie. 'I don't know.'

'You must know, a bit.' His voice is gentle, concerned. I shift a bit closer, warm under the duvet. 'You must have something on your mind, if you jolt wide awake at . . .' He looks at the clock. 'Three forty-seven a.m. Not a time to be up, if you can help it, is it?'

34

I feel sick. 'It's just. I don't know. I feel a bit out of sync.'

'Could you stop drinking, do you think?'

I laugh. 'It's not that. Honestly, it's nothing to do with that.'

'So? Anything that's going to make you feel better, you must do it.'

I take a deep breath.

'It's Elly's email. A week ago. You know. I can't get it out of my head. I feel I'm hiding away from things here. We're so . . . sheltered. Living such a routine. And now, I can't stop thinking about . . . Well, about my mother. And we always said we'd go to Pondicherry, just like we would have done . . . Take the children, when they were old enough. Joe's nearly four. They *are* old enough. Elly needs some help. What if . . .' My voice is trembling, but every fibre of my being is telling me to do this. 'What if you took a month off? What if we all went? Or you could take a year off. A career break. And we could have a different sort of life. Have an adventure. Do something different. You could dust off your TEFL certificate. It would be fun.'

Max is staring at me. I reach over, and switch the light on, so I can see his reaction. He screws his eyes up, rubs them.

'Sweetheart,' he says. 'I'm really sorry if all this has flared up for you again. But you're not actually serious about us doing that. Are you?'

'No one in India cares if there's an "I" in "team".'

'Sure,' he says, at last. The blood has drained from his face. 'But Tansy. I can't go. The boys can't go.'

The clock ticks. I say nothing. I hear one of the boys turning over in bed.

'Don't you think it could be fun? All of us together?' My voice has transmuted into a tiny little thing. It is a wavery voice that I have to force through my throat.

Neither of us speaks. We have instinctively shifted away from each other. I look at my hands, at my short, practical nails and their slightly chipped clear varnish. I twist my engagement and wedding rings. I sense Max trying to make eye contact. I turn my face away.

'Look,' he says. 'Tansy. Darling. We *did* say we'd go. But that was an ancient plan from before we had children. This is our life now. We're not hiding out; we're living a great life in an amazing city. We can't just chuck it all in.'

'Yes we can.'

'You know what you should do.'

'Do I?'

'Go by yourself.'

'No. Absolutely no way.'

'Are you sure?'

'We always said we'd do it,' I repeat. 'Together.'

'Think about it,' he says. 'I can't chuck everything in. This is *not* the time to be resigning on a whim. We have a mortgage, the boys are settled . . .'

I filter him out, and listen, instead, to the high-pitched, desperate scream coming from within.

chapter six

Alexia's thoughts
2.10 a.m. EST

Now, I am never going to be the sort of person who says, 'Did you see my blog?' I am not about to email everybody I know with the web address. I'm not likely to be filling out the profile section to your right any time soon, or attaching my photo either, or even mentioning my family name.

This is my special place, and it is particular to me.

So here's the deal: if you have stumbled across this, great. Welcome to my tiny corner of the World Wide Web. If nobody reads it, also great. But for anyone who is reading, my name is Alexia. I live somewhere between the East and West Coasts of the USA, and not very close to either.

This is my story.

I am thirty-eight years old. I am married to Duncan, who is my childhood sweetheart. We were together at school when we were thirteen, went our separate ways, and then came back together at twenty-six, and I realised that I had been right all along, that my first love had truthfully been my true love.

We were married at twenty-eight. We started trying for a baby right away.

At this point, my story should go something like this: we were blessed with a little boy and then a little girl. They drive me crazy but I would be nothing without them.

And, in fact, I *am* nothing without them. I'm not complete.

After a while we stopped talking about it. Duncan was able to put it from his mind, up to a point. At least, that's what I've always thought he was doing. I don't know – sometimes I think he's just as caught up as I am, but there are only so many times you can have the same conversation. Over the years, we've come to a bit of an understanding that we're happier if we don't talk about it.

For me, even now, ten years on, I hold out a tiny bit of hope each month. It's insane, but that's how it is. Every time, even with the odds stacked against us, we might get the million to one. Every time I get my AF (which is what we call it in online support groups), I feel someone has taken my baby away from me, yet again. (AF means Auntie Flow. I think it's a nicer expression, to be honest, than anything more direct – and I like to think of her as a person because it gives me someone to blame.)

So every time AF comes a-knocking at the door, I grieve for yet another one of my poor little eggs that has never had the chance to bloom. There can't be too many of them left by now. All of them wasted. I think of AF as a witch – spelled with a 'b'.

We went for tests. Oh, the tests we've had. Nothing. No concrete reason at all. Duncan's count is average. My cycles are more or less regular. My hormones seem to be doing the right things at the right times, according to all the blood work. We do so much BD that it became a chore years ago, but all the same, we do it on exactly the right days, whether we feel like it or not. (BD is another expression we use – baby dancing. Again, I find it nicer than anything cruder. I do wish it would live up to its name, just once.)

We had three cycles of IVF, to no avail. We agreed when we started out that three cycles was our limit. It takes its toll. I would go for a fourth try like a shot, but Duncan stands firm. From time to time I read about a baby conceived on the fourth or fifth attempt, and it just breaks my heart in two.

Years ago we started to think about adoption. It has been a rocky path: if you are not a big enough person for a child with special needs, or an older child, then domestic adoption is a difficult thing to pull off and you soon find yourselves looking elsewhere. And we have concluded that we are just not big enough for that. Actually I think I could perhaps provide enough love for a special needs child, but Duncan says no, which is his prerogative.

But let me fill you in on the other things in our life. We are blessed to have two cats, Milly and Brian. They are our prince and princess. Milly doesn't have our problems: we have been lucky enough to have been given three litters of adorable little kittens over the past five years, all given away to good homes (apart from Brian, who is Milly's son, and we had him fixed so he's not going to be a daddy any time at all – I was freaked by the idea that he might end up as daddy to his own brothers and sisters). Milly is black and white, sleek and queenly. She's my girl, my little beautiful baby girl. Duncan says she's a snobby witch, but I say, that's cats for you. Brian's fat and snugglesome. He often sleeps on our bed, and when Duncan's away, he curls up with me, cuddled into my stomach, right where the baby would be if there was one tucked in there.

I know that people laugh. My own sister laughs at me. She says I treat the cats like children. She thinks this is a great insight on her part. I'm like, no shlt, Sherlock. What other choice do I have?

So, Duncan manages a garage. He is a top mechanic, and that is how he started out, but he's area manager now. I work at the candy store. I have rows and rows of different types of candy. You might guess, I see a heck of a lot of children during the day. People think I must mind that. I don't, at all. I love kids. I just love watching them growing up, as the years pass. Making them flabby, rotting their teeth . . . only kidding.

I'm 38, Duncan's 38, and we don't have a huge amount of time. We see the big 4–0 approaching and we have to have a child before we get there. And this brings me to the purpose of this blog. I'm sitting up now, typing as quietly as I can (how nuts does that sound?), while Duncan sleeps upstairs and Milly pushes against my legs. I think that we need to push the adoption thing further, to start looking abroad. To follow a path blazed by such people as Madonna Ciccone, Angelina Jolie and others. For some reason, I am all caught up in the idea of India, even though the above celebs did not adopt from that country.

I have lived for too many years now with the fact that, where other people have their children easily, I will have to fight for mine. And, as long as we get the right outcome, that will be all right. As long as she or he is there at the end of this journey, the battle will only make me love the child all the more. And he or she will know what we went through to get there, and she will know exactly how much Mommy longed for her.

And you know what? The more I think about it, the more excited I am. I am going to post this entry now and go and Google for everything I need to know.

So now I shall sign off.

Bye, nobody

Alexia. x

Comments: 0

chapter seven

The voices are out of tune. We all stagger painfully to our jolly conclusion: 'Happy birthday, dear Roger . . . Happy birthday to you!'

There is a general cheer, and my father looks embarrassed. He shuffles, and looks at the ground, and clears his throat.

'Thank you,' he says eventually. 'I'd, er, like to thank everybody for coming.'

Dad is looking good for his age, and I suppose he must have some inbuilt charisma, something that appeals to women. One of those things that a daughter cannot see; but I do love him, for all his social awkwardness and general ineptitude. So, it seems, do many other people. His house is filled with family and friends, all here to wish him a happy birthday. His hair is white and flyaway. He reminds me of someone like Trevor Howard, ageing in a devilish, British way, but without the smooth patter. I find it impossible to dredge up a single memory of him being married to my mother. If I weren't here as proof, I could never have believed that it happened.

Lola takes over, as she always does.

'Yes,' she says. 'Thank you all for coming. Roger is a very lucky man to have his five children here.' Briony and I cheer; we are on our fourth or fifth vodka and tonic. This, I know, is bad. 'So, thank you, Jessica, for coming from Edinburgh for the surprise party, thank you, Tansy, Jake, Briony and Archie. Also of course to Max, and to the very apples of Roger's eye, our delicious grandsons, Toby and Joe!' Toby cheers too, and Max joins him. Joe beams around the room. Lola carries on speaking, thanking various people for various things, but I suddenly lose my sense of hearing.

The nausea reaches me abruptly. When I was in my teens and twenties, I managed to forget that I was poisoning myself until after the event. Now I feel it at the time. This is one of the reasons why I don't drink spirits. When I drink spirits, I feel myself beginning to die.

I wend my way urgently through the crowd that is politely listening to Lola thanking each of the neighbours by name, and dash to the bathroom. I skid to a halt in front of the loo just in time. An acidic stream of clear liquid pours into the bowl, and down the front of my red dress, and I cough and choke, and try to close the door with my foot. My throat stings. My eyes water. I slump on the floor.

The black spots expand, and join together. I will just lie here for a while, until I feel better.

'Tansy.'

Strong hands are shaking me. I resist. I only need to rest.

'*Tansy!* Tansy, can you hear me? Jess, you'd better call an ambulance.'

I open one eye, just a fraction. Max and Jessica are staring at me. Jess turns to go.

'No!' I shout. She turns back to me. ''Mfine,' I think I say. 'Not an ambulance.'

'No, you're not fine.' Max is angry. I pout at him.

'Don't be cross,' I slur.

'Shut up. You're embarrassing yourself. All of us. Look, I'm taking the children home before they see you. I think we *should* get you to hospital.'

'No!' I have been hospitalised because of alcohol once before, on the day of my mother's funeral. It is not something you want to happen twice. I prop myself up on my elbows and try to smile. 'I'm *fine*,' I say, as clearly as I can.

I see them looking at each other, my worried husband and my sensible sister.

'Whatever,' Max says, at last. 'But Jessica's going to take care of you and bring you home when you're up to it. Is that OK, Jess? The boys are upstairs with Jake and Archie. I'll whisk them away. Pull yourself together. For fuck's sake, Tans.'

He leaves without saying goodbye. I let Jessica help me to my feet. She leads me to her old bedroom. Then I lie back and close my eyes again.

The next time I open my eyes, the house is quiet, the party clearly over. I squint at a Barbie clock on the bedside table. Half past ten.

Then, I am shocked to realise that my father is sitting on the edge of the bed.

I sit up. Everything lurches, and the bile rises in my throat.

'What?' I demand.

'Tansy,' he says, looking at a spot on the wall above my head. I am lying on top of a pink duvet, in an oppressively girlish room. There is still a disembodied 'Girl's World' head on the plasticky dressing table, its face garishly made up. I know that if I look at it for long enough, it will start to speak to me.

'Dad, I'm fine. I just overdid it. I'm better now.'

He clears his throat. 'Occasionally,' he says, awkwardly, 'you remind me of your mother. That's all. I think you need to talk to someone, to go to somewhere that can help you.'

'My *mother*? That would be my mother, the aggressive alcoholic?' And I am teenage again, although I never said these things to him back then. 'The woman who pissed away twenty years of her life, slobbering drunk in a corner? The one you were kind enough to leave me with when you did the sensible thing and buggered off out of there?'

He looks away, excruciatingly embarrassed. He clears his throat with a little 'Hem'.

'Perhaps,' he tells the Girl's World. 'Perhaps I should have taken you away too. Unquestionably. And I have thought about that many times, and it is my major regret in all my seventy years. So I do hold myself responsible for your problems, yes. However. You are rightly saying that that was not an appropriate life for a seven-year-old. So perhaps . . .'

He does not have to finish his sentence, and I can see that he has no intention of doing so anyway. He is implying all sorts of things. He is talking about Toby. I hate him. *Hate him*. I lie back, close my eyes, and pretend he is not there. After a few more throat-clearings and half-coughs, he shuffles out of the room.

I lie on Jessica's old bed all night long. My head pounds and throbs, and my limbs tremble. I hate them all, and myself most of all. The shame is impossible to acknowledge. At five o'clock, I get up very quietly, unlock the back door, and walk three miles home, still in my party dress, the freezing air sobering me up. I stop at Swiss Cottage, where a café with steamed-up windows is serving hot drinks to early risers.

I feel conspicuous in my red Ghost dress, a pink blanket around my shoulders, my high-heeled shoes in my hand. The clientele is mainly early Sunday workers, but there are a couple of other revellers, and no one takes much notice of me.

The floor is sticky under my feet. I buy a cup of coffee and sit at a formica table by the window. I look out at the stirrings of life in the city streets. I close my eyes, briefly.

'Ha, you're up late,' someone says. I turn and see a woman smiling, at the table behind me. She is a few years older than me, with tightly curled short hair, dressed in a neat little suit with a white blouse. 'And I'm up early,' she adds, with a chuckle. 'Meeting in the middle, you know?'

I nod. 'I feel terrible,' I tell her. 'But sitting here is making it a bit better.'

'I can imagine. Oh, for the opportunity, these days.'

'I don't get them often. I was only at a family party. Got a bit carried away.'

'Well, good on you.' She nods, stands up, smooths down her skirt and hurries away.

I stare at the lightening streets, and consider how easy it is to do this, to step momentarily out of my life. I wonder whether the boys would, as my dad kindly implied, be better off away from me. After all, my mother was the millstone around my neck; she is still fucking me up from beyond the grave. I am

44

one of the few people who doesn't see the mother-child bond as sacred.

I write my name in the condensation on the inside of the window. I sit and stare at it.

chapter eight

'Right, Ms Harris,' says the man. He is looking at the piece of paper in front of him. 'You have been self-employed for seven years?'

'Yes,' I agree.

'And now you're applying for a PA job?'

'I want to get back into the workforce,' I say, remembering to smile. I took against this man the moment I saw him. It is probably defensiveness on my part: he is completely bald, slightly larger than his suit, and he appears to be sneering at me. The woman next to him is just staring into the corner, completely disengaged. I think she might be texting under the desk.

'Do you have a list of your clients?'

'Sure.' I hand it over. Max told me to bring it. I watch the man peruse it and nod. He offers it to the woman, who is much younger than me, but she shakes her head.

'O-kaaay,' he says. 'This is good. Are you familiar with Microsoft Office? Windows Excel?'

'Oh, yes,' I say. 'Of course.'

'And do you consider yourself to be an organised sort of person?' He watches me carefully.

'I do,' I assure him. 'Because I get two children to different places at the right times every morning, I do my work in the time available, to deadline. I collect the kids, I run a household as well as a business . . .' I drone on, while he nods approvingly.

Then I realise I might actually *get* this job. There is no way that

I could be someone's personal assistant. I could not possibly devote my days to reminding somebody about meetings and writing things on spreadsheets (which I have no idea about). I must backtrack, and I must do it immediately.

He asks whether I have any questions, and I do.

'Just out of, er, interest,' I say. 'Do you operate a drugs testing policy?'

He smiles, eyebrows raised. 'Is this to do with prescription medication?'

'Oh, no. Just wondering.'

'Would you have an issue with that if we did?'

'Well. On Mondays, maybe!' I laugh. I see the silent young woman smirking. The bald man looks at her.

'Thanks,' he says. 'We'll let you know.'

Early the next morning, the darkness outside the window is palpable and comforting. It is not real darkness: there is a street light across the road, and another a few metres along. This is darkness that is alive with possibilities; there is life out there, and light. I could, for instance, slip out of the door, and vanish into the city. It would, hypothetically, be easy. I want to go back to the café in Swiss Cottage and sit by the window, cradling a drink, being anyone I want to be. A few steps, a quiet closing of the door behind me.

Elly has written again.

'but have you actually thought about it?' she writes. 'really? have you spoken to max? i KNOW he has a tefl. there's heaps for him to do. and the boys would have a great time. or you could leave them all behind and let your hair down. come on – live a little!'

A woman's feet pass the window with a purposeful tap. Her shoes are ugly, with a low, round heel. In half an hour, I will hear the alarm clock beeping, in a muffled way, in the bedroom of the flat above us, waking a man we don't know.

I tiptoe around the tiny kitchen, knowing that a single stumble might rouse the boys. I make coffee as quietly as I can, wishing I could hush the guttural gurgles of the machine, then sit at the table, cradling my ironic 'World's Greatest Mum!' mug between my hands.

I want to go.

The coffee gives me a masochistic pleasure by making the headache and the dehydration worse. I consider teaming it with a glass of water, but decide against it. I check the time. Twenty past six. I have about half an hour before anyone else is likely to get up. The world map is annoying me and needs taking down a peg or two.

India is there, exactly the right shape, in precisely the correct place. Pondicherry is marked with a little dot and a large grey smear which has entirely erased its name.

When I met Max, he was on his way there, to a job teaching English. That is where we should have ended up.

I stand on a chair, grab the top edge with both hands, and very, very quietly ease the whole thing down. The world rips as it leaves my wall, in spite of my efforts, and I freeze and listen for stirring children. Australia is torn down the middle; Brazil is sundered from Chile; a catastrophic earthquake destroys the planet. I carefully tear around the Indian subcontinent, put that part aside, and fold the rest of the map as quietly as I can, and post it into the bin. It has no place in the recycling: it goes in the real bin, the bad one, the landfill one. India gets special treatment.

First, I pluck Elly's elephant postcard from the wall next to the white rectangle where Planet Earth used to be. As I turn it over, my knees tremble. Elly has it all. I met her, nine years ago, on my first morning in Vietnam. She has not left Asia in all that time, is living the life she wants, and apparently has no idea that it is just not practical for a family to uproot itself and jump on the next plane to do good works on a whim.

I close my eyes and try to picture her. I imagine tiny little blonde Elly, living in austerity in a dormitory full of other ascetics, wearing baggy white clothes and sleeping on nails. I picture them doing yoga at four in the morning, and then queuing for sex with a dodgy guru before sipping at a bowl of gruel. I try to imagine us, among them.

48

Joe loves Elly's postcard, so I force myself not to shove it into the bin with the map. It has been on the wall for years, and will, no doubt, stay there for years more. I turn it over.

'Dear T,' Elly wrote, before Joe was born. 'You know what – I have decided to stay here. Here, in India, in the ashram. It is an amazing place. The place that makes me exhale, that gives my existence the pillars I never even knew were missing. I don't plan to live anywhere else, ever.' She never used to talk like that: Elly is the woman who knew every European city by its Irish and Australian bars. I wonder what she would be like these days, face to face.

I stick the postcard back up, and fight my emotions.

Maybe my horrible father is right: perhaps I should be going to rehab, for the boys. Perhaps it is the drink, and nothing else, that is the problem.

I light one of the rings of the gas hob, and carefully hold India in the flame. When it catches fire, I drop it into the sink, and watch the small yet intense conflagration with satisfaction.

I know he is behind me, but I don't turn round. He puts a heavy hand on my shoulder. I still don't look.

'Histrionics?' Max asks. 'Big gestures?'

I shrug him off. 'There's coffee in the pot.'

'And cinders in the sink.'

'Do you want toast?'

'Did you burn the whole map?'

'Just India.'

'You burned India?'

'And some of Pakistan and Bangladesh. Collateral damage. Toast? Coffee?'

He puts both arms around my waist and pulls me into him, backwards.

I refuse to look round. I stay stiff and unyielding.

'Sweetheart,' he says quietly, into my ear. 'This is no good.'

I swallow. 'I kind of know that.'

'Look, if—'

We are interrupted by a plaintive, 'Mummy, where's the map?' I turn round to see Joe standing, flushed with sleep, his wet nappy making his pyjama trousers droop down to his knees. He is staring, in a disgruntled way, at the space on the wall. His thumb is in his mouth.

'Morning, darling,' I say carefully. I look at the wall. All three of us stare at it. The rest of the walls are covered in the children's pictures, the photographs of Max and me on our wedding day, the boys as babies, and the children with Max's parents, and my dad and his family.

My head is throbbing. I hold out my arms, and Joe wanders in my direction.

'An evil goblin broke in and stole it in the night,' I tell him as he approaches. He gasps and steps back.

'Mummy's joking,' Max says firmly. 'Mummy wanted to make some more space to put your lovely pictures up.'

Joe frowns for a second, and then nods. He strolls into my embrace, and I hold him close. The thumb comes out.

'Not really an evil goblin?' he says.

'No,' I admit. 'Space for drawings.'

'Can I have warm milk?'

Max bustles around, getting cereal boxes out of cupboards, making more coffee, diluting fruit juice. Toby ambles along, eyes bright after a long night's sleep.

'Do you know that babies are born without kneecaps?' he asks conversationally.

'No,' I admit. 'Is it true or did you dream it?'

'It's true. It said in my magazine.'

I refill my coffee, edge out of the dining area, and sit on the furthest point of the sofa. I imagine myself in a wide open space, on a stony beach looking out at the sea. I breathe in the fresh salty air. For a second, I am there.

Then I am back in the centrally-heated flat, gagging at the smell of toast and coffee. Max is looking after the boys now, but at ten past eight he gets to put on his overcoat and close the door behind him. He gets to sit on the tube and read the paper for half an hour. At work, he can talk to people, drink all the coffee he likes, mess around on the internet, and focus his mental energies on being annoyed by people who say things like 'I need it by copt', when they mean 'close of play today', and pronounce ASAP as a word: asap.

I don't speak because I am so afraid of what I might say, or do. I look at the wall: India has gone. My eyes pass over Toby's laboured drawings of superheroes flying through the air, rockets, Tardises, unidentifiable shapes, and I feel ashamed that I have no real idea of what goes on in his head, beyond the interminable Doctor Who. I ask him, regularly, but he just finds me irritating and tuts at me.

I don't feel great, either, about the fact that I kissed his teacher. I put it from my mind, again.

Joe's blobby people are roughly circular, with stick arms and legs coming off them, and two eyes, no noses, and occasionally a mouth. These are easier to comprehend.

Tears are trickling down my face.

I stand up and run my hand over a family portrait drawn by Toby. I am there, in pink felt tip, with pink hair sticking up all around my face, the word 'Mumee' written under me. I notice that Toby has placed himself, in blue, next to Max, who is green, and who has DAD written approvingly beneath his feet. Pink Mumee is at the edge of the paper. What am I doing to us all?

When Max grabs my shoulder, I jerk back to reality and I scream at the shock. It is too loud: I am used to keeping things in, these days, and the sound of it surprises me.

'Shhh!' he says.

'*What*, Mummy?' asks Joe, frightened. Toby just stares at me, looking like Max.

I turn on Max. 'What?' I ask. 'What was that for?'

'Nothing,' he says, in a soft voice. He lowers his voice still further. 'Hey. Can we meet for lunch today?'

I turn and look at him. I look deep into his eyes. Once upon a time, Max and I were the best thing that had ever happened, to anyone, in the history of the world. Now, I think he's going to leave me.

chapter nine

Lola laughs when she sees me. 'Oh, Tansy,' she says. 'You were in the shower!'

'Bath,' I say, listening to the gurgling as the water drains away. Then I smile. 'Come in, then.'

I did not invite Lola, but after my performance at the party, I knew she would turn up sometime this week. My dressing gown is belted tightly around my waist, and I have a towel on my head, but I am pleased to see her.

'You had a job interview,' she says. 'You went to it?'

'I did,' I assure her.

'And?'

I shrug. 'Don't call us, we'll call you – that sort of idea.'

'They would be mad to turn you down.' She smirks as she says it. I smirk back.

'Sorry about the party,' I say quietly.

'Is forgotten,' she assures me, and she hugs me so violently that the towel falls off my head. I hated my stepmother for years. She resented my very existence. We avoided each other, communicated through my father (who is constitutionally unsuited to being a communications channel) and each looked away while the other spoke. Lola would not come to any event if I was going to be there, though she never admitted it, and I used to turn up at their house to visit the children unannounced, just to annoy her.

It changed when I got pregnant. We got married, and a baby

was the obvious next step, as far as Max was concerned. I was terrified of the very idea, and held out against it for as long as I could, while he told me everything that he knew I needed to hear. We would be parents together, I would not be doing it on my own. We would help each other. We wouldn't have to be like the other parents we saw in the parks and cafés, who, in my eyes, lived in terrifyingly mundane shrunken worlds. Seven years ago, we sat on the esplanade at Brighton, and Max talked me round.

'If we have them now,' he said, as the wind whipped my hair around my face, 'when we're not quite thirty, then we keep our future options wide open. We'll have the energy to have adventures with them. And we can leave them with my parents. Send them to stay with your dad and Lola. We can go away by ourselves for a week or two – back to Thailand, to China, whatever you like.'

I realise, now, that he just said whatever he thought it was going to take to make me agree. Not only have we not been to Thailand or China, we have not been to Italy or even France. We have been to Cornwall, Scotland, and Brighton. When the boys were small, I never saw the attraction of trying to tiptoe around them in a hotel room, or of staying in a crummy gite without a dishwasher. Max's precious holiday from work is family time, not couple time.

The rest of Max's promises were the part that mattered.

'Just because we'll have children, that doesn't have to hold us back,' he swore. I can recapture the smell of frying food and sea water, just by recalling his words. 'I'll always have my TEFL certificate. We can still go to Pondicherry. We could go to Hong Kong, the three of us. Or Singapore. We could go back to Thailand and set up home there. We could live in Beijing, send the children to International School. If we become parents, Tans, it'll just focus our plans. It doesn't mean we have to be like everybody else.'

I remember him putting his hands on my shoulders and looking hard into my eyes. I remember knowing, at that point, that he was right, that I was going to agree, that we were going to reproduce.

'Are we like everybody else?' he asked. 'So?'

I wanted a boy, and I got the very one I had hoped for. Toby was long and thin, a carbon copy of Max from the start. He had big dark eyes, like Max. He was calm and indulgent of my follies, and I loved him. Sometimes I would sit staring in wonderment at his face, his ears, his cheeks. I would count his tiny toes, stroke the indentation at the back of his neck that was exactly the width of my finger. He was, after all, a distillation of our union. Those were the good moments.

Toby was perfect; I was the problem. Toby was, apparently, a 'good sleeper', but I couldn't bear being dragged from the blissful depths by his mewling every few hours. I managed to breastfeed, and was impressed by its convenience, but I spent twenty hours a day feeling overwhelmed. He depended on me for everything: I made his food and I fed it to him, I kept him warm and sheltered and clean. I kept him alive: without me, he would die.

Two weeks after Toby's arrival, Max went back to work. The prospect was so unthinkable that I shrugged off all remnants of dignity. I lay at the threshold of our flat, held his ankle with both hands, and begged him not to leave. I sobbed and hyper-ventilated and pretended I had mastitis so he would stay at home.

'Sweetheart,' he said, crouching down and cupping his hands around my blotchy face. 'I have to go to work. I've been off for a fortnight. You need to look after Toby. And you can do it. Look, he's asleep.'

'He'll wake up!'

'I'll be back at six.'

'That's ten hours! Don't leave me!' I looked at Max, who was blurry through my tears. 'I can't look after him on my own,' I told him, and it was true. It was so true that I had to look away.

He came back in and sat me down on the sofa. I waited for him to tell me that I could go to work, and he would stay at home with the baby.

'I'll call Lola,' he said instead.

That was the day when everything changed between us. Lola had driven me insane through my pregnancy with her smug advice and knowing looks. Every time we saw her, we had a game of 'You two won't know what's hit you' bingo. After she said it, one of us had to slip the word 'bingo' into the conversation in such a way that no one else thought it was odd. It kept us amused for months.

Lola was a beautiful, South American 27-year-old when she lured my dad away from his alcoholic wife and annoying daughter. He could have taken me, but he decided not to, and I knew from the day he left that it was Lola who had persuaded him on that front.

They had four children, whose ages now range from nineteen to nine. Jessica is twenty times more sensible than I am, headed directly for a career in law. Briony is quite the goth, and a bad influence on me, as has been demonstrated this week where spirits are concerned (and honestly, what sort of pathetic 36-year-old is led astray by a girl of sixteen?). Jake is obsessed by climbing, and Archie is a nine-year-old computer whizz and Doctor Who fanatic, and thus Toby's idol. Lola is no longer the sultry temptress: she is in her fifties, and she is rounder and nicer and she doesn't resent me any more.

She came along as soon as Max phoned, thrilled to be needed, and looked after Toby and me while Archie, who was three or four, drew blobby men on the walls and sent nonsensical emails to everyone in my address book. She came every weekday for two months. It is impossible to carry on hating someone when they carry you through the worst weeks of your life without ever uttering the words 'pull yourself together'.

She came with me to Toby's six-week check, and sat next to me in front of the doctor, and told my bored GP that she had to prescribe me some antidepressants. When I told the doctor that my stepmother was talking nonsense and I was absolutely fine, Lola held my hand and stroked it until I started wailing.

I took the pills. It got better. It got so much better that I came to an understanding with myself. I would stick it out. I loved Toby. I enjoyed marching around pushing a pushchair and making old people walk in the road. I liked looking at him when he was asleep, and I liked making breastfeeds last as long as they possibly could, so that I could watch hours of daytime television every day without having to feel guilty.

Then, one day, Lola took me to the breastfeeding group.

'You need a friend,' she said.

'I don't,' I told her. 'I've got you. And Max. And all my other friends.'

'No,' she said. 'Your other friends don't have babies. They have no clue. Most of your friends live abroad anyway, don't you think? And me and Max, we're family, not friends. You need a mummy friend. Trust me. It will make the world of difference.'

She took me to the door of the church hall. I watched a few glossy women going in, most of them with babies in slings. Intimidated, I stood back. One woman half smiled, and the rest ignored me and marched in, knowing that they were better dressed than I was, and that they were wearing lipstick. I felt weak at the number of other things that must have to be in place before you could think about lipstick.

'Do you want me to come in with you?' Lola threatened. 'Sit next to you? Hold the baby?'

'No!' I told her.

'So, go on.'

'I don't want to.'

'You have to.'

'I don't like them.'

'You are stupid sometimes!'

I left the pushchair in the porch, girded myself, and walked into the hall, clutching Toby so tightly that, after a while, I had to check he was breathing. Plastic chairs were arranged in a circle, and most of them were occupied by women who were probably as desperately insecure as I was. I couldn't bear to look at them. The room was a bit dusty and very tatty.

'Hello, there,' said the woman in charge. 'Come and take a seat! I'm Margaret.'

I sat down, holding my infant son in front of me for protection. I sat for an hour and scarcely said a word. I avoided the eyes of the other women. I convinced myself that they were muttering to each other about me. When Margaret asked how the feeding was going, I squeaked, 'Fine,' and looked down at my baby. I hated the timid person I was being, and as soon as proceedings were wound up and everyone was offered a biscuit, I ran away and never went back.

The woman who half smiled at me turned out to be Sarah, with baby Lucy, and she was feeling exactly the same as me, except that she stuck it out.

I make more coffee, and drink a pint of juice followed by a pint of water. Lola sits at the kitchen table eating chocolate biscuits, and looks at me appraisingly.

'OK, you want to go to the Priory?' she asks. 'Your daddy will pay, if you want.'

I laugh. I can only laugh because it's Lola.

'No!' I tell her. 'Honestly. Look, I'm fine. I'm all washed and clean, and I'm meeting Max for lunch. I am, actually, managing to stumble through the days. I'm really sorry about my perform-ance. I don't quite know what . . .'

'So, you want to go back to the doctor? More pills?' she asks, crumbs around her mouth. Her hair is in a chignon, but a few strands have come loose, which suits her. She is wearing a pink Monsoon blouse and a blue Monsoon cardigan; I know this because everything Lola wears is from Monsoon.

'No,' I tell her. 'Not at the moment. Thanks, though.' I take a biscuit. It turns out to be exactly what I needed.

'So, tell me what's going on. Meeting Max for lunch? Special lunch?'

'I don't know. I'm a bit, well, nervous. He asked me to meet him, but he didn't say why.'

She shrugs. 'You and Max – it's seven years?'

'Ten.'

'Well, seven years married. Difficulties are normal. You have to make an effort, you know. You have to understand that you're not going to meet someone and be swept off your feet again. You have to work with what you have, not go running off to someone or something new. It's a good time for another baby. Maybe a little girl this time.'

'Lola!' I am tempted to mention Dad running away to someone new, after seven years of fatherhood, but I step in just in time and tell myself not to be vicious.

'Well?'

'You know perfectly well that another baby is totally out of the question! Joe's my baby. And I wouldn't even want a girl.'

During both pregnancies, I was terrified of the idea of a daughter. Even today, the notion makes me shiver. The mother-daughter relationship is a dark and tangled thing.

'So, what is really wrong?'

I look at the table. 'Nothing. The boys are fine and Max is fine, though he might be about to leave me, admittedly, and I'm – well, it's like you just said. I'm just adjusting to this being the way my life is, now.' I say it with the best air of finality that I can muster. 'And I have to get ready now, Lola. Or I'll be late for lunch.' I look at her and relent. 'Maybe you can help me get ready.'

Max has chosen a smart, slick establishment, light and airy even on a drizzly day. People in suits bustle in and out, talking loudly on their phones, secure in their own importance. I look down at myself, in an inappropriately summery dress that (according to Lola) makes me look carefree and desirable, with incongruous black tights and a white mac, and I pull the raincoat tightly around me, and do up its belt.

The low-level hangover is still with me, but it is no longer a black cloud over my head; it now resembles a skein of slightly alcoholic rainbow mist that trails after me, easy to manage and only occasionally rendering me dizzy when I turn corners.

My hair is wet, after my walk, despite my careful blow-drying under Lola's instructions, so I quickly pull it back into a ponytail. My umbrella is broken, because, last week, the children used it to re-enact the Winnie the Pooh story where he floats away across the flood. I nearly cried when I saw them, sitting in their 'boat', rocking back and forth, laughing as the spokes snapped beneath them. I wanted to shout, but I managed not to. It was nearly, but not quite, as bad as the time they unrolled every loo roll in the flat and filled bags and bags with it, explaining afterwards that, 'We're going to spin it into gold.' That time, I managed to bite back my nastiness, and say nothing more acidic than, 'If only.'

At least, under Lola's care, I am wearing what she called 'a nice gentle make-up'. She stood over me and forced me to put on mascara, eyeliner, a little bit of brown eye shadow, and a deep red lipstick. It made me realise how much I haven't bothered with anything like that lately. I wonder whether the eye make-up has run in the rain and given me panda eyes.

There are white linen tablecloths, and several knives and forks. I suspect that Max has lunch in places like this most days, though he claims he works too hard.

He sits opposite me, blending in perfectly in his white shirt and purple tie, his dark hair just right, his jacket over the back of his chair. He smiles when he sees me, and I see his eyes flick across my face. I touch my right cheek, self-conscious.

I order a glass of wine and drink it in two minutes. It makes me nervy and jumpy, and slightly nauseous. Max looks amused, in a way that lets me know that he isn't.

I look at him. He looks at me.

'Well?' I say, and I listen to my voice, high and tight in the clattery room.

'Hmmm,' says Max. 'Sorry to dive straight in with a cliché but, sweetheart, we really need to talk.'

I look at him, and he is a stranger, speaking someone else's lines.

'What do we need to talk about?' I ask. I look over his shoulder, at three men and a woman at the table behind us, all in shirt sleeves, looking businesslike. The men are eating steak and chips, the woman a salad. He is going to leave me. Everything I fear is about to come to pass. I picture myself, living in a bedsit on the outskirts of town, having the boys to stay at the weekend, drinking all week, wearing the same clothes for months at a time, my teeth unbrushed, my hair tangled and smelly. Max would get custody of the boys in a heartbeat.

'You,' says Max. 'We need to talk about you.'

'Me?'

'Things aren't right, are they? You've got things you need to do.'

'I'm fine,' I say over his shoulder. 'Honestly, I am.'

Max leans over, ducking into my eyeline. 'Tansy,' he says. 'You have to look at me. You wanted us to go to India.'

I sigh. 'I know. We covered that one.'

'It's not practical for all of us.'

'Apparently not.'

We smile at each other, but they are not real smiles.

'But . . . Look. I got you something.' He slides his gift across the table. It is an envelope.

I stare at it. I know exactly what is in there, and my stomach falls away, my legs shake, and the ringing starts up in my ears. I am not sure whether to laugh, or to kiss him, or to cry. So I laugh, and then I cry until my eyes are red and I have to wipe my nose on a napkin. Everyone looks at us, and we don't care.

chapter ten

It is a frosty morning. There are patterns on the outside of the windows, and the feet walk by quickly. As I watch, a woman's boots slip on a patch of ice. She skids around, and then slips over. Suddenly, her whole body is framed by the window. She has short blonde hair, a tired face. I step back quickly, but not before she has seen me watching her.

I put the curtain down, and turn back to the breakfast table.

It is warm in here, cosy in a way only central heating can manage. The children are tousle-haired, eating breakfast in their pyjamas, fuelling up to face the cold. Toby is reading a Doctor Who magazine, turning the pages with his left hand while shovelling in Rice Krispies with his right. Joe swings his legs and looks idly around the room.

And suddenly I see my family, all together, all belonging; the children, in spite of everything, happy.

'Why are there windows?' Joe asks Max.

'So the light can come in,' Max answers, without looking up from his *Guardian*.

'Why is there a light, when there's windows?'

'Because sometimes it's dark outside.'

Joe considers this and nods, satisfied. He watches me coming back to the table, picking up my coffee, in its World's Greatest Mum mug. I can't eat. Joe picks up his spoon and starts making faces at his upside-down reflection. I stare at him, my chunky, solemn little boy.

I have my ticket, I've wriggled out of the small amount of work I still have, and submitted my visa application. I cannot put off the next part any longer.

'Boys?' I say. Joe gazes at me with clear grey eyes. Toby keeps his head down, busy with his reading and his eating.

'Tobe?'

He looks up. 'What?'

I feel Max watching me. When I look at him, he nods in brisk encouragement. He is in his dressing gown. Seeing him sitting there with part of his chest exposed and a pillow crease on his cheek brings a lump to my throat for some reason.

'Toby,' I say. 'Joe. There's something we all need to talk about. Um.' I have planned this speech down to the last word. I cannot do it. It is a horrible thing to do, a selfish thing. I can't go. But, for some reason, I have to. I hesitate, forget everything I was going to say, and blurt out, 'I'm going away to India, on my own.'

Toby frowns, and goes back to his cereal. 'OK. Can I have toast and honey?'

'In a minute. Daddy and you can't come because of work and school.' I pause, to give myself time to roll my eyes in secret. Max knows that's what I'm doing. My real eyes don't move, just the inner ones. 'But *I* can, because it's easier for me. So Daddy will be in charge while I'm not here.' I pick up my mug and drain my coffee. Then I stand up and walk briskly to the toaster. I busy myself with bread, butter, honey, plates.

'How long for?' Toby has stopped his frenzied eating, and has twisted in his chair, towards me. His cheeks are still rosy with sleep.

I picture myself, in India, back in my backpacker clothes, with a rucksack on my back, hanging out with Elly, relaxing, reading books all day long. I have no right to relish such an idea.

'Maybe a month?' I turn my attention to Joe. His eyes are fixed on my face.

'And I will come too, with you,' he says carefully. 'To Injia.'

I sigh. 'When you're older we'll go somewhere together,' I say, in the lightest voice I can muster. 'You and Toby and Daddy will have lots and lots of fun. I'll bring you back *so* many presents.'

This is not enough. I see it on his face, as clearly as if I had taken a marker pen and written 'rejected by my mummy' across his forehead. His face darkens, literally, until he is a deep shade of puce. The bottom lip juts and judders. I try to look away, but I cannot do it, and I walk to him and scoop him up instead. Finally, the climax: his face contorts itself, his mouth opens, and dribbles of saliva dangle out of it as he starts to wail.

I close my eyes to try to summon the strength. I nuzzle his neck and tell myself that I am a perfect, caring mother. I am the sort of woman who says the right thing, cheers her child up, lets him know that he is the most important thing in her world, even though what I have just told him clearly implies the opposite. I blink back my own tears.

I sit down, and arrange him on my lap. I stroke his hair. He turns his face into my neck. I am soiled and guilty.

'It's OK,' I tell him, treacherous. 'You have to be grown up to go to India. It's all right. I won't be gone for long. It's OK.'

My platitudes have no effect. I throw daggers across the table at Max. I shoot him with an enormous machine gun. This is his fault, because if I'd had my way, we would all be going together, and it would be permanent.

'It's not definite,' I say pathetically.

Everything is crumbling in the face of Joe's tears. I cannot manage without him, any more than he can manage without me. I will stay behind. I will martyr myself a bit longer, cherish my children a bit more, and learn a valuable, clichéd lesson of some sort. At the same time, I will stop drinking, and will turn, instead, to antidepressants or, possibly, to religion as my crutch.

'Yes, it is definite,' Max says sharply. 'Tans, you're going. Just go for a few weeks if you like. We'll miss you. You'll have an adventure, see Elly, have a break because you need one, get your head together. It's not the first time a mother's needed a break. While you're away, me and the boys will have hot chocolate and pancakes every morning. We'll have puddings from Marks and Spencer every night. We'll go to the park and the cinema, and we'll go to Bakewell to stay with Grandma and Grandad. We might even manage a trip to Legoland. A boys' adventure.'

Joe stops crying and looks at Max through narrowed eyes.

'Can we go to Toys-R-Us? With sixteen pounds?' Joe's grasp of numbers is extremely random. Sixteen is currently as high as he goes.

'Absolutely.'

'Mum?' asks Toby nonchalantly. 'Does this mean you and Dad are getting divorced?'

I find my old backpack, in a box stuffed into a cupboard. My fingers tremble as I take it out. It is crumpled and dusty, and bright blue.

'Go on your own,' Max told me.

My first reaction was to refuse; I wanted us all to go, and I wanted it to be a real change for us. Then I imagined walking out of the flat, closing the door behind me.

'Yeah?' I said, trying to catch his eye.

'It's a risk,' he said quickly, looking down at his plate. The clattering and the clinking all around us faded out to nothing. There was no one in the restaurant but us. 'You need to get away, for your sake, for the boys' sake, and for mine. I emailed Elly. Sorry. She says you can stay with her. It sounds as if life in her community is fairly structured, and I think you'd be OK. More than OK, probably. I think it would do you the absolute world of good and at the moment it's the only thing I can think of that might smooth family life for the boys.'

I focused hard on the bigger picture, and managed not to take offence, because I knew he was right.

I sponge the backpack down, and hang it in the shower to dry. Then I put it on the steps outside, instead. I want it to be out in the world, seeing the sun, preparing for its adventure.

I book myself in for a few jabs, though, to my delight, there is not a lot that I need. I email Elly again, telling her that I will spend five days in Chennai and then come to the ashram to stay with her.

'I have been told,' I write, with forced nonchalance, 'to stay at the ashram until I am "better". Sorry the plan is so open-ended. I guess I will know "better" when it happens. Is that all right?'

She replies five minutes later.

'Sure,' she writes. 'You just turn up whenever you like, and stay as long as you want. I'm always around, generally busy, and there's loads here for you to get your teeth into, if you like.'

I stare out of the window as hail starts to fall. This, without a doubt, is a good sign. It marks a good time to be leaving the country, in one month. I wrap myself up in jumper, coat, scarf and hat, fill my shoulder bag with extra hats and gloves for the boys, and venture out with an umbrella, to fetch the boys on the dot of half past three.

I have, of course, forgotten that there is a backpack drying in the autumn sunshine directly outside the door. It is hidden under a pile of ice.

chapter eleven

Alexia's thoughts
4.14a.m.

I haven't written for weeks, although I've been thinking all the time about adopting from overseas. I have spent a heck of a lot of time online, searching for information. The more time I spend looking at India – well, even though it seems to be difficult, I just cannot think of anything else.

Every day, I imagine doing whatever I'm doing – working at the store, shopping for groceries, tidying the garden – with my little Indian daughter next to me (I think it would be a girl, because there seem to be more girls available in most places, but I would be just as happy with a boy – after about six months of trying, you certainly stop having a gender preference!). Of course I wouldn't be working once we had her, but I can see myself taking her to the store and showing her where Mommy used to work, and buying her a bag of candy as a treat.

I think of India, and I imagine danger, excitement. I think of beggars and poverty and people with leprosy and terrible diseases. There are snakes and tigers in India. There are snake charmers and holy gurus and mysterious temples. There are elephants. It is a scary place but a magic one.

I see me and Duncan there, which makes for a strange vision (we are noticeable), and we find our little daughter and bring her away with us, to safety and security and a life where we will give her everything, everything that will make her happy.

I said it to Duncan a couple of days ago.

'I've been thinking,' I said, as casually as I could, as if it was something really quite unimportant. 'Thinking about India. I'd like us to try adopting from there.'

He snorted. 'Er, I know,' he said.

'How do you know that?'

'Alexia,' he said. 'You spend half of every freaking night on the computer! And you never tell me why! I had to check you weren't chatting to guys on there.'

'I would never do that!'

He put his arm around my shoulders. 'I know,' he said. 'But you can be too trusting, sweetie. You could meet a guy pretending to be a girl. It happens. So I've been checking over the history. And it didn't take long to discover that we were adopting from India.'

I kissed him then. He's happy to follow my lead, and if I say 'India' he's hardly going to turn around and say 'China'. 'You're the mom,' he said, and I kissed him harder.

It does appear that India is going to be hard work. They don't have many children adopted internationally, and most of the ones that do leave the country are adopted by folk of Indian ancestry. But it's supposed to be getting easier.

5.23

I still can't sleep. Here I am, tapping away quietly again.

Here's the thing: when I think about India, then I think about me and Duncan, it seems so exotic, and the comparison makes me a little sad. And I think: look at me. I'm not morbidly overweight, not like some of the people I see around here, but I could do with losing a few pounds. My hair is no colour at all, somewhere between light brown and dirty blonde. I don't look after myself the way a few women do, so I have my hair tied back every day, and make-up is only for particular occasions when I need to feel pretty. In truth, I am not so confident applying it, not like my sister Dee.

And I dress in jeans for winter and shorts for summer, with sweaters and T-shirts depending on what's appropriate. My shoes are comfortable.

In short, I am seeing myself through India's eyes, and I look very very drab. If we manage to adopt, we will need to travel (which is a very frightening, exciting idea), and if I'm going to India, I want to be more interesting.

As soon as morning arrives, I'm going to make an appointment for a haircut. That will give them all something to talk about. Perhaps I will even get my fat butt down the gym.

Comments: 2

Hi there Alexia – I stumbled on your blog when Googling for adoption from India. You appeared on page 12 of Google! I am looking into this thoroughly! I wish you the very very best of luck in your search for a child. My husband and I have decided to look to Russia. I take comfort from hearing of other people on similar journeys. I hope you do too. Warmest wishes, Jennifer

You don't know me, but I think I can help you. Send an email to CC@gmail.com. This is an orphanage in India which is very good at helping people in your situation. Give them a try. We are of Indian heritage, but even for us, the official channels seemed very onerous, and CC take charge of so much of the paperwork. They know how to get things done – it costs but can you put a price on a family? Good luck to you. H.

chapter twelve

Everything at the airport is hyper-real. It feels as if I have stepped
into one of those seventies paintings where blocks of colour cast
sharp shadows. I drink cup after cup of coffee, and become scared
of the security people. Someone asks me to take my shoes off
to go through security. I don't blink, just obey unquestioningly.
People are everywhere, but they are moving shop dummies as
far as I am concerned.

I stop, suddenly, and take out my purse. The pictures of Toby
and Joe are there. I stare at them, as if I were not still, just, in
the same city. Every step takes me away from them.

Then I am on the plane. There is a scrum, and I am lucid again.
I make slow progress down the aisle to my seat, past people who
are trying to squeeze outsized pieces of hand luggage into spaces
that are too small. I elbow my way to a seat that is at the very
back of the plane. I asked for a seat by the emergency exit, but
the check-in woman laughed and said, 'You'd have needed to have
been here four hours ago for that. Everyone's wise to that one.'

'Window?' I asked.

She tapped on her keyboard. 'Sorry. You're quite late, actually.
Middle is all I've got. Lucky you're on your own.'

I have said goodbye to the boys, wearing my bravest Cheerful
Face. I have booked Toby into the Mountview Nursery for 'wrap-
around care', which means someone like Alison will drop him off
at school, and collect him from Mr Trelawney in the afternoon.

I have said goodbye to Jim, knowing beyond a doubt that, had

I stayed, I would have been drawn back to him, again and again. It was a wrench to walk away, but when I had done it, had turned my back on the horrific mess that might have been, I was so pleased with myself that I actually skipped.

It has been surprisingly easy to extract myself from my life.

I am crammed into the middle of a row that would barely have had enough leg room for a six-year-old. There is a tiny woman on my left, who is gazing out of the window in a rapt manner, seemingly fascinated by wintry half-light and concrete. I stare past her, trying to force myself to appreciate my last moments in the same country as my family, on the same continent. I feel dangerously nauseous. I have to fight hard to control my impulse to unbuckle my belt and run away while we are still earthbound. I only stay on the plane to avoid looking stupid.

The man to my right is the epitome of the Modern India that is in the paper all the time: he is young, polite and well-dressed, and looks as though he might very well be a technology wizard. I manage a quick *hello* in his direction, before I turn away.

I don't want to go. I desperately want not to go. And yet I am feeling a small, treacherous build-up of excitement. I am not away until the doors are closed. Until we are in the air. Until I have had a drink. Until I have landed. Then I have no idea what will happen.

The plane starts to taxi, and I watch a blonde, heavily made-up member of the cabin crew carrying out the demonstrations with half an eye on a steward who is making her laugh. The noise of the engines fills the cabin. We speed up, then travel impossibly fast, then rise above it all. London, England, Europe drop away beneath me.

It has happened so suddenly. Everything was juddering along normally, and now it has changed.

I spent yesterday evening in the sitting room with Max, my head full of bad things that have happened, full of fear. I didn't say much to him, because I was afraid to open my mouth. We watched a game show instead. I bit my lip continuously, until the metallic taste of blood filled my mouth. His mother, Delia, phoned, full of anxiety.

'You will look after yourself,' she said, over and over again. 'Don't talk to strange men. Don't drink the water. Stick to crowded places. Careful of Delhi belly.'

I said all the right things, and looked at Max, who was watching me. I thought he was looking pleased to see the back of me, but he said he was excited on my behalf.

At three o'clock, I dressed quickly, in the darkness, in the travelling clothes I had laid out. I put on cotton trousers, a flowery top from Monsoon (a present from Lola), and a cardigan, and I crept into the boys' room, and stood for a moment on the threshold, my head spinning as I listened to their untroubled breathing.

I kissed Toby first, my poor little Toby who assures me that he will not miss me. He brushed his cheek with his hand, wiping away the touch of my lips. I touched his springy hair. I smelled his sleepy little-boy smell, the smell he has always had.

Then I lay down next to Joe, on his bottom bunk, and took him in my arms. I buried my head in his hair, and hugged him, and kissed him. Joe did not wake at all, but obligingly moved where I wanted him to, and unconsciously accepted my farewell. I struggled, and kept my composure.

I stood against Max, and he pulled me close to him, and nuzzled my hair. This felt strange: we have not been affectionate to one another, not in that friendly, unthinking way, recently. We should have been.

'I feel that you're sending me away,' I said.

'You're sending yourself away,' he said mildly. 'And you're going to have an amazing time.' He stepped back, and took my face in his hands. 'Just come back happy,' he said.

'Don't make me go!' I begged him.

'Tans, you have to.'

'Why?'

'Because you deserve it. Because you need it. Don't worry about us – you know we'll miss you and you know we'll be fine. You need to get yourself straight. I love to think of you out there, with Elly. It will be *wonderful*. Do it for us, and do it properly. This is a holiday, Tans. It's allowed.'

*   *   *

71

It is half past seven in the morning in Britain but, under the circumstances, and considering that, despite my father's threats, I am *not* in rehab, I decide that I am allowed to flip to Indian time, and order myself a vodka and tonic.

'Cheers,' I whisper. I am talking to myself, but the young man in the next seat answers.

'Cheers,' he replies, holding up a plastic cup of lemonade towards me. I clink cups with him, in a dull collision of plastic. My cup wobbles and trembles in my hand so the liquid almost spills over.

I do not care that the seat is uncomfortable, that my legs are squashed and in imminent danger of deep-vein thrombosis. I shift around and, in a perverse way, I relish the fact that I am crammed into the smallest space an airline can get away with giving someone.

At some point, a tray of lunch arrives: Indian and vegetarian, and I start eating just because it's there, and carry on because it is surprisingly pleasing for an airline meal. I watch the Simpsons movie and drink two little bottles of wine. Then I find myself desperate for the loo. The Technology Guru next to me appears to be out cold, his head lolling uncomfortably in the aisle, his blanket tucked fastidiously around his body.

I unbuckle my seat belt and shift in my seat. I can't bear to wake this man and make him get up, just so I can have a wee. I decide to squeeze past. I am thankful for my long legs, as I am able to step over him, though it does involve an undignified straddle. I am standing with one leg up on my own seat, and the other planted desperately on the edge of the aisle, my hands on the headrest of my neighbour's seat, above his lolling head. I must be slightly drunk, or I would not be attempting this.

This, of course, is the moment when he opens his eyes. He looks at me blearily, then is suddenly, and understandably, alert.

'Um, sorry,' I say quickly. After spending the first few hours of the flight carefully cold-shouldering him, I am now apparently simulating sex as he sleeps. I hoist my leg over him. 'Just trying. Sorry. Toilet . . .' I cannot form distinct sentences. I am beyond mortified. I make a small twisting jump, into the aisle, glad that I am wearing trousers.

'Oh, you should have woken me,' he says, recovering himself

with impeccable politeness. He leaps to his feet. 'Next time,' he adds, 'please do wake me. Don't hesitate.'

I keep buzzing the stewardesses and asking for wine, until the one with the garish make-up refuses to serve me any more.

'I think you've had enough,' she says lightly. 'Why don't you try to get some sleep?'

Everyone else is sleeping. She is right: I have drunk too much. I am already swaying, half focusing, terrified. My whole body is clenched tight, taut, ready to run but with nowhere to go.

'Oh, please,' I say, with a smile, and using my poshest voice. 'I'm on holiday without my children for the first time ever. I won't be loud, I promise.'

She relents. 'Oh, go on then. Only one.'

I make it last. It tips me over the edge, and I fall into a weird, hallucinatory version of oblivion.

Elly runs around my dreams. There is a guru who looks like Jesus. Toby and Joe are there. Max is there. We are all in the paradise that is Pondicherry.

I jolt awake, my heart pounding for no reason. We are beginning our descent into Chennai. The palms of my hands are tingling, my very hair static with anticipation. The tiny woman has creased her face up against her pillow, against the window. I crane my neck to see past her.

It is dark. It is the middle of the night. India is below us. Chennai is not lit up like a Western city: there are pockets of light and patches of darkness. I look around the plane and realise what I hadn't noticed before: that almost all of the passengers are of Indian origin in some way, and that I am already visibly foreign.

I am petrified. I have no idea what I am doing here.

'That's Chennai,' I hear a mother behind me saying to her child. 'Can you say Chennai? Mummy was born in Chennai.'

'Chennai,' says a little voice. I sneak a glance through the gap between the seats. The little girl looks about three, and she is dressed in magenta, with gold earrings. I smile, and she looks away.

* * *

The very air of India knocks me sideways. It is so foreign. I stand at the top of the steps, one foot still on the plane, rooted to the spot. I am dizzy from wine, and sick with fear. I have left a London winter for this, and the very warmth of the Chennai night confounds me.

I am aware that I am holding everyone up, and very slowly I manage to edge down the steps, hanging on to the handrail, and step on to Indian soil.

The terminal building is concrete, and the air inside is humid. I stand in a queue for passport control, eyeing up the other passengers warily. Almost all of them are either Indian or British with Indian origins, and the prevailing mood is one of great jollity. I stand alone, avoiding eye contact or conversation.

There are a few other Westerners: two nice-looking women in their fifties or sixties, and a tall, bearded man in a white suit. The man looks at me, and I look away. I stand with my fists clenched, my heart in my mouth.

I go through the motions. I manage to smile as I hand my passport over, and receive an inky stamp in it. At a branch of Thomas Cook, I change all my sterling cash into thousands upon thousands of rupees. My limp backpack appears on the conveyor belt, half full, half empty. I have never been to this country before, but everyone knows about the hassle. Everybody knows that Indian cities are full of beggars and squalor and that as soon as you eat or drink anything, you start losing weight. I have been elsewhere on this continent, but India is in a league of its own.

I am pale and conspicuous. A crowd of people waits behind a barrier, outside the airport. Many of them are holding up name boards, bobbing, jostling, and scrutinising the passengers. I have heard stories of people being swept up by taxi drivers, shown official-looking price lists in laminated covers, and being forced to pay ten or more times the going rate to get from an airport into a city. I cannot let myself be ripped off; it would be too demoralising.

The pre-paid taxi booth is right in front of me. I ignore the calls of 'Taxi?', march towards it, and fish out a few hundred rupees. I pay, get a voucher, and a man grabs my backpack and leads me through the warm night to an old, shiny car. I put the smallest note I can find into the hand of the man who carried my bag, who turns out not to be the driver, and who is after *baksheesh*.

The interior of the car is crackly leather. I settle back, and stare at the window. The driver sets off, at top speed, veering around obstacles. This is all too strange.

'Hotel Shiva?' he asks, with a smile. 'Hello, madam. First time in India?'

'Hello,' I say, looking out of the window, anxious to see Chennai, even though the darkness shrouds almost everything. A few advertising hoardings are lit, and beyond them all I can make out are the shapes of buildings. When I look at the road ahead, I see that we, along with every other vehicle, are making eccentric progress, swinging apparently randomly from one side to the other. The driver turns around again, grins, and opens his mouth to make conversation.

'Look at the road!' I shout, pointing.

He smiles and rolls his eyes and says, 'Yes, yes, madam,' in a condescending way, and turns his attention languidly back to the dual carriageway in front of him, which I realise is not a dual carriageway at all; he is just treating it like one. He swerves from one side to the other, and back again, either for fun, or to avoid dark-disguised obstacles.

'So,' he says, skirting a sleeping cow and turning back again. 'First time in India.'

There is wailing Hindi music playing quietly on the stereo. It is foreign, dissonant, completely alien to Western ears.

'Yes,' I tell him. I yawn. It is three in the morning. I look at the man, who, after all, is a professional taxi driver and has made it this far. He probably knows what he is doing. 'First time in India.'

I caught Max online a week ago, booking me into the Sheraton for my first few nights. I talked him out of it. We would have had a huge argument about it if I'd had any fight in me. 'If I was going to the Sheraton,' I told him, in my pathetic, limp way, 'I'd prefer just to trek to Knightsbridge or something. It was your idea for me to go to India. At least let me stay somewhere that feels like India.'

He tried for a fight. 'You have responsibilities,' he told me.'You're a mother. And as a lone woman, you're vulnerable. You can't go sleeping in random hovels just for the hell of it. We can afford to put you up somewhere nice, this time.'

'I'll only be in Chennai for a few days before I go to see Elly. You can't send me in a cotton-wool case. If you didn't want me to go, you shouldn't have bought me the bloody ticket. Let me do it properly. I'm not asking for a *hovel*.'

In the end, he spent a lot of time online and consented to the Shiva. The worst thing he could find said about it was that the staff weren't always friendly, and some of the rooms were a bit tatty.

'Check for holes in the walls,' he warned threateningly. 'Specially in the bathroom.'

'Somehow,' I told him mildly, 'I managed to get through life before I met you. I even managed to get through several Asian countries without you. And if I managed without you before, I can probably do it again.' We looked at each other, both aghast at my words. It was not an argument; it was something worse than that.

The foyer of the hotel is bare stone, and it echoes. I walk to the reception desk as if I were walking across a stage. The man on duty has a moustache and a freshly pressed mauve shirt, and is getting on with some paperwork, apparently unbothered by the fact that it is nearly four in the morning. He makes me fill in three different forms, which he adds to various piles.

Another man grabs my backpack and takes me past several buildings to my room. As we cross a courtyard, an aeroplane passes overhead. The man looks up.

'We see the plane,' he says. 'Two hours after, people come.'

It is all too surreal. I cannot walk straight. As soon as the porter has left the room, I run to the bathroom and vomit all the vodka and wine I had in the plane into the loo. Then I crawl between the tightly tucked sheets, and cry myself to sleep.

I am on my own. It is the strangest feeling in the world.

chapter thirteen

I wake to the sound of a telephone ringing, and sit bolt upright, instantly wide awake.

I am in India. My backpack is there, in the corner. Yesterday was real. I am ill.

The room is bathed in daylight, which is pouring through a flimsy white curtain. There are all sorts of noises going on outside, including a repetitive metallic clinking that seems to be taking place right outside the window. I realise that I have been listening to it for hours. It is my phone that's ringing.

Two nights ago, Max fussed around looking up international tariffs and checking that my phone was going to work here. He went through all the numbers in my address book and carefully added '0044' to the front of them and took off the first zero.

'Who's Olivia?' he said, without looking up.

I was flustered. 'Oh. You know. Olivia's in Toby's class. Little stressed girl.'

'You hate her mum.'

'I still needed her number,' I improvised. 'It was for the nativity play. She was sourcing sheep outfits.'

'Do you text her vitriol from time to time?'

'I should do,' I told him. I prayed that he wouldn't go through the messages in my inbox and find out exactly what I do text to 'Olivia's Mum'.

My head hurts and I cannot see properly, but I manage to

locate my phone blearily in the bottom of my handbag. The word 'home' reproaches me on its screen.

'Mmm,' I say, in greeting.

'You're there, then,' says Max. I yawn and try to get my voice out, to say the right words in the right order. 'Woke you up?' he asks.

'Mmm.'

'Oh. The internet told me it was eleven thirty a.m. in Chennai, so I thought it would be OK.'

'Half eleven?'

'According to the World Wide Web. But you tell me. You're the one who's there.'

I blink and look around for a clock. There is nothing in this room: just a bed, table, and a copy of the Yellow Pages. I heave myself off the bed and switch on the ceiling fan. The blades start turning slowly, then faster, and faster. I find myself unable to look away.

'I believe you.'

'Tans, you said you'd text when you arrived.'

I squeeze my eyes shut. 'It was the middle of the night and I was feeling . . . odd . . . and I could barely walk, let alone text. Sorry.'

'That's OK. Don't mind me, tossing and turning for hours, checking my phone obsessively and at one point switching on News 24 just to make sure there hadn't been any plane crashes. It's seven thirty in the morning here. The place is quiet without your early-morning coffee thing, you know? I hardly knew what to do with myself when no one woke me up by staring at me at half past three.'

'Sorry. Really. I didn't think.'

His voice is light. 'I'm sure. So – how is it so far?'

I throw myself back on the bed and watch the dusty blades rotating above my head. The ceiling behind them is yellow, and the leading edge of each fan blade is furry with dust. I try to think what I should say. All I can do is stick to the facts.

'I got a cab from the airport,' I tell him. 'Scary driving. The hotel's fine. Someone's clinking something outside the window. That's it. I haven't done anything or spoken to anyone.'

'Going out exploring today?'

'I guess so.'

'Be careful.'

'I know.'

'Tans,' he says. 'You haven't been to India. The level of hassle in the cities can be something else. Look after yourself. Wear your money belt. Travel by rickshaw or taxi. Haggle on rickshaw fares. Don't go round handing out money to everyone who asks, because you're just making it more worthwhile for people to beg than for them to do anything else, and that's not a healthy economy.'

'You already said.'

'You should be going straight to Elly.'

'I know. But I'm here. I have to explore. How are the boys?'

'Asleep. Fine. We had a good day. Went over to Sarah and Gav's and everyone did plenty of playing. Sarah's gutted that you're gone. She was trying to get me to have a drink with her at ten in the morning. Gav left the room when she suggested it. I told her she'd got the wrong person. Joe asked if India was near Waitrose.'

I squeeze my eyes tight shut.

'Look,' I say. 'This'll be costing a fortune. I'll ring on a landline later on and talk to Joe and Toby. Max?'

'Mmm?'

'Miss you. Love you.' I wonder why I can say this, when I would find it a lot harder to say 'I miss you' and 'I love you'. If I take myself out of the equation, it becomes easier.

'We miss you too,' says Max. 'And it goes without saying that we all love you.'

I recognise at once that he has done the same thing: *It goes without saying that we all love you* is a lot easier to say than 'I love you'. We used to say we loved each other over and over again, every single day. I suppose I am reading too much into this.

I don't want to leave the room. I decide to do everything as slowly as I possibly can. The room feels bland and slightly stale, with a disquieting edge of foreignness to it. I am in limbo, and I cannot bear to haul myself out of it.

I am helped by the fact that the shower doesn't work. I stand to one side, turn the taps, and look, in a hopeful manner, at the shower head that is clipped to the wall. All I can do is to make cold water gush out of a tap at waist height.

When I see the bucket in the corner, I remember, and smile, in spite of myself, at the sudden onslaught of memories. The shower was never supposed to work. I stand, naked, and watch water gurgle down the drain as I am transported back to the good old days, when I was young and confident, and had freedom to drift around in a world that, it seems to me now, was a thousand times more innocent.

I fill the big bucket with lukewarm water, and remember, suddenly, how elegant I used to feel, naked but for a necklace, in a tiled room with a bucket of water. I used to pretend to be a woman in an Ingres painting. I take a deep breath, and tip water over myself using a plastic bowl that is hanging on the wall. I shiver, and my skin stands up in goosebumps.

My body is approaching forty, and I don't feel like a nubile artist's model any more, but as I tip cold water over my head, I manage a very small, nostalgic smile.

Two men are working on a lorry that is parked in the courtyard outside. Both have chunky phones clipped to their belts. They pause to greet me with a friendly, 'Hello.'

I walk across the gravelly ground. Nothing happens. I look around: the hotel complex is bigger than I thought, and I am still in something of a safe zone. There are buildings all around, with paths between them and hand-painted signs showing the way to the restaurant, the snack bar, pool. No beggars are going to get me here.

The warmth of the still air is strange, a reminder of how far I am from the comfort zone. I stand still, and take in a deep breath. I feel it warm inside me. I can smell Indian food, kerosene, rotting greenery. The sky is dark blue, studded with tiny wispy clouds.

The smell of the restaurant, with fragrant spices, makes my stomach gurgle. It would be the easiest thing to follow the sign, to sit in the restaurant, to read the guidebook and put off my first experience of India, to stay safe for a little while longer. It is midday, a perfectly reasonable time to sit down and eat, particularly when you've slept through breakfast.

On my first day in Asia, years ago, I sat in the breakfast room at my hotel in Ho Chi Minh City, and lingered for as long as I could over a fried egg, trying, as now, to postpone the moment when I had to step outside. There were two other people in the room: Elly and Eddy. They ended up being my companions, on and off, for months; and here I am, ten years later, still so connected to Elly that I have turned my life upside down for her.

So I decide that I will try it again. It worked before. I could do with somebody to talk to.

I poke my head around the doorway of the dining room. It is a large room with little light. There is hardly anyone there, and I step back. Breakfast people have already gone; and I don't want to sit in an empty room.

A waiter, smart and smiling, walks over to me.

'Just you, madam?' he asks, ushering me forward.

I step back. 'I'll come back later,' I tell him quickly. 'I'm a bit early, I think.'

He shakes his head. 'No,' he says. 'Kitchen is always open.'

The idea of sitting, alone, in a murky dark room holds even less appeal than the streets of Chennai.

'No, sorry,' I tell him. 'I'll come back.'

I walk backwards away from him, and turn towards the exit sign.

If we had all come to India together, I would not be walking around the hotel complex, pretending to be interested in the snack bar and the pool, just to put off the moment when I step out into the city. I would not be so far from my comfort zone, so debilitatingly terrified, and I would not be cowering from the imminent onslaught of beggars and ghosts from my past.

Max would be by my side, and we would conduct our days within the reassuring parameters of children's needs. We would stay relentlessly safe, stop regularly in air-conditioned cafés. We would go out in short, controlled bursts and retire back to the safety of the hotel for most of the day.

As it is, I can do anything.

Suddenly, I wonder whether I have ever done anything unusual, or even had fun, with Toby. I have spent six years containing him, dealing with him, making sure he is fed, rested, warm and safe. I have given him pens and paper and cleared a space at the table, then stuck the masterpieces on the wall. I have set him loose in a park or on a field several times a week since he learned to walk. I have dragged him along footpaths, and rationed television time. I have cooked nutritious meals or, failing that, defrosted pizzas. I have gone through the motions, carefully fulfilled my duties.

But when Toby has screamed with laughter, it was Max who was chasing him. When he gasped with suspense and gave away his hiding place, it was Max who was saying, 'I wonder where Toby could be.' He has cuddled up with Max to read Harry Potter, and they have had involved, obsessive discussions that have gone on for days about Snape and Voldemort and house elves, while I was pouring my second drink of the evening, and watching the clock, anticipating children's bedtime.

Toby and I have never really enjoyed being together. I should have insisted that he, at least, came with me.

'Hello, madam,' say the rickshaw drivers, their voices on top of each other, all of them. There are at least ten men, jostling on the pavement outside the hotel, and all of them are keen for my custom. I watch them staying behind an invisible line, while a uniformed guard surveys them carefully. Beyond them, traffic is careening along the road.

'Hello, madam,' they say. 'Rickshaw, madam?'

As I step across the line, they rush forward, crowding me, each desperate to be the one to snare me. I see their rickshaws, squat, yellow and doorless, parked around the corner in a great mass.

'No, thanks,' I say. I try not to look intimidated. I hold my head up and walk through the middle of the group. I have given birth twice: I can get through a bunch of rickshaw-wallahs.

'I'm walking,' I explain.

I turn left, for the beach, and set off briskly along the side of the terrifying road. They move with me, en masse. A thickset man bars the path, and I step off the pavement to get past him. A van bounces past, close to me, sounding its horn, with a tone that changes as it disappears down the road. The man, who is frowning, does not look away from my face.

'Rickshaw,' he says, looking as though I have personally affronted him.

'I want to walk,' I tell him firmly. 'I'm walking to the beach.'

'But the beach,' he says, 'is ten kilometres. Very bad idea.'

'It's not ten kilometres,' I tell him, attempting to give him the look of someone who is truly not going to be taken for a ride.

'Very far,' he says. 'And the pavement is very bad. And then you want a rickshaw at the beach, but the men at the beach are very bad men. They are crooks.'

'Is that right?'

'You have a pen?'

'Don't tell me – you want "one pen"?' This is what everyone, particularly children, used to ask for in Vietnam, and Laos, and Thailand. One pen, coin from your country, sweets, shake hand.

But he is looking at me as if I were mad. 'I want to write my phone number,' he says, pointing to the chunky mobile that is clipped on to his belt. 'Then you call me. When you need a rickshaw.'

'Oh,' I say. 'Oh, OK.'

I find a pen in my bag, and give him a piece of paper. He writes his name – Ganesh – and a number. He smiles.

'You all alone? You have husband?'

'Yes,' I say. 'And two children. Boys.'

'Boys! Very lucky. Where's your husband and two boys?'

I am walking off by now. 'In London,' I call over my shoulder. London: a far-off city, a place everyone has heard of; my boys' home.

The pavement is uneven, and the traffic is strange, foreign. I hope I will never have to cross the road. There are enamel-painted buses, with masses of humanity crushed inside them, spilling out of the doorway. At least I can afford not to travel by bus. There are surprising numbers of cars, and there are bikes and motor-bikes, and everyone has a life that I cannot imagine, and is getting on with it.

Once I have started walking, the edge of the fear starts to fall away from me. I put one foot in front of the other, and again, and again, and nothing shocking happens.

This is, clearly, not an area frequented by beggars. I reach the first corner, and nobody has asked me for money. No one has even looked at me. I have not been propositioned by men who assume a lone Western woman to be game for pornographic adventures (or perhaps I am too old for such attention). I cross the road, which is a side road, easily.

By the second corner, I should have little children hanging off my clothes. I walk through air that is not as thick, nor as humid, nor as fetid, as I expected it to be. It is warmer, different from London air, mildly polluted but fresher than the air at home because of the tantalising top notes of ocean. Even the traffic, when I watch it, turns out to be working to a system. Every vehicle expertly avoids all the others, and no one pays me any attention apart from rickshaw drivers.

Two men are walking towards me. Both of them are in their twenties, and both are dressed in Aertex polo shirts and trousers. One has a small moustache, the other a beard and turban. My heart speeds up, and my palms tingle. I wait for them to say something, to do something. I think I see one of them glance at me and look quickly away.

I wait for the approach, the comment, the hassle. But they walk on by, as if I were not there. It is not my wedding ring: they didn't even look. I almost trip on the edge of a paving stone as I turn to check they're not talking about me. It is baffling.

The same road leads all the way to the beach. I cross side roads without any problems. I pass a few old men sitting on wooden stools watching the traffic, but they look at me with no interest. Occasionally, I cough at the stench of stale urine, though most of the time the sea air is surprisingly fresh. I learn how to step up and down the kerb, into the road, and out of it, avoiding broken paving stones and sudden holes.

The buildings I pass vary between crumbling concrete and brand-new stucco offices. Cars and taxis and buses thunder by, black exhaust often belching into my face, and rickshaws shadow me constantly, touting for business. A cloud moves, and the sun shines straight on to the top of my head.

The only attention I get, and it is ceaseless, comes from rickshaw drivers. I walk with an awkward self-consciousness, while drivers hover beside me, waiting for me to change my mind. When one gets fed up and leaves, his places is taken within seconds.

I walk under a thundering flyover, and suddenly there is a road to cross, and it is a main road and I have no idea how to get over it.

Two skinny cows are lying on the side of the road. They are entirely unmoved by the overloaded blue bus which is belching out smoke within an inch of their jutting ribs.

After a few minutes, two confident young women, in tight jeans and T-shirts, come and stand near me, looking at their phones, wiggling and giggling. They are in their early twenties, and are smooth-skinned, healthy, glistening, beautiful. They are wearing designer clothes and expensive-looking jewellery. One has a spiky gamine haircut, the other shiny long layers.

When they step out into the road, I step with them. I follow at their Ferragamo heels as they nonchalantly dodge between the cars. As we all reach the opposite pavement, the gamine one turns to look at me. I watch her sparkling youthful eyes taking in my limp skirt and messy hair. She turns away without a word.

'I saw a little Western girl yesterday,' she says to her friend as they walk away. 'I wanted to eat her up. I just love baby Westerners. *So* cute.'

By the time I reach the beach, I want to throw my arms in the air and yell, just to make Chennai notice me. It is extraordinarily disconcerting to step on to Asian soil expecting to be mobbed and to be roundly ignored.

The beach is wide and long; the sea is a silvery line on the horizon. At the edge of the sand, families are walking, or sitting on rugs, and men sell ice cream from carts, while countless good-natured games of cricket take place all around.

'The Bay of Bengal,' I say to myself. I like the way that sounds.

I stand on the edge of the sand, and say it again, louder. I am inaudible as well as invisible. I buy a creamy vanilla ice cream, and sit on the sand. I feel its warmth through my skirt. I lean back on my elbows and watch a family of four, the mother in a beautiful purple sari, ambling along together. I am the worst-dressed woman on the beach. Perhaps this is why no one is interested in troubling me.

I text Max: 'Absolutely no hassle. Am fine. Will call. xxx'

Then, against my better judgement, I text Jim, too.

'Hey, I'm here,' I write. 'No one's noticed. Look after my son. T x'

I erase the kiss, and send it.

'Rickshaw, madam?' asks a man as I meander between cricket games, back towards the road.

'OK,' I agree. He looks astonished, and hurriedly leads me to his chariot, which is parked at the edge of the busy road.

'How much to Saravana Bhavan restaurant?' I ask, reading from the guidebook.

'Get in, madam,' says the driver. 'Then we discuss how much.'

'No. Tell me the price first.'

'OK! OK, no problem. To restaurant, is free. Then, you pay forty rupees for one hour. I take you everywhere, museums, tourist place.'

'I don't believe you,' I tell him. 'How much are you really going to charge?'

'Forty rupees is the price!' he says fiercely. 'Other rickshaws? More expensive! I like you. Good price for a good lady.'

The engine starts, third time, and the whole contraption starts buzzing beneath me. We take a sharp left, across lines of traffic, and the seafront vanishes. We are swallowed up by the vast city, moving fast. I hold on to the edge of the seat with both hands and, for the first time, I feel my freedom, and I let the city slap me in the face.

Cars close in on either side of us. The rickshaw ploughs a plucky little path between a stinking lorry full of squealing, invisible animals, and a bus, and I pull my elbows to my sides, unconsciously trying to fit through the gap.

There are hoardings everywhere, many of them advertising mobile phones. A man in a lunghi is crouching by a small oil burner, directly outside a Vodafone shop, cooking something in a pan. A woman with a baby on her back is selling garlands of bright fake flowers. Two men in suits, carrying briefcases, carefully step around a resting cow, whose bones are painfully jutting under its skin.

We weave between cars and motorbikes, and screech to a sudden halt. I lurch forwards and throw my arms out to save myself.

'Very sorry, madam,' says the driver, smiling back. A cow, it seems, has stepped into the road. All the traffic is swerving to avoid it, or making emergency stops.

The waiter ushers me through the busy restaurant, to a table by the wall, and as I see and smell the food, I realise that I am starving. The only other visible foreigners are a couple in the corner. I glimpse them briefly, she red-headed and he dark-skinned but, somehow, definitely Western. People look up, and when they see me, they look down again, uninterested. A couple of people say 'Hello' as I pass, and I am careful to say it back, pleased for even this tiny interaction.

I have a good view of the rest of the restaurant, and am in a perfect position for people-watching.

I look down the menu. My stomach rumbles loudly, and the waiter chuckles.

'Hungry, madam?' he says.

I look at the menu. 'One business lunch, please,' I say.

A business lunch, it turns out, comes on a round aluminium plate with many compartments. There are several types of vegetable curry, there is rice, there are chapattis, and yogurt, and spicy chutney. A couple of things I cannot identify, but I eat them anyway. I adore every mouthful of it. There is just one thing that would make this perfect.

I catch the waiter's eye.

'Could I have a beer, please?' I ask.

He smiles and shakes his head. 'No, sorry, madam,' he says

politely (though I can see from his eyes that lone women do not usually ask for beer in this restaurant).

'Don't you serve alcohol?'

'No, madam. Tamil Nadu is more or less dry,' he tells me. I read this in the guidebook, but since it was followed by a list of cocktail bars, I assumed the modern, alcoholic world had caught up with Tamil Nadu. I vaguely recall something about a high tax on alcohol in this state.

'I don't mind paying the extra tax,' I offer.

'Very sorry,' he says. 'Beer is not stocked.'

I make an effort not to look disappointed.

'OK,' I say. 'I'll have another bottle of water then, thanks.'

When I finish my lunch, a man comes around with a couple of pots and dollops some more food into every compartment of the serving dish. I nibble at this, knowing that I am full, but prolonging my time here, finding space for yet more vegetarian curry, drinking every drop of my litre of water.

I watch the backpackerish couple in the corner. They seem to be arguing, but though I scrutinise them, and strain my ears, I cannot hear what they are saying.

My next stop is the Fort Museum, which turns out to be in a deserted and preserved garrison built by the British way back in the seventeenth century. It is entered by crossing a little bridge and walking through a metal detector. The metal detector is a frame, with heavy wires trailing away from it, and it looks surreal on an Indian bridge on a sunny day. It is staffed by two men and a woman, who are wearing blue uniforms and kicking back, smoking, and chewing gum. One of the men barely looks up from his conversation to wave me through.

I try not to think about cold beer. Particularly not about the way the outside of the bottle would be wet with condensation, and the bubbles would almost reach the top of the glass when I poured it out. I am careful not to think of that at all.

The compound is like Toytown, the colonial structure preserved. After the teeming streets, it is bland, dull and, inevitably, shaming for a Briton. There are a few other tourists mooching around. I look out hungrily for potential friends, but all the foreigners here are older, more staid, and clearly on a holiday rather than travelling. All the Indians are in security guards' uniforms, or working as tour guides to the Westerners.

My energy slumps as soon as I step into the actual museum. I look dutifully at display cases of soldiers' uniforms, and register the appropriate level of colonial guilt. I look at a display of hand-written letters from Clive of India and others of his ilk, detailing their negotiations with local leaders, complete with offers of elephants and jewels. I stand and think about the minutiae of colonial power tussles. I see the security guard watching me, stony-faced. When I smile, he looks away.

And the pull of home is too much. I wobble on my feet, and try to work out what I am doing here. Why am I in a random museum, playing the dutiful tourist, all alone, when I have a family in London, and a life there? I find a quiet room, at the top of the building, where sombre portraits of British colonial officials watch me take the photographs of my boys from my handbag, and touch them with my fingertips.

Toby is standing in front of our front door, wearing his school uniform and smiling a proud smile. Joe is jumping in a pile of autumn leaves at the park. Max is holding both of them on his lap, in the flat. I sit on a hard bench, and spread the three pictures out, and touch them with my fingertips. I let the tears come, since there is no one to see them.

People come into the room and pretend not to see me, or leave again quickly. I don't care. For two hours, I wander around this strange little concrete place. I wish I could go and sit in a bar and have a drink.

Eventually, though, I have to go. On my way out, I pass the two backpackers I saw in the restaurant. The woman has long, red hair and is dressed in proper travelling clothes that I envy. She wears loose Thai fishermen's trousers, and an embroidered cotton top, and she has a sturdy little backpack on her back, of a type that I still wince to hear described as a 'day pack'. The man looks Asian, but something in his manner makes me certain that he is a Westerner. As we pass them, I give a little grin that

I hope is friendly, but which probably appears desperate. This is what I need. If I could just have a conversation, I would be able to get through the rest of the day.

'Sam!' the woman calls. She sounds Scottish. 'Sam, would you have two hundred rupees? Could you pay for both of us?'

'Oh, yeah,' he says. 'Sure.' He looks at me. 'Hello, there,' he says.

'Hello.' I pause, but cannot think of anything else to say, so I walk on.

I wanted to go back to the hotel, but the rickshaw swings to the right and pulls into a car park. The driver turns in his seat and looks at me with beseeching eyes. Before he says anything, I look at the front of the building to which he has brought us.

'No,' I say. 'Absolutely no fucking way. I said I wanted to go to the hotel, and I meant it.'

'Let me explain,' says the driver. 'A *very good* handicraft emporium. You buy nothing. It's OK. Just go in and look. Very nice fabric, jewels, souvenirs. Then they give me T-shirts for my children.' He holds my gaze, unblinking. 'For my *children*.'

'How many children have you got?' I ask, although I shouldn't.

'Me? I have two. One boy, one girl. Nine years and seven years.'

'I'll pay you more than we agreed for the journeys,' I tell him, 'if you don't make me go in this place.' The last place in the world I want to go is into an overpriced, hassle-rich 'emporium'. I want to lock myself away, and then go out to find the internet.

'For my children,' he mutters, ruthlessly holding eye contact.

'No way,' I say, trying to stare him out.

'You have children, madam?'

I sigh. He knows I have, because I have already told him.

'How long do I have to stay?'

'Only fifteen minutes, they give me T-shirts.'

'For fuck's sake,' I mutter, and I trail up the steps and into a cold blast of brutal air conditioning.

The emporium is worse for the soul than I could have imagined. It is entirely bland. A counter in front of us is stacked

with rolls of cloth of different colours, but they are as neatly
arranged, with precise pleats and artful drapery, as they would
be in a shop in Knightsbridge. Across the room, a different counter,
staffed by a man with an enormous insincere smile, is displaying
stones and jewels in glass cases. I don't want to look at anything.
The life and joy drains away from me and oozes around the door
and out into the street. I detest places like this.

'Hello, madam,' says the man at the cloth stall.

''Lo,' I say quickly, and avoid eye contact.

I have a cursory look at the fabric, although nothing could
interest me less, and wander into another room. This one has a
large and sterile display of metallic elephants. I cannot bear it. I
turn and walk back towards the door.

The shop owners are impassive as I leave. 'Goodbye, madam,'
says the one nearest the door as I pass. My Birkenstocks clump
on the fake-marble floor. The hairs on my arms are standing on
end. I step gratefully back into the heat and the life and the chaos.

The driver is not pleased.

'Take me to the Shiva Hotel, thanks,' I say. I am trying to be
crisp, someone who brooks no discussion.

'You don't stay long,' he grumps.

'You said I didn't have to buy anything. You said I just had to
go in there and look. That's what I did.'

'Five minutes! Too short!'

'It was horrible in there. You know it was. It's a vile place and
they'd never sell anything if they didn't bribe people like you to
bring them customers. Take me back to the hotel.'

'One thousand and forty rupees,' he says, as we pull up.

'Right,' I say. I am ready for a fight, itching for one. 'Can you
tell me how you got from forty to a thousand? Because I have to
warn you, you're messing with the wrong person.'

I flash back to myself in Vietnam, to a moment that still
makes me cringe. I was far more belligerent in those days. I
still had spirit, then. I remember being so angry when my cycle-
rickshaw man insisted that the price had gone up to five dollars
on a random pretext that I took a five dollar bill, ripped it into
quarters, and threw it at his feet. I watched, with great satisfaction,

as he leapt off his bike and scrabbled around on the Saigon pavement for the pieces of the note, and then I walked into the hotel without looking back.

I am just as angry now, and I have a strong urge to perform the same stunt. This time, however, I restrain myself because I know all sorts of things that I didn't know back then: the man is trying to make a living. He is doing what he needs to do for his children's sake. The world is strongly unfair, but in my favour, not his.

'Forty was for go to Fort Museum,' he is saying quickly. 'Two hundred rupees for waiting at lunch – long time. To go to San Thome Cathedral, two hundred rupees. Waiting one hundred. To go to Wandering Monk, two hundred. Waiting one hundred. Back to hotel two hundred rupees. I don't do you a special rate after you don't go to splendid handicraft shop.'

'But I didn't go to San Thome Cathedral or the Wandering Monk,' I say, laughing at the absurdity of this.

'Yes but rickshaw rate incorporates.'

I decide against following this line of discussion, because in spite of myself, I greatly admire his cheek.

'One hundred,' I say instead.

'No, no, no. One hundred was for if you went to splendid handicraft shop. OK, OK, eight hundred and fifty.'

'One hundred and fifty.'

'No good.'

I do some mental arithmetic. Eight hundred and fifty rupees is less than ten pounds. One hundred and fifty is less than two pounds. I spend 850 rupees at home without noticing. I spend ten times that amount without noticing. I like the working methods of someone who includes charges for places you didn't go to, on the grounds that he would have taken you there, had you asked.

All the same, my pride is stopping me from paying the full whack. I scrabble in my purse.

'Here,' I tell him. 'Four hundred and fifty. Even though I know it's too much. What the hell?'

'Whatta hell,' he agrees, pocketing it with a smile. 'I come and look for you tomorrow.'

'Don't even fucking think about it.'

I lie on the bed, look at the ceiling fan. The dust is, perhaps, slightly thicker this afternoon. There is something satisfying in the fact that the blades catch the dirt from the air as they move.

I fought tooth and nail against labelling myself a backpacker, years ago. I hated the word and despised everything it stood for: I took my designer clothes to Vietnam, and was annoyed when I never managed to drift around playing at being a French colonial aristocrat. I could not see any romance in being known by the sort of bag I carried. I did not want to be swept up into a category with hordes of uncouth Australians, or demobbed Israelis. I wanted to be a traveller; I wanted to be somebody who just happened to be in Asia.

Now, that is exactly what I am. I am not in the least bit special. Chennai is full of people who are better dressed than I am, who carry better phones, and who are clearly not living out of bags of any description. India is supposed to be stinky and poor and gruelling and mind-blowing. Parts of the city I visited today have been those things, but it is also rich and stately and well-dressed and playful. It accommodates everyone, just like London.

chapter fourteen

I sit and think about nothing, gathering my strength for a few hours, and then I venture out again. It is almost dark when I set off on foot, and I am rested and ready for an adventure. I know that there is an internet place on the other side of the road. I know it's not worth getting a rickshaw there. I steel myself and step into the fray, almost relishing it this time.

Ganesh is among the crowd that materialises out of the dusk.

'Rickshaw, madam?' he says, his voice cutting through the rest.

'I'm only going over the road,' I tell him quickly, looking at him over everyone else's heads. 'To iWay.'

He looks into my eyes for a second, then steps aside. 'Tomorrow.'

'Tomorrow,' I promise.

The crowd clears with tuts and mutters of resentment.

Traffic thunders by, in four lanes. I stand for a while, waiting for somebody to come and cross with me. The darkness deepens by the second.

'If I give you ten rupees,' I say to Ganesh, when he materialises at my shoulder, 'could you walk me over the road?'

He grins, showing a row of glinting white teeth that would make a Hollywood (or Bollywood) star proud.

'Ten rupees, I'll take you to iWay. Tomorrow I take you everywhere.' He grins at me. 'I saw you come back today. Four hundred and fifty! Very expensive rickshaw!'

iWay is like every internet centre in the world. It smells of cheap carpet, paper and ink. I stare at the computer, and wonder what to say. Should I be honest, or should I let everyone think I am ecstatically happy?

I write to Elly first, a quick, urgent message.

Dear Elly,
I can't believe it, but I appear to be in Chennai . . . am still
not quite sure how you managed to get me here.
But I can't wait to see you. Can I come sooner? What
about if I got a cab, say, tomorrow?
I'll check mails in the morning – hope to hear from you
and hope to see you very very soon.
Lots & lots of love
T xxx

Then I write to Max. I imagine him at home, worrying about me, checking his mails, and I know what I have to do. I keep it brief.

Darling x 3,
I'm here, and it's amazing. Like being hit in the face by a
spicy-scented hairdryer set to hot.
The hassle factor is low except from rickshaw drivers, and
nothing I can't handle. It's weird being away, but clearing
my head slightly. I miss you all more than I can say and
have shown your photo to a few random people.
Love you so much, thinking of you all the time.
M, don't worry about me, I am fine and appear to be
pretty much invisible anyway.
With so much love
Mummy xxxx

There is something unhealthy about signing an email to my husband 'Mummy', but I send it anyway. Then I write similarly jaunty messages to Lola, Jessica, Briony, and Sarah. I read a message from Jim, but manage not to reply just yet.

'Jesus,' he has written, 'but I wish I was where you are. Have a cool time. You've got me all worked up about heading to India myself. You know I'll miss you. Keep me posted. J'

A young man next to me is hitting the space bar hard, repeatedly, with an expression of pained concentration on his face. Toby does that too, given the opportunity. I had to ban him from clicking on any link from his approved games sites when I found him staring, baffled, at a chat site with alarmingly adult avatars.

I remember that I promised to contact Max's parents.

'Just to let you know,' I write to Delia, 'that I arrived safely, and have not yet been affected by dysentery, malaria, or even Delhi belly. I'll be off to see my friend in a few days and in the meantime am staying in a nice, clean hotel and visiting museums.'

I blind-copy Max in, to make sure he sees this rare evidence of impeccable daughter-in-law behaviour on my part, and send it off to the Peak District. I wonder why it is that I find it so hard to be considerate to my in-laws. I sometimes try to say that it's because I have never known a normal family life, and so the very ordinariness, the positive niceness, of Max's family unnerves me. Max has been known to suggest that it's because I can't find it in myself to bother with people who are not going to be professionally useful to me, and who are not in the least bit glamorous.

I think it's a bit of both.

Though, now that I think about it, Max's mother, Delia, is meek and unassertive, and was baffled by me and nervous of me the first time we met. Now I might be more like her than I would care to admit.

chapter fifteen

When I leave iWay, it is so dark that it could be midnight. The pavement is less navigable in the dark. No one gives me a second glance, even as I stagger and stumble along the uneven, treacherous walkway.

The smells seem to be intensified. As I can't see anything, I picture Smell as a shifting monster that follows me around. It is made of wisps of rotting food, droplets of stale urine, bodies, and exhaust. Every time it seems unbearable, a waft of spices drifts into the mix, or a scent of frying samosas that is so all-encompassing, so glorious, that I want to buy whatever is for sale at the roadside stall, and eat it quickly, greedily, with my fingers, out of newspaper.

I buy a wrapper full of onion pakora, and walk along the road, devouring it, savouring the grease and the spice.

People loom in front of me as dark shapes, because the roads are not lit. They are not lit, and many vehicles do not have headlights – most are not capable of headlights – but there is life and ceaseless activity everywhere around. I hear it, but I don't see it.

I am disorientated, and wish I had let Ganesh wait outside iWay, and bring me to the temple. Even the rickshaw drivers ignore me, now that I am out of the touristy area, and, in the dark, not obviously foreign. A group of young men passes, chatting seriously, and pays me no attention at all. A man is pissing heavily against a wall, and the stream of liquid creeps towards my feet, out of the half-light. I am in such haste to avoid it that I trip over the edge of my own shoe, and my left foot receives a warm and revolting splash through its sensible sandal. I scream and gag, and screw up my eyes in disgust, but there is nothing I can do, so I carry on walking with this man's urine drying slowly on my foot. I need a wee myself, and I know I could just lift my skirt and do one here, and no one would even notice.

When I reach a wide, crowded shopping street, full of shoes and clothes and textiles which spill out on to the night-time pavement, in the most different sales display possible from the Emporium's, I know I have missed the temple.

'Bollocks,' I say, and a woman walking past looks at me sharply. At least she has seen me. When I smile, she backs away.

I have been walking the streets for nearly an hour, and I am starting to feel reckless. I am lost, but it doesn't matter. I have overshot my destination, though I have no idea how that could possibly have happened, considering that, according to the map, I have walked past an enormous busy temple with a water tank in front of it. I stare at the shop building opposite, as if it might somehow help me to get my bearings.

'I'm lost,' I whisper. I scan the area. There is nothing so mundane as a road sign.

I am lost in Chennai, and tired, and disorientated. For a moment, the whole world seems wildly random. For years I have chafed against London, and I never realised what a small step it would take to become immersed in an Indian city, alone in the dark. Yesterday I woke up in London. Now I am lost in search of a Hindu temple. It is impossible.

When I nervously stop a young woman carrying a baby, her husband turns round and guffaws. He shows me the blank wall behind me.

'But this is the Kapaleeshwarar Temple!' he explains, with a laugh. The woman joins in. They chuckle at me more than I think is strictly necessary. 'It's just here! Directly where you are standing!'

'There?' I stare. 'But there's nothing . . .' I notice that there are railings on the top of the wall, then a blank space, and further back there is a building, which does, indeed, look a bit like a temple might look. 'OK,' I say. 'Thanks.'

*   *   *

A man at a flower stall motions me over with his head, and nods to a pile of shoes by his feet. He turns his attention straight back to his sickly-smelling blooms. I look at the shoes he is guarding: they are high-end, top of the range shoes, a mixture of designer and Bollywood, shiny and sequinned; he is clearly only soliciting the shoes of the rich. My Birkenstocks are the dullest ones there, by a long way. I look around, wildly hoping that it might be good form to wash one's feet before entering the temple, so that I could be rid of the stranger's urine. 'Is there a tap?' I ask, but he frowns in incomprehension, and anyway, I can see that there isn't.

He hands me an orange flower that immediately covers my hand with thick bright powder.

My feet barely touch the ground. I walk with the crowd, to the temple and around it. Little bells ring, and there is incense in the air. I follow the people, caught up in their energy, and stare around at the gods and the altars and the flowers everywhere. I walk past the queues for shrines, become a part of the noisy crowds. The heady scent of pollen mixed with incense makes me light-headed. I twizzle the flower round and round.

'Hindus have more fun,' I say to myself.

'Indeed we do,' says a middle-aged man, beaming at me. He is dressed in a kurta pyjama and is carrying armfuls of flowers. I follow him at a discreet distance, and put my bloom down next to his.

Elly should have become a Hindu. I imagine it appealing to the hedonist in her, as it does to me. Who would need wine and beer as distractions when you could go to the temple instead? Yet you never hear of anybody converting to Hinduism, and I have no idea what the process would involve. Everyone becomes Buddhists instead. It would be one way of surprising Max.

'How do I become a Hindu?' I ask the kurta man, when our paths cross again.

He grins, his round face lighting up.

'Oh, Hindus are not made,' he says, in a genial voice. 'They are born. I can assure you, madam, you will never be a Hindu!'

The dark street outside is still thronged with people, and I scan it, again, for someone like me. It is lit by lanterns that are strung along by the temple wall, and it is hard to see faces, but I peer around anyway. Although I hate myself for needing to do this, I know that company would be a lifeline. I want to see someone, through a crowd, and share a smile of recognition because we know that we are both far from home and experiencing the same things. I desperately want to share this experience; I want to hear someone else's perspective, to validate my own. If someone else were here, my experience would be normal, plausible, less hallucinatory. Also, I would quite like to speak.

Some women seem to fall into a backpackerish easy friendship when they have babies. I have seen it happening: they look at each other at adjacent café tables, look at each other's children, and say, casually, 'How old is she, then?' The next moment, they are apparently friends for life. I have even, on occasion, been so desperate that I have tried the same thing myself but, as with everything else connected with parenthood, I have spectacularly failed to pull it off.

I remember the first time I tried it, in a café in North London. Max was at work, Lola had told me to 'stand on your own two feet', and I was desperate for human interaction. I sat at a table in Matt's Café and attempted to drink a cup of coffee without dripping hot caffeinated milk on to Toby, who was sleeping in a sling on my front. I started to stare at a dark-haired woman a couple of tables away. She had an older baby sitting on her lap, and she was feeding him the froth from the top of her coffee, with a teaspoon. She was chatting to him happily, singing, 'This is the way we slurp our bubbles,' while he giggled at her.

After a few minutes, I decided I would do it.

'Hello there,' I said, in a stupid bright voice. 'How old is he, then?'

She looked at me as if I'd asked her bra size.

'Ten months,' she said, out of the corner of her mouth. 'And she's a girl. Come on, Matilda, we mustn't keep Daddy waiting.'

She was out of there before I could even try to reply. She left half a coffee behind. I left mine, too, and took Toby for his first, urgent, trip to the pub.

I am cringing at this memory when, all of a sudden, I am on the ground. I sprawl on the pavement, so shocked that I cannot move. People step around me and carry on with their journeys, unbothered. I think I have scraped the skin off both my knees. They are stinging horribly. My hands tingle with pain.

I swivel around, and sit up. I blink hard. The pavement feels rough and grubby, and I am quite glad that I can't see it. I wonder whether I should try to get some disinfectant, because I am sure that my legs are bleeding.

This is the last straw. Tears roll down my cheeks. I gulp and sniff, and long for home. I want to howl, to wail, to have a tantrum. I don't want to be here, on my own.

'Sorry about that,' says a voice. It is a croaky, hollow voice, with, I think, an English accent. I do not move from my position, sitting in the middle of the pavement.

'What?' I ask, without looking around. There is no reply. I start to get to my feet, as this is, clearly, the only thing I can do.

'I might've tripped you. Didn't mean to.'

There is a dark figure, closer to me than I had realised. He could put out a hand and touch me. I shift away, and stand up. I need to grab a rickshaw back to the hotel.

'No, don't go,' he says. 'You looked nice. Wanted to talk to you.'

'So you did mean to, then,' I manage to point out, edging away. Then I stop, and try to see his face. I can just see the outline. The lanterns are high up at the top of the wall. In spite of myself, I take a small step closer.

A pair of eyes stares at me from a face that is so haggard, so dirty, so lined and so creased that I know at once that he can only be a drugs casualty. This man's hair is thick and matted, his clothes falling away from him. His arms are both skeletal and muscular. If I saw him in London, I would walk away, as quickly as I could. The muscles of his face are twitching, and his head jerks from side to side, from time to time.

'Well, anyway,' I say. 'Hello.' My voice comes out sounding like Alison's from the nursery, patronising and sing-song. I back away, now that I have seen him. 'And goodbye.'

'You got a few rupees?' says the man.

'Yes. Of course.'

'You laughing?'

'No,' I protest. 'I'm smiling.'

'You're laughing.'

'I'm not.'

'Yeah?'

'It's just that, well, everyone told me India would be full of people asking me for money. But you're the first I've met. And you're a Westerner. It's a bit unexpected. That's all. So I'm not laughing at you. I'm smiling at the irony.'

He nods, apparently absorbing my words. His head jerks. He laughs; at least, I think it was a laugh.

'The first?' he rasps. 'How long've you been here?'

I am almost embarrassed to admit it. 'I arrived at three this morning.'

He grunts, not looking at me. 'Think I waved to your plane.'

I picture this man, wherever he spends his nights, waving at passing aircraft.

'You didn't really?'

'No.'

'Are you taking the piss?'

He shrugs.

'Are you English?' I try instead.

'Are you a squirrel?' he counters.

'Er. No.'

'Do you like cake?'

'Do you?'

'Girls all love cake.'

People are milling around us. We are provoking a few curious glances, though only from people who wander very close to us. I suppose we make a strange tableau. I hand the man four hundred and fifty rupees, deliberately paying him the same as the rickshaw driver.

'Fucking hell,' he says, looking at it, then quickly tucking it away somewhere about his person.

'No problem,' I say, as if he had thanked me.

He inclines his head. 'Grab a pew.' He nods encouragement, his eyes twitching.

Max would hate it if I sat down with this man. I remember him talking about the Western down-and-outs he saw from time to time when he was in India. 'When they ask you for money,' he ranted one day, back when we were in China together, 'that's when I want to kick them.'

This was so out of character that I laughed.

'Someone's lost the plot and ended up living on the streets in India, and you want to *kick* them? Are you sure?'

He shrugged. 'Well, I never *would* kick them, but yes. In Mumbai, I walked through the slums, handing out rupees even though I knew I should be donating to charity instead – because you can hardly not, when someone's thrusting a tiny skinny baby in your face, and I wanted to see the slums so giving out cash was the price I paid – and there were children with elephantiasis, which meant they had huge swollen limbs, and which is incurable, and flies everywhere, and mosquitoes and disease. And then when I'm on the way back to my nice comfy guest house, some white guy with dreads taps me on the shoulder and asks for two hundred rupees.'

'But maybe he had a crisis of his own.'

'He didn't. Not in the way the kid with elephantiasis had a crisis, or the woman with the dying baby. I'm not normally one to say this, particularly not when it comes to mental health, but he needed to look around, put things in perspective, and pull himself together. I mean, there is no better place in the world for making your problems look small than Mumbai.'

'So you didn't give him the two hundred rupees?'

'I gave him ten and told him to use it to make a reverse charge call home and get someone to wire him the money for a ticket. He told me to fuck myself.'

Now, I look down. 'I did not enjoy my moments on this pavement,' I tell the man. 'I don't think I will sit down, if that's OK.'

It smells bad all around him. Max would insist that, now I have given him some cash, I should walk quickly away, back to my safe hotel room. I would have been long gone by now if I wasn't so desperate to speak.

I can do what I like. Changing my mind, I sit down, and feel my skirt sticking to the ground.

'Do you want to see my children?' I ask him, because I want to see their faces myself. When he doesn't reply, I look at my photos and hold them up before him. He grunts. I stroke their faces with my little finger, careful not to smear dirt on them.

'What's your name?' I ask. I look sideways at his face. He is freaky, shivery, constantly making little movements.

'Bush,' he says, with a manic smile. 'George W.'

'What's your real name?'

'No one asks me that.'

'I just did.'

He pauses, plucking an answer from thin air. I am surprised that, when he replies, it is with a name at all.

'Ethan.'

'I'm Tansy.'

'Sorry I tripped you up. It was so . . . tempting. There you were, walking by.' He stops talking, and laughs his odd hollow laugh.

'Look, can I get you some food, or water?'

He shakes his head. 'You have,' he says, patting the place where he hid the money. 'But any time you have any more, like, spare rupees you want to offload . . . you can find me here. Near a temple – karma . . .' His voice trails off and he stares straight forward, into the darkness.

'But what did you . . . How did you . . . ?'

He shrugs. ''Tis a long story.'

'Do you sleep right here?'

'Folks give me a wide berth,' he tells me in his croaky voice. 'No hassle. Just the police, and when they're coming, away I run.' He mimes himself running away, with two of his fingers. 'I get food one way or another. Try not to look too white, but it's hard.'

I look at him. It is difficult to tell in the dark, but I think that his hair and beard are very light brown and his skin, although hard to the point of scaliness, is fair.

I stand up. 'Right,' I tell him. 'I'm off, then. I'll come back and see you again. Do *you* love cake, then? I could bring you some cake.'

He does not reply; he looks as if he might be asleep, but when I look back, I see the whites of his narrowed eyes, as he watches me.

chapter sixteen

Alexia's thoughts

Finally, things are happening. It's happening faster than I ever thought could be possible. All these years I've imagined us with a child. For the past few years, I've known that our child would be adopted. But a part of me has felt it was a dream, and every time we seemed to get anywhere the barriers would come down and we'd be back to square one. But now, I have a photograph of my future daughter!

Yes, this is the news: Duncan and I have been matched with a little girl in India!

Her name is Sasika, and she is just two years old. She is an orphan, living in a place in southern India. I will never, ever be able to thank the lady called 'H' who posted on my last blog entry. Whoever you are, H, we owe you everything.

Although her name is Sasika, we are going to change it to Saskia. It is the most straightforward thing to do. Although I'd imagined my little girl to be named Dolly (because it means Gift From God), we can just switch two letters of her real name and make a pretty, unusual American name, and that way we keep something of her origins. So that's who's going to be coming to live with us: Miss Saskia Smith. (Although our surname is not actually Smith – it is not a million miles away but I am trying to preserve our anonymity here.)

The photograph came by email. Most of this has been done by email. I am so grateful for the invention of email as it would have taken months longer to have done all this by post. I have saved it as my desktop photo.

'You shouldn't do that,' Duncan said. 'You'll jinx it.' But I'm jinxing nothing. I know, now, that this was all meant to be. As soon as I saw her little face, I knew that she was my little girl, that the years of crying every time AF visited, the frustration with domestic adoption were for this. It all happened for a reason: to bring Saskia and me together, across the continents.

We are going to go to India and fetch her. Simple as that. We have struggled through a lot of paperwork, and the agency are taking care of the Indian side of things. There is a hefty fee, but I would pay it ten times over.

I worked all day today. People kept asking me why I was smiling so much. I was glad when they did. I took out the photograph.

'Look,' I said. 'This is Saskia. We're going to go to India and adopt her.'

It certainly gave me a little taste of the reaction we'll get when we bring her back.

'From India?' said Mrs O'Brien. 'Poor little thing. Why didn't you get an American baby?'

'She'll certainly stand out around here,' said Chloe Johnson.

'You will get her tested for *things*,' said old Marianne Myers. 'Before you bring her to this town?'

I knew what she meant by things. She meant HIV. I was actually very angry, but as I was serving her a bag of strawberry CremeSavers at the time, I managed to hold it back.

'She is in perfect health,' I said, 'and I have a medical certificate to prove it.'

'Yes,' she said. 'From *India*!'

But we can rise above them. Duncan is just as excited as I am. She is a beautiful little girl. We are already in love with her. After work I went to the store and bought some things for her bedroom. I'm going to decorate it in pink and purple. Duncan tried to tell me not to, but by the end of the evening, we were doing it together, transforming our guest bedroom, the one that has always needed a baby, into Saskia's room. It is adorable, amazing. I feel as if I'm going to wake up some day soon.

Duncan is still up. He is making a sign for her bedroom door. It says 'Saskia's Room' on it, in sparkly pink paint.

As soon as I hear back from the agency, I'm going to book our tickets.

Comments: 0

chapter seventeen

I order at the bar, and savour the familiarity of the words. I am rather proud to have managed to stay away from establishments that serve alcohol until my second evening here.

'One beer, please,' I say, with relish. I am being sensible. The easiest thing in the world would be to order a cocktail from the extensive list and to sit and get drunk by myself, but I know I am too far from the comfort zone.

The bar could easily be in London. It is too air-conditioned, and goosebumps are appearing on my arms. There are varnished floorboards, and there is abstract art on the walls. Tables are dotted around the room, many of them empty, some inhabited by people in suits or well-assembled designer outfits. The women here are wearing high heels, not dirty Birkenstocks, and they do not have filthy feet on display through their footwear. No women are drinking without a man at their table, and most of them seem to have soft drinks in front of them. I have heard Hindi music all day today. In here, the soundtrack is provided by Dido. Well-groomed heads swivel at my progress across the room. I glue a smile to my face, wishing I had stopped to put on some make-up or to do something with my hair. I cannot believe I am here on my own.

I wanted company. I practised saying, 'Actually, there's a list of bars in here – shall we nip out for a beer?' in a casual way, but there was no one to say it to. I walked around the hotel smiling at people, but only found smug couples, and big Indian families.

One family had set up camp in the snack bar. I stood and watched them. The children played in the centre of the room, while the others talked and laughed. I looked at a large woman in a green sari, and knew that there had to be something I could say, a magic formula that would have made her invite me over, become a part of the group.

I take the large glass of Kingfisher over to an empty table in the corner, and I sit back and prepare to savour the first sip. As I lift the glass to my lips, I realise that I am a little bit cross with Max, though I have no right to be. He has sent me out of my own life because he thinks he knows better than I do.

Max has changed; I have not. I wonder whether this is true. I would not have moped around Chennai feeling nervous ten years ago, so I must have changed.

I gulp back half the beer in one mouthful, and I take my phone out of my bag, and put it on the table. It looks at me, and I look back at it.

I had better not. I finish my beer instead, and buy another.

I am halfway through a terse text to my husband, when the first man comes over. He is tall, and good looking, and he knows it. There is a cricket jumper tied around his shoulders. When I was sixteen, I found nothing more attractive than a man with a cricket jumper over his shoulders. Twenty years later, I still find it pleasing.

'Excuse me,' he says, with a small smile. 'But are you waiting for somebody?'

I wonder whether to lie. 'No,' I say.

He grins at this. 'Then would you mind terribly if I joined you?'

I can sense his friends, a few tables away, watching us and laughing.

'I'm sorry,' I tell him. 'You can if you like, but I'm married. I'm just here because I wanted a quiet drink.'

'In civilised surroundings,' he agrees.

'No, not that.' I stop short of telling him that it's the alcohol I need, not the Western ambience. 'Well. Kind of.'

'I do apologise for disturbing you. The wedding ring was not visible.' He leaves.

I buy myself another beer, and pretend I can't hear them sniggering about me.

Half an hour later, the same thing happens. This man is wearing a business suit, and has brought his briefcase over to the table.

'I'm waiting for my friend,' I tell him. 'My friend Ethan,' I add, randomly.

'You have been here a considerable amount of time,' he points out. 'Your friend Ethan is not gentlemanly.'

I picture him, crouched by the temple wall, giggling and twitching.

'True,' I agree.

I stay at the bar for another hour. I hate it.

chapter eighteen

In a cramped, hot booth with breeze-block walls, I call home.

'It's me,' I say. 'Again.'

'Why, hello,' says Max. 'Here's Toby.'

I bite my lip with frustration. I wanted to talk to Max. Instead, I converse in a stupid, stilted way with Toby. I can't tell him anything. I ask about his reading book, and he tells me about last night's television. When I ask what he has been doing, he says, 'Nothing.' When I ask what happened at school, he says, 'Nothing.' When I run out of questions, I ask to speak to Daddy again.

Joe comes on instead. I can almost see him as he breathes heavily down the line.

'Hello, Joe,' I say.

'Hello, Mummy.' He sounds more babyish on the phone.

'Is Daddy looking after you properly?'

There is a silence. Max's voice in the background calls, 'He's nodding.'

'I miss you,' I tell him.

'Mummy,' he says. It is unbearable.

'I love you so much, darling,' I say quickly. 'And Toby. I show your photos to people.'

Max is brisk with me, in the middle of something. There is so much I want to say, but I tell him nothing. He tells me nothing. We are both like Toby: unforthcoming and awkward. I lean against the wall and watch a woman going past, outside on the street.

She has a large parcel on her head, and a baby tied to her back.
I gulp down the stale air, and close my eyes.

Ethan looks worse by daylight. I can see his hair moving up and
down, infested with creatures. His skin is peeling off in places.
His body is hollowed out. The day is unrelentingly hot.

I stand at a distance for a while, and watch. Indian city life
goes by around him, through the furnace-like heat. People
throw him the occasional curious glance, but that is all. They
hurry past, bustle away, everyone focused on getting to work,
or getting food, or water, or going to the temple. He sits with
his back against the wall, looking at nothing, twitching and
shifting.

'Saw you watching,' he says when I approach.

'I was interested.'

'Did you glean any new information?'

'Are you taking the piss? Aren't you meant to be too down and
out to take the piss?'

He taps the side of his head. 'Still got faculties. Ain't nothing
missing up there.'

'Brought you stuff.' I hand him a newspaper full of pakora, a
bag of samosas, a sticky cake, a T-shirt and a pair of shorts.

He grabs the food, and snorts. 'What are you? Mother Teresa?'

I look away as he stuffs it into his mouth. It seems too intimate
an act to witness.

'She's dead.'

He laughs his strange laugh again. 'Yeah. I know that. Come
on. Tell me something.'

I decide that I will. 'Sometimes I drink too much,' I say. 'It's
the only way I can relax. Sometimes I drink wine from a teacup.'

He is not remotely interested. 'Don't worry. Now you've got
me. You'll be fine.' He twitches and laughs. 'Don't go! I'm only
trying to freak you out.'

'It's working. So, tell me what you're doing here?'

He shrugs. 'You know. Got to India with some mates. Didn't
go so well.'

'Where are you from?'

He narrows his eyes at me. 'I don't want to
you try to find someone to come and fetch m

'But I could call the Embassy. Get them to he
what they're for.'

'It's fucking not what they're for. They're shit. They're r
they can go to parties and drink champagne and toast the fucking
Queen's fucking birthday. Believe me. I've been there, done that.'

'What, you've toasted the Queen's birthday?'

'In piss I have.'

We sit in silence. A middle-aged man stops to stare at us.

'Madam,' he says. 'Is this fellow bothering you?'

'No. It's fine, thanks.'

He stares for a while, and walks away.

'So, what happened?'

He shrugs. 'Got in some trouble, down at Hampi. Got away.
No particular place to go. Here I am. *Voilà.*'

'But what—'

I break off when I see Ethan's eyes widen. In a split second,
he is on his feet.

I leap up too, and see the police heading towards us. Ethan
runs, surprisingly fast, vanishing into the crowd. I run after
him, feeling beads of sweat forming on my forehead. I follow
the blur, ducking down a side street after him, running to the
end of an alley as my shoes flip and flop loudly, and skidding
to a halt at a dead end. I am so hot I can barely breathe. I
look back. The police are at the end of the road, coming
towards me.

Ethan is nowhere. I look around, desperate, realising that I
should never have followed him. It was madness. The buildings
here are ramshackle, with blackened fronts and glassless windows.
What paint there is is peeling. The bricks are bare. The wood is
rotting. A pair of dark eyes watches me from inside one of the
houses. The smell is pungent and fetid. A pile of rubbish by the
kerb stirs, and a rat runs out of it.

I turn to the police.

'Hello,' I say. 'He's gone.'

They look at me suspiciously.

'What is your name?' asks one of them.

'Tansy Harris.'

'Address in Chennai?'

'Shiva Hotel.'

'You know this character?'

'I stopped to talk to him. I gave him some food.'

'Madam, you must leave him alone in future.'

By late afternoon, he is back by the temple. He takes me for an adventure, and I find myself sitting with him, in an illegal bar, in a back street, drinking homemade liquor from cloudy glasses. The room is dark and muggy, the clientele almost invisible in the clouds of smoke.

'You're crazy,' he says, jerking suddenly to his right. 'Never do that. If they see you running off again, they'll have you. They will fucking *have* you. You shouldn't even talk to me.' He nods several times in quick succession. 'No. You should not.'

I knock back my drink. It immediately makes me queasy.

'Last night I went to a bar,' I tell him. 'This one's better.'

'What, you went to a yuppie place?'

'You know them?'

'Sat outside them.' He sinks down, miming himself sitting outside. 'Not good.'

'It was like being in London. In the City. The men came over, one by one.'

Ethan nods, many times. 'Lady alone.'

I do my best to imitate one of them: '"It is very unethical for a married woman to be drinking alcohol in public!" They were nice, well-spoken, polite, but they didn't take to my morals.'

'In this place, no one has morals. Morals, go home!' He looks at me, puzzlement cracking his face. 'Are you as stupid as you seem to be? I don't mean that in a bad way.' He laughs. 'I mean, I'm curious as to what a married woman with kids is doing hanging around with me, let alone in a dive like this. Drinking.'

'I'm interested. And in search of adventure.'

'Back on the tourist circuit.'

A man stands over us, and refills both our glasses. I sip my second drink, and abruptly feel violently ill.

I vomit copiously in the gutter outside. It splashes in my hair. Ethan stands a little distance away, watching me and laughing, looking delighted, his skin appearing to crack.

chapter nineteen

Six days pass in a blur of bad tourism. I suspect I am too jumpy to look like an attractive prospect for friendship to anyone but Ethan, because I find myself alone, apart from Ganesh, who drives me everywhere and kindly admires the photos of the boys every couple of days. Elly replied to my email with an instruction that I must not come earlier because she is away on Children's Centre business, so I have no option but to wait it out.

And now, finally, I am checking out of this stale old hotel. I am kicking my heels waiting for the taxi that will take me to the ashram, where I know that at least one person will want to speak to me. I look at the clock. Ten to twelve. The cab is coming at midday. I notice my legs jiggling in anticipation.

The reception area is a little bit tatty, with damp stains on the painted walls and chips out of the floor tiles. The only seating provided consists of three hard, churchy benches in an alcove.

A woman sitting on the next bench, dressed in tight Diesel jeans and a magenta top, keeps smiling at me. Her features are beautifully made-up, just on the right side of garish. I know why she likes me: I am wearing my best clothes and I look like a Londoner. Clearly, this woman recognises Prada when she sees it.

I have dutifully played the tourist over the past six days; I have, finally, actually visited the Catholic Cathedral, which houses the remains of Doubting Thomas. I have seen the display about a man who was called the Wandering Monk, a character called

Vivedananda who seems to have been the first Hindu missionary to the West. This conflicts with the advice of the man at the temple, who assured me that Hindus are born not made, and I make a mental note that one day I will find out for sure whether I could convert, purely as an academic exercise. I had to admire the 'Swami', as his vocation seemed to have led him into the orbit of an impressive number of wealthy white women, many of whom were pictured gazing adoringly at him.

I have walked randomly and got lost, again and again. It transpires that it is not difficult to wander away from the parts of Chennai where they are used to seeing foreigners, but still, no one takes any notice of me. I have pounded the streets just to keep myself busy, to give myself distractions. It is a foolproof activity: I walk and walk, look at everything around me, and feel that I am wearing an invisibility cloak. Whenever I have had enough, I just flag down a rickshaw and get delivered straight back to the hotel.

Yesterday, I sat in my hotel room staring at the fan, and thinking about Max and the boys. The longing and loneliness comes over me in unpredictable waves: it appears when I least expect it, and fells me. The urge to grab a taxi to the airport and to go straight home was so strong that I leapt to my feet and cast around for something to do. I could not bear the prospect of traipsing around another tourist destination. I did not have the strength for Ethan.

The local paper, delivered to the room every morning, was on the table, open at the classified ads. I was fascinated by the huge number of call centre jobs advertised. 'Walk up,' they all said, and gave a location for presentable English speakers to go to seek well-paid work. With nothing else to do, I snatched up the paper, slid my feet into my sandals, and went out to get Ganesh to take me to one of the centres.

It was up some stairs, in a refurbished, yet tatty, office building. The receptionist was dragonish, in a mustard-coloured salwaar khameez, with glasses perched on the end of her nose.

'You want work?' she asked, looking at me over her specs. 'Proper, want work?'

'I'm just interested,' I muttered, looking around the room,

which was lined with eager applicants, every single one of them breaking off from their form-filling to look at me. Every one of them was well-dressed, twenty-something, and Indian. Every eye was on me. 'Would you let me work for an afternoon, maybe?' I asked, lowering my voice. 'Just to see?'

'You want to take work from a Chennai person?'

'No.'

She nodded to the door.

'Which companies do you provide this service for?' I asked as I edged away.

'Not at liberty to tell you. Industrial espionage,' she said happily, and came out from behind her desk to shoo me away, to everyone's amusement.

I have set up a little altar to my sons in my bedroom. It is dismantled now, the pictures carefully pressed between the pages of my book. I have talked to them every time I am in the room. I have cried. I have had a panic attack, in my room on my own. I have drunk beer every day and have stopped caring what the handsome men think of me. I have eaten every single meal alone.

I have written cheerful emails home, peppered with phrases like 'amazing experience', 'sights and smells' and 'back on the road'. I have implied that I am learning some vaguely defined life lessons. I am surprised at how glad I am to be going to an ashram, a place where I will do as I am told, where my life will be structured.

Ethan barely acknowledged me when I told him I was off. I told him I was going to see my friend at an ashram, but he twitched at me and looked away. Either he is cross with me for leaving or he really doesn't give a shit.

The two backpackers come and sit down, in a flurry of bags and guidebooks, on the third bench, the one opposite me. The man nods, as he always does, and the woman ignores me, as she always does.

I have seen them everywhere this week. I have stumbled past them drunk, walked too close to them when I was bored, hoping for them to speak to me. I have told persistent drivers that 'my friends want a rickshaw' when they have been following me out of the hotel, to offload the hassle. We have always said hello and walked on. The girl always marches away looking miserable. I have to remind myself that, for once, I cannot possibly have done anything to offend her.

'Let's head to Pondy for a while, though,' she is saying. 'You can contact them from there. Firm up a date and a plan.' Her ginger hair is loose and thick, her face freckled, her tone wheedling.

'You know they're desperate to see us,' he says. 'Don't be nervous. It's going to be amazing. A real milestone. We can get all the family stuff out of the way and then head off to Nepal. The Annapurna circuit.' I see him look at her. 'Or whatever you want to do,' he adds quickly. He has a London accent. 'But the village – you know we have to. You know it's why we're here. You used to love the idea. Admittedly it won't be luxurious, but we're not about the luxury, are we? It'll be one for the blog.'

'I don't have a blog.'

'But if you did.'

'Yeah,' the girl mutters. 'But I won't be able to bloody speak to anyone.'

'You're going to Nepal?' I ask.

This girl has an impressive scowl: her whole face crinkles and although she could be pretty, she becomes ugly. I smile a nice bright smile, to annoy her.

'Yes we are,' her boyfriend says, looking at me, smiling back. 'Just as soon as we've done what we have to do here.'

'I don't even know if I want to go to Nepal,' she says sulkily. 'Haven't they got a civil war or something?'

'Not where the tourists go, they haven't. It's like everyone tells you Laos is dangerous. It wasn't, was it?'

I lean forward. 'You've been to Laos?'

The skinny redhead tries to kill me with a look. The boyfriend smiles.

'Sure,' he says. 'We were there this autumn. We've only been in India two weeks. What about you? Have you been to Laos?'

At last. I grin, relieved.

'I was there a few years ago,' I say carefully, not wanting to tell them exactly how long it has been. 'I loved it. Laos is one of my favourite places in the world. Did you go to Champasak?' I have a blast of memories of Max and me in Champasak. It was a perfect time in my life. I see us in the photograph, on bicycles, surrounded by lush greenery. I remember the sensation of everything I had ever worried about falling away from me.

He nods and laughs. 'We went everywhere.'

'The Plain of Jars?'

'No, not there. That was a bit remote.'

'It's amazing.'

He nods. 'So, I thought I'd seen Laos, and you've pulled rank on me already.'

'Sorry. Where else have you been?'

'We crossed into Thailand at Pakse and spent a month there, you know. Ko Lanta, Bangkok, Chiang Mai. Then we flew into Delhi, and our friends went off to Dharamsala, because they wanted to touch the Dalai Lama's robes, or whatever it is that people do, and we came here, by train. Scraped the cash together for first class. It was the greatest. So, how long are you in India? I keep thinking we should stop and talk to you, you know, but you looked like you were enjoying your own company.'

I don't contradict him. 'I'm here for about a month.'

'All on your own?'

'Completely on my own – here in Chennai, at least. I've spoken to a few people this week, but I haven't found anyone to hang out with. Well, not anyone conventional.'

The girl looks at me over the top of her *Lonely Planet*. 'Are *we* conventional?'

'More conventional than some.'

'Oh right.' She pretends to read her book.

'Sorry,' he mutters. 'She's not herself.'

'I heard that,' she snaps.

He shrugs, and opens his mouth to say something. Then he closes it. 'We'll talk later,' he says quietly, to her.

'Oh, this is it, is it? "We need to talk"?'

He looks at me. He is short and thickset, with huge dark eyes and thick eyebrows. 'I do apologise,' he says quietly.

I look sideways. The woman in magenta is following our conversation with interest, and I wonder how to include her in it.

'No problem,' I say.

'So what's it like, a single woman in India?' he asks. 'I'm Sam, by the way, and the ray of sunshine here is Amber.'

I nod to them, though she is still hiding behind her book. I nod to the magenta woman too, but she looks away.

'Well, it's not easy,' I tell them. 'But in a different way from how I'd expected it not to be easy. It's weird and, well, I don't know.' I grind to a halt. I have no idea what to say. 'The only person I actually met was a beggar from London who calls himself Ethan.'

He nods. 'That white guy? He looked a bit hardcore. So, where now?'

I just have time to say, 'An ashram near Pondicherry,' before magenta woman leans forward to interrupt.

'Excuse me,' she says, in what I have come to recognise as a posh Indian accent. 'But your trousers are stunning. May I take a snap of you?' She shakes her mobile phone, indicating that this will be her camera.

'Oh,' I say. I sense Amber giggling behind her book. 'Sure, why not – go ahead.'

I stand up, cringingly self-conscious, and let the woman take my photograph. I try to rise above it and pose, ironically, as a model, twisting my upper body, hands resting lightly on hips, my head thrown back. I know it doesn't work.

'They are Prada?' she says.

'They are,' I confirm. I have made a big effort for my reunion with Elly.

'London?'

'Yes.'

'Thank you.'

'Is that the Singapore phone?' asks a man as he sits down heavily next to her. Again, the upmarket Indian accent. There is, I realise, something deeply attractive about it in a man.

The smart woman looks up. 'No!' she says furiously. 'No! You never gave me the Singapore phone! This is the India phone!

Does it *look* like the Singapore phone? I have just taken a photograph of the trousers I *have* to have.' She looks at me critically. 'But two sizes smaller, and in ecru.'

'Excuse me? Mrs Harris?' A man is smiling, next to me. I nod. 'I am your driver.'

I look at Sam. 'Hop in?'

The two of them look at each other.

'The place you're going? How near is it to Pondy?'

'We can't afford to split a cab,' Amber tells me, dismissing the idea. 'We were going to spend all day on the bus. We can't be extravagant with our travel any more.'

'It's fine,' I insist. 'I'll pay. I'm going anyway, and there are empty seats.'

I have rarely been so pleased to leave a place as I am now that I am leaving Chennai. I stare out of the window, immensely happy, as the taxi wends its way through apparently unending city streets. There are huge chunks of this place that I have not seen, that I will never see, and that is fine by me.

Sam sits in the front, by unspoken agreement. It is my cab, but he is the man. This is the sort of sexism I would normally chafe against, but I am happy, here, to sit back and let someone else make the small talk. I am surprised, however, when he starts talking to the driver in a language I don't understand.

I lean forward. 'Is that Tamil or Hindi?' I ask. 'Or something else?'

Sam looks back. 'Tamil,' he says. 'My parents are Tamil. Which means, I guess, that I am, too. I come to Tamil Nadu via Tooting Broadway. I come with baggage.' He turns back to the driver.

'He's finding his roots,' Amber says, her voice low and, I think, slightly cutting. 'Finding himself. The village his parents came from is a few hours from Pondicherry. That's why we're here. That's why we're heading in this direction. A few days in Pondicherry, and then we have to go to the depths of beyond to find Sam's cousins.'

'And you're not relishing that idea?'

She shrugs and turns away. 'He is,' she says.

I watch the city from my window, listening to Sam chattering to the driver. They both laugh often, and Sam's obvious excitement begins to infect me. Joy at the idea of seeing Elly again, after all this time, creeps up inside me. I am not alone any more. I have done it; the grim part of my trip is over. The relief makes me giggle.

I stare and stare, at snapshots of everyday lives: at little girls in pristine navy blue uniforms on their way to school, their hair pulled into perfectly neat, agonising-looking plaits; at men and women on motorbikes, bumping around the roads, as fast as they can go, on their way to places I cannot imagine. I watch older women stepping carefully over obstacles, on and off the kerb, keeping their dignity as they pick their way to their destinations. We do not pass anyone begging, nor anyone who looks destitute. Ethan swears he is not the only one, laughed in scorn at the very suggestion, told me I was stupid and naive.

I wonder whether London looks like this, whether it is possible to travel through it, as a stranger, to look out of the window and be fascinated by snippets of people's lives. London is huge and diverse and cosmopolitan; it's just that I am stifled in the corner of it where we live, surrounded by families like us, everyone competing and struggling and muddling through. We should, I decide, move to a more interesting suburb. I make a mental note to inform Max. I know that he will say no, because of schools, and commutes, and the mortgage.

Finally, the city peters out. The streets become quieter, the houses more spread out. The road is tarmacked, but every side road is now dust and stone. Hand-painted signs every now and then show the way to 'International School'.

I lean forward.

'How old are you, Sam?' I ask.

He looks surprised. 'Twenty-four.'

'God, I was older than that when I came to Asia the first time. All on my own then, as well. It's funny. In between I've hardly had five minutes to myself.'

'You like travelling by yourself then?' Sam asks. 'It must take confidence. I wouldn't want to do it.'

'No. Anything can happen. I met my husband last time, in Vietnam.'

'You're *married*?' says Amber. I show her my wedding ring. 'Yeah,' she says. 'I saw that. I just thought you were wearing it to scare off the men. You're really married?'

'Really.'

'Have you left him?'

I try to hide my shock at the baldness of her question.

'Only for a few weeks.' I try to keep my voice casual. 'He has a job. A proper one that pays the mortgage. Hence, he's not here.'

'Oh. I thought you were divorced, or maybe gay.'

I laugh. 'You could have asked.'

She nods and goes back to staring out of the window. A minute passes before she looks round again.

'You haven't got children, then?'

'What makes you think that?'

'The fact that you're in India on your own. Yes, that'll be it.'

'If you met a man in India, visiting a friend, you wouldn't assume he didn't have children. Would you?'

Sam turns round, and stares. 'Have you got *kids*?'

'Two boys.'

'Did you have them when you were really young?'

'No. I had Toby when I was thirty and Joe three years later. Not young at all.'

'So where are they?'

Amber is frowning. 'I'm trying to work out,' she says, 'whether it's more shocking if they're in India with you, tucked away somewhere, or if you've left them behind.'

'What's your conclusion? Which is worse?' Their amazement is unnerving. 'They're in London,' I say quickly. 'With Max, their father – my husband. They are absolutely fine. I miss them horribly, by the way. In case you were wondering.'

Sam nods slowly. 'Sorry. It just seems a bit strange to us that you're here when you're a mother of children who are really little.'

'Six and three.'

'And,' says Amber, 'that you're here just for fun.'

'Hey,' I tell her. 'I never said I'm here "just for fun". An old friend of mine lives at this ashram. She runs a kind of orphanage there, and she asked me to come and help her for a few weeks. Said she desperately needs another pair of hands and someone she can trust. For what it's worth, I said no several times. Then I tried to work it out so all four of us could come. Then I decided that the world wouldn't fall apart if I left my boys in the care of their dad, my parents, and the Mountview Nursery for a few weeks and came to give Elly a hand. Is that OK? I stopped in Chennai because I kind of felt I should see the city. God knows why.'

They are staring at me. Amber puts a hand to her mouth.

'Oh, Jesus,' she says. 'That's amazing. Look, I, well, I apologise. I thought you'd just left your kids with a nanny or something and buggered off on holiday. Though admittedly most of us wouldn't choose to go round the sights of Chennai when there are tropical islands in the world. But you're here to do good stuff. That's impressive, hey, Sam?' She is grinning at me all of a sudden.

'I'd say. It's fucking amazing, is what it is.'

'It's really not,' I protest. 'I feel a bit of a fraud. There's lots of other background, too.'

'Yeah,' says Sam. 'Sure. So tell us about your friend. And the ashram. And the orphanage. Tell us all about it.'

We pass rice paddies and little villages on one side, and holiday resorts on the other, the coastal side. In the middle of nowhere, next to a field, I see a backpacker, standing next to her bag, looking down the road. There is a French flag stitched to her rucksack. She looks as if she has sprung from nowhere.

'Can you stop?' I ask suddenly. She reminds me of myself, years ago.

The driver doesn't question me but slams on the brakes so hard that we all jolt forward.

'Apologies,' he says, with a little laugh.

I open my door, step out of the cab, and call back to the woman, who is perhaps twenty metres behind us.

'Need a lift?' I shout, the sun shining on to the top of my head.

She grabs her bag and comes running. The driver gets out and opens the boot. There is no room for a fourth backpack.

'OK,' she says cheerfully. 'I hold it.'

We have driven into a different world. Dust blows around my ankles. The sky is bluer than is plausible. The air is different. It smells like greenery, pollen, and lingering kerosene, with a hint of the sea.

Our new passenger is wearing short dungarees over a red vest. She has dark brown hair that is wild around her face, and there is an impressive crust of dirt under her fingernails. Her body is tiny and angular, and she is swamped by her clothes.

'*Bonjour*,' she says. 'I am Delphine. Thank you. You go to Pondy?'

'I'm going to an ashram near by,' I tell her. 'And these guys, Sam and Amber, are headed for Pondicherry, yes. How about you?'

She shrugs. 'I go where the car goes.'

Delphine talks and talks. We discover that she is French, that she has been in India for ten months, that she hitches between places and works where she can.

'I come to India because I have a dream,' she tells us. 'A real, sleeping dream, I mean, not a desire. I don't even remember it now, but when I wake up I know I must come to India. So I do. I rely on strangers. So far, it works. Today, I go to the ashram. You pick me up, so I go there with you. It's destiny. I have seen other people who travel that way. It has a good energy, I think.'

We swap stories, and I discover that Sam and Amber met through a friend, Amy, currently in Dharamsala in the Indian Himalayas.

'So we met in a pub at Amy's twenty-fifth birthday drinks,' Sam says. 'She'd talked about Amber, her Scottish friend from college. It was always, "You'll never ever guess what Amber's done now!" That sort of thing. Going to lectures drunk. Falling asleep in tutorials when there were only four people in the room. Dancing on the tables in her underwear. Shagging a tutor.'

Amber hits him in the face with the back of her hand. 'Sam!'

He laughs. 'Sorry.'

I have great empathy for anyone who loses control and behaves badly.

'Really?' I ask.

Amber half smiles. She seems to have undergone a radical mood swing. There are many undercurrents here that I do not understand, but there is no doubting the fact that, as soon as I mentioned orphans, she became as devoted to me as she had been hostile before.

'Sorry,' she says. 'You must think I'm awful. You've left your children behind to come and do good works. Delphine's following her dream. And I'm just . . . stupid. And scared.'

'You're not!' I am aghast.

'Amber, that's ridiculous,' says Sam.

'Oh, I am,' says Amber. 'And Sam, you know I am.'

They are all fascinated by Max's existence; it amuses me to be in a situation where our conventional family set-up is seen as exotic.

'So,' Amber says. 'You met your husband in Vietnam? Did you know straight away that you'd met the one? Was it boof, flash of lightning, life partner?'

This part of my history, in itself, is relatively straightforward. 'Yes,' I say. 'Not straight away, but as soon as I realised, that was it. Then I had to make quite a play for him.'

Sam nods. 'But when you realised it, you never had doubts afterwards? None at all? Simple as that? Slam dunk, happy ever after?'

I nod. 'Absolutely.'

Delphine appears to live her life entirely on impulse, judges no one, and takes whatever happens in her stride. Every single thing that happens to her is 'destiny'. She sees ghosts, is guided by crystals, believes in karma. I zone out of the conversation after a while. We pass through towns that are gone in the blink of an eye, and we overtake men and women, and occasionally entire families, on motorbikes. We pass a cheerful-looking theme park called Dizzee Land. Hours later, we start coming into a town.

'This must be Pondicherry,' I hazard. 'Who wants to be dropped off?'

Sam and Amber look at each other.

'There's accommodation at the ashram,' says Sam. 'Isn't there?

It might be cool to check it out. I mean, there'll be a phone there, I imagine? So I can call the village, can't I?'

'And maybe,' adds Amber. 'I don't know. If I could do something at the orphanage. That might, kind of, be good? Would you let me tag along with you?'

We all look to Delphine. 'Oh, sure,' she agrees. 'I go to the ashram. I go where you go. I follow the path in front of me.'

'Oh!' Amber calls suddenly. She reaches forward and taps the driver's shoulder. 'Sorry, could you stop just for a second? That was a postbox back there, wasn't it?'

The car stops. Sam puts out a hand, and Amber gives him a card. He sprints back down the crowded street, pushes the postcard through into the letter box, and runs back.

Suddenly, we are in full-blown backpackers' terrain. We pass a Tibetan restaurant, and a stall with a rack of the clothes I have been craving outside it. I watch with satisfaction, through my open window, as the hot air blasts into my face.

A large white sign is next to the road. The words 'The Ashram of Fortitude' are painted on to it in heavy black paint, with some Hindi or Tamil writing next to it. Underneath is a lot of small print.

The pace slows. There are thick clumps of trees on either side of the road. There are speed bumps every few metres. We pass people on mopeds, on bicycles, and on foot, in little groups. They look peaceful.

'So,' says Amber. 'Now we get to meet Elly.'

I lean back, and inhale deeply. I am with people. I am about to see a familiar face, to be reunited with one of my best friends. I am going to do something good, and see some children.

As we slow down to go over a speed bump, I hug myself with excitement and bounce in my seat in anticipation and pre-emptive relief.

chapter twenty

The car draws up in a dusty clearing, and we step out into quiet, heavy air. There is a rustling in the leaves, but, for a few seconds, nothing happens. Then an Indian woman steps briskly from between some trees and walks towards us, extending a tiny hand. She has thick black hair, a nose ring, and a shiny purple tunic.

'Good afternoon,' she says. A huge leaf from an enormous palm tree comes crashing towards the ground. She catches it, folds it quickly and expertly, and throws it away, a foliage aeroplane. It glides into the car and falls to the ground. 'Tansy Harris?' she continues, unperturbed. She looks at Amber and Delphine, then settles on me, probably because I am more than a decade older than the other two. 'I am Maya, the manager of the Peaceful Haven guest accommodation block. Elly asked me to meet you and to make you comfortable.'

A hot wind springs from nowhere, rippling through the treetops. The trees are everywhere. She nods at me, her hair whipping suddenly around her face.

'Good afternoon,' she says to the others.

'*Bonjour*,' says Delphine. 'Good leaf aeroplane.' She picks up a leaf, and starts folding it. Then she kicks off a flip-flop and picks up the one Maya made, using her toes, and starts to copy it.

'I don't understand,' I say. 'I thought I was staying with Elly. She asked me to come. And she said she had space in her house for me. And she said she was going to meet my car. Peaceful Haven? That sounds like a hospice.'

Maya is graceful and petite. I am feeling enormous and clumsy.

'She intended to meet you,' she tells me calmly. 'She sends her apologies. Here.' She passes me a folded piece of paper. 'She will seek you out in due course. The Peaceful Haven, meanwhile, offers simple accommodation and I can assure you that your well-being is our priority. We are not a hospice, but we *are* hospitable.'

I unfold the note.

'Dear T,' Elly has written. 'Sorry. Had to go away for a few days on CC business. There are people staying at my place. Maya's great, though, and she'll look after you. Will make it up to you, OK? Do yoga even if you hate it. Chill out and I'll come and find you in a day or so. E xxx'

I put it in my pocket.

'O-kaaay,' I tell everyone. 'I travel five thousand miles because she apparently needs me, and she's not here and she doesn't even tell me where she is. She tells me to "do yoga"? I guess she knows what she's doing.'

'Oh,' says Maya. 'Don't take it badly. Enid is one of our best teachers.'

I let Enid drop, whoever she may be.

'What's CC business?' I ask instead.

'The CC is the Children's Centre.'

'Right. Well, I'll go there. I didn't leave my babies at home so that I could do bloody yoga. That's for sure. If I wanted to do *yoga*, I'd have stayed in North London.'

We are standing on a patch of packed-down red earth, a clearing in the woods, which we have reached by a bumpy track. The driver has unloaded our backpacks and stands at a polite distance, waiting for his money. Through the trees, I can see the edge of a building.

When I stop and breathe, I have to admit that this seems like a pleasant environment. The sun is hazy, and the treetops are waving in the wind all around us. The whole place is bigger than I expected: the cab drove for ten minutes after we passed the 'Ashram of Fortitude' sign. I thought it was going to be a few people living in huts around a guru, with some malnourished children hanging off them. It all seems rather more impressive than that.

Maya gestures with her head. 'Come on,' she says, indicating the guest house. 'The Peaceful Haven is well-located. Central.'

I look at Amber, and we both snigger.

'Central?' Sam says politely. 'Really?' He says something in Tamil. She replies, and they both laugh.

'So,' says Amber. 'Where's the ashram?'

Maya points to a path leading through the woods. 'That way. You'll see.'

'And the Children's Centre?' I add.

'Oh, the children aren't far. I'll point you in the right direction tomorrow.'

Delphine has been bouncing on the balls of her dirty, bare feet, desperate to speak. Finally, she manages it.

'*Bonjour*, Maya,' she says. '*Namaste*. I would like to stay at Peaceful Haven. I hear that you have farms too? I have not much money. After some ashram time, can I work in the farms? I will do anything.'

Maya smiles a genuine smile, and nods. She starts walking towards the building, and we pick up our backpacks and follow her. Delphine slips her feet back into her flip-flops.

'Of course,' Maya says, as she walks. 'The farming families on our land readily accommodate casual labourers. Is it just you? Your name?'

'Delphine Brunel. *Oui*, just me.'

'I'd like to help out with the children,' Amber says quickly, looking at me sideways.

'By all means,' Maya says. 'Delphine, you please tell me when you wish to move to the farm, and I will have one of our staff take you to the central farming unit, where you'll be assigned to a family. Amber, you visit the CC with Tansy tomorrow.'

Delphine gives a double thumbs-up, looking briefly and incongruously like Paul McCartney.

A couple of women walk through the clearing, their long hair tied back in buns, their mouths glinting with gold teeth. They are carrying old-fashioned, witchy broomsticks. They stare at us with a certain world-weariness. One says something, and the other nods, her mouth glinting. I wonder how many times they have seen fat, white people like us rocking up.

'What did she say?' I ask Sam.

'She said I must be a very well-hung lad to have such a gorgeous harem at my feet.'

Amber looks back at me. 'He does that all the time. Honestly. Don't encourage it.'

The compound feels as if it had been carved out of the rainforest. I have the impression that, were the place left unattended for half a day, the vegetation would slip in and take over, growing up between cracks, pushing through masonry, splitting the whole place apart. The single-storey whitewashed building forms a horseshoe shape around a dusty red courtyard. The windows are small, covered by insect screens, and there is a concrete veranda along the front of the building, with many doors opening on to it. The veranda is messy, dotted with chairs and people and stuff.

At the end nearest to us, a blonde woman with ropy long hair is sitting in the lotus position, her eyes closed and a pained expression on her face, and I can't help suspecting that she knows we are here and is performing. Beyond that, another woman, this one tiny with dark hair, is lethargically wringing out clothes into a bucket of grey water. A man with a sunburned face and a paunch that strains against his pale green T-shirt sits on one white plastic chair, with his feet up on another, reading the first Harry Potter book in English, a bead of sweat trickling down his forehead. All but the meditator look up and scrutinise us as we arrive. I make a point of scrutinising them right back. Nobody smiles.

The two women with broomsticks are sweeping the dirt on the path, talking fast to each other. Two Indian children are playing at the edge of the forest. They look at us for a while, their faces expressionless. A girl and a boy, aged, I think, a little bit older than Toby, and a little bit older than Joe. I want to follow them, for a moment.

'Are those children from the Children's Centre?' I ask Maya.

She looks up briefly. The children turn and run. 'Yes,' she says.

'Now, this is the female side.' She waves an arm at the left-hand side of the horseshoe, the side that is closer to us. 'And this the male.'

Sam speaks at once. 'What about couples?'

Maya shakes her head. 'We do not offer couples' accommodation here at the Peaceful Haven.'

'Is there anywhere at the ashram that does?'

She holds her head on one side and purses her mouth a little. 'Well, there is. But it is reserved accommodation, to be used by invitation only, for particular guests.'

Amber shakes her head. 'And I guess if we asked you to invite us to use it, you'd say no?'

'I would indeed.'

'Thought so. Basically, if we want to stay here, we have to sleep apart? Is it dormitories, or what?'

Maya's eyes sparkle. 'No, no, no. Not dormitories. Shared rooms. We have a maximum of four beds to a room, so really it is not on the industrial scale that the word "dormitory" might imply.'

In my youth, I managed to travel extensively and avoid dormitories in every country except China, where things were so surreal, and frightening, that I was glad of the company. A room of four won't be so bad.

'Sounds fine to me,' I say. 'But Amber? Sam?'

'Fine,' Amber says quickly. 'It's only going to be a couple of nights, isn't it, Sam? We should live by ashram rules.'

Sam shrugs. 'I guess.'

'You complain about this – do you live at Buckingham Palace?' Delphine throws herself on to her bed.

Amber sits on the edge of hers, looking nervous. I lie on mine, between them, and prop myself up on my elbows to look around the room. The word I am seeking is 'austere'. There are four beds in here, lined up along the wall, opposite the door and the tiny, barred window. I know I could easily roll over on to either Amber's or Delphine's beds without slipping through the gap on to the floor. The fourth bed shows signs of occupation: a

Lonely Planet South India guide in German, a white cotton tunic that I covet.

Other than that, there is a ceiling fan, and absolutely nothing else. The walls are a greyish white, the floor tiled with peeling squares of plastic linoleum. The air is stifling. I open the door, which leads only to the outside, as wide as I can, and prop it open with my backpack.

'No,' I tell Delphine. 'I don't live in Buckingham Palace, and this will actually do me fine.' I look at the narrow beds, with white sheets and orange blankets. 'I have three Laura Ashley duvet covers at home,' I tell them. 'We rotate them. All of them match the curtains though the patterns are slightly different.'

Amber laughs. 'I have an Ikea duvet cover that my parents gave me, but it's the only one I've got, so every couple of weeks I put it in the washing machine first thing in the morning, and I dry it on the radiator all afternoon. Sometimes I have to finish it with a hairdryer before bedtime.'

Delphine is laughing. 'When I am at my parents' home, in Mont de Marsan, which you know is a very *yokel* town in France, I have a pink bed. You know "Charlotte aux Fraises"? Is a cartoon character. She is on it. Very nice for a girl of four years old. But last week I sleep under nothing at all, so this is good for me.'

'Yokel,' says Amber. 'That's a great word to know.'

Maya reappears in the doorway, having shown Sam to his room. She draws herself up and embarks on a speech she has clearly made many times before. The look on her face is unaccountably mischievous.

'This is an ashram,' she announces, 'devoted to the well-being of mind and body. We have strict rules and any deviation from them will result in your being asked to leave. No alcohol, no drugs, and chastity is paramount. We all rise before five every morning, and spend the first hour of the day in silent meditation in the Great Hall.'

'Jesus Christ,' says Amber. 'But this is going to be a blast.'

'Isn't it?' I agree.

'Breakfast is taken communally after meditation, the whole community together. Dinner is here at the Peaceful Haven, for a

cost of forty rupees. There are yoga classes throughout the day
– Tansy, you will have three hours in the morning, three in the
afternoon, with Enid.'

'I don't think so.'

'Yes you will. We are a contemplative community, but this is
the real world, and much of our income comes from tourism.
You will be pleasantly surprised by the visitors' centre and its café,
for example.'

Amber puts her hand up, as if she were at school.

'How big is this place?' she asks.

'Oh, we are one of the largest ashrams in India: the settlement
is twenty kilometres wide, and in places runs down to the beach.
We have two thousand residents, and several working farms, as
Delphine knows. We produce garments, dairy produce, cashew
nuts, souvenirs, bricks, toys . . . I would urge you, therefore, to
visit our shops, which also supply much of Tamil Nadu. Kitchen
block this side.' She waves a hand vaguely to her right. 'And toilet
block the other. That's it, I think. No smoking, no meat, and try
to be nice. Any questions?'

'Yes! When's Elly back?'

Maya shrugs, and steps out on to the veranda. We follow her.

'She will find you,' she says. 'Don't fret.'

Suddenly, she dashes forward. A huge black bird, the size of a
baby, has landed nearby, and Maya chases it off by running at it.

'Begone!' she yells. I catch Dephine's eye and try not to laugh.
'These pesky birds,' Maya explains, coming back. 'I could kill
them, every last blasted one of them. Pestering for food.'

'Very yogic,' says Amber.

'Would you use a gun, or your bare hands?' I ask. I watch her
consider this.

'Catapult,' she decides. 'With stone.'

Something moves in the trees. I have no idea whether it is a
child, an animal, or the wind.

chapter twenty-one

Someone is ringing a handbell, outside, a proper, jangly, brass-sounding one. It comes closer, close enough to make my ears ring, then fades away.

I lunge at my phone: it is nearly five. There is a stirring around the room, a yawn, a shifting. I don't manage to speak, but I do manage to move, to pull on the nearest clothes (though I am not completely sure that they are mine), to get my feet into my sandals, to shuffle, bleary-eyed, to the door.

The early morning light slaps me around the face, and wakes me up like a bucket of cold water. The world is touched with gold, the shadows slanting: everything is new and fresh. Everyone from the guest house, several hundred of them, is walking, en masse, in the same direction. I join the throng, with Delphine. We follow a path between the trees, the wood fragrant, the world reborn.

The Great Hall looks disappointingly mundane. It is a concrete building, with dirty white paint peeling away in places. As soon as we step inside, however, it changes, becoming huge and airy, with fabric billowing on the ceiling like a sail, and a sanded wooden floor. Thousands of people are here, sitting in rows, staring forward, most of them in the lotus position with ramrod-straight backs. I take my place in a row near the back, with Delphine, cross my legs (there is no way I am getting my foot up on my inner thighs like some of these people are doing) and try not to feel ridiculous while I wait for something to happen. My only reference point for a gathering like this is a vague recollection of what it was like to sit in school assembly.

The woman who drifts on to the platform looks young, perhaps thirty, and has ruler-straight hair and a smiling face. Even from this distance, with thousands of other people in the room, I can see her charisma. She says nothing, but sits on a cushion, crosses her legs, and looks searchingly around the room.

'That's Anjali,' whispers Maya, who is sitting behind me.

Someone, somewhere, rings a tinkling little bell.

Other people close their eyes. Nothing is said, so I make sure I stay quiet. I stare at the sea of heads for a while, trying to spot Elly's. There are Indians and foreigners, about half and half, in the room. Several small blond heads could belong to Elly, but it is impossible, from behind, to know which one, if any, is hers. Almost certainly none of them.

When I catch the woman on the platform looking at me, I stare into her eyes for as long as I dare. I try to look away, but it turns out that I don't want to. This is ridiculous: she is younger than me and I want to laugh at her, sitting on a cushion at dawn, as if she was doing something heroic and important. Yet I cannot quite summon up a smirk.

When she looks away, I am strangely deflated. I screw my eyes tight shut and try to think of nothing, because I'm sure that's what you are meant to do. I imagine a great thought bubble of nothingness rising above the hall, popping in the sky, showering glittery blankness and peace all over the countryside.

The glittery peace lasts for several seconds. Then the bad things notice the space, and crowd into it.

I see my children, through a thick pane of glass, getting on with life without me, laughing with Max. I wave, but they look straight through me, as if I were a stranger, and not even an interesting one. I see myself and Jim, sneaking into a cheap hotel together, making everything spiral out of control, so I lose it all. As the meditation plods endlessly onwards, my breathing becomes laboured, my muscles tense. I see myself, thousands of miles from home, letting it all fall apart. I know that something worse would have happened with Jim if I hadn't come. My mother appears, behind my eyelids, taunting me, reminding me that I am as bad as she ever was. 'You've failed,' she slurs.

I try my hardest to push her away. I clench my eyes tightly shut, although this does not keep anything out, and concentrate on breathing. My breath hisses through my teeth. The good things in my life are Max, Toby and Joe, and I have walked away from all of them. I make the boys stroll into my mind, holding hands, looking cheeky. I remember being pregnant: the panic, the terror. I feel a phantom baby kicking inside me. I tell myself that there is no way I could possibly be incubating anyone now.

This place, this ashram, is self-consciously about motherhood, in a glib way. They have no fucking idea of how twisted the mother-child relationship can be. According to the rubbish display in the visitors' centre, 'Everyone needs a mother'. The spiritual leader here is always a woman: currently it's Anjali, who is, apparently, the woman in front of me. Now that I am not looking at her, I can scoff at the fact that she is far too young and inexperienced to be a spiritual leader of anything. She looks like someone doing work experience as a guru. She wouldn't have a clue.

I feel more capable of 'mothering' the orphans at the Children's Centre here than I am of looking after my own children. And I don't need a mother. I have never bloody needed one. I open my eyes to escape from my thoughts, and find her staring at me again. I am disconcertingly sure that she can see into my mind, and am ashamed of myself.

When the bell rings again, and people start to stir, I am stiff with tension and bubbling over with stupid emotion. If this is what happens when I empty my mind, I think I had better not bother again.

I decide to skip the communal breakfast and go and hide until I have missed the yoga class.

Sam and Amber are easily persuaded to duck away from the crowds with me. The ashram members en masse are a mixture of the very wholesome and the alarmingly bizarre. There are many people, male and female, in random flowing robes. There are women with plaits. There are earnest-looking men with a convert's zeal in their eyes, who make me want to turn and run as far away from them as I can possibly get. The white people are much the more odd-looking ones.

We end up in the visitors' centre café, and although it is half past seven, it feels like midday. There are outdoor tables, in a paved yard where an eclectic mixture of people has congregated. A pale girl is scribbling in a book, a couple of tables away, biting her lip. Two women are arguing in fast Tamil, or what I assume to be Tamil, behind us, with much gesticulating.

'What are they saying?' I ask.

Sam listens for a while.

'They're talking about whose turn it is to go to Pondy,' he says, and listens harder. 'And they're talking about "the children". They're sorting something out for the orphans.'

'Ask them about the Children's Centre,' Amber urges him.

He rolls his eyes, and goes over to their table. We watch him talking, pointing over to us, and nodding while the women reply. A minute later he is back.

'They know all about you, Tansy,' he says, nodding to me. Amber is impressed. I had never realised how easy it is to seem impressive to young people. She seems to be latching on to me. 'They say Elly's been talking about you and even *Anjali* has been asking when you're arriving.'

'Anjali, the "spiritual leader"? You know, she was sitting at the front this morning. According to Maya.'

'She can't be. The way they were talking about her, she must be at least forty or so.'

'Oooh,' I say. 'Ancient.'

'Well, she must be. That woman today must be a different Anjali. They said, go over to the CC today and say hello.'

I look at the women. They smile and wave.

I wonder whether there is another Anjali. I imagine someone who is about sixty, with a kind face and a straight back. That would make more sense than the beautiful young woman I saw today, magnetic though she was. I recall Maya's tone, 'That's Anjali,' and I remember the way she looked at me, and I know it was her.

Some men are poring over technical diagrams, to my right,

discussing some sort of engineering project in French. They are clad in identical white T-shirts and white shorts, and they look as though they are about to step on to a tennis court, possibly on the set of a gay porn movie. Three women in flowing robes walk slowly by. One of them carries a plate of worthy-looking biscuits and pastries.

Sam grins. 'Hey, they've got cakes. Mum, can I have a cake?'

'You sound like Toby,' I say. 'Except that I'm not your mum. But yes, as the senior person present – much the most senior person – I will allow you to eat cake. Watch out, though. It might not be nice. You know the rules, Sam. Stick to the local cuisine, and you can't really go wrong.'

'You *so* can,' argues Amber. 'My brother, my stepbrother. He got really, really ill in Pakistan by eating local cuisine. I think it was goat.'

I consider this. 'True. But if you don't eat meat you're on firmer ground. And I don't mean the cake might be poisonous, I just mean it might not be very nice.'

'Well.' Sam stands up. 'Wish me luck. I'm going to risk it.'

The cake is stodgy, like a polystyrene sponge. The tea is milky, cardamom-scented, and perfect. I sit in the café and scrutinise the people who pass me.

I watch a group of children playing an involved game, keeping their distance from the café and its strange occupants. A boy draws something in the dirt with a stick, and the others, three girls, run and jump over it, ritualistically. They laugh, jostle each other. Then, from time to time, they look up at us, watching the strangers, with expressions that are far too knowing.

chapter twenty-two

The Children's Centre is another ugly concrete building, this time with a reed roof. There is a fence around it, enclosing a large grassy area with a shiny, new-looking climbing frame and slide. A middle-aged man dressed in a white suit is walking away, and greets us with a 'Good morning'. I nod back to him, and look at the children playing outside.

A boy who looks a bit older than Toby stares at me, unblinking, unsmiling. Two girls run up to the fence and say, 'Hello,' over and over again. Both of them are wearing their hair in tight plaits, and they are holding hands. I stroke the photographs of Toby and Joe, in my pocket, with my fingertip.

'Hello,' I say.

The sun beats down. The leaves rustle in the distant wind.

'How are you?' asks the elder of the two, who I guess to be around five.

'I'm fine, thanks. How are you?'

'Fine.'

'Can we come in?' asks Amber, nodding to the building. The girls smile, and run in ahead of us.

Five minutes later, I am on the floor, with children sitting at a respectful distance, staring at me. The children range from babies up to nine or ten years old. They are watching us, with dark velvety eyes. A tiny child crawls over, and I pick her up and settle her on my lap. The others inch closer. Amber sits next to me, clearly ill at ease, and soon she has a bigger child on her lap, stroking her ginger hair.

'What shall we do?' she hisses. She puts an arm awkwardly around the child.

'Um.' I am thrown by this; we knocked on the door to see if we could help, and were immediately ushered into a room, and left here. I try to imagine what Toby and Joe would like. 'We could tell them a story,' I hazard. 'Or sing a song.'

'I can't sing a song!'

'The wheels on the bus?'

'No!'

'A story, then.'

'Will they understand?'

'It doesn't matter.'

I start trying to think of a story from my head. I can't just make one up as I go along. It needs to be something that will be striking, even if they don't understand the words. Then I remember.

'We're going on a bear hunt,' I say, in as dramatic voice as I can muster. I feel extremely silly, but I carry on, stepping outside myself. If you can't make a fool of yourself in a roomful of grateful orphans, there's not much you can do. I throw myself into the performance. I stand up, holding the baby with one arm while using the other for random miming. 'We're going to catch a big one!' I exclaim. 'What a *beautiful* day.' I gesture to the sky. 'We're not scared!'

I get through the whole Bear Hunt book, from memory, with Joe's chubby face in my head all the time, smiling along with the familiar words. When I finish, with a relieved, 'We're not going on a bear hunt again,' I look at my audience. There are a few tentative smiles among the baffled faces.

'Again,' says a boy.

'What was *that*?' asks Amber. 'That was great. Did you make it up?'

'No! It's a favourite from home,' I tell her. 'Come on. You join in, this time. It's not difficult.'

We spend hours there, hiding from yoga. We change cloth nappies, brush hair, sort the laundry, and recite the Bear Hunt book again and again. The Children's Centre is far better funded than I had expected. Only twenty children live here (I was expecting hundreds), and they sleep in bunk beds and cots, five to a room, but each with their own space. It is clean, and tidy, and the children look well fed and clothed. The older ones get to roam the ashram at will, and attend yoga and meditation, while the younger ones are supervised by volunteer workers, namely, at the moment, Amber and me.

I decide to take four of the children to the café for lunch, and select them randomly, promising the others that they will get their turn. Three girls and a boy, Amber and me, all settle at a table. The children speak a little English, and we talk to each other as best we can, with lots of smiling.

'Speak English,' says the boy, over and over again. The younger girls whisper to each other.

'Do you think they think we're going to adopt them?' I ask Amber. 'Maybe we shouldn't be so nice.'

'Show them your boys,' she advises. 'Then they'll know you've already got children.'

So I do. I take out my pictures of Toby and Joe, and pass them around. The children laugh, and the littlest girl carefully kisses each of them.

'My brother,' says the boy.

'No!' I tell him. 'Not your brother. Sorry. Well, in spirit maybe.' I look at Amber. 'But children don't actually get adopted from here, do they? Elly just traces their families. Do you think they know that?'

'Um, I have no idea.'

The voice that interrupts is harsh and hostile.

'You are Mrs Tansy?'

I look round, to see an Indian woman with bulbous glasses standing next to me. Her eyes are magnified, and she looks like a frog. She is wearing a purple salwaar khameez, with bare feet and long hair.

'Yes,' I tell her. 'I am Mrs Tansy.'

'I am Enid. You miss the session this morning! This is intolerable.'

I laugh. 'No. Sorry, Enid, but there's been a misunderstanding. I'm here for the children.' I gesture to them. 'Not for yoga. Elly booked me on to your course because she's not here and she thought I'd need something to do. But I'm actually helping out with these guys instead. So, do give someone else the place.'

She shakes her head, her mouth pointing downwards. 'Payment has been made. Attendance is compulsory.'

'*Payment?*'

'Of course. Two weeks' intensive.'

'But I'm only here for a few weeks! I'm sure your course is great, but there's no way I'm doing it. Who paid?'

She shrugs. 'Elly paid on your behalf. You must come this afternoon. Otherwise Anjali will ask you to leave the ashram.'

I stare at her. Amber giggles. The children are wide-eyed and nervous. They obviously know Enid: they are shrinking away from her.

'What?' I say to her. 'Are you mad?'

'Not at all.'

'Anjali wouldn't do that.'

'Anjali most certainly would.'

When darkness falls, I am hobbling along the path that leads from the forest back to the Children's Centre, vowing never to darken the doors of a yoga studio ever again. I hate Enid, I hate everything she stands for, and everything she does. She has tortured me for three straight hours, this afternoon, when I should have been with the children.

When it gets dark, it is like a curtain falling. One moment, I am admiring the dusky sunset, and then, all of a sudden, I cannot see the path in front of me. I stop. I reach out in front of me, then sideways, trying to get my bearings. I start edging forward with baby steps. Nothing is lit here; nothing at all. The trees block any lingering daylight. I lean sideways, grasping for a tree to lean on.

I stand still for what feels like hours, wondering, as I veer between amusement and terror, how I am supposed to get back to the Peaceful Haven when I am nowhere near it. I wait for someone to come along on a bike, but they don't. I hear the noises of the forest, and my heart is in my mouth. For the first time in days, I think of past dangers.

When a pair of hands gently closes around my waist, I start and gasp.

'It's OK,' says a female voice. It is a soft voice, heavily accented. 'I have a torch. Where are you going?'

'Peaceful Haven,' I manage to say.

'This way. It's OK. Here. Take my hand.'

Her hand is soft and strong. She leads me quickly along paths between trees, occasionally saying things like 'large stone ahead', until we emerge beside the Great Hall. Then she takes me along the short path towards the guest house, and stops as soon as we can see the light. I cannot see her at all. She has been careful not to illuminate herself with her torch.

'Thank you so much,' I say. 'Who are you?'

She reaches out and strokes my hair. An unexpected current of electricity courses through my body.

'I am Anjali,' she says, and she is gone.

chapter twenty-three

I lie on the veranda, under the dim outside lights, and offer myself up to the swarming mosquitoes. It is dark, but still hot, and I have no energy for anything. The backs of my legs are on fire. My arms are trembling.

'So?' asks Sam. 'What was yoga like, hey? I can't believe you actually went.'

'Nor can I. She's evil.'

'You didn't take to it?'

'I spent all afternoon in a room with Germans,' I tell him, 'being ordered into stupid positions by the bloody Taliban. She actually yanked my limbs into place if I couldn't manage it by myself. I was just waiting for the ripping of the hamstring.'

He is laughing. 'Sounds fun. I don't think the Taliban quite go in for all that, though.'

'But it does sound fun!' says Delphine. 'It is something far from your ordinary! This is good.'

'You go instead of me, tomorrow,' I tell her.

'Yes please!'

'And there's not even a clock in there. I was just waiting and waiting for it to end. I thought she'd have a break halfway through but she just ploughed on. And that room was the hottest, smelliest, stuffiest . . .' I stop, because I haven't got the energy. 'And then I got lost on the way back, in the dark.'

'Yes,' Amber agrees. 'You did rather appear from nowhere.'

'I was rescued,' I tell her, but something stops me from telling her more.

The electric lights come on, suddenly. There are fluorescent strips along the top of the veranda. Swarms of insects rush to them, like iron filings to a magnet.

Women bring pots of food to a side table, and leave several baskets of chapattis on the dining table, at intervals. The woman who was ostentatiously meditating yesterday busily fetches piles of plates and glasses, and jugs of water.

People congregate all at once. Very few of them speak. They just form a line and start dishing rice, curry and whatever else is in the pots on to their plates. As I did yesterday, I try to slot in. I notice people looking at me, although no one says anything, and I try to stare them out. A few faces are familiar from yoga, but none of them appears to recognise me.

Sam and Amber mutter to each other, keeping up an unhappy-sounding private conversation that I can't hear. I take a seat at the long outdoor table, opposite them. A woman with cropped grey hair and a severe face sits down next to me. I recognise her.

'Hello,' says the grey-haired woman. 'Welcome. I am Helga.' To my surprise, she leans over and kisses my cheek. I try to take this in my stride, and air-kiss her back quickly, as if I were at a London media party.

'Hello, Helga,' I say. 'I'm Tansy. You're in Enid's yoga class. How long have you been here?'

'Four weeks. Soon my programme will end and I will leave for a while, but I plan to return several weeks after that.'

'Really? You like it here, then? You've been doing a four-week programme? How do you stand Enid for that long?'

'It becomes easier. You will see.'

'You're German?'

'Yes, from the former East Germany. How long do you plan to stay?'

'I have no idea.'

'This is the best way.'

We are interrupted by a shout from a little way down the table.

'Hello there!' calls the man with the big stomach, the one who seems to spend all his time reading Harry Potter. He is American, by the sound of it. He sounds as if he is hailing another boat, from his deck.

'Hello,' I tell him.

'Ha!' he shouts. 'Fellow English speakers! We must stick together!'

I look at Helga. She is smiling indulgently.

'Sure,' I agree, and turn away from him.

I help myself to three plates of carrot and okra curry with brown rice. I drink five glasses of water, and realise that I don't even want alcohol. There is nothing like a five o'clock start and an afternoon of yoga to put you off beer. When I finish my own bottle of mineral water, I stop drinking, as I am rather scared of the tap water in the jug on the table.

I talk to Helga. This is what I wanted: random conversation with people who just happen to be in the same place at the same time.

'So, what actually made you come here?'

Helga tells me about a messy divorce, a crisis, a midnight revelation that she should go to India, that her grown-up children would be fine if she did.

'You know Elly, and you know the Children's Centre,' she says. 'I am fully behind the work they do. As you know, there are some places at the centre coming free in the foreseeable future. I am going to Chennai, to visit some orphanages there, to see which children we can help, here at the ashram.'

'Oh, that's great.' I wonder whether this is what Elly wants me to do. I imagine it might be. 'Are there many orphanages in Chennai?'

'Of course.'

'I was surprised how little real poverty I saw when I was there. I was looking out for children but most of the kids I saw were well-dressed and nicely fed. Yeah, there were a few beggars, but everyone had told me it was going to be horrific and distressing, and it, well – it wasn't.'

Helga smiles sadly. 'It is not *in your face*, is it? You have to know where to look, but, oh yes, it is not as rosy as the powers that be would like it to appear.'

I reach for another chapatti to mop up the remains of my curry.

'Oh, sure, it's *vegetarian* food,' the American man is saying loudly. 'But you know, there's a difference between vegetarian and vegetables!'

No one challenges this statement, so I lean forward.

'Is there *really*?' I ask.

'Oh,' says the man. 'Absolutely. In India, they don't like to eat vegetables.'

I laugh loudly, but several of the women at the table are nodding in agreement. This man seems to enjoy holding court, and the women appear to submit to it. Typical, I think crossly. The only man at the table is the one who's doing all the talking.

Actually, there are two men at the table. Sam is folding a chapatti into quarters; he looks half asleep, though when he sees me looking, he winks. I turn back towards the American, and watch him noticing my cleavage in the lantern light.

'What on earth do you mean,' I ask, 'when you say they don't eat vegetables? What a ridiculous thing to say.' I look down at my plate. 'Look,' I say, jabbing it with my fork. 'Carrot! Green stuff! Vegetable curry! Made from vegetables.'

'But honey pie, that is my point!' he explains to my breasts. '*Here*, they use vegetables. They grow them and then they eat them. I meant *elsewhere* in India.'

'Yeah, right,' I tell him. 'Aloo gobi? Channa masala? Vegetable biryani contains vegetables – the clue is in the name. And so on, and on. At Saravana Bhavan in Chennai, there were so many vegetables that I had to have third helpings, because I liked them so much.'

He forces his gaze up at my face.

'You are a fine-looking woman,' he says. 'I'm Nick, and I like a girl with a bit of spirit. Tell me, though, sweetheart, how long have you been in India?'

I am furious.

'A week,' I admit. 'But I live in London, and—'

'One week. First visit?'

'Yes, but I've been to—'

He beams at his audience, and spreads his hands. 'I rest my case.'

'Oh, fuck off,' I tell him. 'A billion people in India, and only the residents of this ashram have discovered the joys of the *vegetable*? Are you fucking *kidding me?*'

People edge away from me. I hate Nick. I ostentatiously turn back to Helga, though I feel Nick's eyes on me.

'Tell me about the children,' I say to her quickly. 'How do you decide who to pick? And then what happens?'

'Oh,' she says. 'Well, you are Tansy. Elly's colleague. You know how it works. We look for relatives, or for people who could take them in. Whenever a child is housed, we fill the space with another in need. We have a lot of rehousing coming up, as you know.'

I pretend I know what she means, and nod sagely. I rather like the idea of being Elly's colleague.

'There's more wealth here than you expect, coming from Europe,' I say, a while later, going off at a tangent. 'I mean, yesterday morning I had my expensive trousers on and a woman took a photo of them because she wanted to get them herself.'

'Two sizes smaller and in ecru,' Amber calls across the table, with a giggle.

'Exactly. But the beggars weren't out in force. The only people who noticed me were rickshaw drivers.'

'Oh yes – they become tiresome,' Helga is saying, but Nick interrupts her, leaning across the table.

'Don't judge by the surface, Tamsin!' he calls.

I glare. 'Tansy.'

'Candy,' he says.

'Tansy,' I repeat.

'So Tammy,' he says quickly. 'You don't see beggars hanging off your clothes, so you think they don't exist? India's quietly solved the poverty problem, right? And you'd know because you've been here – hey! – a week!'

'You have no idea what we're talking about,' I shout down the table. 'You weren't even listening.' I give him one of my special glares. 'Look, *Mick*,' I say, 'I can be offensive if I try, and that was *not* me being offensive. I was interested in . . .' I gesture to the nice woman, momentarily forgetting her name in my ire.

'Helga,' she says.

'In what Helga was saying. And I *wasn't talking to you*. Novel concept as that clearly is.'

Nick widens his eyes and leans exaggeratedly away from me, holding up both hands to fend me off.

'Well, ladies,' he says. 'I think mealtimes around here just got a whole lot livelier.'

'Go fuck yourself,' I tell him. 'What a fucking lovely way to welcome someone to your fucking table. Most people are actually here to do something, not to sit around reading a kids' book in a T-shirt that is *many* sizes too small.'

There is a laugh from somewhere out in the darkness. We all look round, staring into the night.

I hear someone leaping over the low wall.

'I don't need to ask whether I've found the right place,' Elly says, striding over to me. She still sounds Australian, and is as tiny as she ever was. She laughs again, as I get to my feet, beaming. 'Years and years gone by since I saw her, and she hasn't changed a bit.'

chapter twenty-four

Elly is a fast and skilful rider, and I muffle my screams as the motorbike bumps up and down the uneven track through the Indian night. The sky is patchy with cloud: the bright pinpoints of the stars interspersed with areas of ominous blackness. Everything feels strange and foreign again.

I can feel the muscles of Elly's tight little body. The warm wind blows in my face, blows my hair out behind me. I have no idea where we are going. Toby and Joe are eating dinner with Max, right now, and missing me. I think of Max, coming home to them, sleeping in our bed every night without me, stretching out into my side, relishing the extra space.

I throw my head back, look at the sky, smell the warm night air.

We veer off the track on to a narrow stony path. The long grass and the small, red-earthed path are momentarily lit when we pass them, as in a horror film. The darkness presses down everywhere else. The path enters the forest, and the trees on either side reach out over the path, occasionally brushing us. The bike bumps over a big stone, and I grip Elly tighter, certain I will fall.

She really does live in a hut. There is a lantern lit outside, and a few other dwellings are visible through the trees. There is a bonfire built, but not yet lit, a little way from the house. Elly carefully parks her motorbike, turns to me with a grin, and ushers me in, wordlessly. I drink in the sight of her.

The hut is wooden, with a reed roof, but inside, it feels flimsy, almost like a tent. The floors are pale wood, the walls hung with white cloth, just like the Great Hall. I blunder around, afraid to touch anything, certain that I could send the entire structure crashing to the ground. It is surprisingly big inside, with rooms opening off one another, doors closed.

'It's like the Tardis,' I say, and I think of Toby.

'Yeah,' says Elly, turning to me and smiling. She used to be plain and boyish, but somehow over the years she has blossomed. 'What is that? Some other British people were here the other week, and that's the exact same thing they said when they came through the door: "It's like the Tardis." I was just like, yeah, I know, but what the fuck is a *Tardis*?'

I watch as she picks up four cups from a table and puts them in a bucket, ready for washing up.

'Didn't you get a BBC series called *Doctor Who* in Australia?'

She frowns. 'Maybe it used to be on when I was a kid. I didn't take much notice of TV. I was an odd fish.'

'It's come back lately. It's brilliant. I guess it's passed you by. You must have had your forty-two-inch plasma screen tuned to *The Wire* instead.'

'So I have no freaking idea what you're talking about.'

'Well, the Doctor is a time lord, and he travels around time and space in a blue police box. It's much bigger on the inside than it is on the outside. It stands for Time And Relative Dimensions In Space.'

Elly looks at me somewhat quizzically, then looks around her home and nods. 'Cool. The Tardis. I think I'll name the house that. Get the kids to make me a little sign to hang outside. Everyone else tends to call their houses 'Truth and harmony' or other bloody crap.'

'Sure.'

Elly walks quickly over to a wooden desk and picks up a pile of papers. She opens a drawer, drops it all in, closes it, turns the key, and threads the key on a thin silver chain round her neck. All this takes ten seconds, perhaps less.

'Where have you been?' I ask her.

'Delhi. Sorry. Maya gave you my note?'

153

'Yeah. Elly was in Delhi.'

'Elly was in Delhi,' she agrees. 'Hey, look. I got you beer.' She takes a huge bottle of Kingfisher from a bucket of water in the corner, shakes the drops off it, and opens it on a metal opener that seems to be embedded in the wall.

'Oh,' I say. I take it. 'Thanks. Cheers.'

'I may not have seen you for nearly ten years,' she says happily, 'but I know you'll still need a drink. Max filled me in on that. Bet you didn't even know Tamil Nadu's dry. Dry-ish. Sit.'

There are large, coloured cushions ranged against one wall. I sit down, slowly, on a dark red one, and stare at her. She is busy, sprinkling what can only be cannabis into a roll-up.

'Max filled you in?' I manage to say.

She licks the paper, and closes her spliff.

'Yeah. Did you like yoga?'

'Hated it.'

'Bummer. That was Max, too.'

I stare at her. 'And I thought I'd left him in London. What?'

'Oh, he asked me to sort out something nice for you. So I sorted out yoga. I'm not sure it's what he had in mind but we don't exactly have a spa. Don't tell him I wasn't here when you arrived. I said most people enjoy Enid's yoga. He said he'd like to see you in the lotus position.'

'I fucking hate Enid's yoga. And I hate Enid.'

'You'll love her before you know it. Stockholm Syndrome? You'll love her because she has total control over your life when you're in her room. People always do. They always start off hating her. They always end up worshipping her.'

'I don't think I'm going again.'

'Oh, no way will she let you get away.'

'Anyway,' I say, and I look at her properly, and grin. 'Here I am! And here you are! I can't really believe it.' She puts the cigarette to her lips and inhales deeply. I sip my beer.

'It's so good to see you,' she says. 'You haven't really changed.'

'You have. You look so calm and peaceful. You used to be hidden behind your glasses, looking like the Milky Bar kid. You looked about ten but it was all deceptive. Now you look like . . .'

I look at her. Her pale blond hair is longer than it was, down to her shoulders, and slightly curly. She has either ditched the glasses altogether, or got contact lenses. She has the impeccable posture of the yoga devotee. She is dressed in a loose yellow top, and a pair of orange silk trousers. 'Well, now you look like someone who lives in an ashram. And you look all of twelve, too.'

'Well, what's it been? Five years?'

She is so skinny that I am sure I could pick her up with one arm. I notice that her face, in repose, is severe. She seems less straightforward than she used to be.

'Eight years,' I tell her. 'Not five. Toby's six, for one thing.'

'Right. Well, I don't keep great track. Specially not of other people's children's ages. There's not a lot of things more tedious than that.'

'Oh, right. Yeah, I suppose so. I can imagine.'

She leans against a turquoise cushion, closes her eyes and inhales deeply, then exhales in contentment. Then she offers the spliff to me.

'No thanks,' I tell her. 'I don't do downers. They're bad for me.'

'Alcohol's a downer.'

'It's different. It's legal. I got used to it.'

Something screeches outside. I jump. 'What was that?'

'Mr Owl. Tans, it really is good to see you. I've thought about you heaps of times. I wish Max had come along too. I said that to him. He didn't really have a good reason.'

'It looks like that from here. But he's busy over there. Happy in his life, and all that.'

The tiny room is filled with druggy smoke.

'So are you two splitting up?' she says languidly. 'I mean, really. Max was so concerned about you. Something's not quite right, hey?'

I kick my sandals off and lean back. It feels odd drinking warm lager from a massive bottle, but something stops me asking for a glass. Everything feels odd, but I am suffused with a weird sensation of well-being, all the same.

'No!' I tell her. 'Of course not. I'm here because you asked me to come. He kind of encouraged me to go away to get happy, but it's not a marital thing. Why, what did he say to you?'

'Nothing much. So he never wanted to finish his journey?'

I look down. 'It wasn't as important to him. He'd been here before. Pondicherry doesn't have the mythical pull for him that it's had for me, down the years. Pondicherry is just another place as far as he's concerned. For me, it's been Shangri-La. It's been the most exciting, most exotic, most alternative-to-the-norm place on earth. It hasn't just been Pondicherry, a town in southern India where Max was going to work as a TEFL teacher. It's Pondicherry, the place where, in a parallel universe, we would all be living a life of seaside bliss. Where I would be perfect and so would everyone and everything else.'

Elly smiles. I wonder why, years ago, I never noticed how pretty her features were.

'Yeah,' she says, with a giggle. 'That's what brought me here, too.'

I stare. 'Seriously? How did that happen?'

She shrugs. 'I didn't have a destination of my own, so I borrowed yours. You went home, and it was all strife like none of us had ever known before.' She looks at me, and grins, and at last the years fall away. 'Suddenly, you'd gone,' she says. 'I was desperately scared, and I hung around in Kathmandu with Greg and Juliette till Max mailed from England to say you were all right. Then it was: now what? I was single for the first time in forever. You and Max were gone. I wasn't speaking to Eddy. Greg and Juliette headed back to Laos. Gabe stayed in Tibet. I was all on my own. So I thought I'd steal your journey.' She leans back, a faraway look in her eyes. 'I did it slowly. I went to Dharamsala to try to find the Dalai Lama, but I got pissed off because there were too many other people like me, and they were really severely annoying, which gave me a small existential crisis. I drifted down through India. I kept having to sort out new visas, but since I had no plans or deadlines I was cool to hang around government buildings for days and weeks at a time. Ended up in Pondy, as planned.' She laughs. 'It was pretty cool, actually. It's not like other places, Pondy. It doesn't disappoint. Then I came out here because it seemed like an interesting place to hang while I worked out what was next. The years passed. And here I am.'

'I never would have expected you to end up somewhere like this.'

There is a sudden squeal from the other room. At first, I think it is an animal. Then, as it happens again, a little high wail, I realise that it is a baby.

Elly looks around, and sighs.

'I'll give her a couple of minutes,' she says.

'You have a *baby*?'

Elly laughs. 'No, I fucking don't have a baby! And I never will. It's a little kid, Tara. You'll have seen her at the CC. They are ravished by your story about the bear, by the way.'

'It's not my story.'

'Well, it is to them. So, Tara's a sweet little thing but she doesn't sleep. I found some of her family in Kashmir, and they've come back with me, to collect her. Met them in Delhi. They're just at the "getting to know you" stage.'

'That's who's in your "quarters"? Tara's family are right here, right now?'

Elly is leaning back and nodding. 'Exactly. It's one of Anjali's rules. We take in the kids, try to track down their families and get them settled. We help out with paperwork. Not that anyone official could give a shit, but you do need the right piece of paper to wave under the right person's nose.'

'Where are the Kashmir people, then?'

'Out in Pondy for the evening.'

'So you left the baby on her own when you came to get me?' I am surprised at how shocking this is to me, me who fantasises about walking out on my family all the time, and who has now finally done it.

Elly laughs. 'Don't look like that! It's fine. She's perfectly safe here.'

'What if your house caught fire?'

'And how often does that happen, spontaneously? It could only catch light if I was in here smoking, and the whole point is that I wasn't.'

I can't bear the crying any more, so I stand up and follow the noise. 'Can I get her?'

Elly nods. I push open a door and stumble towards the wailing. When my eyes become accustomed to the darkness, I see the shape of a child, under a twisted sheet in the corner of a bedroom. I reach for her and pick her up. She neither resists me nor wants to come to me.

'Remember the tsunami?' Elly asks, when I come back, holding Tara, who is tiny but definitely older than her size would suggest, on my hip.

'Of course.'

'Right, well, you remember the tsunami because you switched the TV on in your big comfy house in London and saw dreadful things happening in Asia and you probably switched it off after a while because the pictures were too distressing and you didn't want your children to see them.'

I let the 'big comfy house' thing pass, as this is not really the point, and I nod.

'Here, it was unimaginable, apocalyptic devastation. In Pondy. In all those villages you passed along the Chennai road. In a place called Mamallapuram, in particular. It's a fishing port, and it was devastated. You have no idea of the scale of it, because you really and truly cannot imagine such a thing.'

I nod.

'And,' she continues, 'now, years later, the ones whose lives have been ruined are mainly children. They've lost their families. Tara was a tiny newborn baby, the only survivor from her immediate family, because her mother managed to throw her to someone on a roof. There are actual orphanages, but believe me, they are grim. The CC isn't an orphanage, and we only take a few kids at a time. You've seen that. We tap into the community thing so everyone can keep an eye on them, everyone can be a bit responsible. The actual orphanages round here are run by amazing people and in the main they do an incredible job, but it's grim as all fuck. We take children out of them whenever we can.'

'Those poor, poor darlings.' I stroke Tara's hair. 'I'm so glad I came. What do you want me to do?'

She looks at me. 'You've got two boys. I often wish international adoption was easier. Most of the orphans are girls. You could have had one. That would have been the best thing you could possibly have done – solve the whole world's problems for one person.'

I laugh. 'Elly, I am a crap mother.'

She looks at me over the top of her cigarette. 'You're a crap mother? So you'd leave an orphaned girl living in a flea-infested room she shares with forty others, sleeping on a concrete floor, shitting in the corner?'

The beer has made me light-headed. I forget my fear of the mother-daughter relationship. I forget the fact that I know there are complex issues behind international, cross-cultural adoption.

'You're right,' I tell her. 'Of course we'd have one, if it was possible. Absolutely, we would. But what can I *actually* do for them?'

'A bit of what I just did, to be honest. Smoothing things over when we're sorting them out with homes. You're a mum. You can take a child to its family, if need be?'

'Course I can.'

'You're ultra-responsible these days.' She laughs. 'On the outside, anyway. You're very nervous. You shouldn't be.'

We sit in silence for a while. Elly hands me a third beer. Tara shifts on my lap, leans into me, and goes to sleep. I look at the top of her head, at her soft black hair, and I stroke the back of her delicate little hand.

The hours pass. Suddenly, Elly and I are outside, lying on the grass beside the fire that she must have lit. I have drunk all of the beer that Elly bought me, but it is the fumes from her cigarettes that are knocking me out.

The night is warm, and the flames are leaping into the sky. Tara is back in bed. Her Kashmiri family came back from Pondy, picked her up, and disappeared into another room with barely a word, looking at me warily. I think the woman was wearing Top Shop, but was too befuddled to ask.

We both lie on our backs, our bare feet hot next to the fire.

The cloud has vanished and the stars above are remarkable: bright and defined.

'Toby's teacher's a traveller,' I say. 'Mr Trelawney. He got me thinking about coming away again.'

'Mr Trelawney?' says Elly. 'Is he sexy?'

'No. Well, yes. Well, kind of. It's a good thing I came away when I did. Really. I didn't want to do anything but I might've done.' I am talking nonsense. I know this, even as I say it.

'What? You might've or you did?' Her words are slurred, lazy.

'Might've. Only because he's a traveller. He's like Max used to be.'

Elly is unruffled. 'How far did you go?'

'Nowhere much. Flirting. Texting. Oh, and I kissed him once. In the classroom. That's bad, isn't it?'

'Do you think about him, now you're away?'

'No. Not really. I've texted him a few times. He replies after a day or so. All quite above board.'

'So you'd tell Max?'

'No! But it's nothing. It could have been something but it isn't.'

'Well, even if you'd been fucking his brains out, who cares? It's your body. You do what you like with it.' Elly has smoked so much grass that I am amazed that she can move her mouth and form words with it. 'It's nothing. Look around you. Doesn't it blow your mind that we can see millions of miles into outer space? I mean, you can climb a hill, look at a view, and people get excited about that. But no one cares very much that you can look across the universe whenever you want to. Even in the day, that blue, that's space. Infinity.'

I look up. 'Don't they think the universe has limits, these days?'

'Yeah?' Elly turns her head towards me. 'It hasn't really, though, has it? I mean, it goes on for ever, as far as I'm concerned. See those stars.' She waves her joint at them, in an imprecise manner. 'The human eye deserves more credit than it gets. I mean, you and I, we can see that star, a huge burning sun, millions and billions of miles away, and years ago. We can see across space and time. We can do that with something this big.' She is holding up her cigarette, which is about the diameter of an eyeball.

'Yeah,' I agree. 'It makes you feel small. And that's before you get on to the hows and the whys.'

'You mean, how did it start? And why? You know, that shit doesn't bother me any more. You only have to look at it to realise that we're nothing, and that nothing we do or say is going to change anything, in any significant way. We're less than ants. Kiss who you want, do what you want: we're random little energy swirls. In the cosmic sense, nothing matters. If you do your bit to make the world a slightly better place, then that's your work done. Have a good effect on the world around you, leave no footprint, and don't sit around stressing about the small stuff, because it's all small stuff.'

I prop myself up on my elbows and look at her. 'But – but Elly? You live in a cult – I mean in a religious community. You meditate and do yoga all the time. You must have a more rigorous philosophy than that.'

She laughs. 'Why?'

'But don't you have to believe in, I don't know, cosmic forces or karma or something? Not to mention some sort of god? Or that Mother business? Or Anjali? I thought you'd be banging on about channelling the universal spirit of blah-de-blah. Surely you see everything as meaningful and significant?'

'Meaningless and insignificant. Best way.' She waves the joint around. 'Anjali, by the way, would say the same, if you caught her off guard. Which you never would. And anyway, humanity's in its last days. Radical upheavals are coming. You're going to need to supply your own food, batten down the hatches and look after your own. And this place isn't a religion. We don't have a god here. People supply whatever gods they want. We're just about ways of living. I take Anjali's laws a lot more seriously than I take the police.

'I ignore earthly laws at my discretion,' she adds, after a few seconds. 'I mean, earthly laws are arbitrary, historical nonsenses. Why is all the beer you just drank legal, and this cone not? Why are the laws applied differently so that if, say, a local guy without any connections was caught with a bag of hash, he'd be banged up for years and years, but if it was, say, you, they'd let you off with a warning and the Ambassador would make sure you had a window seat on your flight home? You could get away with anything.'

'I met a down-and-out in Chennai,' I tell her. 'He was British, white. He got in some trouble at Hampi, and he's still here, living on the street. I hung out with him because no one else would talk to me.'

'Then he's mad. Was he mad?'

I think about Ethan. This is an easy question to answer.

'Of course he was. In a strange way, I liked him. I felt a bit "There, but for the grace of God . . ." about him.'

She shrugs. 'Of course. Could be any one of us, I guess. You just have to deal with what life throws at you, do the best you can, try to make the world a better place than it was when you arrived. That's all there is.'

The grass is comfortable under my head. I close my eyes, and listen to the strange noises of the Indian night.

chapter twenty-five

I have been asleep for two hours when someone starts ringing a bell, very loudly.

'Meditation!' a voice calls, and I recognise it as Maya's. This morning, I am not receptive to the idea. 'Up you get! To the Great Hall!'

People are shifting around. There is a general air of activity.

I swallow down my nausea and pull the sheet over my head. People are moving in the room. Delphine shifts around, crawls to the end of her bed, gets off it. I hear Amber muttering. I am still drunk. I close my eyes, swallow the bile that has risen to my throat.

When the bell rings again, directly next to my ear, I scream.

'Sorry,' says Maya. I still don't open my eyes, but I imagine that she looks anything but sorry. 'Meditation. No excuses, no exceptions.'

'I'm ill.'

'No you're not. Get up.'

'No.'

The sheet is whisked away. I am lying on my bed in a T-shirt and a pair of knickers. I force my eyes open, and glare at her, while feeling around blearily for my covers.

'No doubt Elly will be feeling similar,' she says, 'but I can promise you that she is already there.'

'What will you do if I refuse?'

'I will go to Anjali and tell her, and I will also tell her that you were drinking alcohol within ashram grounds last night – don't deny, I can smell it – and she will ask you to leave the community and never to return.'

I start to pull on some trousers. 'Why does everyone go on about Anjali all the time? Why's she such a goddess?' I grumble, as I scrape my hair into a ponytail, tying it with an elastic band that is probably Delphine's.

'Come on. Everyone else has already left. We'll catch them up if we cycle. You can use Youssef's bike.'

Ten minutes later, I am sitting cross-legged at the very back of the room. I cannot possibly spend an hour here. I shoot a glance at the man to my right. His eyes are closed. I look at Maya, to my left. She opens her eyes, winks, and closes them again.

I concentrate on Anjali. She is the only person who can see me, but, today, she is not looking, and I am stupidly affronted by this. I keep looking at her, even though I don't want to. At least I am not going to be tormented by my own demons today. With a certain degree of relief, I edge backwards, and manage to lean my back against the wall. Then I close my eyes.

'Hey,' says Amber, shaking me. 'Get up. It's lunchtime.'

The bedroom is bathed in daylight, and there is a clatter coming from outside. My head is thumping, my mouth as dry as the earth outside, and about as dusty. I try to go back to sleep, but it's too late; I am awake, and I need water.

'How did I get here?' I vaguely remember staggering back to bed. 'What am I doing?'

'Duh. Sleeping. You've missed loads of yoga and the woman was on the warpath again, but we told her we hadn't seen you and we locked the door so she couldn't get you up. She wasn't happy. You're going to have to go this afternoon. I spent the morning with the children. I sang them "Row Row Row Your Boat". It was great.'

I sit up. 'Christ. I'm never drinking again. Did you do the bit about "if you see the crocodile, don't forget to scream"?'

'The *what*?'

My eyes are closing by themselves. I make a considerable effort to focus.

'Row your boat. It has all these verses now that everyone knows. Gently down the river. If you see the jellyfish, don't forget to quiver. Stuff like that.'

'No. I didn't do those bits. Look, Sam and I thought we'd get you up for lunch because three hours' yoga on an empty stomach, with a hangover . . . Get yourself up and dressed, wash your face, and I'll see you back here in a minute.'

I walk carefully past the meditating woman on the veranda, and find my feet propelling me to the middle of the hard earth in front of the guest block, where I stop abruptly, stand and look around, the whole world spinning around me. The sun instantly makes my headache worse. Veins are standing up in my temples. I vaguely hear Nick's voice in the background. I am assaulted by twenty-seven different layers of sound. Indian music drifts over the treetops. A dog is barking, somewhere in the distance. Insects are shouting at the tops of their little voices. I put a hand to the side of my head. I cannot believe I ever thought this place was quiet.

Nick is walking towards me, and I realise I am only wearing a big T-shirt and knickers. I break into a run, as I make no secret of escaping from him. I run into the woods before I realise my mistake. Still, it is quiet in there, and soothing. It is a different, muted world, and I sit down and lean against a tree. This would be a good haven, if ever I should need one.

I eat the most enormous lunch I can manage, with as many forms of carbohydrate as possible.

'I honestly didn't want to drink,' I tell Amber. 'It was Elly. She'd bought me all these beers, and she was so proud. But why do I have to drink everything that's there? Why can't I stop?' I think of my mother. I am not an alcoholic. I am not like her. All the same, I know that plenty of alcoholics can manage a night, or several nights, off. It is moderation that is the key.

Amber shrugs. 'Just because it's there. I guess. It's no big deal.

Loads of people are like that. It's not as if you're going to have much opportunity, round here. It's hardly Wetherspoons.'

'I guess.' I tear off a piece of chapatti. 'Where's Sam?'

'Calling the famous village.' She clamps her lips together until they are white and bloodless. Then she smiles a tight smile. 'It's funny, isn't it? He calls the village. Not any particular person, just the whole settlement, en masse. Then he wonders why I'm intimidated.'

'So, what is the deal, exactly?'

'Mobile coverage isn't very good. So he has to call on the payphone at the right time.'

'I didn't mean that! I mean, you two are going to visit? But you don't want to and he can't wait?'

Amber twirls her hair around her finger. 'Before we got here I totally wanted to. When you're in London it sounds fantastic, doesn't it? Come to my village in south India. Now, I'm absolutely dreading it. And yes, he's wildly and fantastically excited – stupidly excited. Different from how I've ever seen him before. I think that's why he's let me put it off a bit, because he's actually savouring the anticipation so much. It's his total raison d'être.'

'Why are you dreading it?'

Amber eats a chunk of potato before replying.

'Because I'm absolutely fucking terrified. Obviously. He speaks Tamil at home – you know that – it's his first language. Whereas I can just about say hello. *Vanakkam*. Although when I try, it makes people laugh. People in tiny Tamil villages – Poosarippatti in this case – aren't going to speak English, are they? So I'll be sitting there like a stupid white ginger lemon, not understanding a word. And they'll all wish I hadn't come so they'd have Sam to themselves. And . . .' Her voice tails off, and she suddenly looks close to tears.

'And what?' I demand. 'Tell me.' The sun is hot, now. A beam has slipped between the strands of the flimsy roof, and is pounding at my head.

'Oh, this is stupid.' She looks around, then leans forward. 'Promise me you won't say anything to him?'

'I promise. Of course I do.'

'You must absolutely and completely promise, even if you want to tell him, and you must promise not to try to make me tell him, too.'

'Yes, yes, absolutely and completely.'

She nods. 'Well, I read a letter they sent him. I didn't mean to. I was looking for his passport and it was just kind of there. Obviously I didn't actually *read* it because it was in Tamil. But there was a photo in there. Of a girl. Formally posed, smiling her best toothy smile, wearing her best clothes. And you know what? I think they want him to marry her.'

I look at her, and when I see that she is serious, I cannot help but laugh.

'But that's hilarious,' I tell her. 'Don't be ridiculous. He's your boyfriend. If they've got a girl lined up, that's something to *laugh* about with him. Not something to stress about in secret.'

'Yeah, it would be, if he'd mentioned it to me. She was very pretty. And incredibly young. I can't really compete, can I?'

'If he hasn't mentioned it, it's only because he knew you'd be upset, and you wouldn't want to go.'

'Can you blame me for not wanting to go? Would you?'

I think about that. 'Well, no, not the way things stand for you now. But I would definitely have had it out with him as soon as I found the photo and so things would be fine. First of all, they probably don't want him to marry her. He's just got a picture of his cousin or something – it's not a crime. You have to find out who she is and why he has the picture, and what the letter says. Talk to him. He just has to say to whoever's in the village, "I have a girlfriend, thanks," and it's all sorted. They know you're coming, don't they? He's probably said it already.'

I see Amber perking up a bit. 'Do you think so? God, it must be *amazing* to be married. Is it the greatest feeling, not having to worry about this crap any more?'

I think about Jim, then Max. 'Mmm,' I agree weakly. 'Pretty much.'

Sam flings himself down in the chair next to Amber, and this, happily, stops me from having to elaborate.

'Hey,' he says to me. 'Sleeping beauty. You snored all through

167

meditation. Some of us were giggling. Most were very dis-approving.' He pushes his hair out of his face.

'I did not!'

He looks pleased with himself. 'Maybe you did. Maybe you didn't. You'll never know now.'

'Shut up.'

'So, Ambs, it's sorted. We get the bus on Wednesday. They'll be there to meet us. I've got all the instructions. Everyone's very excited. I don't think they've ever played host to a redhead before.'

'Oh,' Amber says, with a thin smile. 'What's it going to be? Me Big Man Come From City?'

He looks annoyed. 'Not at all. This is my family. My actual close family – my aunts and uncles and my first cousins. As you know. Not me-big-man-from-city at all.'

'I'm going to be sitting there while everyone talks around me. Would it be rude to read a book, do you think?'

'If you're going to be funny about it,' Sam adds, 'you don't *have* to come. God, you've made no secret of the fact that you don't want to.'

'Well, maybe I won't, then' she says, and she stands up and stalks off. 'I wouldn't want to cramp your style,' she calls acidly, over her shoulder.

Sam turns to me. 'What was *that* about?' he asks, but before I can tell him, and I would have told him, he has run after her.

Yoga is torture. Enid hates me, and I hate her. I hate her straight parting, her convex glasses, and her purple tunic. I hate her rush mat, and her knobbly feet.

She doesn't believe I was ill this morning, and she threatens to make me leave if I miss a lesson again. I don't say anything, but I think the glare I give her says it all.

I contort myself, stretch my muscles, stand on one leg. I always thought this was supposed to be gentle exercise, but it is horrible. An hour or so in, I realise I will only get through by surrendering myself to it entirely, as if I were a child. I make a mammoth effort, switch off the part of my mind that is chafing, and do as I am told, unquestioning.

And in spite of everything, by the end of the session I am feeling strangely exhilarated.

I teach the children as many verses of 'Row Your Boat' as I can remember, and make up a few more. They are fairly dire:

> Row, row, row your boat
> Very, very far.
> If you see the pirate ship
> Don't forget to Arrrrrgghh.

That one goes down well. We transform the Indian orphans, briefly, into fetishised pirates, and I vow to text Jim, later, and tell him. Then I vow not to.

After that, we start on our project, which is to get them acting out the Bear Hunt story. We split them into groups, and work on their parts. Everyone wants to be the bear. I pick the tallest child, a boy called Mani, and watch him running around scaring the others, who shriek with laughter.

I am surprised, when I look up to check the daylight, to see Elly and Anjali, deep in furtive conversation at the back of the room. They are, quite obviously, muttering about me. Elly says, 'Of course. She'll do anything,' quite clearly, before she sees me looking. We all stare for a second or two, and then she rushes across the room, kisses me, and says, 'Oh, Tansy, you're the greatest. We need you to stay here for ever and ever, and I'm going to mail Max and tell him that right now.'

'You're going to mail him?'

'Sure.'

'Where from?'

chapter twenty-six

The twilight is edging in through a window set into the roof, lengthening shadows and making everything look eery. There are very few people here. Elly sits at one side of the room, and I take a cubbyhole on the other, and log on to my email. I had no idea there was an internet centre here.

A strong arm grabs me round the neck.

I shout. Then I whip round, fists up, ready to defend myself.

'Hey, you *are* a firecracker!' says my attacker.

'Nick! Jesus. What are you *doing*?'

He is wearing tight shorts which reveal meaty pink thighs, and a Fairtrade ashram T-shirt (I can tell this because it says 'Fairtrade @ The Ashram' on it, in embroidery).

'I thought I was being friendly You didn't look so well earlier.'

'And grabbing me by the neck makes me so much better. I know what you were really up to.'

'Oh yes? And what was I really up to?'

'Groping a defenceless woman. Taking your opportunities where you find them.'

He laughs. 'Apologies. But I don't think you can really, in all conscience, call yourself "defenceless".'

Elly is looking round, her blond hair falling over her face. 'Don't mess with this lady, Nick. I bought her beer last night. We both feel like a sack of shit today.'

'And you weren't even drinking,' I remind her.

'You both slept through meditation,' Nick informs us, grabbing a computer in a far corner. 'Both of you. I saw you. Or should I say, heard you. Nice snoring.'

'I didn't snore!' I protest, but he raises both eyebrows and turns away. Damn it.

I turn my attention back to the email I am reading.

'Hey, Elly,' I say. 'Here's some photos Max has sent. I know I showed you the boys, but do you want to see them again?'

She smiles. 'Sure I do. Your little guys.'

I click to enlarge them. Nick comes over to look, too.

'This is Toby.' I point to him, standing on the top of a climbing frame, his arms up like Superman. 'And this is Joe.' I scroll down and indicate my baby boy, who, in the photograph, is holding an unseasonal ice cream in the rain, and smiling a happy little smile.

'Wow,' says Elly, leaning in. 'Look at them!' She takes the mouse and scrolls back up to Toby. 'I know I said it before, but that one looks so much like Max. It's uncanny. Like it's actually one of Max's baby photos. I still can't believe you've got people like this in your life. That these are actually your kids. That you and Max made some little people. I couldn't do it. Hey, who's that woman with Maxy?'

I look closely at the screen. She has scrolled down to the third photograph, taken, clearly, by one of the children. Max is standing close to Sarah, laughing, looking into her face.

'That's Sarah,' I say. I swallow hard. 'She's one of my best friends.'

Elly says nothing for a while. 'Do you trust her?' she asks, after a while.

'Yes.' I hear the uncertainty in my own voice.

'Are you sure about that?' Nick interjects. 'I'd want to be fairly sure.'

'Oh, fuck off,' I tell him, and close the file.

Elly sits back down at her computer and turns the screen round slightly, so I can't see what she is doing.

I go back to my own emails. I open one from Sarah and attempt to read between its lines.

Hey. Just to reassure you that max and t & j are doing fine. gav's away in singapore as per bloody usual, so we've been keeping an eye on them for you. max is a lot more fun than I'd realised. I had it in mind that he was a career obsessed, well, banker (not to mention all the choice epithets you had for him before you left). but he's a lovely man, isn't he?

Alarm bells are ringing so loudly that I'm surprised Elly and Nick can't hear them from across the room. I start crafting a message to Max that will, I hope, explore this avenue without sounding paranoid. I tell myself that I am being stupid. But still, I can't help feeling that my poor husband is finding life easier in my absence

I picture them getting closer, thrown together by circumstance, slowly and deliciously falling in love, trying to hold off but, eventually, overcome by passion, sharing a bottle of wine or two, and tearing each other's clothes off. It is not only possible; in my tired, hungover state, it seems inevitable.

I write to him more affectionately than I would have done normally. I decide I will call them all later, too.

The woman with long ropy hair, who meditates on the veranda ceaselessly, comes into the room, looks unsmilingly at me, and walks over to Elly. They talk in low voices, the woman constantly looking over to me with a suspicious face. She puts her back between me and Elly, and they carry out a transaction of some sort. I watch her handing money over, and pocketing something tiny in return. Then she leaves the room without another glance at me.

'What was that about?' I ask Elly.

She looks over, smiling. 'Oh, that was Melinda. She's been around a few months. Ray of sunshine. Wouldn't you say, Nick?'

'Oh,' he says. 'She is charm and grace personified. I entirely heart her, as you young people say.'

In the absence of absolutely anything else to do, I try to find out what happened to Ethan. Max would hate me doing this.

I have a feeling that, if it was indeed something dramatic that brought him here, then I might be able to find a trace of it online. The name 'Ethan' and 'India' together prompt Google to ask whether I might mean 'then India'. I try to remember his home town. He once mentioned Norfolk. I add Norfolk to my search. Then I add Norwich. Then I add Hampi.

I am entirely thwarted by the fact that his name is not, in fact, Ethan. I have no idea how to trace a man with no name. 'Missing man Norfolk' is the best search I can do but, contrary to my hopes, this brings up no trace of him at all. I try it as an image search, but apart from a poster looking for someone who is definitely not him, nothing remotely relevant comes up.

'Tansy?'

I look round. Elly is tipping her chair back, and waving to me. 'Yes?'

'I've been calling. What are you up to?'

I smile. 'Oh, absolutely nothing. Just Googling someone for the hell of it.'

'Not the handsome surfer teacher?'

'No. That guy on the streets in Chennai.'

'Most of those guys don't have email, you know. Or Facebook pages. Look, could you do something for us? You're amazing with those kids. Could you take Tara to Pondy for her medical check-up? What do you reckon?'

'Go to Pondicherry?'

'You have to start calling it Pondy, now you're here. Everyone does. You know, it's not even called Pondicherry any more. It's Puducherry, if you're being correct.'

'I know, but it will always be Pondicherry to me. And if you need someone to go, that is what Delphine would call a sign. I don't think I'll ever call it Pondy. It seems a bit too familiar, when I've been obsessing about the place for ten years.'

'You'll get there. Do you want to go in the morning?'

'Can it live up to my expectations?'

'Sure it can.'

'Are you coming?'

'Actually not. I'm all busy tomorrow. We'll go there for dinner sometime, though, when you've been here long enough to crave some cosmopolitan cuisine. Tomorrow, you'll be on business.'

Nick has turned round. 'I can come if you like. Hold your hand.'

'No you fucking can't.'

chapter twenty-seven

Alexia's thoughts 5.12a.m.

For once I am writing this after going to bed. Normally I'm up late not sleeping. Tonight I have slept, but I woke early and knew that was me done.

Duncan tells me I am obsessed. 'Quit thinking about her,' he says. 'It's making you crazy. Everything is in hand. She's fine. You just have to wait.'

It is making me crazy, but, although I don't tell him, I think I'm crazy in a good way. I mean, since I got this idea and started to imagine the two of us, in India, becoming a family of three (becoming a family – at the moment, we're a couple, not a family, because the cats so don't count), then I think I have changed for the better.

I have an India guidebook and I read it all the time. I know that in New Delhi, the nice hotels are in South Delhi, and the backpackers stay in Paharganj. I know the government is in New Delhi and that the British used to be in charge until Gandhi made them leave (yes, this simplifies things somewhat). I know that Calcutta is now called Kolkata. I know that there are lots of old hippies in Goa. I know the Sikh temple is in Amritsar, and I can point to Amritsar on the map. I know that Sri Lanka is not actually a part of India.

I realise just how ignorant I have always been about the

world out there. In all honesty, before this, 'abroad' meant Canada, Mexico, London. That's all.

I tell these things to Duncan, but he laughs. I tell them to Dee, and she looks at me funny and says there are plenty of American children needing a family, and if I want to save someone I should look closer to home. Why do people always say this? They don't believe that we tried that route. I tell things to Milly and Brian. They don't judge me. I talk to Brian about India a lot. Brian knows it all.

I am trying to read novels set in India, because I think that will give me a good idea of what it is like. I must admit, though, that I am struggling with some of these books and have not picked one up in a few days.

And I am obsessed with Saskia. Perhaps we will call her Sas or Sassy. Maybe she'll like to spell it Sasi. That would be kind of cool, I think. Although we will be cash-poor for many years to come because of the expense of the adoption, we will give her the best life ever.

I try not to think about where she is right now, and yet it is impossible not to. Unfortunately, I have, in the course of my research, discovered that the poor little orphans tend to sit in orphanages in India for their entire childhood, and that conditions are horrible. I know that's where she is now. I hope she knows that we are coming to rescue her, just as soon as we possibly can. I hope she knows she has a bedroom and a bike and a cupboard full of toys.

I wonder what the change will be like for her. It's going to take her a while to adapt, I can see that. Folks out there worry about taking a child so far away from its culture – because we really are a thousand miles away – more than a thousand miles away of course but I meant in spirit. So I will keep up my interest in all things Indian. I will take my daughter back there every couple of years. I will seek out the Indian community around here, if there is such a thing. I will do everything I can to let that child grow up Indian-American, and I think that Indian-American might be just about the best thing in the world to be.

I'm even getting myself in shape. I'm walking around town instead of taking my car. I had my hair cut and everyone says it looks better. I want to be a mom that my little Saskia will be proud of. I want us to be the very best we can.

Comments: 1

Alexia, hi. We don't know each other but I'm another potential mom on a similar journey. We looked at India but the hurdles seemed too great, and we're heading to China in two weeks to pick up our little girl, Wei. I am SO excited. We live in Canton, Ohio, appropriately! If you're anywhere nearby, I'd like to invite you to join our Overseas Adopters group. I think it does everyone good to meet someone in the same situation, and it certainly sounds to me as if you need to talk to someone who understands, other than your cats.

I am thrilled that you have been matched with your little Saskia. All the very best of luck to you, my dear.

Love to you and your little family,

Pam

chapter twenty-eight

The rickshaw bumps along the road, and all I can think of is Max. I am waiting for the triumphant entry into Pondicherry and am looking out for some sort of 'Welcome to Pondicherry' sign. Of course, it doesn't exist, and I realise, as the roads become ever more built up, that I am already there. My heart thumps and I clench my fists and feel sick. This is it: this is the end of my journey, after an eight-year hiatus.

The road is not particularly busy but the pavements are teeming with life. Dust floats in the hot air. There are people everywhere, squatting by the road, cooking, shouting, carrying things, talking on mobile phones, smoking.

Our rickshaw bumps along, and I watch, through the open side, and drink in every detail. This is Pondicherry. The roads, I think, are wider here. There are trees at intervals. The people are happier. Lots of them are walking in the road.

I tighten my grip on Tara. I wanted to be here with my own children, but I am with someone else's baby. A child of a dead mother. She doesn't look at me; she is fiddling with the catch of my handbag. The rickshaw swings around a corner, and I almost don't want it to stop. We swerve through the streets, alongside a dry, stinking canal. Then the driver pulls across a lane of traffic, and stops.

'Government Square,' he announces.

I am not sure why I am so nervous. My first step on to the Pondicherry tarmac seems more momentous than my first step on to Indian tarmac did. I feel that something has shifted, just by my being here.

I see Max and Sarah, laughing together. I wonder why he sent me that picture, what he is trying to tell me, whether he is trying to provoke me.

Tara stands close to my legs as I pay the driver, and I take her hand, which is small but strong. The air smells of the sea. A breeze lifts my hair.

'Come on, Tara,' I say, though I have never heard her say a word. She is always hidden behind Elly, or hanging on to the bigger children at the CC. 'Look, there's a playground there, just like Elly said. Let's go and play, and then we can go to your appointment.'

I never expected a playground in India. I particularly did not expect it to be exactly the same as the playground I take my boys to, after school, in North London. But for its situation, in the centre of a bustling Indian city, it could be the same place. It has the same primary-coloured equipment, but here it is shinier and less well-worn. I wonder whether this is globalisation in action, whether a company somewhere is manufacturing slides and rope bridges with red, yellow and blue frames, and selling them to every municipal authority in the world.

Indian children, I would have supposed, play either with old bits of cardboard box they find on the street or, in the case of the privileged uber-minority, with expensive and intricate toys imported from FAO Schwarz. Instead, this place is teeming with children playing exactly like my boys, with the same sense of focus on the task in hand: the climbing, the sliding, the hanging on.

I stick close to Tara, much more afraid for her than I ever am for Toby and Joe. I am acting like Olivia's Mum, sticking by her side, helping her up steps, holding my arms in case she falls. I am terrified that she might be hurt, or lost, while in my care.

She is four. That is to say, slightly older than Joe. I imagine him next to her: she is tiny and slight. Were I to ask him to look after her, he would put an arm round her shoulders and steer her around. I picture his solemn face, hear the way he would take his duties as her guardian seriously. He would be affronted if he realised he was younger than she is. All the same, there is something in her eyes that I hope never to see in Joe's.

She plays seriously, scrambling up the climbing frame, turning round, and cautiously walking back down, watching the other children carefully. I try to read her expression.

Elly told me that, after the tsunami, she ended up in a suddenly overflowing orphanage in Mamallapuram, where she was the only child without extended family visiting her. 'I went to call,' Elly said, 'because we could take a couple in at the CC. All the kids were crowding around me – I tell you, it's heartbreaking, when you make those visits, and they're all, like, "Me! Pick me! Mama!" shoving each other out of the way, survival of the fittest in action. And there was this tiny little girl standing by herself, a little way away, looking at the floor. I asked about her, and they said no one ever came to visit Tara. They thought her family were in Kashmir.' She shrugged. '*I* thought someone had better track them down.'

Tara is entirely self-contained. As I watch her carefully sitting at the top of the small slide, lifting both hands at once, and shimmying forward to reach a point where gravity will take her down, I find myself blinking hard. Even at this age, she has learned to keep her emotions bottled up inside. I wonder what her new life will be like, up in the mountains in Kashmir.

I am aware that the mothers and grandmothers in the square are looking at us with open curiosity. When I take Tara's hand and walk her in what I hope is the right direction, the crowds part around us. Nobody smiles, and no one looks hostile. For the first time since I arrive here, they just look at me.

There is a group of schoolgirls walking in front of us. Every one of them has hair that is shiny and perfectly styled. Indian schoolgirls look like schoolgirls ought to look. Many of them wear their hair in two long plaits. They look innocent and vulnerable.

I watch a girl in a modest blue uniform, and she stares back. After a few seconds of blank eye contact, I make an effort, and smile. She stares for a moment longer, then looks down to Tara, looks back at me, and smiles back. I raise my hand and give her a little wave. She does the same.

There are elderly people out walking with sticks, in groups of two or three. Tara walks slowly, and I think she must be tired, so I pick her up and march towards the doctor's surgery, returning every stare, daring anyone to be rude.

An hour later, we are crossing the road that will lead to the promenade, and the sea. I feel terribly empty, here without my boys. I look around for something to do, to make me stop thinking about it.

'Come on, Tara,' I say, and the little girl looks up at me with placid dark eyes. 'Let's go over here.' I hold her hand tightly.

Then, finally, I am on the seafront. The waves are arching and splashing, obviously dangerous. Instinctively, I pick Tara up, swing her into my arms, hating the fact that she lost her family to a wave here. I wonder how much she knows about it. Spray flies into the air. The water is a dark, murky grey, and the beach is narrow and stony.

The Pondicherry of my mind had a white sandy beach, with a row of pastel bungalows, palm trees swaying in the sea breeze, clear water, fusion cuisine. Reality is different, but, somehow, it is better, and more intense, than I imagined. Elly is right: this town cannot disappoint. There is something magical about it.

Pondicherry is not just another Indian town: the roads are colonial and stately, some of them still bearing their French names; the seafront buildings are grand in places, and the atmosphere is fearsomely relaxed. Despite the stares, nobody is interested in hassling me, not even the man, clad in a lunghi and a long shirt, who is dragging an ice-cream trolley behind him. He offers his wares to everyone he passes, apart from me. I try to catch his eye, but he looks away. If he had approached us, I might have bought an ice cream for Tara, although that might have made her ill, and now that I have her clean bill of health tucked safely into my bag, I do not dare take any chances. It is not as if she is asking. Toby and Joe would be, if they were here. They would be pulling on my sleeve: 'Can we have an ice cream? Can we, Mum? Please, Mum?'

We could have lived here. We still could. Exhilaration sweeps over me at the very idea.

I glance at families with beautiful dark-eyed offspring, at young men and women in Western dress, at the man with rickety legs, sitting at the edge of the path holding a tin up for coins. I throw in all the coins in my purse, aware of Tara watching me, wide-eyed but silent.

There are other Westerners around. A young couple with back-packs are haggling with a rickshaw driver. A silver-haired woman in sensible trousers clutches a guidebook close to her chest, and smiles briefly at me but doesn't pause. I watch her eyes flicker from me to Tara, and back to me again.

When the brass band starts playing, I jump, and then look around. Speakers are rigged up on the lamp posts, thin wires trailing between them. A cloud passes over the sun. In the sudden shade, it looks like a British beach at high tide. After a while, I locate a large brass band made up of men in military uniform, sitting in precise formation behind a statue of Gandhi. When they start playing the *Mission Impossible* music, I smile to myself.

I wish I had someone to share it with. I squeeze Tara's hand in encouragement. I want her to enjoy this. She looks at me until I look away. I smile. After a while, she smiles back, though I think she is imitating me, rather than happy.

Toby and Joe would love this. Max would be laughing at the incongruity of the brass band. I push the idea of them away. I am used to the slightly hollow feeling of only having myself to worry about. It is good. It must be doing me good.

Out to sea, half hidden by mist, a group of unwieldy boats is performing unlikely manoeuvres. There is a small cracking sound, and a few people point to the sky. The world's least impressive fireworks have been let off. I wish they had waited till it was dark. I imagine the ships lit up, out in the Bay of Bengal in the night. That would have been the time for fireworks.

I am the only one who is being churlish. Everybody else seems delighted with the display. People are milling about, chatting, eating. They are happy and busy. I stroll on. I suppose it is good that the navy around here have so little to do that they spend their time entertaining the people of Pondy with their prowess, their music and damp squibs.

It is lunchtime. There is a café across the road which looks like a genuine, non-tourist, non-rich-people's café. I can see a little way into its dark interior, to formica tables and packing crates stacked against the walls. In front of us, on the promenade, is a far more attractive-looking establishment. This one is white stucco, surrounded by a patch of fenced-off grass, and its clientele seems to consist of a white tour group with Australian accents, and a few rich families. I hesitate, weighing up the sea views and gorgeous location of the tourist one against the normality of the one across the street. Then I pick Tara up and carry her over the road, stepping easily out of the path of three rickshaws, two of which slow down so the drivers can lean over and shout, 'Rickshaw, madam?'

We sit at the table closest to the open front of the establishment. Here, I can watch Pondicherry going past. We would come here all the time, if we lived here.

'OK?' I ask, pulling Tara's chair closer to the table. She nods. She is so small that she should really be in a high chair.

'What would you like for lunch?'

She looks away.

'Rice?'

She nods.

'And something else?'

She nods again. I wish I knew how much she understood.

The room is dark, despite being open to the street, and it smells of spices and dust. I look at the people passing by. I am watching an elderly couple edging along slowly, each with a walking stick, when someone speaks loudly behind me.

'Excuse me, madam?'

I jump and spin round. When I look at the speaker, I see that he is a middle-aged man wearing a pale summer suit.

'Hello,' I say.

'I'm sorry to disturb you,' he says. 'I am sorry to be so forward. But the fact is, I recognise you from the ashram. Is this your little girl?'

'I think I've seen you too,' I tell him, narrowing my eyes. He does look familiar. 'No, she's not mine. I've just brought her into town for an appointment. She lives at the Children's Centre at the moment. This is Tara.'

He laughs. 'Hello, Tara,' he says, and addresses her with a stream of fast Tamil. She shakes her head and looks away, refusing to engage.

'Do you live up at the ashram?' I ask, annoyed to be left out of the conversation, and wondering what he is saying to my charge.

'No!' he says. 'No, I am most certainly not a resident. I tend to visit rather frequently as the environment agrees with me. And in truth I am interested in what they get up to up there.'

'Yes. And if you don't live there, you don't have to do five o'clock meditation every morning.'

'Indeed.' He clears his throat. I sip my chai, and look at dust dancing in the beams of sunlight. 'Tell me, are you residing there? Working with the children, perhaps?'

I take a sip of warm water from the bottle that I have been carrying in my bag all morning. I wish I could order a beer.

'Definitely not. I'll probably move on soon. I'm enrolled on a yoga course, but they're letting me off today because I've brought Tara for her appointment. It's actually Pondy that I came to see. I came all the way to India for that. It has a particular meaning for me and my husband. I might come here for a while. Or I might go home to my own children. I don't know.'

The man nods. 'Freedom is a powerful drug,' he says. 'But I should introduce myself.' He holds out his hand for a formal shake. 'Brian Thevar.'

I smile, in spite of myself. 'Brian? Your name is Brian? Really?'

He is laughing too. 'Oh yes. I often have such a reaction from foreigners. Brian, it is true, is not an Indian name. My parents were inexplicably drawn to it. I must say after the Monty Python movie its cachet rose somewhat.'

'I'm Brian! No, I'm Brian!'

'Exactly.'

'That film was big?'

'Big enough. And you?'

'Oh, sorry. I'm Brian too.' He laughs. 'Not really. I'm Tansy.'

'Like the bitter herb?'

'Yes! Thank you! Not many people manage to get it right.'

Our food arrives, and I spoon rice and a vegetarian curry on to Tara's plate, and then on to my own. There are obvious pieces of tomato, potato and okra in it, among other things. I take out my phone and quickly photograph it, just to prove to Nick that there are vegetables outside the ashram.

'So, what do you do, Brian?' I ask, putting the phone away. 'Do you work?'

'Me? Oh, I am a retired man these days,' he says. 'I am ex-police.'

I shift around in my chair. 'Seriously?'

'Oh, yes, indeed.'

'That's nice. Makes me feel safe.'

'Pleased to hear it. You should not feel unsafe, however. Pondy is not at all a dangerous town. I keep my hand in, you know. Keep an eye on things, in an unofficial capacity, when necessary. Now tell me, why did you photograph your lunch? Is this a London habit?'

A young man approaches as Tara and I are finishing our food. I watch him coming closer. Our eyes meet and I look away, nervous about nothing. He has a soft little moustache, probably his first one.

I look back at Brian, who is busy with his lunch.

The man wears a crisp burgundy polo shirt, and trousers with the creases ironed in. His eyes are chocolatey, and focused completely on mine.

'Hello,' he says, with a sudden flash of a smile. 'Please. May I take my photograph with you?'

I blink at him. 'What?'

'My photograph.' He holds up his mobile phone and waggles it. Then he looks over his shoulder. I follow his glance. There are five other young men, all wearing crisp burgundy polo shirts, all watching us with interest, from a safe distance. They are in uniform; probably, they are still at school.

I mentally run through reasons why I shouldn't have my photograph taken with a polite young man. They are not compelling.

'OK then,' I tell him. 'What the hell. Don't get the little girl in them, though.'

He turns to his friends and gives them a double thumbs-up. They rush over, and one of them takes his phone from him. The young man pulls up a chair next to me, and grins for the photo. I force a smile. I am aware of Brian, behind me, watching the scene.

'How old is your mother?' I ask the young man as he starts to stand up. He looks perplexed.

'Thirty-seven years old,' he says, after a pause. I decide not to tell him that I am a year younger.

His friends sit beside me one by one, give the camera the thumbs-up, and race away to look at the pictures. The last one, who seems to be the group clown, a well-built young man with longer hair than his friends, puts an arm around my shoulders and attempts to yank me closer to him. His hand is far too close to my breast for comfort, and moving closer. I pull his arm away, and stand up

'No photo for you,' I tell him. I look at Brian, who is half out of his seat.

'Oh, I'm sorry,' says the young man. 'Come on. Please.'

'No way. Go on, go away.'

'But I am most dreadfully sorry.'

I enjoy being horrible to him. 'No. Leave me alone. This man is an ex-police officer.' He looks at Brian, who says something stern in Tamil, and he backs away. His friends are laughing, and I feel mildly better as he mooches away, looking grumpy and humiliated. It serves him right.

'Would you like to join us?' I ask Brian, with a smile.

'I would be entirely delighted,' he says, and shifts himself and his plate to our table, where he sits opposite me.

'So tell me, Miss Tansy,' he says. 'What brings you to India?'

I grin at him, and start to tell him about my sons, and my husband, and my friend Elly who lives at the ashram.

chapter twenty-nine

A week later.

When Sam finally announces that this time he really is off to his village, I cannot imagine why he would want to go. I realise I have become institutionalised.

We are standing on the veranda, and he has his backpack on his back, and sturdy shoes on his feet.

'You're actually going?' I say. '*Really?* Leaving here? Why?'

He looks at me sideways, and laughs. 'Er, to see my family? The big wide world? The reason I'm here? Remember? Tamil boy in Tamil Nadu for the first time in his life? That one? I've already put it off about twenty-three times because it was so pleasant hanging here. I can't do it again.'

'I know, but . . . Don't you want to stay here a bit longer, though?'

'Tansy! No I don't. You and Amber have a great thing going on with the kids. I can see that. It's not been easy reminding her that I have to drag her away. But no, I actually have a life outside this place, and I'm absolutely fucking beside myself with excitement. I mean, I grew up British first and Tamil second. I had friends from all over the place. I was slightly embarrassed, if I took a white friend home, that my parents spoke with such heavy accents. I shoved aside the Tamil thing because I wasn't at one of those multi-ethnic schools. I was in a minority and I did what it took to fit in. And it's taken me this long to think, hang on a sec, this village is me, it's where I come from, and that's something to be proud of. There's so much of me here. I just can't wait to immerse myself in it. Is that OK?'

'Yes,' I tell him. 'That's fine.'

'Very kind of you.'

'Erm, don't do anything rash, though.'

He looks at me rather puzzled and, I think, slightly guilty.

'What do you mean?'

'Oh, don't drink from the well. Don't eat dodgy meat. Don't marry a teenage cousin. Anything like that.'

'They don't eat meat.' He looks back at me. He has extraordinarily long, curling eyelashes. 'I won't drink from the well.'

'And?'

'Did Nick tell you?'

'Nick?' I take this in. 'Well, let's say he did. Is it true, then? There's a potential bride lined up for you?'

He sighs. 'They're just trying their luck. I could, as far as they're concerned, take her back to London and give her a great life. Which, although I'm not exactly rolling in cash, is true, up to a point. A visa, a roof over her head, electricity . . . You can't blame them for giving it a go.'

'Have you mentioned that to Amber?'

'No, of course not. It's been hard enough trying to tear her away from this place as it is. She wouldn't go anywhere near the village if she knew about Amirtha. Who, by the way, I've never met, never corresponded with, and have no intention of marrying.'

'And you decided to confide in Nick, of all the people in the world?'

'Well, there's only me and him in the room.'

'Right. I don't think I'd tell him anything even if he *was* the only one in the room.' I wonder whether to break Amber's confidence. I cannot watch him waiting around for her when I am sure she has no intention of going with him. 'I'd tell Amber instead, if I were you,' I say quickly, getting it out before I change my mind. 'Because what if she'd found the photo and worked it out for herself and decided that the reason you hadn't said anything was because you were taking it seriously?'

He stares at me. A group of women walk past, chanting a mantra as they go. I hold eye contact.

'She didn't, though?' he says, after a while.

'You'll have to ask her that.'

'Well, I will. When she turns up. Our bus leaves from Pondy in an hour. We really have to get into the rickshaw.' We stand in silence, waiting. Birds fly overhead. Ashram life meanders around us. 'I've tried to broach the subject, you know,' he says, after a couple of minutes. 'She doesn't much want to know me any more. It's all "Tansy this" and "Children's Centre that". She's bought into the chastity thing, too. I can see that it's a traumatic thing for her, that travelling was always going to churn her up, and it's like a haven for her, being here. She's built herself a little comfort zone, and I guess she doesn't want to leave it.'

I am baffled. 'Why does it churn up lots of emotions? Why does she need a comfort zone?'

'Oh, she must have told you.' He is staring at the dusty earth, kicking up the topsoil. 'She's not coming, is she?'

'So go and bloody find her, you idiot.'

He nods. 'Coming?'

'I think you have to do this one on your own.'

He starts to walk away, towards the guest house, then turns back.

'But if things were different for me,' he says, 'well, are arranged marriages necessarily a terrible thing? Are people happier in "love matches" than they are in any other sort of arrangement?' He starts to walk back. 'Maybe, if it wasn't for Amber, I *would* marry Amirtha. I mean, Delphine would say I should seize the day, act on impulse. And it would be a good thing, wouldn't it, to give her opportunities, and if it didn't work out, we'd be in the West, we could split up without it being a source of shame? Hypothetically speaking, that is.'

'Oh Sam. Don't be ridiculous. That's just stupid. Go and find her.'

'I know.'

*   *   *

The whole ashram, it seems to me, hears their argument. Amber doesn't go. Sam storms off in high dudgeon, threatening to go through with his arranged marriage. Amber lies on her bed and speaks to no one for a whole day and a whole night.

Meanwhile, I succumb, gratefully, to the routine. I have awoken to the delights of the structured day, and I don't want to set foot out of the grounds until it is time for me to go home to my boys. I don't even want a beer, because I cannot bear the idea of being woken by Maya's bell before five o'clock with even the hint of a hangover. Every day follows the same pattern. I walk to meditation, half listening to Delphine telling me, 'The spirit of Gaia has been disturbed and the Earth Goddess is angry,' or 'Amber has a very powerful golden aura,' depending on which seminar she has most recently attended.

I sit still, cross-legged, for an hour, and the silence and the solidarity is better than any drug. I am entirely unable to empty my mind and meditate properly, so I use the time to think about my boys, to send them mental messages, and to concentrate on making myself as calm as I can, so I will be best placed to go home, sometime, and renegotiate our life. Somehow, I have developed an ability to sit and think without going mad. When I start to panic, I open my eyes and look at Anjali.

Everyone is starving by the time breakfast is put out, and I dive in with the best of them, grabbing puris and chapattis and the remains of the previous night's dinners from all the guest houses, folded into pieces of bread, with yogurt dripped over them.

I walk back to the guest house with Amber and Delphine, and we shower with buckets of cold water, and brush our teeth with mineral water. Then I walk to yoga. I spend three hours contorting myself, taking a perverse pleasure in the aches and pains, and pushing myself a little further each time. I am strangely dependent on the grumpy Enid, even though I do still hate her.

Since I started embracing the yoga, on the grounds that it is a temporary boot camp, I have realised that most of the other people in the room are fiercely competitive about it. Swiss Daniella and German Helga are regularly and conspicuously trying to outdo each other at head stands. They look over at each other, determined not to be the first down. They stay for ages, until Enid tells them they have to stop. When they do get down, I am the only one who sniggers at the fanny-farts. Everyone else looks innocently at the ceiling and no one comes close to smirking.

I have lunch with whoever is around, at the visitors' centre. Even my lunch has become routine: I have something called a 'healthy platter', and eat all of whatever is on it. There is always rice, always some form of vegetable curry, always something incongruous, Western and vegan on the side. I like it best when this is cold pasta, because it reminds me of how very far I am from that other life, where I used to eat cold pasta from the fridge for lunch. The afternoon is filled with yoga again, but Enid lets me out early to go to the CC. We are working on our production of the Bear Hunt, and the children are drawing posters that we will stick up all over the ashram.

'You have to do this thing in the next week,' Elly warned me. 'We have a high turnover of kids at the mo. You know that.' So, the children are variously playing the grass, the snow, the mud, dressed in random pieces of appropriately coloured clothing that I have borrowed from anyone I can find at the ashram. Kamatchi, who is playing a tree in the big dark forest, is wearing a T-shirt of Nick's, which has a picture of a tree on the front of it, and the words 'Save the trees' written underneath. It goes down past her knees and she is heartbreakingly proud of it. I hope that Nick will let her keep it.

Dinner is at the guest house at seven, and I make sure I sit close enough to Nick to bicker with him, because we are the official entertainment.

Nick is so rude to me that I am almost starting to like him. Last night he called me 'some overprivileged, arrogant colonist who thinks she knows it all'.

I was laughing so much that it was a job even to get the words out, to counter, 'But at least I'm not fat, and I'm fairly sure I don't have BO.'

Everything is simple. I had no idea life could be this straightforward. Mentally, I feel I am swimming in crystal water, refreshing myself, gathering my strength. I do not worry about Max, because there is nothing I can do about it while I am here. I don't fret about the boys, even Joe, because I am certain that by living like this, I am making myself into a slightly more worthy mother for them. I do not give more than a fleeting, occasional thought to Jim Trelawney. I am completely contented.

Amber is initially awkward about the fact that she didn't go with Sam.

'You think I'm pathetic,' she tells me and Delphine, many times over, when she resurfaces.

'I don't,' I say. 'I don't want to go anywhere either. I want to stay in this weird place for as long as I possibly can.' It is all about Anjali, I have realised, in a strange way. The entire place is permeated by her presence, even when she isn't there.

'I don't think so neither,' Delphine agrees. 'Because you follow your heart and this is good.'

We have this exchange on three consecutive days before Amber looks at us both searchingly, laughs, and says, 'OK, I believe you now. I think. So, whew,' she continues. 'Who knew you could start the day at five and feel OK about it?'

'It's like those people who swim in the sea every day,' I say. 'If you did that every morning, you'd feel pretty good. Probably.' Although it is relentlessly dry, and a little more humid every day, water seems to be the only metaphor for the way I am feeling. The life here is cleansing me. I can understand why people want to live here permanently, why Elly stayed: it is terrifyingly different from the way things are in London.

'Yes,' says Amber. 'The village. I mean, interesting anthropological experience and everything, but really, what would I have done? Without an hour's meditation to start the day? Without being woken by a madwoman ringing a bell?'

'You could always have got up at five and meditated for an hour anyway.'

She snorts. 'Yeah. Right.'

'I know. I keep telling myself I'll keep all this up in London.

Of course I bloody won't. That's the worst thing of all. The idea that things will slip back into the way they used to be.'

A few days after Sam's departure, early in the evening, we sit on a clump of prickly grass at the edge of the Peaceful Haven, and I watch Amber smoking a spliff she has made. Maya is sitting on the veranda but she just gives us an indulgent smile.

'Why are you "churned up" about travelling?' I ask her.

She chokes on her cigarette. 'I beg your pardon?'

'There's a reason why you were all tense when I met you. And now you've relaxed because you're somewhere safe. What is it?'

She looks carefully straight ahead, and blows smoke out of her nose.

'Is that something that you get in your thirties? Special levels of spooky insight?'

'Delphine lent me a crystal ball,' I assure her. 'It told me. Alternatively, Sam alluded to something but didn't elaborate.'

She looks at me with a small smile. 'Right. Um, yes. I've had to face a few fears, I guess. Yes.'

The grass is prickling me through my thin trousers.

'Me too,' I admit.

'No.' She shakes her head. 'Not normal travelling fears. You've left your children to come and help out with the kids, and obviously that's a worry for you. But I . . . well, I have a stepbrother. Alex. I mentioned him a few times, I think. His dad married my mum when I was eleven. He's ten years older than me.'

'And?'

She is gazing into the distance. 'He was travelling.'

'What happened?'

'Just an accident. He was in Pakistan, in a taxi. A road accident. The sort of thing that happens every day.'

'He died?'

She leans back on her hands, her flimsy dress flapping slightly in the wind. She turns to me suddenly, smiling. 'No. Thank God. He was hurt. He's at home. Badly hurt, I mean. He's quadriplegic. He can't do anything for himself. I mean, he's still there, himself, and mentally he's the same as ever, and I love him to absolute bits. But, to see what happened to him . . . I don't know if it's worth taking any risk, but then how can you live without a risk?'

'Oh, Amber.'

'I wouldn't have come away if it hadn't been for Sam. My mum and stepdad didn't want me to go but they didn't say so. They were happier that I'd be with Sam, I think. I knew it was silly. This is a huge continent, and accidents happen every day in Britain – it's not as if I was retracing Alex's steps or anything, and even then . . . But it was still hard. Because I knew he'd been to India, and he'd sent me postcards from here, and now here I am, and he . . . Well, his horizons have shrunk. He's not going anywhere.'

'What did he think you should do?'

She laughs. 'Well, that's why I went, in the end. Alex was desperate for me to go. He couldn't bear the idea of me staying at home because of him. He told me to do it for him, to live life for him. He talked the parents into it, too. I try to send him a card every couple of days. You've probably seen me posting them.'

I put an arm round her shoulders and hug her. 'He must be proud of you.'

She grins. 'He says he is. The thing we never talk about is the future. But when Mum and John can't look after him any more, it's going to be my job. So, although he didn't say it, I know he wants me to get my adventures in now. While I can. And I'm OK with that.'

'How long ago was it?'

'Nine years.'

'That's when I was travelling before.'

'There were people being murdered, but we all thought Alex would be OK. He was a big strong man, after all. Well, until a taxi drove up on to the pavement, he was.'

'How old is he?'

'Now? Thirty-four. Then, he was twenty-five. I'll be twenty-five next year.'

We sit in silence for a while. I wonder whether to tell her my whole story, but I cannot bear to be defined by it, so I decide not to.

'And here you are. So you're doing really well.'

'What, hiding away at an ashram? Shrinking away from every-thing? Too scared to go to some lovely village where we would have had a hero's welcome, because it's away from my comfort zone? I have to make myself little lists any time I actually have to do anything, you know. Sometimes I write one that goes: have breakfast, do washing, be happy. It's pathetic.'

'No it's not. Those are good goals.'

'He used to come and stay with us on alternate weekends, when we were growing up. I looked up to him *so* much. I would mark off the days to his next visit on a little chart.' She looks at me. 'I'd love you to meet him.'

'So I'll come to Scotland when we're back. Bring my boys.'

We smile at each other. There are people milling around, but no one comes close to us. I watch Melinda sitting on the concrete, her ankles behind her ears.

'Have you got any brothers and sisters?' Amber asks.

I nod. 'Halves. Two sisters, two brothers, all from my dad's second marriage.' I edit out the rest of the story. 'They're great. They're my family.' As I say it, I realise it is true. I thought I was so alone in London, but I wasn't, not really. That is a big family, by any standards.

The air is getting muggy, and threatening rain.

'You shouldn't leave things the way they are with Sam,' I tell her. 'Everyone heard you. You accused him of wanting to saunter in being the Big Man from the West and have all the young girls lined up for him to take his pick of. Have you called him? Or even texted him?'

'He said some rubbish stuff too,' she says, with an exaggerated carelessness. 'He can ring me when he wants. I've got my mobile. His won't work over there.'

'Ring the village phone. Ask for big man from city.'

'Yeah. Right. He's on home turf – and don't we all know it. He'll be all full of his family. I'll leave him to it for a while. Let him decide what to do about the child bride.'

I consider pushing the point. 'Whatever you want,' I say instead.

'Jeeze, you are so calm. I should do that yoga with you, shouldn't I?'

'Of course you should, you stupid woman.'

'Maybe I will. But now that Sam's gone, I shouldn't just sit here pathetically. I could have a little trip somewhere on my own. Just a day or two to show that I can be brave. Prove to myself that I can do it. Maybe I'll go to Mamallapuram.'

I squeeze her arm. 'You are allowed to stay here, if you like, Amber,' I remind her. 'It's OK to find a peaceful haven. Or yes, go off for a bit. Ask Anjali if you can do anything for the CC. Or just go and hang out by yourself with a book. It's the greatest feeling in the world.'

The following day, Delphine bounces up to us, with her Tricolore-bedecked rucksack on her back.

'*Allez les filles,*' she says. 'I'm off. *A très bientôt.*'

I stand up and kiss her cheek. She pulls me to her with surprisingly strong arms. 'Going to the cashew fields?'

She shakes her head happily. 'Not this time. I had a dream that I must go to Madurai. A real, sleepy dream. I asked Anjali and she said if it's pulling my soul, I must go. I think I come back later. This place has good energy.'

'Oh. OK. Well, we'll miss you.'

'We will see each other again. I am certain.'

When she has gone, Amber and I look at each other and laugh.

'She's fabulous,' I say, 'but she *really* makes me glad that I'm not twenty-one any more. I couldn't take the pace if I just got to bounce around wherever my soul was pulled.'

'Me too.'

I narrow my eyes. 'But I think your soul would pull you to Sam.'

'It would not.'

'You were so grumpy when I met you. Was that because of the village?'

She nods. 'I found that letter the first day we were in Chennai. I was waiting for him to tell me. Each day that he didn't, I got a little bit crosser. And I was feeling bad about Alex, and things were just getting on top of me. You know, I was petrified every time we went in a rickshaw, obsessing over the fact that a couple of seconds can send your life tumbling down for ever. I kept imagining our rickshaw going under the wheels of a juggernaut. You know how it is, you're inches from that happening all the time. And Sam wasn't exactly sympathetic. He just blathered on about his stupid village all the time.'

'Do you think you've split up?'

'Do you?'

'No, I don't. But maybe you should have a few days away on your own and then make sure you sort things out. You've just been preoccupied with different things, each of you. Anyway, it's Friday, isn't it?'

'I think so.'

'Then it's half-term.'

'What are your family doing?'

'Max has taken the week off work. They're going to do all sorts of things. I think they start tomorrow with a trip to Legoland. With . . .' I swallow hard and make myself use a nice voice. 'Some friends.'

I picture them: Max, Sarah, and their four offspring. It is too cosy, sickeningly cosy.

'Why aren't they coming here?' Amber asks. 'They could come and visit you. I know the flights wouldn't be cheap, but if he works in the City . . .'

I try to marshal reasons. 'It would be too much for Max to do that flight with two children.'

'He'd manage.'

'And too much travelling for the children, when they've only got a week.'

'Oh, they'd be fine, and you know it.'

I think about it some more, seeking the killer reason.

'I don't want him to,' I say. 'Because I'd have to say goodbye to them all over again, or else I'd have to go home with them.'

It is a lie, but it saves a bit of face.

Amber packs a bag, and leaves on a bus for Mamallapuram. Although she is only planning to be away for three days, I am surprised at how alone I feel.

I imagine Joe, crying for me. I picture Toby, quietly missing me, in a way that is perhaps more heartbreaking. Both of them must be turning to Sarah for maternal affection. I resolve to call Lola and ask her what she thinks is going on.

I am wandering to the CC when someone rushes up behind me and lays a hand on my arm. I turn in surprise and discover that it is Anjali. I see her every day at meditation, and occasionally at the Children's Centre, but I rarely exchange a word with her. Although she is so young, I am as awed by her as everyone else is.

'Hello, Tansy,' she says.

Max could be coming out here. If my babies were arriving now, I would be ready for them. They would see me like this, better and calmer than I have ever been before. If I went home right now, Max would resent me for stepping into the cosy little set-up he has created with Sarah. He would hate me to muscle in on their half-term plans.

I look into Anjali's face. I have never believed in people having auras, but this woman has something, some charisma on a scale that I have never seen before. It is overwhelming.

'What?' Anjali asks. 'Tansy, are you OK?'

I look into her clear dark eyes.

'It's OK,' I mutter. Her skin is so smooth that for a second I want to touch it. 'Nothing, really.' Close up, this woman makes me want to beg her to let me walk next to her, all day, and fetch her drinks and food whenever she wants them, and fan her with a little homemade fan. The ashram is shaped by her; the calm and the peace I feel every day emanate directly from Anjali.

She shakes her head.

'I hope you are finding some spiritual sustenance here,' she says. 'From what Elly tells me, you need something. I want to thank you for your help with Tara.'

At this I have to smile. 'It's nothing. She's lovely.'

'And you are phenomenal with the children. They love the bear play.'

'Oh, it's as much fun for Amber and me as it is for them.'

197

She touches my arm. 'We appreciate everything you do. I need you to know that.'

'Oh, but what I do is nothing. If there's anything else, ever . . . I mean, I came here because I thought I was needed. I'd be happy, more than happy, to do much more. If there's anything more I can do, ever, just ask.'

She looks thoughtful. 'Really? You would do anything?'

I feel stupid, big, pink, and too eager. 'Anything,' I assure her. 'Elly implied, once, that I might help with the children's families, bring them together, that sort of thing.'

'Yes,' she says. 'Well, if this is something you would like to do, I will bear your offer in mind. Thank you.'

Later, Elly and I are sitting in her Tardis, drinking green tea. I am still excited about my encounter with Anjali, and am doing my best not to analyse why that is. Elly has been talking about the children's show, when I interrupt her.

'Are you selling drugs?' I ask. I am certain that she is, on a small scale. Everyone seems to smoke. Everyone seems to get it from Elly.

She snorts. '"Selling drugs"? What are you, the magistrate?'

'No. Sorry. I just don't want you to do anything that might get you into trouble.' I pause. 'Do you think I'm an alcoholic?'

Elly laughs. 'What is this? Twenty paranoid questions?'

'Well, do you?'

'I do not. But . . .'

'What?'

'Well, before you arrived, Max mailed me. You know that. He said he thought you had –' She puts on a deep voice and an English accent to quote Max. '"An alcohol problem, or drink dependency." Which I must admit I took to be a rich man's alcoholism. But actually, I think he was quite right. I think you can function just fine without it. I think it's the circumstances of your daily life that made you like it so much. Living somewhere where it's so available and acceptable. Living a life that bores you to tears, so you have to take steps to change your reality.'

'Bloody hell. Tell me what you really think, why don't you?'

I feel it rising inside me, the fury. I close my eyes and clench all my muscles, but I cannot stop it. It spills out. 'Max said that to you?' My voice is rising. 'He said that to you, and he never said it to me. He goes behind my back to say things like that to you – things that aren't even true? Who the fuck does he think he is? What's he doing?'

Elly interrupts with a tiny hand on my arm.

'Hey,' she says. 'Just live your life. Like you are now. Run off with the teacher man if that's what you want to do. Stay here, get a hut. Help us out with the children as much as you want, as long as you can. Bring your kids to live here with you. But *do* something. Think about the sort of life you want. Don't just go back to Max because it's the easiest thing to do. Make it change. Otherwise, you could easily be your own mother, five years from now. And you know all about that.'

Until she mentioned my mother, I was with her. Now, I turn on her.

'I am not *ever* going to be my own mother,' I snarl. 'You know nothing about her. Fuck off, Elly.'

And I storm out, slamming the door so hard that I hope the hut falls down, and I set off back to the guest house, running blindly. I never want to speak to her again.

chapter thirty

I am letting my paranoia run away with me. In my mind, Max and Sarah are at our local swimming pool. It is mysteriously filled with sparkling turquoise water. Max hangs on to the edge of the pool, and looks up at Sarah, who stands in front of him in a tiny pink bikini. She grins at him. He gapes at her, devotion in his eyes. She reaches behind her back, and unfastens her top, looking teasingly at him as she does it.

I open my eyes. I am lying on my bed, alone in the room, and it is dark. I can hear everyone having dinner outside. The light is off, and I know that the ceiling fan is not moving, because if it was, I would be able to hear it. That means there is a power cut.

My eyes are puffy, and I am scared. I hate Elly for what she said, but what I hate most is the fact that she was right. Sarah and I were both halfway to becoming our own mothers. We validated each other. We were playing an incredibly dangerous game, and now she is playing a different sort of dangerous game with my husband, a man who is clearly drawn to screwed-up semi-alcoholic women.

And Max. Treacherous Max, who pretended to be my best friend and my soul mate, has been slagging me off to Elly, in secret. I picture him, at work, on his computer, tapping out a quick email about my 'drink dependency' to my friend, then going home to take the boys off my hands and pour me a drink. He is a two-faced bastard and I know that things will never be the same between us, ever again.

I wonder whether I could come and live here with the boys, leaving Max with his precious job and mortgage. I would do it, like a shot. It would be good for Toby and Joe, apart from the small fact that they would miss their dad. But Max would never let me take them away. He would stand up in court and tell a judge all about my drinking until I lost them. I know he would do that, if he had to, for the boys' sake. Because he thinks I have 'a drink problem'.

I put my head back down on the bed. I wish I could imagine a future, something clear and simple and obvious. Do I return to London, and let everything go back to the way it used to be, but worse because now I have seen the truth, that I can be better than I was at home? Or do I tear our family apart by demanding that we all come and live in India? I cannot see myself in five years, anywhere.

She comes in without knocking.

'Right, Miss Harris,' she says. 'Up you get. Maya says you've missed dinner. She said you can forage for scraps in the kitchen, but I've got a better idea.'

'Fuck off, Elly,' I mutter, into the pillow.

'We're going out. We're going to have dinner in Pondy. My treat. To say sorry. I don't always think, and things don't always come out right. You're doing great work for us here, and Anjali's just torn a strip off me when I said I upset you.'

'Fuck off. I don't want dinner in Pondy. I'll forage when I feel up to it.' I lift my neck from the pillow. 'And I'm not doing any sort of good work. Nothing that a hundred other volunteers wouldn't do. I have no idea why you summoned me.'

'Nah, you'll come now.'

'Won't.'

'Will.' To prove her determination, Elly scrabbles around for the bottle of water that is beside my bed, and carefully tips it over my head. I shriek, and sit up, and push her off the edge of the bed. She lands on the floor, looking tiny and cute, and laughs up at me.

'You coming then?'

Maybe I should just stay here indefinitely, submitting to the routine. Max could send the boys out to visit me from time to time. Everyone would think I'd had a breakdown, and life would carry on.

As I follow Elly along the path that leads to the car park in front of the Great Hall, I talk to the back of her head. It is easier that way.

'She used to sit in the same chair every day,' I say. 'With a bottle of whisky. She only left the house to buy booze, and everyone – *everyone* – laughed at her, and they laughed at me because I lived with her. They adored her in the offy, thought she was hilarious. She'd say things like, "Having some friends over for drinkies, you know," and they'd say, "Of course you are, Mrs H." She'd draw a face on to go out, with make-up, but she was so shaky that she looked like a grotesque clown from some avant-garde movie. She pissed herself in her chair. Once she did it in the offy. I was glad. It served them right for serving her.'

Elly pauses, and I almost walk into the back of her. Then she starts walking again.

'Christ,' she says. She looks at me, and away again. 'I had no idea. Why didn't you tell me all that?'

I laugh, though it is not funny. 'Why would I?'

'Tansy – I'm so sorry. I thought she'd just been a bit of a tippler, and then her liver gave out. Obviously you won't end up like her, then. Totally retracted.'

I screw my eyes up. I want to ask whether we can divert to the Children's Centre, just so I can hug someone, pull them close, stroke their hair, feel the comfort of another body. I almost do, and then I decide against it. I cannot use those poor children as teddy bears.

chapter thirty-one

It is getting dark as we enter the town. There were no rickshaws, so Elly and I are in an old Ambassador taxi, hand-painted black, like the one that brought me from the airport in Chennai, four weeks and a lifetime ago. I stare out of the rattly open window. Flashes of dusky Indian life pass us by. Men shout on chunky mobile phones. An old woman squats beside a kerosene stove on the pavement, shaking a frying pan. Two young women walk together, deep in conversation, laughing, looking at their phones.

On cue, my phone beeps, with a text. I hold it up to the light to look at it.

'RU still @ cult?' it reads.

My heart jumps, in spite of myself. Thinking of Jim is a lot more straightforward than thinking of Max, right now. I answer at once. He is, after all, thousands of miles away. It has never been as safe to flirt with him as it is now.

'Yes,' I write. 'It's fabulous. Not a cult. Am in rickshaw to Pondy. Love it. x'

Elly doesn't ask. I don't tell her.

Every time I come here, however many times I do it, I will feel I am finishing Max's journey, the one he doesn't care about. I push my face out of the window and inhale deeply, thousands of scents mingled together.

'Le Club,' the driver announces, sooner than I had expected.

'You'll like the Club,' Elly says cheerfully. 'And then, the Rendez-Vous. You won't appreciate the Rendez-Vous one bit, but I will.'

'Australian people sound hilarious when they say French words,' I can't help telling her. 'I don't know why. It just makes you sound so incredibly uncultured.'

'Ah, who gives a shit?'

'Why won't I appreciate the "Rondai-Veeew"?'

She laughs. 'You just won't.'

Rue Dumas is wide and lovely, a French colonial street that is sleepier and calmer than any Indian road could expect to be. The houses that line it are mainly white, and all of them look grand, with the exception of a hallucinogenic painted guest house opposite the bar. Elly takes me, as if to test me, to a bar that serves alcohol: with its dark wooden panelling and tropical theme, it could be in a five-star resort in Malaysia just as much as on a street in Pondicherry. When it is quiet, I can hear the waves breaking on the stony beach near by.

We order gin and tonic.

'You do actually drink, then?' I ask Elly.

'Occasionally. I'm a cheap date these days, I can tell you.'

'That's funny. How much things have changed for you. You and Eddy used to knock it back with the best of them. I remember you telling me about the Australian pub in Paris. And you went to Brighton and got so drunk you didn't notice the sea. You gave me a run for my money. I never knew how you did it, with your tiny little body.'

'Well, I don't do it any more. That's for fucking sure.'

'I'm going to drink what you drink,' I decide. 'Because I do have to admit that, if I start, it's hard for me to stop. I can do *not drinking at all*. And I can do *massive, ugly binges*. I can't do anything in between. I'd like to be able to do moderation.'

'So, tonight we do moderation. A G & T here. A beer or something at the restaurant. Water. The end.'

'Deal.'

I smile at her, all my anger forgotten. This is, after all, Pondicherry. This is a bar. This is Elly and me. It is a rare treat.

'I'll tell you what,' I tell her. 'You've got the right idea.'

The drink is cold and gorgeous. The ice clinks as I tip the glass. The lemon has infused the liquid with exactly the right acidity.

Nothing, I think, could beat the perfection of a gin and tonic in India.

'Right idea in what way?'

'Lots of ways, but I'm thinking of the celibacy thing.'

'What makes you think I'm celibate?'

I stare at her. 'Well, I just assumed. I mean, according to Maya there's no sex in the ashram. And you never mentioned . . .'

'According to Maya there's no alcohol at the ashram. According to Maya there are no drugs. Anyway, Maya's a fine one to talk about celibacy.'

'*Is* there someone?'

'There have been plenty of them over the years. Last year I broke up with this French guy. Pierre. He was at the ashram for a while, and then he left. That was cool. And yeah. There is someone now. Someone a hell of a lot cooler than Pierre.'

'That's great! Who is he?'

'I'll tell you later.'

By the time we arrive at the Rendez-Vous, the single gin and tonic has made me slightly dizzy. This is a marker of how sober I have been for the past week: normally one drink has no effect whatsoever. Now, I stumble slightly on the stairs. We are ushered up to a roof terrace and emerge into a babble of chatter from tables that are clearly filled with tourists. These are tourists from afar; pink people. They are eating pasta, pizzas. Elly looks at me, and we both laugh.

'This place looks like hell on earth to you,' she says. 'Eh? You're only away from home for whatever time, so the last thing you want is a mediocre Westernised menu with expensive yet bad wine, and garlic bread. Right?'

I consider denying it.

'Absolutely right,' I say.

'Funnily enough, though, we quite like it. There're a few of us at the ashram who come here from time to time. In my crass Aussie way, I see it as a treat. You can take the girl out of Australia . . .'

We take a table next to a half-wall, with the dark street down below. It is pitch dark outside, more like midnight than half past eight. I have no interest in eating spaghetti or garlic bread, not here in Pondicherry. There is a small section of the menu offering Indian food; not South Indian, but the sort of dishes we get for takeaways at home.

'Beer, then?' I ask.

'Or a glass of wine? I like it better than beer, because lager sits in my stomach a bit.'

'Sure.'

'White OK? Red gives me a headache.'

'You know what? I only ever drink white. Never red. Rosé at a push. Champagne. Not red, though. I'm quite fussy. So my fucking husband can—'

'Enough!'

'Why?' I look at her. 'Oh, OK.'

I try to push aside my ongoing confusion. Max hardly ever commented on my drinking. If I actually had been an alcoholic, as he said to Elly, he would have been my 'enabler'. I imagine, with some dread, the conversations he must have had with Lola and Dad.

Max is not stupid. If he thinks I had a problem, much as I hate the way he has handled it, he was probably right. I don't want to go back to being the heavy drinker, the dependent drinker, I was in London. My mother used to drink wine from teacups, just like me.

I push the glass away. I am not sure I am strong enough to go back to London without taking up boozing again.

I am distracted by a familiar figure coming through the door. A tiny figure, holding an adult's hand on either side, with an expressionless face.

'Tara!' I call. I can't help myself. I stand up and walk over to her. She looks up at me, and her face cracks in a huge smile.

'Going on a bear hunt,' she says. I pick her up and kiss her. The adults with her – presumably the family from Kashmir – are taken aback.

'Sorry,' I say. I try to put her down, but she hangs on. I have no idea how much English her family speak, so I talk to them as clearly as I can, in the absence of the appropriate words of Hindi at my fingertips. 'My name is *Tansy*,' I say. 'I am from *England*. I know *Tara* from the *ashram*.'

'Oh, right,' says the woman. 'Hi. I'm Gita, and this is Sanjiv. We're from Liverpool. Nice to meet you.'

I turn and look back to Elly, who is on her way over to us.

'I thought you were from Kashmir,' I say quickly. 'That's what Elly told me. Tara's family from Srinigar.'

'Oh, yeah,' the woman agrees. 'We're from Liverpool, sure, but we decided to return to our roots, and come home. Sanjiv's family are originally from Kashmir, so that's where we've settled. We've come a long way to pick up little Tara but . . .' The woman looks down at her, and pats her head. 'It was the least we could do.'

'She's lucky.'

Elly is at my side. 'Isn't she just? Nice to see you guys. Hey, Tara. You OK, sweetheart?'

Tara nods and hides her face. I put her down, unpeeling her fingers from my clothes, and I kiss her. She stays close to me until Gita takes her by the hand and leads her to a table on the other side of the room, where a waiter is standing, chairs pulled out for them, menus at the ready. She looks back at me over her shoulder.

'Going to catch a big one,' she says. I blow her a kiss.

'Kashmir's an amazing place,' Elly says as we sit back down. There is a certain steely aspect to her gaze. 'There's so much more to it than the conflict, which is, of course, the only thing anyone knows about. I've never been but I might make it there one day.'

'You never told me they were from Liverpool.'

Her eyes widen. 'Sorry. I didn't realise I had to tell you every detail of every part of the Children's Centre business.'

'Of course you don't.'

I look at her for a while, and wonder what is going on. Then I have another sip of mediocre wine, and stop caring. Tara has people to look after her. She lost her immediate family in the most shocking of circumstances, and now she has a home again. The rest is details.

'There's a theory that Jesus ended up in Kashmir,' Elly says. 'That he died there.'

'I thought he ended up on the cross?'

'Oh, you know nothing! He survived the crucifixion and I can't remember how the story goes after that, but he came to Kashmir. There's a tomb there that a lot of people reckon belongs to him.'

'Some people think he went to Cornwall,' I counter. 'I read about it in the paper once.'

'Well, he didn't. What would he go to Cornwall for? He went to Kashmir because it's full of lovely clear lakes and beautiful boats and crystal-clear air. That's what they say.'

'I guess he got to choose. Son of God, and all. The world was his oyster.'

I let the topic go, and we start reminiscing about the old days. This is the safest possible ground for us, at the moment.

'It's funny,' she says, picking up the last slice of her pizza and folding it in half, 'but there was just something different about those months. I mean, Eddy and I'd been on the road for ever. We'd lived in that squatty house in London. We'd dashed around Europe as if we were being pursued by Nazis, pausing only to get "maggot" in Aussie or Irish bars every day or so. We'd been in Malaysia and Singapore. But those months, ten years ago, they were something different. When I think about it, it still, to this day, makes me want to head off.'

'Does it? Where would you head off to?'

She smiles. 'Fantasy travelling. I've found myself doing that more and more lately. Bet you've done it too. I really am settled in the ashram, but one day I might hit the road, on my own, for a month or two. I'd head straight out of India, that's for sure, and get my ass back to Nepal, first off. I'd get a bus to the mountains and spend weeks just walking the paths. I'd be cold. I think I'd like to get cold. I'd walk along the edges of mountains, and I'd look at the snowy peaks in the distance. Can you imagine that? Being *cold*?'

'I love the idea of those mountain kingdoms,' I say. 'Bhutan. Ladakh.'

'Oh, too right!' And before long, we have a cold trip planned, just the two of us.

'Now, I guessed I might find you here, you two!'

Anjali is standing beside the table. She looks incongruous and out of place in this setting. It seems, somehow, too crass for her. Despite myself, I am excited.

'Hello!' I say, too forcefully. 'Wow, this is quite the meeting place.'

She slips into the seat next to Elly's. 'I was in Pondy visiting someone, and I recalled that Elly had said she was taking you here.'

Elly looks at her, with the same puppyish expression that I am certain is on my own face.

'What's up?' Elly says. 'We were just talking about old times.'

'Yes. How intriguing. Tansy, Elly has mentioned the time you both spent elsewhere in Asia. It was dramatic.'

'Too dramatic,' I say quickly. 'Have a drink?'

She laughs. 'Oh, no thank you. Alcohol doesn't agree with me in any way.' She picks up Elly's water glass instead, a surprisingly intimate act, tips her head back, and swallows it all. Her throat is peachy and vulnerable. 'So, Tansy. Are you happy?'

I giggle. This is too big a question. 'Yes,' I say. 'I think so, anyway.'

She turns to Elly. 'Elly, I have some good news,' she says. 'Helga has the family of Kamatchi and Haniska, in England. We need to get the children to London and they can be collected from there.'

Elly frowns. 'OK. We can do that, I guess. When the paperwork's in place. That's great news, anyway. Good on Helga.'

I lean forward. 'If you need some children taken to London,' I say, 'and they'll have passports and everything, they could come on my flight.'

Anjali smiles at me. 'But Tansy, you're not going any time soon? And it is not something I would ever ask you to do. It is a big responsibility.'

'Of course I'll do it. As long as the paperwork's in order and everything.'

'There would undoubtedly be some time spent with immigration officers, explaining the children's situation.'

'But it's all above board, isn't it? I'm planning to go home in a week or two. I'd love to help you. I said that before.'

'You could personally inspect all the paperwork before you set off.'

'Yes, of course. But I wouldn't be breaking any laws, would I?'

'No, no,' says Anjali. 'Quite the opposite.'

'So, yes, let me do it.'

She grins. 'Thank you! That is hugely appreciated. You know, we hope you will return. We could use you as a part of the Children's Centre on a more permanent basis.'

'But I don't *do* anything.' The constant insistence that I am amazing is baffling me. But Anjali has not finished yet.

'And another thing,' she says. 'In the meantime. Since you genuinely wish to help. Would you make a trip to Mamallapuram for us? I know you like the backpacking lifestyle. Would you consider going for a couple of days, and collecting a package of paperwork for the Children's Centre? As you know, we deal with a lot of Mamallapuram children, and we are extraordinarily careful to keep their papers in order. It is a full-time job, honestly.'

I grin. 'You want me to go to Mamallapuram?'

'If you don't mind.'

'Mamallapuram is the backpackers' place?'

'It most certainly is. And a centre of sculpture.'

'Of course I'll go! I'd love to. Amber headed off there today.'

'We will provide a taxi to take you there and bring you back. Tomorrow. If that is possible? I'll arrange the cab to take you directly after breakfast. I will mollify Enid, and she will make an exception, and let you carry over your last two days of yoga until you come back.'

I smile. 'Thanks.'

Elly reaches for Anjali's hand, and squeezes it. Anjali looks at her. They smile a private smile at each other. I look at their hands, entwined. Elly looks up at me, smiles slightly, and looks away.

I glance down at the dark street below. A couple of unlit rickshaws go by, and a man stumbles from one side of the street to the other.

chapter thirty-two

The first thing I do, when I have checked into my guest house, is to take a book and find a café. This is not difficult, as they are everywhere. I have vowed not to drink alcohol while I am here, unless I feel able to trust myself to do it in moderation. There is, however, no limit to the coffee, and chai, and the fruit lassis I can have. It is the idea of caffeine that is getting me excited. This, surely, is a drug that will do me no harm. Guest-house coffee was terrible: wishy-washy instant stuff. I would kill for a latte.

'Yes, madam! Clothes, madam? Lovely bag, madam?' call various men, at various clothes stalls, as I pass. I smile at them, and they grin back. My phone beeps with a text. I will save it until I am sitting down.

'Maybe later,' I tell the stallholders, eyeing up their wares without slowing my pace. These are the clothes I have been craving: much cheaper than the ashram's upscale Fairtrade offerings, they are simple, loose, and form a kind of uniform. Most of the travellers I see around me are wearing them.

I put my feet up on a chair, order a mango lassi, and sit back, in the shade, to watch the people passing. I will order a coffee next: I am relishing the anticipation.

I came here for this: for the crowds of people, for the woman with bracelets slung over her arm, who is eyeing me up and who will pounce on me the moment I leave. I came to India for the smell of the sea, of the spices that are part of whatever is being cooked at this restaurant and the others along the strip, for the

211

red dirt that has been swept to the sides of the road, for the people on top of each other, the buildings on top of each other, the rails of loose, comfortable clothes and embroidered bags. I came here for the sounds: the repetitive clinking of the sculptors' chisels on stone. The distant whooshing of a sea that is visible between two tall buildings. The hum of conversation, the distant Hindi music. I came here for life.

There are still a lot of grown-ups here: two grey-haired couples walk past with a man who is obviously their guide. A couple of women with ashram-style posture – the ramrod back of the yoga devotee – drift past looking enlightened. A younger woman trudges by, her rucksack on her back, eyes straight ahead, either arriving or leaving.

I look at my text.

'what are you doing right now? is half term and am so tempted to seek you out. jx'

I text back. 'Sitting in a café in Mamallapuram. Is bliss. But you must not seek me out.'

And there are children everywhere. I spot a couple of Western children, looking happy and well-nourished and not ill, and hundreds of local ones. The Indian children are thinner but, on the surface, they look happy. I feel quite the expert, as I compare them with the Children's Centre inmates, and with my own strapping lads. These ones are less hollow-cheeked than the CC children, and not nearly as well-rounded as my little Joe.

He texts back. 'Gorgeous town. enjoy it! don't worry, I am not stalking you. x'

For ten minutes, I watch three boys and a girl playing with an old bicycle tyre. This street slopes gently downhill, towards the sea. The children take turns to attempt to get the tyre all the way to the sand without letting it fall over on its side.

Anjali told me to relax and enjoy the place before I go to pick up the bundle of stuff. I am happy to oblige. All those hours of yoga and meditation have energised me in a way I didn't imagine would be possible.

I am about to order a bottle of water when my phone beeps again.

'off to longleat. come home, we miss you. m, t, j. s, l, r x'

Max is doing this on purpose, ramming home the fact that he is doing family things with another woman to show me that all three of them can manage without me. I screw my face up and eject my paranoia from my mind. I am sitting in a little town on the Bay of Bengal. I am lucky not to be going to Longleat. I am glad to be here.

I walk down to the beach, and stand on the sand. The water in front of me is grey, the waves frighteningly big. There are fishing boats lined up on the beach, brightly painted, some with the names of charities on the sides. A group of men is walking at the edge of the water, laughing and kicking up spray as they go. Along the beach, to the right, the Shore Temple juts out, an ancient survivor of centuries of wind-blasting and tsunami.

I feel a million miles from Longleat. It is rather alarming to find myself here, so far from my old life, becoming preoccupied with the existence of Jim Trelawney again. It is easy to slip into that, to remembering his beautiful, open face, his cheeky eyes. He is straightforward, because he is apart from reality. A part of me wants to push the boundaries, to find out whether he really would dash out here to spend half-term with me. I will not, of course, do it. I stand at the edge of the waves, and decide to be sensible. Much as I hate to be standing on this idyllic beach, amongst the brand-new fishing boats, and staring at a mobile phone, I take it out and write: 'Actually I should stop this conversation now. sorry.'

I send it, and congratulate myself on being more sensible, regarding Jim, than I have ever been.

I step out of my shoes and into the shallow water. It laps around my feet, cleansing them. The edge of my skirt gets wet and heavy.

'Spoilsport,' he texts back, 'and here I am at the airport.'

The wind blows my hair around my face. I look down the beach, to the ancient Shore Temple that juts above the water; that has withstood storm and tsunami for centuries.

'You'd better be joking,' I write, and I switch my phone off, and put it away.

The backpackers take no notice of me. The young men walking

213

along the sand take no notice of me. The woman selling the sandalwood necklaces rushes over and walks with me.

'Sandalwood necklace,' she says. 'Very nice. One hundred rupees – I give you four necklace. OK, five. Five necklace. OK, six. Six necklace.'

I duck into an internet centre, and log on to my emails. There are a few paragraphs of family news from Max, with three photographs attached. Two of them have Sarah in them. In the second of these, she is wearing a top that Max will not have identified as the one that she calls her 'sexy' top. The sight of it chills me to the bone, because I know exactly what it means.

It is a crossover cardigan with a low V-neck that she keeps decent with a T-shirt underneath. When she wears it, she puts her shoulders back and says, 'I'm after nookie tonight.' She says it works on Gav every time.

But Gav is away. And she is wearing it on a day at the Science Museum with my husband.

I write the shortest possible email to Sarah.

'Hi S,' I type, my fingers shaking. 'Max sent me photos. Nice to see you all looking so happy. And is that your "sexy top" I see making an appearance? Is Gav back, then? India great, I will be back soon, prob with some orphans in tow who are going to live with their aunts and uncles in London. See you soon, lots of love. T x'

I don't even read it through before I send it. I could not let that pass without comment. I head to the nearest café, doubled up with dread. I look for Amber, everywhere I go: our paths will cross, sooner or later.

At the top of the stairs, a double shelf is overflowing with shoes: there are beaten-up leather sandals, lurid plastic Crocs, canvas shoes that, in my youth, would have been called plimsolls, and an incongruous pair of fur-lined boots. I kick off my sandals.

The café stops me in my tracks. It is exactly the place I have been looking for. It is the essence of a travellers' restaurant. There are a few tables in the centre of the room and next to the balcony, while the edges where the roof slopes down, reducing the headroom, have low tables and floor cushions. There is wicker matting over a concrete floor. Papery lampshades with Buddha and vaguely Tibetan-looking motifs on them hang from every part of the ceiling. A bookshelf of battered paperbacks, a Scrabble set, and a few toys complete the ambience. This, finally, is real backpacker country.

I walk to a table with a view down between the top of the low wall and the roof. This way, I can see the street. There is Kingfisher beer on the menu, but I manage to order a large coffee instead.

The café is populated by a mixture of the usual types of people, from earnest yogics to sensible sculpture buffs, to well-dressed Indians. I look down to the street, where any number of narratives are being played out. As I look down at it, a man in the clothes shop opposite catches my eye and calls up.

'Hello, madam! Very nice bag?'

This is what I wanted. A shifting travellers' town, with me occupying a space somewhere on its periphery. Not drunk. Not champing at the bit, wanting to be somewhere else. Just sitting and obsessing over Max and Sarah.

I know, now, that my instinct has been right all along. Until recently, I would have assumed that Max would never cheat on me. Now, however, I know that he has told people about my drinking, behind my back. He has said things to Elly that he would never have said to me. And how can I trust him, when I have kissed Jim Trelawney? I know how easily boundaries are crossed, and it is frightening.

chapter thirty-three

Alexia's thoughts

We are flying tomorrow! I am so excited that I can barely
manage to type. We are all packed. The best thing – the
thing I was despairing of ever happening – is this: in the
case I have clothes for me, clothes for Duncan, and
clothes for Saskia! Yes, I have bought her some little
outfits, from the Gap, and more everyday ones from
Target, and when we come back, she will be wearing
them. I hope the size is right. Although she's four, I
bought her clothes smaller because I figure she's probably
not the size of an American kid. My little Indian goddess.

Some are pink, some are not, although I have discovered
that it is pretty hard to get her clothes which are not. I
don't think little girls should be in pink all the time as
it might get a bit dull. I think bright colours will suit
her.

People have commented on the change in me.
Everyone in town knows about Saskia now. I think that
just about everyone has seen the photograph they sent
me. Some of my customers have even asked for copies of
her photo, and when they do, I always pop into the back
room, log on to my emails, and print one off for them,
there and then.

To the anonymous H, if you're reading this, I will

never be able to thank you enough for providing the contact address for the CC. I know I said this last time, but I just need to repeat it over and over. I wish I had an email address for you. After all we've been through in the past ten years, the CC were a breath of fresh air. Although I am not a religious girl, I actually prayed the other night, thanking God, or Buddha, or Krishna, or just the universal life spirit (my sister Dee likes to talk about that) for the fact that I started this blog, and that one of the very few people who read it was able to put me in touch with someone who could make my dreams come true.

The CC have taken care of the bureaucratic side of things most efficiently, and it is worth every penny. All we have to do is to turn up and collect her. She will have a full medical report, all her paperwork in place, and she will be ready to go.

They told us we have to say we're her family's representatives, rather than her real-life family, if anyone outside of the circle asks, and that, they say, is just to stop the gossips. There are a lot of people, the CC lady says, who think that Indian babies should go to Indian families, and so we pretend we're not her new family just to smooth things over. We say she's going to live with her cousins in the States. More than happy to oblige.

We're going to spend a few days with her in India, as they recommend, so the three of us can start to get to know each other.

Did I mention that I'm excited? I have decorated the house for her arrival, with balloons everywhere and a banner saying 'Welcome Saskia!' Mom says it's stupid to have the balloons up now as they'll just deflate, but then she smiled and said she'll pop in the day we come home with some fresh ones for her little granddaughter.

Duncan has just come in to say he's booked the cab for five o'clock in the morning. We have a lot of flights: from here to La Guardia, to Delhi, to Chennai, and then three hours in a taxi. I don't think I even need to say that it's going to be worth it.

Comments: 2

Alexia! You never said you have a blog. My crazy sister. Look, I see below that you've quoted me as saying you should have adopted an American babe. Scratch that comment. Apologies. Good luck to you my sweetheart, and all the love in the world. Come back safely with my niece. Love you. Deanna xxx

Hello there. No need to thank me. I'm so glad it's working out for you as it did for us. We will be with you in spirit on your journey. Much luck and love to you all, H

chapter thirty-four

Once I step away from the three streets that could be the Khao San Road, Mamallapuram is a sculpture town. There must be hundreds of men chipping away at blocks of stone with chisels and hammers, each ensconced in a little workshop, while their wares, ranging from tiny stone elephants to enormous gods which would need to be lifted by crane, are displayed on the pavement outside. There are little shops selling warm drinks and random items, there are food stalls, and there are people of all ages, from every walk of life, going about their business and barely glancing at me. The air is thick with stone dust.

I adore it. I could walk around this little town for ever.

I amble along in the direction of the Five Rathas temple complex, trying hard to push Max from my mind.

When I think I am nearly there, a man appears beside me.

'Hello,' he says. 'Guide?'

I laugh. 'No thanks.'

'Very cheap?'

'No. Sorry.'

The man walks close to me, just in case I change my mind. He has a nice smile, and I can see that he is only doing a job.

'Have a nice visit,' he says, after a while, and he wanders off towards a group of extremely well-heeled men and women who are stepping out of a four-by-four. One look at them shows me two women with St Tropez tans, two hundred pound haircuts, and Gucci leisurewear, accompanied by two men in Ralph Lauren.

Every freelance guide in the vicinity descends upon them at the same time.

'Wankers,' I mutter happily.

I buy a ticket for the temple complex, and go through the gate, running a gauntlet of unusually persistent shoe-sellers on the way.

I laugh when I see Amber, standing by an elephant sculpture. It was inevitable: this is such a small place. As I walk over, I watch her. Her mouth is set in a straight line, her hair loose, unbrushed, blowing in the hot breeze. Her shoulders are hunched, and she is all turned in on herself.

I look at the guidebook, and stand next to her.

'This is one of the greatest elephant representations in Indian history,' I say. She turns round and gasps, a hand on her chest.

'Oh, Tansy!' she manages to say, after a few seconds. 'Oh, sorry. You scared me. How amazing to see you. What on earth are you doing, out of the ashram?'

'Some stuff for Anjali and Elly,' I tell her proudly. 'But first, a bit of time off. How are things?'

She looks down at the sandy ground. 'OK. Better now you're here.' She smiles suddenly. 'The elephant's fabulous, isn't he?'

I run my hand over its warm stone leg. 'It's very big,' I point out, unnecessarily. 'And smooth.' I point to the temple behind it. 'Have you been here long? What's that?'

'It's the chariot of Arjuna Ratha,' Amber tells me.

'It's gorgeous. God, I could set up home in a place like that.'

'What? Inside a temple? It might not be very comfy.'

'Oh, I don't need much,' I assure her. 'And I'd be looked after by all these gods. They'd feed me nectar and let me lounge on goosedown pillows and silken cushions.'

She laughs. 'So what would you do? Live in there?' She pokes her head into the temple, and quickly re-emerges. 'Your silk cushions would go mouldy and your goosedown pillows would get all claggy. I don't think you'd get many house guests. Though on the other hand, I think you've already got one.'

'Who is it?'

'The Rat family.'

After a while we stop looking at the guidebook and content

ourselves with wandering around looking at the five chariots, squeezing into nooks and crannies, feeling the warm sand beneath our feet. This complex is next to the sand dunes and was uncovered by the British.

'Really?' I ask. 'We found this?'

'Apparently so.'

I smile. 'That's the first nice thing I've heard of us doing. Thank God for that. Here, Amber. Stand by the elephant again. Let me take your photo.'

We see all the sights together. My favourite is a rock called Krishna's Butterball. It is vast and spherical, balanced on a steep slope. It looks precarious, but it is firmly stuck in place. I pose pretending to hold it up with a finger, and then Amber lies on her back and keeps it at bay with her feet, carefully preserving her modesty in front of some very interested teenagers by holding her skirt up to her knees. Every other tourist is taking the same photographs. I notice a thin blonde Westerner watching me critically, and when I smile at her, she grins, and runs to catch up with a thickset man.

A monkey jumps out at me and tries to grab my bag. I scream. Amber yells with me, and a family who are having a rest on a rock laugh heartily at us. The monkey leaps up and down, reaching up with its creepy child-like hands, and making authentic 'aah aah' noises, until someone takes pity on us and chases it away.

'I guess monkeys are all right really,' Amber suggests when it has vanished over a rock. 'Cute at least.'

'They are fucking *not*,' I tell her. 'They can jump on to you and bite you, and they might have rabies. I don't like those attributes in a creature.'

Late in the afternoon, we walk across a strip of scrubland to the beach and pass two teenage couples hiding, I presume, from the eyes of their elders. They lean apart from each other as we approach, and giggle together.

I am on holiday, from my holiday, and I have a friend. I have not thought about Max and Sarah for hours.

On the way back, we duck down a side street. Clouds have

gathered overhead, and the air is humid. We pass a rubbish heap, where a tiny road turns an abrupt corner.

'Whoa,' says Amber. 'Smelly.'

'Mmm.'

She stops. 'Look! Pigs!'

Three black piglets are snuffling around in the rubbish, one of them almost buried in it.

'They're eating it!' I note. I remember that I did know this about pigs but that I had forgotten.

'I'm never going to eat pork,' Amber says. 'Ever, ever again.'

'You are what you eat,' I agree. 'Pigs eat poo. We eat pigs. Therefore . . . Yes, let's not eat pork. I guess this is why so many religions ban it.'

We walk on. I look up at the sky. It is definitely about to rain. Moisture hangs in the air. We turn into an alley that I hope will lead to the road with my guest house on it. The first drops of rain fall as I realise that this is not the backstreet that I thought it was.

We pass a woman and four children, the youngest around Toby's age. The children stare and giggle, but the woman glances at us, then away. We are not interesting. After we have passed them, one of the children says, 'Hello!'

When they have gone, Amber turns to me. There are tears in her eyes.

'I can't do this, Tansy,' she says. 'I mean, look at you. You're everything I want to be. I've messed up my relationship. I can't bear my own company even for a couple of hours. I'm useless at everything I do. I think I just want to go back home.'

I put a hand on her shoulder. 'Hey,' I tell her. 'For one thing, you're not useless at anything. For another, any capability you may imagine you see in me is an illusion. Look, let me tell you a few things.'

As we walk slowly back, through the rain, to the street where the cafés are, I tell Amber about Max, and Sarah, and me and Jim. I chronicle it all for her, and then we go for a beer.

chapter thirty-five

It is an enormous luxury to wake up at eight o'clock. I have had three hours more sleep than I ever get at the ashram, and I feel as if I have been steamrollered. I stretch out in my single bed, thinking idly back to the night before, and checking myself for a hangover.

It is there: I had three beers, and I feel decidedly fuzzy. This is, I decide, good; it means that my tolerance levels have gone down. I am not sure whether three big bottles of beer counts as a binge. It probably does, technically, but it is very different from the way I used to drink.

Amber and I sat in the restaurant by the beach and talked and laughed, over huge fish that were caught that day from the water that crashed and splashed to our right. For some reason, now that she has taken me off the pedestal that she put me on as soon as she discovered I was working with orphans, we have become proper friends. We laughed about poo-eating pigs, about our own inept way of handling relationships. We did not talk about the future. We lived in the moment, in the Indian night, beside the beach. Amber asked if she could share my cab back to the ashram today, to my delight. I think we agreed to meet for breakfast, in half an hour, back at the Yogi café.

I jump out of bed, in the half-light, and stumble to the shower, where I tip buckets of water over myself. I dress in the least creased items in my backpack, which turn out to be a pair of blue trousers and a white cotton blouse. I turn my phone on to send a quick text to Max. It starts beeping furiously as soon as it finds a signal. There are five texts from Jim.

'I would have come to see you, you know,' says the first, 'if you'd asked.'

'And I actually was at the airport,' says the second.

'But on my way to Lanza, not India – surf ahoy,' says the third.

'PS – heard on grapevine that you and max have parted?' says the fourth. 'if true, hope you're ok. I wasn't going to mention this but consider myself your friend so i think i should. Is toby all right? and your little boy? v sorry. J x'

And the last says, 'having a wicked time in the surf btw. feel free to pop to lanza on your way through.'

I stare at the phone. Then I click on Jim's number. To my surprise, he answers the phone, sounding groggy.

'Ugh?' he says.

'Oh, sorry,' I say. 'Is it the middle of the night? You should have switched your phone off.'

'Yeah. Hello.'

'What grapevine?'

'Um. School. Mothers. You know.'

'No, I don't know. Because this is the first I've heard of it. Did you just say that to wind me up?'

I can almost hear his brain ticking over. 'Yeah. Yeah, I did.'

'No you didn't. Who said it? Was it Sarah?'

'No. Sorry. I'm really sorry. I shouldn't have said.'

There is another voice in the background. 'Who's that?' I ask him. 'Mr Trelawney, do you have company?'

He laughs a small laugh. 'It's allowed, isn't it?'

'Of course it is, you horrible flirt. Look, sorry. Go back to sleep. Text me an explanation when it's morning. I want names, dates and exact quotes. OK?'

'Sure.'

I hang up, burning with anger, wobbly with insecurity.

The taxi is coming at midday, and my instructions are to swing by the orphanage, get the paperwork, and carry on to the ashram.

I am not entirely sure that I want to go back there, right now.

224

Now that I have had a day of freedom hanging out with the other travellers, I just want to stay here. Then I want to change my flight home, and get back to my boys, to gather Toby and Joe, my real children, the fruits of my womb, into my arms. I want to do everything I can to make things work with Max because if word is going around the school that we have split up, things are clearly even worse than I had realised.

chapter thirty-six

Alexia's thoughts.

So I'm updating you, my imaginary reader, from a cybercafé in Chennai, which is the same place as Madras. And all I can say is, 'Wow!' India is even more full-on than I imagined it could be.

Here are my impressions so far: the heat is not as bad as I thought it would be, but sometimes it's very humid. There are so many people! They are everywhere, just getting on with daily life. The people we have spoken to are kind, although I feel we stand out a bit in a crowd and sometimes we find someone staring. Things are pretty rudimentary. We could not believe it earlier when we saw a bus going past our taxi. It was so full! There were literally three times as many people on that bus as there would have been in the States. It would certainly not have been legal to drive a vehicle so overloaded back home.

We saw some sights today (and smelled some smells!). We went to the cathedral which was a little haven for us. It is a big white place and to my amazement it houses the remains of St Thomas the Apostle (Doubting Thomas). Duncan and I are not great churchgoers, but he and I do remember that guy from Sunday School. He lies in a crypt and we took our shoes off and filed in to see his last resting place. There was a nice statue of him, over an ornate tomb, in a small underground room, looked after by nuns in brown habits. There were signs up saying SILENCE and it was a little oasis of peace. So much so that if Saskia was a boy, I would be giving her the name Thomas.

I am fascinated to learn about Saskia's homeland. Now I will be able to tell her about St Thomas. I will be able to tell her every little thing about how we went to India to fetch her. I will be able to talk about the little buzzy autorickshaws that we haven't travelled in because Duncan insists on proper taxis, though I would like a rickshaw ride just once, to see what it feels like with the wind in your hair. And the food: I can tell her how I wanted to eat Indian curry, and her daddy wanted to go to Pizza Hut and literally could not believe his luck when he spotted it from the taxi window first thing this morning. And I will tell the story of our compromise, how we had lunch in a very nice Indian restaurant where Duncan forgot he was being cautious and gorged on curry, and then dinner in Pizza Hut which was a little taste of home. I hope we will bring her up to like both, also.

I am saving everything for her scrapbook: the tickets, the Pizza Hut receipt, the hotel stationery, everything.

We are only here for one night. We have a pretty good hotel, with proper bathroom and running water, a normal toilet and comfy bed. This surprised us – I think we both thought there might be a plank of wood on the floor for a bed and a hole in the ground for a bathroom. I don't think I'll sleep tonight, however homely it is. Because tomorrow we go to the Center, and we get to meet our little daughter. The thought that she is out there, only a few hours away from us, is almost impossible to contemplate.

Comments: 1

Forgive me for laughing. Tell that husband of yours to
loosen up. And – GOOD LUCK. We are all thinking of
you, literally the whole town. Take care of you. Love you
to pieces. Dee xxx

chapter thirty-seven

The orphanage is in an alley, tucked away in a part of Mamallapuram that is minutes' walk away from the backpackers' quarter, but in a different universe. It looks like all the other buildings around it: crumbling rather, but still standing in spite of everything. The alley is close, narrow, claustrophobic. It smells strongly of sewage.

The woman stands in the doorway, holding a baby, and smiles. 'Welcome,' she says. 'Tansy?'

She is thin, and dark-skinned. Her mouth twinkles with shiny fillings. Her long hair is gathered into a single plait, which reaches almost to her waist. She looks as if she is in her mid-twenties, but then something in her eyes makes me wonder if she might be much older. Amber stands a couple of paces behind me.

'You *are* Tansy?' she asks again quickly, looking at Amber. A few drops of rain start to fall from the low, full sky. I am glad; I hope it will wash away some of the smell.

'Yes,' I agree. 'I'm Tansy. Elly and Anjali asked me to come. This is Amber, who's from the ashram as well.'

'Hello, Amber,' says the woman. 'Welcome.'

A bead curtain separates a dark room from the lacklustre world outside. A faded black plastic sign outside the door reads: 'The Happy Children's Home'.

Because I have grown used to the comfortable Children's Centre at the ashram, because I did not see distressed children on the streets of Chennai or Pondicherry, because I think of myself as a dab hand with unfortunate children these days, my first experience of this place makes me retch. It is a slap in the face, a completely unexpected descent into hell.

The room is small and so gloomy that it takes a long time for my eyes to adjust. The walls are unpainted plasterboard. I count nine little faces looking up at us, but I know there are more lurking in the shadows. For a few seconds, everyone just stares. I try to hide my shock, and reach up to tuck my hair behind my ears. I am aware of Amber's shrinking, horrified presence at my side, but I cannot look at her.

The children, all of whom appear to be girls, start to smile. One of them, a little girl who I guess is about four, walks up to me and grabs my skirt with both hands, holding tight. She smiles up at me and says, 'Hello!' carefully. The others follow. Some go to Amber. They swarm around us, reaching for our hands, our clothes. 'Hello,' they say. 'Hello. Hello. Hello.'

'Hello,' I tell them. I try to ignore the desperation on their faces, the fact that no child in the world should have to beg for care like these girls are doing. 'Hello, everyone,' I say, swallowing a mouthful of bile. 'How are you?'

They all smile and nod to me.

'Very fine, thank you,' says one of the older girls. The others repeat the mantra. They push and shove each other, trying to get close to us. 'Very fine, very fine, very fine.' One girl hooks her legs around mine, so I have to reach out to stop her falling backwards. She grabs me and jumps so her legs are round my waist. I pick her up.

The babies don't wear nappies. They are dressed in thread-bare clothes, and the room smells horrible. There is not a single piece of furniture.

'Are they orphans?' I ask the woman.

She wobbles her head from side to side. 'In the main. A few have parents who are unable to support them, who come to visit on a weekly or so basis. Many of the older children, you know, are tsunami orphans. This town was hit badly. We are far from the only such establishment.'

I look at the little girls, the eager faces. One girl, who looks about two, runs over to me and hugs my knees tightly. 'Mama,' she says. The one I am holding, who is about Joe's age, tightens her grip with her knees.

Again, I picture the massive wave sweeping into the town, and taking people away, randomly.

'Are they all girls?' I ask.

She nods. 'We have a few boys. We have many more children than those you see here. Three boys. Just over forty girls. As a general rule, orphaned boys will be taken in by extended family, and girls will not.'

The girls are exuding a desperate sort of hope, imagining, I assume, that Amber and I will whisk one of them away to a life of unimaginable richness and love.

However much I complain about motherhood, I could give one of these girls a life. I could fit another child into my comfortable existence. What, otherwise, are they growing up to? A life on the street, a life of rape and prostitution and nothing. No life at all. Anything that takes them away from here is worth doing. Anything at all.

The woman speaks to the girls in Tamil, and they crowd even closer to us, grabbing at our hands and clothes.

'The girls will show you around,' she says, 'while I gather together everything you will need.'

'We don't need a tour,' I protest, but the girls have got me, and are propelling me, with hundreds of firm, spiky fingers, into the next room.

One girl holds each of my hands, and several others cling on to my clothes, while the one I was holding clings on to me with all four limbs, like a baby koala. Little hands grab me from every direction, everywhere we go.

Each room is worse than the last. I can see that the woman does her best, but this is not a place for anybody to live, let alone children. The crowd increases until the whole orphanage surrounds us. Each child gets as close as possible. They push and shove each other out of the way. Desperation and hope are in the air like static. The bedrooms are crammed with smelly mattresses, pressed up against one another. There is, perhaps, one mattress for every six children.

The juxtaposition of this place, this tiny home to fifty children, with the luxury afforded the backpackers, who are just down the road living in conditions many of them probably consider basic, makes me tremble. The hopelessness of these girls' situations makes me cry. I think of Toby and Joe, of the food they eat, the roof over their heads, the three pound coins Max's aunt sends them each birthday – money that, at home, I would barely bother to pick up if I dropped it on the street but that could feed all these children easily.

I could pull one, or even two, of these children out of this life and into something unimaginable. Whatever the laws are, a bit of bribery would sort it out. I know, now, why Elly and Anjali are doing what they do. I feel viscerally that I must stay at the ashram, and do it with them. To take one child out of here would make everything worthwhile. If laws occasionally get broken, as I suspect they must do from time to time, nothing could matter less. I am looking straight into the context of Elly's 'earthly laws' philosophy, and I know, now, exactly what she means.

'Are many of these children likely to be adopted?' I ask the woman when she returns. A tiny girl is clinging on to her dress, and she prises her fingers away, tutting.

She shakes her head. 'No. In India, an orphanage needs to be on the Cara list. Licensed for adoption. Otherwise, adoption is not legal. Adoption from here is not legal at all.' She hands a file of papers to Amber. 'This is the paperwork you need.'

I am turning to go when she picks up one of the little girls who has clung to my leg for the past half hour. She holds her out to me. I look at the girl. She is small and pretty, her features like a doll's. She is gazing at me, unsmiling, with huge brown eyes.

'And here,' says the woman, 'is the other part of your delivery. This is Sasika.'

chapter thirty-eight

We sit in the car, largely in silence, and head back to the ashram.

'So, no idea at all, then?' says Amber, again.

'No,' I tell her. 'None. They knew I would agree to fetch a child. I've said I'll escort some to London, for God's sake.'

'It's odd, isn't it?' Amber muses. 'A bit weird. To spring a little kid on you like that.'

I sigh, and look down at Sasika. 'I guess it makes sense. They wouldn't have paid for a car just for me to go and get a bundle of papers. They'd have got them posted. It's just the fact that they never mentioned her. Poor little sweetheart. I mean, it's wonderful that we get to carry a child out of that place. Amazing. The best thing I've ever done, in my life.'

It is getting dark, and the rain is falling so hard that the taxi is moving at a snail's pace.

I stroke Sasika's soft little head. 'So, we've kind of avoided future plans, but – what now, for you?'

Amber smiles and sighs. 'God knows. Back to Anjali for as long as I can manage it, I think. I sent Sam a text this morning, but I don't think he'll have got it. I'm crap on my own, we've established that.' She takes something out of her pocket and hands it to me. 'Look, this is how bad I felt, before you showed up.'

I hold it up to the window, steadying Sasika's head with my left hand, so I can read it in the twilight. It is written in purple ink, loopy messy writing, on a lined page torn from a notebook.

THINGS TO DO
Breakfast in café – take book.
See temples, as many as poss.
Proper coffee.
Walk on beach.
Be confident.
Don't be accosted or ripped off.
Be happy.
Talk to someone.

I smile at her. 'And?'

She laughs. 'Most of it. You know that. But how flipping tragic to have to write it down. On my first night I took a book, and went for a beer at Moonrakers. I felt like a sore thumb on my own. There was an awful English group at the next table – stepped out of an air-con jeep, all fake tan and designer clothes. I knew they were looking at me and talking about me.'

'I saw them,' I say. 'They were at the Five Rathas temple.'

'Yes, they were. Well, they were awful. They were being so obnoxious to the waiter – 'Write that down because if you get it wrong I am not paying. Do you understand?' – lots of that. And I thought, I'm not really sure I like the real world. It's weird being out of the ashram, isn't it? I want to get that Bear Hunt play on stage. Look after people like Sasika.'

Sasika is far lighter than either Toby or Joe. She is lighter, even, than Tara. As she sleeps, her head falls into my lap. I am wildly relieved that she is coming to live at the Children's Centre, somewhere comfortable, where there is always food. I stroke her hair, and think about taking her home.

'Dare I ask any more about Sam, then?' I ask, smiling sideways at her.

'Oh, feel free,' Amber tells me. 'So. I sent a text that he won't get. And then I rang the payphone this morning. I knew I should. So, someone answered in the end, and I asked for him, and they had no idea what I was on about. So I was shouting "SAM", very loudly. And they were going on at me and I wasn't understanding. Then I hung up. That was it. Not a roaring success.'

I nod. 'Good work, all the same.'

'Do you think word will reach him that a shouty foreigner rang up? Do you think he'll guess it was me? Do you think the man who answered was trying to tell me that he couldn't fetch Sam because he was in the middle of his wedding?'

'No to the last one. Obviously. Yes to the first two.'

It is pitch dark by the time we reach the ashram. I suppose we hung about for too long at the orphanage and missed the last of the daylight.

I am already planning where to slot Sasika into the children's show. I can't wait to ask Elly why they didn't tell me I was picking up a new resident for the CC. I cannot wait to ask if I can get more heavily involved. Nothing has any value compared to what they are doing.

This girl is less wary than Tara was. Sasika is wearing the same threadbare clothes as the other girls at the orphanage. She smells strong but not offensively so. She is precious and fragile and every fibre of my being wants to protect her.

The rain is falling heavily now, bouncing off the road as if it were rubber. I can hear the torrents of water on either side of the road, though I tell myself they sound worse than they are.

As we splash through huge puddles on the approach to the ashram, I notice that a car is parked at the side of the road, and that as we pass, it pulls out, and cruises behind us with its lights off. When we reach the visitors' centre, where the driver pulls over to drop us off, all is quiet, and I am relieved.

The rain soaks us instantly, as if we had stepped under a bucket of water that just keeps pouring.

'Hey, Sasika,' I say in a cheerful voice. I pull her into the shelter of a tree. 'We're here. Now, let's get to the Children's Centre, and get you settled in.'

'Tansy?' says Amber. 'Let's go to the guest house. Nick's got loads of torches. He's always whipping them out and trying to lend them to people. And we can use bikes then, and get Sasika to the centre perched on a handlebar. You know, the kind of thing you wouldn't ever do at home?'

Sasika is trembling in her rubbish clothes. My long skirt immediately clings to my legs, and my hair is flat, stuck to the sides of my face. I heave my backpack out of the boot.

This is my own fault, for delaying the taxi. I should have warned Elly, should have made sure that, at the very least, someone would be here for Sasika.

We walk together through the rain, across the parking area. My feet, sliding around in flip-flops, are instantly covered in mud, and I have to keep a tight hold of Sasika because I am afraid she will slip right out of my grasp. The path to the guest house is better: it is still muddy, but it has been reinforced with so many stones that walking becomes marginally possible. We walk side by side. There are, of course, no cyclists or bikers out. There is nobody. The only sound I can hear is the rain, pounding close to my ears, and thudding on to the path, slapping on to the wide leaves, and splashing into the puddles. After a few minutes, we are away from the lamp post that illuminated the little muddy car park, and darkness envelops us completely.

'I trod in a puddle,' says Amber. 'It's gross. My foot's all slimy.'

'Yuck.'

We tramp on, through the rain.

'Nearly there,' I say after a while, because we must be. We keep walking. I am on edge, desperate for food, a bed, for Elly and Anjali. I want to cede control of this odd little escapade.

I see a vague glimmer of a light over to our left. 'Look,' I say. I point, knowing that it is a futile gesture. My arm whacks Amber somewhere on her head or shoulder. 'Sorry.'

''S fine.'

'But look. That must be the light from the guest house. This is definitely the right track.'

It is hard to negotiate the area outside the Peaceful Haven because it is, normally, an open area with a hard earth floor, where bikes and motorbikes are parked. I had never noticed that it dips down in the middle, but I see now that it must because, between us and the dim light, the surface of a lake of muddy rainwater is shimmering. There is no way around it.

236

'We can't go over it,' I say to Amber, going back to the Bear Hunt story.

'We can't go under it,' she agrees.

'Oh no!' we chorus stupidly. 'We've got to go through it!' We laugh too hard.

My feet are submerged instantly. I try walking forward, through it, and hitch my skirt up with one hand, clutching Sasika with the other, as the water reaches halfway up my shins. Each step I take feels like the one that will trip me up and send me splashing to the depths with my tiny charge.

I can hear splashing and breathing close to me as Amber navigates it too.

'You OK?' I ask, after a while.

'I've been better.'

We reach the archway that leads to the guest-house courtyard. The dim light is dazzling. I look at the long table in the dining area, and am shocked to remember that it is not really night. People are sitting there, apparently barely noticing the torrential rain outside their roofed area, still picking over the remains of their curry. I look at the food, on the side table, and am pleased to be home.

Helga sees me first.

'Tansy!' she says. 'And a little girl! Is she for the CC? And Amber too. Hello. How wet you are, but how pleasant to see you.'

'Good to see you, Helga.' I kiss her cheeks. 'Sorry. I'm *really* wet, and now you are too. Aren't you in Chennai?'

'Clearly, I am not! I will go, perhaps tomorrow.'

Nick tips his chair back. 'She sets off to fetch a package. She comes back with a third baby! Sheesh, but you work fast.'

'You wouldn't understand,' I tell him. 'People flock to me wherever I go. No, you *really* wouldn't understand.'

'Truly, you are irresistible.' His hair is damp with sweat, and his face shiny. There are large sweat patches spreading across his off-white T-shirt.

'So are you,' I assure him.

He chuckles. 'So, what's with the kid?'

'Off to the Children's Centre. We got here a bit later than planned. I might take her over there now.'

Helga shakes her head. 'Oh no, we can keep her tonight. Let her sleep with us, poor thing.'

The rain is falling harder, and I know that Helga is right. The tiny wet child in my arms wriggles, gets down on to the ground and runs to the table, unabashed by all the strangers looking at her. She stands and stares at the food until the nearest person – Melinda, the woman with the ropy long hair, who has still never said a word to me – passes her a chapatti.

When I see Sasika starting to eat, I realise how hungry I am.

'Tansy,' says Helga. 'Who is this behind you?'

This makes me jump. I spin round.

'No one,' I say, but as the words leave my lips, I am aware of a small movement. Something, or someone, is coming. There is a splash as they walk through the puddle, and a muffled noise.

'Who is it?' I shout. 'Elly? Anjali?'

I walk over to Amber and sit gingerly on the seat next to her. Sasika crawls over on to my lap. I hold her tightly. Amber's silk dress is wet through. I am freezing.

'Admittedly,' Nick is saying to a man I have not seen before, 'there is something compelling about the sewers of Los Angeles.' Then, even he stops talking. He looks at us all. 'What?' he asks.

I am edgy, scared of whatever is out there.

'There's someone coming,' I say. Everyone looks around. It is hard to hear anything because of the rain.

Nick sits with his head cocked to one side.

'There *was* someone coming,' he says. 'And it was you.'

'No.'

It seems as if nobody breathes. Then there is a splash, and a squelch. Even though we have just made exactly this entrance, I quiver, and pull Sasika close. She reaches for Helga's plate and takes a handful of okra curry. For a mad half-second, I wish my boys would eat something like okra curry.

'Is that Elly?' I call. I am annoyed by the tremor in my voice.

They come closer. Then two men appear. They are Indian, in their thirties, and they look pissed off.

'Ha,' says the fatter one, and he surveys the dinner table. They

238

talk quietly between themselves for a while, and then the more thickset man claps his hands.

'Ladies and gentlemen,' he says in a loud voice. 'We seek Elly. Where is Elly?'

So many of the guests look at me that he does, too.

'I have no idea where Elly is,' I tell him.

'I was told to find her here. Or any CC person?'

'Well, I work at the CC a bit,' I tell him. 'And so does Amber, and Helga here. Can it wait till morning? Everyone will be here in the morning.'

'Your name, please?' he barks at me.

'Who are you?'

'What is your name?'

I don't want to answer, but eventually I do. 'Tansy,' I mutter. 'What's yours?'

'Thank you. Goodnight.'

We stare at each other. I frown at the darkness into which the men have just disappeared, and wonder whether I should tell Elly that some unpleasant characters are after her.

chapter thirty-nine

At five o'clock, the air is still and heavy, the ground spotted with puddles. Although the rain has stopped, electricity hangs in the air. Sasika is asleep on the end of my bed, her face peaceful, her breathing even. I stare at her for a while, marvelling at the unconscious perfection of her curling eyelashes, her pinkish cheeks, the complexity of her ears. The photographs of Toby and Joe are next to the bed, and my boys look at her, good-natured. Max is not with them. I slept with his picture under the pillow: I could not bear the idea of him looking at me.

I cover Sasika with a sheet, dress quietly, and follow everyone else out to meditation.

Anjali is not there; to my disappointment, the meditation is led by someone else, a man I have never seen before. I sit for an hour and think about my babies, trying, as ever, to work out how Max and I could possibly compromise, whether I could forgive him for a full-blown affair, and how we will manage to add a little Indian daughter to our dysfunctional set-up.

After breakfast, before yoga, Amber and I take Sasika to the Children's Centre. Sasika walks close to me, hanging on to my skirt, taking in her new surroundings through huge, accepting eyes.

We battle through the thick air. Every step is an effort, every movement unnecessary. I am walking in a John Wayne style, trying to avoid my thighs chafing against each other. Amber looks tense, worried.

240

The man who comes to the door of the Children's Centre looks familiar, though I have never spoken to him. The top of his head is entirely bald, and he has a black moustache.

'Hello,' I say. 'How are things?'

He frowns. Again, I wish I had bothered to learn Tamil.

'This is Sasika,' I add. 'We've brought her from Mamallapuram.'

He nods curtly.

'Look at that,' I say to Amber. I point to a homemade poster for the famous Bear Hunt play. 'Tuesday night. Three days' rehearsing time.'

The man glances down at Sasika. She looks up at him, her tiny face heartbreakingly eager to please. He looks away, impassive.

'Children's Centre is full,' he says. 'Anjali and Elly unavailable. Come back tomorrow.'

'But this is Sasika,' I explain. 'Anjali asked me to fetch her from Mamallapuram. You're expecting her. I've got all this paperwork, too. And I work here. Where are the children?'

'No space,' he says. 'Come back later please.'

And he closes the door in my face.

Josiane, a French woman from my yoga class, sits down with Sasika and fusses over her.

'Hello, little soldier girl!' she says. 'Hello, my heart. Hello, you magnificent gorgeous thing.'

Sasika shivers with pleasure. 'Hello,' she says.

Josiane instantly realises her mistake. *'Bonjour!'* she says. *'Bonjour, bonjour, bonjour! Bonjour, ma petite. Bonjour, ma grosse. Bonjour, mon coeur. Bonjour!'*

'Bonjour,' Sasika echoes. Josiane applauds her.

'Bravo!' she cries. I reflect that it must be hard being French, trying to save your language from the unrelenting onslaught of English.

Helga comes along and takes Sasika on her lap and sings her a German song.

'Do you know where Elly or Anjali is?' I ask her. 'And why the CC isn't functioning?'

She looks wary. 'I saw them both yesterday,' she says. 'At the

Children's Centre. There seemed to be some hustle. I think they are around later today. Sometimes Elly takes the children to Pondy. Don't fret.'

By the time I get back from morning yoga, Sasika is revelling in her celebrity status. She beams at the crowd, and echoes whatever is said to her because she has discovered the reaction it garners. Somebody has made her a nap place on the floor. She has a nest made from two blankets to sleep on, a pillow donated by one of the hardcore Germanics who doesn't need such a thing, and a sheet.

Amber leaps up when she sees me coming.

'Hey, Tansy,' she says. 'Sam called. He wants me to go. And I think I will.'

'Too right you will. Come for a walk? I want to get Sasika some clothes, and I need to email Max.'

'Good! Sort things out properly. Like me. Shall we bring Sasika?'

I look at her, entertaining her audience. 'She looks pretty happy where she is, and I'm long overdue contact with home.'

'Sure.'

'Helga?'

Helga looks up, inquiring.

'Can you look after Sasika? I'm going to buy her some clothes and send some emails, and I'll pop over to Elly's house too, to look for her. I've texted her three times but she hasn't replied, but you never know. I don't think her phone's often charged because she has to go to the internet centre to do it. But I don't really want to drag Sasika all over the place with me.'

'Of course.'

'In fact, could you give her a bit of a shower? Use my shampoo if you like.'

'Yes, of course.'

I do everything else before I log on to my emails. I buy Sasika two expensive outfits from the wildly overpriced boutique. They are salwaar khameezes, one blue satin and the other dark pink cotton. The shop is almost empty but for a white couple who are looking at the same rack of clothes as me. The man hangs back,

242

shifting his weight from one foot to the other, clearly bored, while the woman grabs outfits, holds them up with her head on one side, and puts them back, until she has looked at every item for a little girl in the whole shop. She is tall and intense-looking, her light-brown hair cut into a severe bob, her eyes burning. There is so much energy radiating from her that I get warm just by standing next to her.

'Sorry,' she says, in an American accent. 'Oh, I *am* sorry. I'm looking for something for my daughter.'

'They're lovely, aren't they?' I say politely.

'Do you have a daughter?'

'No, I have sons, actually. I'm looking for something for a friend's little girl.'

The woman nods and turns away, continuing with her search.

Max has sent two emails. My fingers tremble as I open them.

'We had a great day out at Longleat,' he writes in the first. 'Sarah and the girls came too, so we were able to pack everyone into her seven-seater and share the driving.'

For some reason, this image makes a tear trickle down my cheek. This is what he deserves: someone funny, bouncy, lovely. Someone who likes doing family things. Someone who has time to be a mother and wife, who makes an effort to wear figure-hugging clothing for him. I wilfully forget, for a few moments, that Sarah has issues of her own, and I picture them all, happy without me. They sing along to 'The Wheels on the Bus'. They listen to the Charlie and Lola CD in the car. They buy a family ticket, and share experiences that will bond them for ever.

Max's second email is a carefully non-emotive reminder that I said I would write every day.

'You must remember,' he says. 'You promised. I know you do email, but I'd be so much happier if it was less sporadic.'

As soon as I read it, I picture his disappointed face. I know he is secretly worried that I have been abducted by dacoits, or robbed, or that I am lying helpless in a dirty bed somewhere, riven by dysentery.

'Right,' I write. 'Putting a lot of things aside for a moment. I need to tell you about a little girl called Sasika. Elly and Anjali (who is Elly's lover, did I tell you that?) asked me to fetch her from an orphanage. Actually they asked me to fetch some paperwork, but she came too, it turned out, included in the bundle. I have no idea why they didn't tell me, but there you go. They've got a bit secretive and at the moment they seem to have disappeared. Some men came looking for Elly last night because they thought she'd be at the guest house, for some reason. Rude fuckers. Anyway, I'm looking after Sasika until they have space at the Children's Centre. I'm not sure what's going on, but I'm sure all will become clear.

'And Max, don't laugh, but I want to bring her home. Obviously I know it's not that simple. It's completely unrealistic. In fact, do laugh, if you want to. But at the heart of it, here is an adorable little girl craving attention. And we have a home and two brothers for her. It should be that simple, even if it isn't.

'And I know I don't do babies, but she's four. I can do four-year-olds. I am serious, by the way.'

The day passes in a static haze. After a few days off from yoga, I go to one of my sessions, and find it torturous. My muscles protest and spasm, and the minutes stretch out. Three hours last forever. I think of Sasika, wonder whether Amber has managed to get back into the CC. We need to get our show sorted out. It seems that I actually like doing things like this with children. I wonder how surprised Toby and Joe would be to hear that. Too surprised.

Before dinner, I end up cross-legged on the veranda, eyes closed, meditating. Most of the other guest-house residents are doing the same, because keeping still is the only way to pass the time in this prickly humidity.

Sasika sits in a corner, fiddling with a Fairtrade wooden puzzle I bought her for an insane amount of money. I would have been better off sending that money to the orphanage and giving Sasika a cardboard box. She does not complain about being left to her own devices, and happily turns to anyone offering attention, with a smile that is so eager that it brings a tear to my eye every time.

I am trying, unsuccessfully, to close my mind. Every time I think

I have emptied it, it fills with children. I am unable to stop thinking of motherhood, and responsibility, and why I am enjoying being away from my babies, and how desperately I want to get back to them. Being responsible for myself is liberating and heady, and a part of me feels I am only just beginning to get going. Another part of me feels I am pushing my luck just being away for this long. I think of Toby: will I be a stranger to him when I get home? Will he even smile at me? I am picturing Joe's trusting little face, and wondering whether he will hate me for ever. Then everything begins to go wrong.

It starts with a gasp and a cry. An American voice shouts, 'It's Saskia!'

I open my eyes. Everyone else does the same.

The woman who was in the clothes shop is running through the courtyard. She looks unhinged, and this, strangely, reassures me (this place attracts the unhinged), until I notice that she is making a dash for my little charge.

There is something in this woman's manner that makes me race her to Sasika, snatch the little girl up, and shield her with my back. Amber reacts in much the same way, and puts her body between me and the woman. The man skids to a halt next to her. I half turn, and we all look at each other.

'You don't understand,' the woman says, with an intensity in her eyes that makes me stare, against my will. I try to look away, but find I can't. 'That's Saskia.'

'No it's not,' I tell her. 'It's *Sasika.*'

'No. Look, I have no idea who you are. Are you Elly? You're not Elly, are you? I'm Alexia Jones, and this is my husband, Duncan. We're . . .' She takes a deep breath, and looks to Duncan, who picks up the story.

'We're representatives of Sasika's family,' he says firmly. 'We've come to take her to a good home in the States, where she has an aunt and uncle and many cousins who are very keen. Very keen. To look after her. This is all agreed. But ma'am, if you are anything at all to do with the CC, you know that we are here in good faith.'

'I'm looking after Sasika on behalf of the CC,' I say, because it is true, 'and I don't know anything about any of the children going to America.'

'Then you don't know much. We have paperwork. Who are you?'

I almost claim to be Elly, just to see what they would say to me.

'It doesn't matter who I am,' I tell them. 'I work closely with Elly, and I brought Sasika here from the orphanage where she was living – after a fashion – yesterday. Elly's not around, and I'm responsible for this little girl until she or Anjali get back. You understand that I can't just hand her to you. Don't you?'

'We have paperwork,' says the woman, and her eyes are burning with something. 'Duncan. Show her the paperwork.'

He takes a blue cardboard file out of a neat little backpack. I see pieces of paper, marked with yellow Post-it notes, with certain phrases highlighted in pink or yellow.

'Well,' I say. 'You're certainly organised.'

'Yes,' Alexia agrees. 'In everyday life I'm not that organised, but when it comes to something important like this, you can't take chances.'

I can feel Sasika's little hands around my neck, gripping my T-shirt. I hold her tightly, and give her a little kiss on the top of her head.

'Here,' says Duncan. 'Look. We're to take her now, to stay in Pondicherry with her for four nights so we all get used to one another. Then we get to take her home. Elly has her passport.'

I tighten my grip on the tiny girl.

'Elly cannot possibly have her passport,' I tell them. 'Elly hasn't even *met* her. And,' I add, 'I definitely don't have the authority to hand her over to you. I won't do it. Ask as much as you like. This is all too weird. Elly and Anjali are in charge here. Not me. The Children's Centre has closed in a bit of an unexpected way. All we can do is stay as we are and wait for them to get back. And anyway, why do you need four days to get used to each other if you're just the couriers?'

The electric clouds are overhead again. The humidity is unbearable. I want the rain to start. People are watching, but they are all keeping their distance. Something is going on here, and I don't like it. I don't like these people with their air of desperation. I don't like the hunger in the woman's eyes when she looks at Sasika.

We stare at each other as the seconds tick by.

'Fine,' Alexia says eventually. 'Fine. But you just call Elly and whoever that other person is, and you just tell them to haul their sorry . . .' She breaks off, and puts her face in her husband's shoulder, overcome.

I try to be gentle.

'You wouldn't want me to let her go with strangers,' I suggest. 'Would you? If everything's in order, like you say, then this is only a temporary hitch.' I am saying anything, whatever it takes to make them leave me alone.

'You bought her those clothes this morning,' says the woman. She is accusing me of something. 'The ones she's wearing right now.'

'And you were buying clothes for your "daughter",' I remind her.

We all look at each other, mistrustful.

'OK,' Duncan says. 'That's fine. It all makes sense. We'll wait for Elly. Can we wait here? Could you call her?'

I look at Amber, who is leaning on a wall, watching and listening. She shrugs, takes her phone from her bag, and starts tapping.

'I'll send a text,' she says.

'Then, sure,' I tell them. 'Stay around while we wait. It's a free country.'

Helga quickly appears with two wicker chairs. Alexia sits in one, and holds her arms out for Sasika.

'Oh, come on,' she says to me. 'You were letting any old person play with her just now. I saw you.'

I nuzzle the little girl closer. These people want her too much. I don't want to give her up. All the same, I put her down. I have a lot of back-up here. Nothing bad could happen.

'Come on, sweetie,' Alexia says. Sasika looks around, sees that all eyes are on her, and walks slowly, deliberately, over to Alexia, who sweeps her up and sits her on her ample thigh. It happens so quickly that none of us so much as draws a breath. There is a loud blast on a whistle. Uniformed men come running out of the woods.

We all stare for a few seconds. It is an utterly surreal sight, the very last thing I would have expected to see.

As they get closer, I see that not only are they real, but they have handcuffs, batons. I take a few steps back.

One of them – a tall, thin man with a hint of a moustache, a man who is probably fifteen years my junior – is looking at me. He is quite far away, but looking straight at me, purposeful, and I know, suddenly, that he is coming to get me. I see the two men who came to the guest house last night looking at me, pointing, shouting.

I turn and run. I sprint as fast as I can, faster than I have ever run, straight into the forest, and when I get there, I keep going. I have no idea what I am doing, but I know that I have to get out of there and I do what I have to do.

chapter forty

My legs are ripped to pieces by the forest. Thorns lodge in my skin. Spiky things scrape and cut me. Branches pull at my clothes and my hair. I keep running. My legs seem to know exactly where they are going, though the rest of me has no idea. My breath comes in short, sharp rasps. I run and run.

I am in a weird different world. It is so close to the ashram world and yet it is entirely different, a parallel universe of spikes and canopies and secrets and hiding places. It is impossible to know what is around the corner, and my legs are torn to pieces with every step I take because I am nowhere near a path.

Perhaps an hour passes before my body slows to a halt. My adrenaline is still pumping but when I reach a tiny clearing, exhaustion and terror overwhelm me, and I sink to the ground. I lie still for a moment, listening. I can hear my blood pumping in my ears, and my ragged breathing, and the noise of the breeze in the tree-tops, and a few unidentifiable forest sounds. I cannot hear the might of the law pursuing me.

The ground is prickly and boggy but nothing could matter less. I lie on my back, and keep listening. Nothing.

I try to piece together what just happened. They came running, as soon as Sasika went to that American woman. They were waiting. It was all because of Sasika.

And there is, of course, no way in the world that that man and that woman were 'representatives' of Sasika's family in America. Of course she hasn't got family in America. If she did, she would not have been living in that fleapit. If she had an aunt and uncle and cousins in America who wanted her to live with them, they would have come for her after the tsunami orphaned her. Not now. It is not possible that those people were telling the truth.

I feel sick. Why were they looking at her like that? Why did the police charge in as soon as they took her? What were they really going to do with her?

Part of me wants to think that all they wanted to do was to adopt her. And if that is the case, I know that, no matter what laws have been bent and twisted, she is better off away from that orphanage. As I try to rationalise it in this way, to myself, I know it is not true. If these people were going to take Sasika home with them, then Elly and Anjali have arranged it. Elly and Anjali haven't even met the Americans. You can't send a child away with strangers. You just cannot. That is not adoption, but something else.

And the Liverpudlians who backtracked and said they lived in Kashmir. That never rang true, but I didn't give it any thought at all. I would bet everything I have that Tara is in Liverpool now, that she has never been anywhere near Srinigar.

I will not allow myself to dwell on my naiveté. The more pressing matter is the fact that I have just run from the law. It is the most stupid thing I could possibly have done. It is an admission of guilt, in the eyes of the police. I scrunch up my eyes and curse myself. If I had stayed, I would have been arrested by the thin policeman, but I would have cleared my name in an instant. I have not actually done anything wrong.

And now I cannot go back because if I do, they will throw me into jail. I have made things a million times worse. I have done the worst possible thing.

I pull leaves out of my hair. If I had my phone, I could call Amber, or even Max. I could sort myself out. Unfortunately, I have nothing; not a single thing.

I try to imagine what it would be like, in Indian prison. I flash on to an image of myself in a cell, looking something like Ethan, while Toby, Joe and Max watch me through the bars.

'Oh, Christ,' I say. I am going to have to give myself up. I have no food, no water, nowhere to go, no plan.

I lie on the ground. It is lumpy, hard, spiky. It is not exactly the magical clearing from the fairy tales, with the bed of moss. The trees are so thick that I cannot see the sky at all. I try to piece things together, but it doesn't work. I make no sense of it at all.

It gets dark, suddenly, as it always does. The forest is full of noises, of animal sounds, birds flying suddenly among the leaves. Insects buzz and hum next to my ear. Everything is spooky, weird, and foreign. I am much too far from home.

I start to sing, because if I'm making my own noise, the other sounds don't seem so scary. I sing any old thing: 'The Wheels on the Bus' because I was thinking of it earlier. 'Twinkle Twinkle Little Star'. 'Rock-a-bye, baby', my boys' night-time song.

'We're going on a bear hunt,' I chant to myself eventually, but find little comfort in the sentiment.

After a while, I start to fall asleep, in spite of everything. I drift in and out of consciousness, plagued by nightmares, plunged into despair such as I have never known before, on the forest floor.

chapter forty-one

Alexia's thoughts.

Hello, this is Dee writing. I know a few people read
Alexia's blog and when she called from India she asked
me to write an update on it for her.

I am her sister. I told her all along that if she needed to
adopt she should do it from home, or use a surrogate.
She was set on India.

Now it has become a nightmare. Because when
she went to get her little girl, she was arrested. She
and Duncan both. From what we can tell, the adoption
was not legitimate, and the paperwork was faked, and
the girl was being trafficked. I mean, trafficked?
'Trafficking' means rape and slavery in my book, not
going to a new home in the world's greatest country
with loving parents who would do every little thing
for you.

So they're being held in a prison in a place called
Pondicherry. The entire town is in shock. It is just plain
impossible. We're trying to set up a lawyer and get the
Ambassador to help them. We know no one over there,
and I think I'm going to have to go there myself. What an
enticing prospect. Mom wants to go but she can't, she's
too frail.

But the purpose of this blog entry is a warning to any of you childless ladies thinking of India. I will keep updating when we know what is going on.

Dee

chapter forty-two

It is starting to get light. I am almost hallucinating, longing to wake up back in my bed in London. I keep seeing snakes out of the corner of my eye, but when I whip round, they are not there.

Monkeys jump in the trees from time to time. Real ones. I freeze when I see or hear them. That is the only time I am glad not to have any food. I gasp at the sounds of breaking sticks. After three long seconds, a huge bird flies into the clearing.

The dawn light is growing stronger. The air is fresh. I am petrified. I cannot start crying or I will never stop. I hear a monkey approaching, and gasp in horror. It stands in the clearing, chattering and jumping.

'Oh, fuck off,' I say. I run at it and kick it, and it retreats.

I lick rainwater off the leaves, drink from murky pools when I find them. At least in prison there will be food. I have no idea which way to go, but I figure that the woods, bound by the ashram, the main roads, the beach, cannot be that big. I set off, weary, in the direction that I think I came from. I want to pick berries and scavenge for food, but I don't dare, so despite the fiery cavern in my stomach, I eat nothing at all.

By the time I get to the edge of the woods, the sun is high in the sky. I can barely put one foot in front of the other. I am entirely ready to collapse.

As the trees start thinning, I have so much adrenaline that I don't know what to do with myself. My palms tingle, my stomach lurches around, and every one of my yoga-toned muscles is poised, ready to flee. I am going to do this. I am giving myself up. Toby and Joe will have a mother in an Indian prison. I try to tell myself blithely that it will be a talking point for them, but find that I cannot manage hard-bitten cynicism yet.

You hear stories like this, all the time. They are usually about drugs, but it is the same. I follow it to the end. The white person is arrested, thrown into prison where they sleep with forty other people in a tiny cell. They languish there for years, while family try to spring them out. After five years or so and as much publicity as the family can manage, the Indian government agrees to extradite them and they finish serving their sentences at home.

I am at the place where the forest meets the beach. There is a road in front of me. A few hundred yards to my right, a police car is parked by the side of it.

I want to run over the road, lie on the sand and sleep. I want to immerse myself in the water, wash it all away. I desperately want to throw myself on the policeman, and beg him to take me somewhere with drinking water and a stretch of dry floor. Yet I hold back.

There are a few people on the beach: a couple of young men, a woman with a child. I stand far enough back not to be seen.

'I have to give myself up,' I mutter to myself. It is so hard to make a plan, to know what to do. 'I can't do this any longer. I have . . .' But I can't even say the word 'children'. I don't trust myself. I stroke their photograph, still in my pocket, instead. 'I have to do the sensible thing.'

There is a choking engine sound from down the road, in the opposite direction from the police. A blue and white painted bus is approaching. I open my hand, and see that it contains a fifty rupee note. I remember stuffing it in there, yesterday morning, my change from Sasika's outfit.

I step to the roadside and flag the bus down. When I glance sideways, the police are not even looking at me. They are engrossed in conversation with each other.

The bus has a lot of boxes and bags strapped to its roof. There is the sound of a chicken crowing. The driver stops at once at the sight of a white girl, even one who has spent the night hallucinating in the forest. I see all the passengers jolting forward.

I step quickly out of the protection of the trees and push my way on board. I hand the driver fifty rupees, don't wait for change or find out the destination, and force my way into the middle of the crowd.

I cannot see through the window. The bus is hugely over-loaded. I don't look at anyone's face because I don't want to know what they are saying about me. I keep my head down and bury myself deep in the scrum. A chicken clucks. A goat-like animal bleats. I can't see either of them. I cannot understand a word of what is being said.

I hold my breath and stare downwards, wishing I looked Indian, trying to vanish.

I should have let them arrest me. Nobody else would have been stupid enough to turn and run, as if I were the mastermind of a criminal gang. Everything is a thousand times worse now. I cannot think straight enough to work out what has happened, beyond my flash of insight, yesterday, about the CC.

The first few seconds are the worst: I know we are driving past the police. If they stop the bus, they will find me in a second. I bend my knees slightly, look at my pink varnished toenails in battered sandals, clench my jaw, concentrate my mind on doing nothing. The seconds tick by. We bump around. I am thrown against a man beside me, a woman in front. In spite of myself, I risk a glance through the back windscreen.

The police car is back there, beside the road. One of the men is looking into the forest, and the other is asleep on the car's bonnet.

I hardly dare breathe. So far, so good. I am chugging away from the police, into the absolute unknown, with no money and no idea what is going on. Things have been turned on their head when this is a good development.

chapter forty-three

Alexia's thoughts

Hello, Dee again here.

I have just come back from visiting Alexia. I need a drink and it turns out this place barely has a single bar. It is godforsaken.

I mean, as an American, you can stay in a reasonably nice hotel and travel by car and ignore all the falling-down buildings and poverty, sure. But when that car stops outside the prison, and when you are going into that prison to visit your own sister, and when that sister is accused of buying a child (implied = for bad purposes) – then any interest the place might once have had does rather seem to evaporate.

A representative of the US Consulate, here in Chennai, is visiting Alexia, and they found her a lawyer. I said it had to be the very best lawyer in all of India, and they laughed and said that person wouldn't be available in Chennai but they've got the best they could. Lexy and Duncan have been moved from the little prison in Pondicherry to the big ones here. They are in completely separate buildings, in different parts of town. We haven't been to see Dunc yet, although he is more centrally located – Lex comes first. Duncan is next on the itinerary. (Ha. Most people go to India with an itinerary like: See Taj Mahal. Visit temples. See mystics and snake charmers. Check out beaches and palm trees. Buy carpets. Not like me: Shout at Ambassador. Visit sister in prison. Call home. Update blog. Check out brother-in-law in prison.)

I cried and cried when I saw her. I am not crying now, because I am the one who has to get her out of there.

She's not in proper prison, it turns out. Although she's in a cell with about 12 other women, NOT A SINGLE ONE OF THEM able to speak English, this is a holding cell. She'll stay there until some paperwork is done and then she'll go to actual prison.

I visited her with George, a guy from the US Consulate. I was glad he was with me. He'd been there before, and he knew some of the people, and he did all the talking, because I was so busy trying to contain my nausea, and not to mention my f—ing fury, that I don't think I could have said a word. And we had the lawyer with us (the one who is not the best lawyer in India), who is oh-so-full of promises to spring her out of there, but I don't see him doing much about it right now.

The building didn't look too bad from the outside, apart from when I thought about my big sister locked away in there. We went through lots of security and walked down corridors through various locking doors, and each step we took, the smell got a bit worse.

When we got there, to the cell, I didn't see her at first. The whole of the wall was bars, if you see what I mean, so we could see all the women easily. They were all Indian women, chatting away to each other, sitting around, just being like people who haven't got much to do. One of them was peeing in the corner, holding her skirts around herself to hide it. I swear, not even on a pot: I just saw the liquid trickling from underneath her.

And then, holy crap. That was A, in the corner. Next to the peeing lady.

Rocking and, I swear, humming. Dirty. Folded in on herself.

I could see straight away that Alexia has given up. She was not built to cope with a place like that. I think if I were in there I'd be shaking the bars and yelling at them until they were so pissed they let me go. I should be the one in there, not A. All the spirit has gone. Her eyes were empty. It was like a horror movie. The most scary thing I have seen in my whole life.

When I called to her, she didn't hear me for the longest time. One of the other women went over and poked her until she looked up.

George put his hand on my shoulder, which was appreciated.

'We'll get her out of there,' he said. 'I know this is hard. We'll do it.'

She was brought to a little room. In f—ing handcuffs. She was barely there. It was not like talking to Alexia at all. I cried and cried. She didn't even react to that. She just stared ahead. Only once, she cracked a bit, and she looked at me and said, very quietly, 'Deanna, this is the only way I can do it. Don't try to make me.' I knew what she meant, so I backed off.

The sight of my big sister in chains. I will never, ever forget it. Alexia is the most conventional person, the most straight, the most normal, that I have ever met. She doesn't even jaywalk.

George and Rajiv said they are trying to work out what's gone on at that 'Children's Centre'. It's in a religious community of some sort, and it's, clearly, totally a scam. Everyone else has run away, even the woman who gave the child to Alexia. The whole children's home has shut down and all the children have vanished.

Only my poor sister and her husband are left. All this, and they only wanted a baby.

George said he'll take me to a bar tonight. Can you believe, in this place they barely even drink? But he said he knows some good places. He even says we can get some food that isn't Indian. Halle-bloody-lujah.

Comments: 3

Sweetie, tell her we're praying for her. Everyone in the shop, everyone in town. We are heartbroken that the adoption has gone so badly wrong. I know you, Dee, and your lawyers will get her out of there. Sending you and Alexia and Duncan all the strength you need.
Mary

Oh my god, I left a comment on Alexia's blog a few months ago. I cannot believe what I have just read. I am so, so sorry. Are the media involved? I would say some publicity would help get her out of there.

My husband and I have just been matched with a little girl in China. If ever anything made sure I triple-check the paperwork with a local lawyer before taking her, this is it.

Much love to you, Dee, and to Alexia and Duncan. Please keep updating. Janice.

Dee. We are counting on you. Mom.

chapter forty-four

I stand on the bus, swaying around, for hours. After a while I sit down on the floor; it is vaguely unsanitary, but I don't care. I pretend not to notice the general disapproval at the dirty Westerner breaking bus etiquette and taking up too much floor space with her big bum.

More people get on, and hardly anyone ever gets off. I am glad of the crowd. It makes me feel safe. I have to stand up again, though, because after a few more stops, there really is not enough space.

I don't look out of the window. I have no idea where we are going, or how long it will take; but as the sunlight comes glaring in, straight into my eyes, I wonder whether we will arrive somewhere before nightfall. I would rather get somewhere in the dark, so I can hide more easily.

I keep running over the plan of action in my mind. Instinct tells me I am travelling south. With this many people on the bus, it must be headed for a fairly big town. Once I get there, I can only travel by foot. So I will walk until I find a telephone kiosk, and then I will make a reverse charge call to Max. Beyond that, I have no idea what to do.

I notice we are in the outskirts of a town. It looks, from the little I can see between people's heads, like any old Indian town. It looks poorer than Chennai, with corrugated iron houses with sacking for doors. We drive through this shantytown area for a while, and then, when, for some reason, I am not expecting it, the bus stops. There is a noisy scramble as everyone gets off. I am the last one standing there, and then I follow.

I am in a city. I try to picture the map, and to imagine any city that might be six hours' drive from the ashram. Could it be Madurai? Delphine is in Madurai. My heart leaps. I could trawl the hostels until I find her. People would remember the impulsive French girl with the crystals and the dreams. I run my fingers through my hair, touch my various cuts, scrapes and bruises, and wonder just how bad I look. Dreadful; worse than I have ever looked in my life. There are still twigs tangled in my hair.

I pull it back, and, in the absence of any form of elastic, force it into a knot around itself, just to get it off my face. I lick my fingers and scrub randomly at my face, in a lame attempt to clean myself. Toby hates it when I do that to him, but I can't dredge up any emotion, at the moment, at the thought of my children.

I am standing in a bus depot. It is almost dark. I walk up to a man who looks as if he might be vaguely in authority.

'Excuse me,' I say, in a tiny little voice. I point to the ground. 'Is this *Madurai*?'

He looks at me. 'Madurai?' he echoes, and looks around. Then he takes me by the arm and leads me to another bus. He talks quickly to a man sitting on its step, smoking a little cigarette. They both nod.

'Madurai night bus,' says the first. He takes a mobile phone out of his pocket, taps in the number eleven, and shows it to me. 'Madurai,' he says. He mimes driving.

So this is not Madurai.

'This bus leaves at eleven?' They both nod. 'Where is *this*?' I ask, pointing to the ground.

'Madurai night bus.'

'Madurai – how far from here?' I try. I tap where my watch would be, if I had one. 'Madurai? What time?'

'Madurai.' He uses his phone again. '10.'

'This bus leaves at eleven and arrives at ten tomorrow morning?'

He nods. 'Madurai very long.'

'From where?'

'Here. Chennai.'

'This is *Chennai?*'

They look at each other and laugh nervously. Both start to edge away from me. The man smoking on the bus retreats back to his driver's seat. The other one melts off into the crowd.

I try to think of the sensible thing to do. I could find a police officer and hand myself in. That would be good, in a terrible sort of way. I could find a quiet place, and sleep on the street. I cannot do that. It cannot have come to that. I must walk, and find a phone, and if I see another white person, I will beg them for ten rupees for some street food.

My vision keeps clouding over. All the terrified energy, the force that kept me walking through the forest, has deserted me. This no longer feels like a hallucination. I cannot go anywhere where the police might find me, because I am a fugitive. I need to find my way, as unobtrusively as possible, to a hiding place, and I need to do everything I can to make myself safe. I am beyond starving. My stomach is digesting itself, in a roar of angry acid.

I feel in my pocket for the photo of the boys. The one thing that will keep me going.

It has gone. It must be lying, abandoned, trampled by strangers' feet, on the bus, or on a pavement. My boys. This pushes me to the edge, and I hyperventilate and stop walking. I give up.

But I cannot give up. There is no easy option. If there was a policeman in front of me, I would surrender myself gratefully and ask him to deport me. They could do what they wanted to me.

My feet keep going, though my mind is gone. The rickshaws don't stop for me any more. I walk straight ahead, noticing my surroundings with a vague, drifting lack of interest. I am on a busy road. It is filled with people and, as before (but differently), none of them is concerned with me. I observe as my trembling legs negotiate uneven pavements, walking in the road, dodging around cows and food stalls. My legs are shaking wildly, and I start to stumble.

There is a man up ahead, selling pakora and other things. The smell hits me in the stomach. I gaze at the wares. They look greasy. They smell like the nectar of heaven itself. I pause, knowing that one of them would cost almost nothing, and that it would give me the energy I need to keep going a while longer. The stall-holder smiles, and gestures to his wares with a sweeping hand.

I stare more, then shake my head.

'No money,' I tell him.

'Five rupee,' he says. I shake my head. I should have got some change from the bus driver. I start to walk away, and he runs after me, and hands me a single deep-fried piece of vegetable. I cannot even find the words to thank him. I nibble it, trying to make it last.

The fog is closing around me, so I can see nothing but the pavement immediately in front of me. I have no idea of what I am doing, no control over myself. I carry on walking because there is nothing else to do. I have lost my boys. There is not much point in anything.

After several hours, or five minutes, I see a telephone centre.

I stand outside for a while, staring in, watching a woman laughing on the phone. This is what I have to do. It is the only thing I can possibly do.

I tell the piece of pakora in my stomach to give me the strength, and I take a deep breath, and attempt to stride in there. I try to pretend that I am not wearing the same stinky clothes I was wearing when I bedded down in a boggy forest, that I have not dodged police, hacked my way through undergrowth and ridden on a random bus to get here. I try not to look like someone who was so pitied by a street food seller that he gave me the single morsel that is sustaining me.

I draw myself up to my full height, and announce, in my poshest voice, that I would like to make a collect call to London, if you please.

The British ring tone is so comforting that it almost breaks me. After four rings, I know that Max is not answering. After six, my own voice cuts in, speaking across the weeks, over the chasm. The kiosk man immediately hangs up, and tries to get me to pay him fifty rupees for the connection. I apologise, and run away.

If I could find my way to the Shiva Hotel, I could, at the very least, jump into their pool and clean myself. I have not the faintest idea where it is, or how to get there. It is almost dark, but in the city, that doesn't matter like it did at the ashram.

I walk in what I guess might be the right direction (it is *a* direction, anyway, so better than standing still), through areas that are busy and bustling, and others that are quieter. In the quiet ones, I feel conspicuous, but no one pays me much attention. A few beggars call out. I look at them, at their arms and legs that are nothing but bone.

After a while, a rickshaw slows to walking pace beside me.

'Rickshaw, madam?' asks the driver.

'I have no money,' I tell him. 'I mean, look at me.'

'Where you going?'

'Shiva Hotel.'

He nods. 'OK, no problem. Forty rupees. You pay me at hotel.'

This is tempting. I shake my head.

'I have no money at the hotel either.'

This confuses him. I imagine asking the hotel reception to lend me forty rupees. I see myself through their eyes. They wouldn't dream of it. I try to think of anyone who might lend me money. I could try. I could run around the public areas, looking for backpackers, pleading with them. Forty rupees is fifty pence. I would give it to me, if I were them. I think I would, at least.

I can't take a ride from this man without the money to pay him. I am defeated. A part of me knows that I am sabotaging myself. I should take the ride and find a way to pay when I get there. I should do whatever it takes to pull myself out of this hole.

The driver is eyeing me thoughtfully.

'I take you to Shiva Hotel,' he says. 'No money, no problem. On the way we stop at shop. You clean your face first. You look. No buy anything . . .'

In spite of everything, I burst out laughing.

'You're a genius,' I tell him. The energy comes from somewhere. 'Let's do it. How long do I have to stay there before they give you your commission?'

He considers this. 'Fifteen minute.'

'Deal. Then straight to the Shiva.'

'Very good.'

I am surprised they let me into the splendid handicrafts emporium, because I am beginning to smell myself. I borrow the rickshaw's rear-view mirror, vaguely surprised that it has such a thing, and clean my face as best I can. The driver gives me an elastic band which was hanging around his rear-view mirror, and I scrape my hair back properly and tie it severely in place, which immediately makes me less of a wild woman. I make an effort with yoga posture, and appropriate the manner of Margaret Thatcher in her prime. My legs are still shaking, and I am desperate with thirst, but I know I can pull this off.

As I step through the door, and the air conditioning hits me like a block of ice, I look at a green clock that hangs above the counter. It says it is five past five. I will stay until twenty past.

I nod graciously and peruse the tinny jewellery, the swathes of cloth, the model elephants. I stand back so they don't suspect that I spent the night on the run from the law, and allow the staff to show me random items. I look at every stall, admire every object presented to me, and go so far as to inquire about the price of a pale pink pashmina. We are starting some negotiations when I break off and ask if I may come back in the morning with my husband. Then I beat a hasty retreat, as exactly fifteen minutes have passed.

'Where your husband?' the driver asks as we bump through the traffic towards the hotel.

'In London. And my children. I have to get back to my children. I have to leave India but I don't think I can.'

'What age?'

'Six and three.'

'Boy girl?'

'Two boys.'

'Very lucky.'

It is a blow to the stomach.

'Yes. Very lucky.'

'Why you no money?' He turns around to ask this question. I look away.

266

'Actually,' I say, on a sudden impulse. 'Could you take me to the Kapaleeshwarar Temple instead?'

'Best of luck,' he says, and pulls up right in front of Ethan.

He does not look at all surprised to see me in this state.

'Oooooh,' he says, when I sit next to him. 'She sits without being asked, now. She's making herself at home.' He is still twitching and spasming away, laughing at something I cannot see.

'What should I do?' I ask him. 'You know this city. You survive with no money. I need to get hold of my husband but he's not answering the phone and I can't reverse charges to a mobile. I haven't eaten for days. I'm going to pass out if I don't get water. The police are after me although I haven't done anything wrong. But I have done things that are stupid. Very much so.'

'Stupid?'

'Yes. But Ethan, where do you get food from? I have to know. I have to sort this mess out and I can't do anything in this state.'

He is looking at me, interested now. I lean towards him, and rest my head on his shoulder, just for a moment. He stretches his arm round and ruffles my hair.

'India got you?'

'Not India. India's been great. I love it.'

'Ha,' he says, and spits on the ground. 'You have no idea.'

I think about it. My experience of India has, I must admit, been sanitised, until yesterday at least.

'Do you think?'

'Oh, Christ. People like you. You come. You think you're "doing India". You hang out with white people and look for beggars because they fit the image you have of yourself, prancing around the poor people. You don't have any idea of what life is like in this shithole.'

'I guess not. But it's changed a bit for me now.'

He laughs loudly. 'You know how I know that? Because I was the same. Here.' He is holding out a fist. 'Have this. Like the parable of the fucking talents.'

I open my hand. 'What do you mean?'

'The Bible, my dear. Take this, and get food and water. Make the money grow.'

It is a fifty rupee note, folded into sixteenths. I unfold it and stare at him.

'I can't take money from *you*! Ethan, for fuck's sake. Where did you get this from?'

He giggles. 'You. Stashed as much as I could. You gave me four fifty, the first time? I saved the fifty. See, it's actually yours. Come, give it back when you can.'

I smile. 'Like that Hancock sketch. Where he gives blood in the morning and gets it back in the afternoon.'

. Ethan nods, probably a hundred times in quick succession. We are still leaning on each other. I hold my breath, lean upwards, and kiss him on the cheek. He recoils, and takes his arm away. I feel people looking at us, but I don't care.

By the time I reach the hotel, I have drunk a small bottle of water, and eaten three vegetable samosas, but I am desperate. I have five rupees left, and I am still starving. I remember myself at the Saravana Bhavan, and wish, madly, that I had stashed the third helping of curry into a napkin and hidden it somewhere in the hotel grounds.

All the same, I am free to roam the compound as I wish without anyone in authority having any idea that I am not a guest, let alone that I am penniless in the extreme and on the run from the law; purely because I am white.

I sit in the courtyard outside my old bedroom, and lean on the building, as darkness engulfs me. I notice an old mineral water bottle at the side of the building. It has a centimetre of liquid in the bottom. I smell it: it is not wee, so I drink it. It's hot, but it is water. My body instantly cries out, again, for more, much more.

I will target backpackers. I will borrow someone's phone and text Max.

There is no one by the pool, so I quickly take off my stinking clothes, and get in, in my underwear. It is blissful. I swim up and down, underwater, and get out refreshed. It is a shame to put my smelly clothes back on, so I give them a quick rinse first, and hope they will dry quickly. When I walk, I drip.

Darkness is descending, and all the lights are coming on. There are a couple of Westerners standing on the path that leads to the restaurant. I gather all my strength, and approach them. I stand back, hoping that, in the dusky light, they won't notice how weird I look. They are deep in conversation, speaking something that sounds like a Scandinavian language. They are in their late forties or fifties, and they have kind faces.

'Excuse me,' I say, dripping water on to the ground. 'Do you speak English?'

They both turn.

'Yes,' says the man, who has greyish hair, messy and wispy yet attractive, and round glasses. 'Of course,' he adds. They both look at me with unabashed curiosity, and something approaching disgust.

'Right. Well. I'm sorry to bother you. But, where to start. I'm in India.' Tears spring to my eyes, and I look around wildly, suddenly convinced the police are here. 'I nearly got arrested by police who thought I was trafficking children, I think, but they were wrong and I've had to come here to get help and call my husband . . .' I am distracted by their sceptical exchange of glances. I know I sound like a ranting madwoman. I am the precise embodiment of someone who has been on the road for too long, and who is delusional and desperate. I don't even believe my own story, though I have lived it. 'I have money and stuff, but it's all at the ashram and if I go back they'll take me to prison. So, what I need is a very small amount of cash for some food, and if you have a phone, I need to send a couple of texts. Is that possible? Is any of it *at all* possible?'

They look at each other, embarrassed. Eyes widen. I know that expression. I have been on their side of this transaction, many times, in London. I have walked away from sob stories, assuming that the person ranting needs the money for drugs. I would think that now, if I met me.

The woman rummages in her bag.

'We can give you some rupees,' she says. She hands me a fifty rupee note, the third that has saved me today. That covers the food and drink I need.

'Thank you!' I manage to say. I fight to control myself. 'Thank you so much!' I am crying and don't bother to hide it.

'Though if what you say is true,' says the man, 'you must contact your British Embassy.'

'I know.'

I run into the foyer. For some reason, now that I have a tiny bit of money (and fifty rupees translates as about sixty pence), I dare to approach them. Max has to be at home by now. He must be. If he isn't, I am lost. If he doesn't answer the phone, I will go back to Ethan, and sleep on the pavement, next to him.

'Can I make a call and reverse the charges?' I ask. I am no longer dripping, but I am very wet.

'Good evening, madam.'

'Good evening. Can I make a call and reverse the charges?'

The man tuts at this annoyance. 'For this, you need the telephone kiosk,' he says.

'Is there one at the hotel?' I know the answer.

'No, madam.' He gestures in the vague direction of across the road and down the road, around some potholes and under the flyover.

'This is an emergency. I am in a lot of trouble. I need to telephone my husband in England. I need to call the British Consul. I will reverse the charges for all the calls. So if you let me use that phone there,' I point at it, it stands big and black and shiny behind the desk, old-fashioned, with a dial, 'it won't cost you anything.'

'British Deputy High Commission may not accept reverse-the-charges,' he objects.

'But my husband will,' I tell him, 'so *he* can call the High Commission, if he wants to.'

'This is a business line. In constant use.'

I stare pointedly at it, willing it not to ring. It doesn't. I look back at him, eyebrows raised.

He sighs and motions me around to his side of the desk. He pushes the phone as far to the side as he can. I count six heavy books with entries made in fountain pen. There are stacks of paperwork everywhere. Everything about this place is reassuring, but I remind myself not to tell him that I'm hiding from the police. He would call them, because he is not necessarily on my side.

He dials a number, and hands over the receiver.

'International operator,' he says. 'Free call.'

I get the operator to place the call to London, and channel all my energy into willing Max to pick up the phone. Every ounce of my spirit goes into this. Everything depends on it. This is the biggest crossroads of all: if he answers, things will be all right. If he doesn't, they won't.

By the time it has rung four times, I know that I am lost. The flat is not that big. It is still half-term: he is out with Sarah. After six rings, the machine gets it. My own voice greets me once more, from five thousand miles to the west, a million years ago. I wait for Max to pick up. He doesn't. He wouldn't. He is not at home.

I know that the operator won't let me leave a message, because even though it's my voice at the end of the line, I can't accept the charges from this end of the call. I hang up before she comes back.

'No one there,' I say. I feel sick. I know, in this moment, that I have lost everything. I can blame Elly, blame Anjali, blame Max, but the truth is, I did this to myself. There is no going back from this: I am going to turn myself in, and go to prison, or else try to forge a life on the street. It will have to be prison.

I used to think I was unhappy. Now that it is too late, I can see that I had no idea, none at all.

The man is looking at me with something approaching sympathy, and I realise that this may be because I have tears pouring down both cheeks. I ignore them, and try to keep a safe distance away from him, because in a minute he is going to see beyond my white skin, and notice that I am scum. I lean on a wall and sob.

'I will telephone your Embassy, madam,' he says. He takes out a large telephone directory. This might be the worst thing to do. It might be the only thing to do.

'No,' I say. 'Don't.' I cannot think straight, but I might be better off with Ethan than behind bars. I will sleep on the street, and then see what happens.

At first I think I am imagining it. Then the voice comes again.

'Tansy?' it says. It is a voice that is so familiar that I wonder, for a fraction of a second, whether it is my own.

Nobody can be saying my name. No one in the world knows that I am here.

He says it again. 'Tansy!'

I take my hands away from my face. I am not imagining it.

It is not my voice, not the voice of anyone in India.

I look up, slowly, incredulous. I am standing behind the desk like a stinking, wailing receptionist in the very worst hotel in the world. The seconds stretch out as my brain makes the connection.

It cannot be Max standing on the other side of the desk. I look at him, at his expensive travelling clothes, black T-shirt and beige Palinesque trousers. I look down at his Reef sandals, and up to his hair which, as ever, needs a cut and is in danger of betraying its natural springiness. It cannot be him, but it is someone who looks very much like him.

He is looking at me with concern, and suspicion, and absolute confusion.

'Max?' I whisper. 'Real Max?'

He smiles. 'Yes,' he says. 'Real Max.'

'What are you doing here?'

'I heard a rumour that you might be in need of a little help.'

'What? By magic?' The world goes blotchy, and the blotches merge into one another, and it is all black. I hold on to the edge of the reception desk, while the high-pitched ringing sounds in my ears. Max is beside me in a moment, taking my shoulders, leading me carefully to the benches where I first spoke to Amber and Sam, where a woman took my photograph because she loved my trousers.

He lies me down along the bench. He holds a water bottle to my lips, and although it spills all over the seat and the floor, enough goes into my mouth to revive me, very slightly.

'Are you staying here?' I ask him.

'I came to get a room. Then I met the new receptionist. She looked familiar but a bit less happy than I was hoping. I was going to use it as a base tonight and spend the evening on the phone trying to work out what in the name of holy fuck is going on.'

'Get a room now,' I tell him. 'And some food. And then talk to me.'

He touches my face. I close my eyes, and reach up, and take his hand. We stay like that, holding on to each other. Then he leans forward, and kisses my cheek. I grab him around the neck and hold him close. After a few minutes, he gently unpeels my fingers, and I vaguely hear him checking into the hotel.

chapter forty-five

When I wake up, he is talking on the landline in our bedroom. I come round gradually, amazed at the way I feel. I am not hungry. I am clean. I have slept, in a bed. The things that I used to take for granted, every single day of my life, are an unimaginable luxury. But I am not out of the woods. Max has no idea of how much trouble I am in.

The daylight is peeking around the edge of the flimsy curtains. The ceiling fan is dusty. This is not the same room I stayed in before, but it might as well be.

'Room forty-one,' he is saying. 'Thanks. See you in a minute.'

'See who in a minute?' I ask, nervous.

'See the room service guy who's bringing breakfast.'

'Oh. Good.'

He smiles. I smile back. He sits on the edge of the bed.

'Now,' he says gently. 'You didn't make a massive amount of sense last night. In fact you made none at all. Shall we start from the beginning?'

'Tell me about the boys. I've had their photo in my pocket all the time. But I lost it. I lost it. In the woods or on the bus. I miss seeing them.' I sniff, and make an effort to control myself.

When Max looks at me, there is so much in his eyes that it makes me nervous, because I know there is a lot he is not saying to me.

'Toby and Joe are absolutely fine,' he says firmly. 'They're staying with your dad and Lola. First day back after half-term today.'

274

'Is it?'

'And they'll be having a ball. Honestly, they will.' He looks at me sideways. 'They're both kind of excited that I've come to get you. You will come back?'

I blink, and make an effort to control myself.

'There's nothing I'd like more,' I say in a tight voice. 'Nothing. But I'm not sure I'm allowed, Max. I don't know when I'm going to get out of here and I don't know . . .' I hiccup and sniff, 'when I'll get to see them again. And all the time I was with them, I was always thinking about going away and now I'm so far from them and I can't see them any more and they'll forget about me and grow up all screwed up because their mother abandoned them, and I don't mean to, I really don't. You can't even bring them to see me in prison because I can't bear for them to see me like that, I'd rather they got on with their lives without that . . .' I watch my husband force a reassuring smile. He shuffles up close to me and puts his arm around my shoulder. I lean on his, just as I did with Ethan yesterday.

'So, tell me all of it again, and this time tell it in a way that allows me to know just exactly what the hell you're talking about. Specifically, tell me who these people are: Anjali, Amber, Ethan. You've mentioned them in emails, but I never really worked it out.'

'First of all,' I say, 'you have to tell me how you did this. How did you manage to turn up, here?

'Because when I read your email, all about how we have to adopt this kid, I thought something was a bit weird. I mean, they sent you to pick her up? And didn't tell you there was going to be a child? I felt you were being a little, well, blinkered, and I thought you were seeing the best in Elly while she clearly had an agenda. I was worried you were getting caught up in something you shouldn't be.

'But *then*, then I had a phone call which changed everything. I discovered that you were on the run from the police and that you were in the woods, and no one had seen you for hours. So I called work, called Lola, and got out here as fast as British Airways would allow me to.'

I feel sick. In fact I might be sick at any moment. All the same, I force myself to ask the question.

'Who called you?' I say

'Your very best friend.'

'Sarah?'

He laughs. 'Of course not Sarah, you idiot. Elly.'

'Elly? Where is she? What did she say?'

He looks grim. 'Almost nothing, is what she said. That you were in trouble, that you'd run away when you hadn't been supposed to, that you needed rescuing. And she said to tell you she's sorry and she had no other options.'

'What has she done?'

'We'll get to that. Over to you.'

I tell Max what I think has happened: Elly and Anjali were rescuing children with a flimsy cover story. I was, apparently, the only person who was stupid enough to believe it. They set me up when they knew the net was closing on them, diverted the upcoming raid to me, and did a runner. That is all we know.

We agree to take a break for an hour. We go out into the city, and for a wonderful, brief time, it feels as if everything is all right. Ganesh takes us to Peters Road, where we duck into a completely random café and sit opposite each other, at a rickety wooden table, and drink three cups of chai each.

Max grins. 'India, hey?' he says. There are other customers coming and going. A very young-looking white man with a backpack comes in and sits at the table nearest us. A man and a woman sit in a corner and have an argument. A tortoiseshell kitten cowers in a corner.

'You said it would be full of hassle,' I remind him. 'It wasn't.'

'I think the south is a bit different,' he says. 'Or maybe things have changed. But, to be fair, you have managed to create your own hassle. We'd better go to the Embassy.'

We have been having this conversation over and over again.

'But I *can't*,' I remind him. 'They'll arrest me.' Tears spring to my eyes again. It is all too much: nothing can change the fact that I ran away from a policeman. Nothing could implicate me quite as much as that does. Yet again, I travel back in time, and stem my urge to flee. I let the thin policeman arrest me. I handle it all like a grown-up.

'They won't arrest you. They might have to tell the authorities, and that would be fine, because it would give you the opportunity to set things straight.'

'I can't. Let's go this afternoon.'

Max sighs. 'We could just try leaving, you know. There's every chance you'll just saunter through passport control.'

'There's every chance I *won't*. My passport is at the ashram, along with everything else I had with me.'

We walk back to the hotel. As I duck on to the road, shake off rickshaw drivers, gratefully ignoring all passers-by, my paranoia begins to grow. By the time I reach the Shiva, I am expecting to be carted off in chains the moment I step across the threshold. I cannot go on like this. I have got Max back, and I am about to be separated from him by handcuffs, locked doors, visiting hours.

Max stops to pick up some water at the stall by the swimming pool.

I step into the room, kick aside the newspaper that is pushed under the door every morning, and switch the fan on. The walls start to close in.

I remember being in Pondy, having lunch with an ex-policeman, who said he 'kept his hand in'. He is the only option I can think of. There is a telephone directory in the room, but it doesn't cover Pondicherry.

I call directory inquiries, and soon a phone is ringing at Brian Thevar's house.

'Good morning?'

I cannot say anything. The ceiling fan seems to speed up, and the walls creep closer.

'Hello?' he barks. 'Is there somebody on the line?'

But he was kind to me. I liked him. We talked about Monty Python.

'Hello?'

He is about to hang up.

'Hello,' I say quietly. 'Brian?'

'Yes, Brian speaking. Who is this?'

'We met in a café in Pondicherry. I had a little girl with me.'

'Tansy!' He is speechless for a few seconds, then recovers himself. 'Goodness gracious, Tansy. Is it really you?'

'Yes.'

He whistles. 'What has happened to you?'

'Brian, do you know what's going on?'

'Of course. You should have stayed to face the music. What on earth have you been up to? You are still in the woods? Mobile telephone?'

I sigh. Of course I could not expect a retired policeman to come riding to my rescue.

'No. Just tell me, am I in a lot of trouble?'

'You ran away. This was unwise. Where did you get to?'

'I can't tell you where I am. Brian, I just need to know what's going on.'

'Can you meet me in Pondy?'

'Not really.'

'Same place as before?'

I laugh, although it's not funny. 'Probably not, you know. What would happen if I tried to leave the country?'

'Do not do that.'

'Brian, I didn't do anything wrong. I didn't know I was doing anything wrong.'

'Oh, I know that.'

'You *know*?'

'Have you seen the newspaper?'

'No. Why?' I stretch the phone cord, and reach for it with my foot. I bring it closer, and pick it up.

We drive south in considerably more comfort than I enjoyed on my ride north. I cannot stop looking at him. We talk, nervously, about how we have missed one another, how I have missed the children, how the boys have missed me. There is too much to say; and this is not the time to say it.

'How's Sarah?' I ask. I watch his reaction. He doesn't meet my eye.

'She's all right,' he mutters, and looks away, out of the window.

'Hey, look, Dizzee World. I went there once. I can't believe Disney haven't sued them in the past ten years.'

Finally, we reach the outskirts of Pondy.

'So, here we are,' Max says lightly. 'Journey's end.'

We look at each other, and smile, but not with happiness. I reach tentatively across the back seat and take Max's hand. He squeezes mine. I close my eyes.

Two hours later, I am quaking in front of a police officer. Everything is old-fashioned and bureaucratic. There are stamps and ink pads, carbon copied documents, computers and mobile phones.

'And that's it,' Max confirms with him. 'A fine.'

'A hefty one,' he tells Max. The policeman is tall and thin. I have not worked out whether he is the same man I ran away from but I think he might be. He is pleased to be able to sort this out with my husband, rather than with the untrustworthy, impulsive woman who ran away into the woods and took days to emerge.

'Do you take Visa?' Max asks him, taking out his wallet.

As soon as I saw the paper, with its blurred photograph of the deserted Children's Centre, our poster still forlornly promising a performance of a play about a bear, I realised that, in spite of everything, it was going to be all right.

'Ashram leaders abscond with children,' said the headline. I was, it turned out, a bit-part player. Elly and the enigmatic Anjali knew the police were watching their adoption racket. They set me up to collect Sasika and her bundle of forged paperwork from the orphanage, set up poor Alexia and Duncan, who thought they were adopting her, and anonymously alerted the authorities about our 'transaction', heaping all the blame on to me. While the entire police operation was focused on the moment when I handed over poor little Sasika, they gathered up every single one of the other children and disappeared with them.

Brian, it turned out, had long had suspicions about the CC. In fact, I am the only one who didn't. That was why he spent his free time visiting, checking it out. He knew the children were being whisked away to new families and, unlike me, he was never taken in by the story about them going to live with distant relatives.

'No one in their right minds could have believed that,' he laughed. 'It was a cover story, just to give everyone something to say. Everybody knew. You know, the orphange conditions? It makes it easy to turn a blind eye. You were turning a blind eye too, Tansy.'

I let him think I was. I suppose I was, subconsciously.

I remember Elly talking about earthly laws, and about the way people like me can always use our natural privileges to get away with things. She left enough evidence, once they broke into the Children's Centre and checked her email account, to exonerate me entirely; and she called Max when she heard, from Helga (who was entirely in on it), that I had run off. Sasika has been placed in a children's home that is on the 'Cara' list, approved for adoption. I hope she will be out of there soon: I have the name of the orphanage, and I vow to check on her, to send her money. Perhaps, even, to try for an international adoption; stranger things have happened. The American couple are going to be allowed home, but they will be banned from India for ever.

And Elly, Anjali, and the children have all vanished, into thin air.

'On this matter,' says Brian, 'she covered her tracks nicely. She was extremely careful. We have no clue where they are, except that we can find no evidence of this number of children leaving on a flight. They will not be able to stay hidden for long.'

As we stand outside the police station, I lean over and kiss Brian on the cheek. He looks embarrassed.

'Thanking me is unnecessary,' he says. 'Now, you must go to the ashram and fetch your belongings. Then you must go home to your sons.'

As we stand in the guest-house courtyard, Nick wanders over.

'Hello there,' he says. 'You're back.'

'Nick,' I say. 'This is Max.'

He laughs. 'Mr Tansy?'

'I suppose I would answer to that,' says Max, 'if I had to.'

'Mucho respect to you,' Nick says. 'I understand you live with her.'

'Have you seen Amber?' I ask him.

'Not a sign of her. She left just after you did, managed to sneak away. I must say,' he tells Max, 'it is a great pleasure to meet you. Your wife has been, erm, entertaining us here at the Peaceful Haven. She's a feisty one.'

'Tell me about it,' Max agrees.

chapter forty-six

The guest house is small, cheap, and almost empty. We have a little suite: two bedrooms and a sitting room with a map of India on the wall and a television in the corner.

Up close, the laminated map makes me realise how right Ethan was. I have barely skated on India's surface. I know now more than I did when we arrived about the lives of Indian people. I know that a huge proportion of people are malnourished, but the only malnourished person I spoke to was a white man. I have meandered along among the well-dressed rich people of Chennai, and run around panicking, while life went on around me.

I put my finger on the map.

'Pondicherry,' I say. I move my finger slightly away from it, to approximately where I think the ashram must be. Then I shift it to the deep countryside, so I am pointing at a spot that represents Sam's village. I imagine that Amber has gone there. I look at Mamallapuram, Chennai. Madurai, where I thought I was, for twenty miserable minutes. Goa. Mumbai up above it. There are Delhi, Rajastan, Agra, Amritsar, Dharamsala.

Then, in between, is the bulk of unknown, mysterious India. I run my finger over the names of random cities. Jabalpur. Hyderabad. Ranchi. I have barely heard of these places. I can see how arrogant I was, to think that India was backpackers and poverty, to have framed it in terms that were so convenient to me. India is vast and I am completely on its periphery. Just a tourist, a tiny speck landing, momentarily, on an enormous, mind-blowing whole. And yet, in my skewed, negligible way, I have ended up where I wanted to be. This is Pondicherry; and this is me and Max. This is where our life together could have started; and it may be where our life together is about to end.

I am in limbo. I spoke to the boys, earlier, sounding as casual and upbeat as I can.

'How was the first day back?' I asked Toby.

'Fine,' he said.

'Was Mr Trelawney there?'

'Of course he was, Mum! When are you and Dad coming back?'

'Soon,' I told him. 'Very soon.'

Joe, as ever, just said 'Mummy' several times, before handing the phone to Lola. I ached to feel him, solid and loving, in my arms.

'They are fine,' she insisted. 'You and Max have a second honeymoon. Enough with your travelling on your own. Don't neglect your husband. Pay him attention.'

Max comes through the main door to the sitting room, holding a clinking carrier bag.

We sit on the tiny balcony, sharing a big bottle of Kingfisher. I remind myself, over and over again, that I must not drink to the point of oblivion. I have to practise the moderation thing again. It is the only way to handle tonight.

'What?' he asks. 'Why are you making that funny face?'

'What do I look like?'

He purses his lips and frowns.

'Oh, a good look. Sorry.'

'What was it for?'

'It was to remind me not to get pissed tonight.'

'Oh. Well, then that's good. You can keep doing it, if you like.'

'I haven't had a drink for ages,' I remind him, slightly stung.

We have crammed two plastic chairs outside; there is no room for anything else. For a moment I wonder whether the balcony is strong enough: I picture the two of us crashing down, beers in hand, still sitting in our chairs, ending up sitting in exactly the same tableau on the pavement below.

'If any masonry cracks,' I tell him, 'we go back in.'

'Deal.'

'Quickly.'

'Sounds like a plan.'

This is how we used to live, when we met. We have not done anything like it since we had the boys. I want to ask Max whether he has missed it, now that he is back.

The air is balmy, the darkness belying the fact that it is only nine o'clock. This is the first time that we have not been able to distract ourselves from the elephant in the room that is our relationship.

A rickshaw passes; I watch its dim headlights approach, and then disappear down the street.

'So,' says Max. 'Here we are.'

'How were your work?'

He shrugs. 'Fine. I didn't give them a choice. What are they going to do? I was hardly not going to come, when you need me, because someone says there's no I in team.'

I smile at him, tentatively.

'I can't believe I got into such a mess,' I tell him. 'And I'm still not sure what happened. Why didn't I spend five days at the ashram, and then get the hell out of there?'

He looks sceptical. 'Because you were with one of your *very best friends*.' His voice is heavy with irony.

I lean back in my chair. 'I think Elly and Anjali think they're working for the greater good, you know. I do. You didn't see the place where Sasika came from. You look at that, and then at their CC, and the difference is . . . well, it's immense. There can't be anything wrong with taking a child from one to the other. They want what's best for the children, and they'll do whatever they have to do to get there. Wherever those children are, I bet they end up being adopted and having good lives.'

'Tossers. I think you're too trusting. God only knows how much money you can get for fifteen Indian kiddies with no families. The adoption thing, we know now that they've been doing that for a while. Scooping children from the orphanages and faking up papers for them – all for the greater good of humanity. God knows how long they've got away with it. And do you think they vet the families? Or do you think they process the paperwork for anyone who emails and says they want to adopt a little girl? Don't be naive. They'd have sold a kid to anybody, no questions asked, and their life would not necessarily have been better.

'Shit hit the fan with those Americans, and Elly wanted it to. You must admit, that's not the behaviour of an idealist. She actually told the police that you were trafficking a little girl, and then she fucked off, and let it happen. And yes, she called me, but so she fucking should have done. Now she's Christ only knows where with all those other kids.' He puts a hand to his head. 'And Tansy. I've been trying to avoid this part. But a lot of this is my fault.'

'Oh, shut up. How could it be? Look, if fifteen children get homes out of it, then perhaps it has been worthwhile. In spite of everything. Really – you didn't see that orphanage, Max.'

'If it made even you want another kid, I can imagine it was bad. But what if fifteen kids *don't* get homes out of it? What if they get something worse?' He pauses. 'But, yes, if you're being nice, then the adoption situation from India seems very complex, a bureaucratic nightmare, in fact. And particularly after the tsunami, of course there are hundreds of children in this area holed up in horrible conditions. If they made any attempt to vet the families, then sure. But Tans, you're not listening to me. I'm trying to confess something.'

'What are you talking about?'

'I'm trying to tell you. Did you ever wonder why Elly contacted you out of the blue like that, asking you to drop everything and fly in to help the babies?'

I look at him, curious. 'Well, I assume, now, that it was because she wanted me to play my part in her dastardly plot.' I look down. 'I was going to bring two of the children to England, you know. I actually offered.'

'Oh, don't tell me. I do not want to know.'

'The children. I'd have done anything. So, carry on.'

Max sighs. He shifts his chair a little closer to mine, and puts a hand on my thigh.

'Obviously, had I had the slightest idea . . . You weren't happy.

You were drinking too much and I didn't know what to do about it. I couldn't bear to tell you to go to rehab, or march you to AA, but that's what everyone was telling me to do. Not just your dad and Lola. Everyone. And I knew you'd been thinking about Asia, and you always wanted to come back here. So I, well, I wrote to Elly and asked her if she could use your help. She said,' he winces, 'that of course she could. But I said it had to come from her, and you must never, ever know that it was me. I'm sorry. I'm not sure I've ever made this bad a call before. I mean, you've made some bad ones, but I started it.'

I stare at him. '*You?* You're behind it all?'

He looks miserable. 'I thought it might be just the thing you needed. Even in London, I could see at once it was a mistake, because all of a sudden you got a thousand times worse. You stopped sleeping. The drinking got worse. You became fixated on the idea of us all going, which wasn't what I'd had in mind at all.'

My head is spinning. 'Elly must have thought it was Christmas when she got your mail.'

'I know.'

'I did wonder why she'd summoned me so urgently, and when I turned up she wasn't even there. I spent most of my time doing yoga and reading books to the children. She obviously *didn't* need me urgently, like she'd said.' I look at him. 'It's all right, though.' I put the beer bottle down. I don't want any more. 'It kind of worked. Drink-wise. In spite of everything, I had an amazing time.'

'I'm proud of you for that.'

'Do you think we'll hear from her again?'

'No.'

I shift my chair closer to his, which is difficult, and listen to the sound of an unlit, invisible motorbike going along the street below. I need to confess something now.

'Um,' I say, as casually as I can. 'When I was in Mamallapuram, I heard a rumour, by text, that the word at school is that you and I had split up.' I look at Max's face, and then away. I have to do this.

'And who texted you that school-based rumour?' Max asks. 'Actually, let me hazard a guess. Jim Trelawney, by any chance?'

I look down. 'What makes you . . . ?'

He sighs. 'I asked Elly to mail me from time to time, because I was outrageously anxious about you. She asked me if I knew that you had a thing for Toby's teacher. Filled me in a bit. I think the thing with Elly is that she really, really doesn't care. Her mind is elsewhere. She did add that you were feeling very bad about it, which was nice. But not bad enough to stop texting. Apparently he's been telling all your news to anyone who'll listen. Seems you tell him rather more than you tell me.'

I am horrified. I have no idea what to say.

'Nothing to add?' Max asks mildly.

'I do not tell him more than I tell you! I text him one or two sentences from time to time. That's all. It's nothing. What else did Elly say?' I swallow and look out into the night. By the dim light of a street lamp, I can see a woman sitting in a doorway opposite. She is swathed in light-coloured fabric and I cannot see how old she is.

Max's voice is tight. 'What do you think?'

'Don't know.'

'I'm sure you could guess.'

A car speeds down the street and away. There is a distant hooting of horns. After what feels like hours, Max sighs.

'Apparently, you've had a crush on him for months.' His voice is expressionless. 'You kissed him in the classroom. If you hadn't come away, you'd have had a full-blown affair. You love him because he's everything you want me to be. It was a bit of an eye-opener.'

I turn to stone. I know what Max has done. He came to India to rescue me. Now that I am safe, he is going to leave me. And who can blame him? I notice that I am furious with Elly, but I do not even have time to process that now. I will get to it later; she is no friend of mine, and I will never have anything to do with her again.

'I didn't do anything,' I say. 'It was nothing. Nothing at all. Just a friend – someone I could talk to. I used to wish he was female so I could be his friend and no one would think anything of it.'

'Apart from when you were kissing him.'

'Only once.'

'Yes?'

I have to tell the truth. 'Yes. Of course only once. It was the biggest mistake I've ever made. I called him the other day when he asked if we'd split up. He was in bed with a woman. Honestly. There's nothing there.'

Max looks at me. He doesn't have to say anything. I swallow and blink back the tears.

There is only one thing I can do. I put my beer bottle down and sit up straight.

'Look,' I say. 'This is how it happened. I went to the school gates one day, and I saw a man who reminded me of you, long ago.'

I sit in the Indian night and tell my husband everything.

chapter forty-seven

Alexia's thoughts

Well it has just been such a whirlwind. I hardly know where to start. This is still Dee, by the way.

I was beginning to despair for her. I mean, they do have a legal system here, but it's not the same as ours, although, when I made some angry comment about the Mickey Mouse way things are done, Rajiv took exception and explained to me about India's legal system, and how it is extremely thorough. And, you know what, I can see that he's right. Everything takes a long time and is thought through very carefully. Which is not, in fact, great for people like Alexia and Duncan.

I went to see them every day, of course. She stopped even looking at me. She was like a shell of a person. She had been so happy, so full of optimism, when she set off, and we had all prepared one enormous celebration for when they got back – we couldn't wait to welcome Sasika into the family.

And it was just breaking my heart more each day, the sight of her in there. Duncan was doing a lot better. We would go to see him too, George and me, and he was so mad with it all. I think it kept him going. He swore and stamped around and ranted and raved. It was a different side of Duncan – Duncan had never left the States before this (he says he never will again). He was always such a homebody. His world was Alexia, the garage, his friends. He's not really prison material, but he did well. The last time I saw him, he was even speaking a little of the local language, Tamil.

Anyway, this was going on, and to be honest I was becoming scared. Rajiv said it would be months before their case came to trial. I did not really relish the idea of staying in Chennai for months, visiting the two prisons every day. Also, George was accompanying me, and I knew that was beyond his remit, really, and that soon he would stop. I love his company and was dreading doing it all on my own, when my own sister won't even speak.

George is a lovely guy, and (I feel bad to admit this) he has been showing me a few of the sights of Chennai in the evenings. The part I feel bad about is that it has opened my eyes, and if I were here in different circumstances, I feel I would absolutely damn love it. We've been to Pizza Hut (a small taste of home!), as well as to some Indian restaurants. It's mostly vegetarian around here – George says that even the restaurants that have 'non veg' written by the door are unlikely to serve actual meat. And this seems to have meant that my stomach has not suffered KNOCK ON WOOD. It's hard to find a drink, but George knows where to go, and has shown me some bars that are, frankly, a hell of a lot more pleasant than the ones at home.

So anyway, you don't want to hear about my evenings out in Chennai, do you. Here is what happened: Rajiv called me at the hotel, totally unexpectedly, yesterday afternoon. 'I have good news for you, Miss Dee,' he said. 'There have been developments.'

The developments turn out to be fabulous ones. The police have checked through the women's paperwork at the ashram place, and have discovered what was really going on. They set the whole Sasika thing up as a diversion while they whisked fifteen other children out of the country. Luckily for all of us, although I would happily see them strung up, they left evidence to show that Alexia and Duncan thought they had the right paperwork – it was all found, faked up, on a computer.

As for where those other little kids are – who knows? Poor little things. I am trying to believe that they have gone on to a better life in loving homes somewhere, but really, I'm not sure. Rajiv says the net is closing on them.

So the upshot is, Rajiv and George pushed for an emergency hearing for Alexia and Duncan, and even the clunky old Indian system managed to hold one. They were dragged up in front of a judge, Alexia under instructions to look at him and to force herself to say something, and Duncan told strictly not to say too much, and not to curse. The judge was OK. He said they'd been a bit stupid (that wasn't his exact words) and that they must pay a fine and never come to India again. Duncan shouted something at that point. And then the judge let them go, and said they would be escorted to the airport tomorrow and put on the plane. Guess who was left to sort out the money for the fine.

So, we are off. Tomorrow. Alexia and Duncan are here at the hotel. I looked in on them earlier. Duncan was sleeping. Alexia was still staring into space. I tried to talk to her. 'Honey,' I said. 'It's over. You're going home.' Even then she didn't say anything. But just as I was giving up and going back to my own room to call George about the evening's arrangements, she said one thing, very quietly. She said: 'I held her.'

And I realised I have no idea what became of Sasika in all this.

chapter forty-eight

I am watching from the balcony, and when I see them coming along Rue Dumas, I turn to run downstairs and meet them. Although we arranged this by email, I still did not expect to see them, ever again.

I skip out on to the pavement, and hug Amber, and then Delphine, and then Sam. I look at Amber and Sam closely, trying to work out how things stand between then.

'Hey, Sam!' I say, and Sam smiles back. He seems different: more relaxed, at ease with himself in a way that he wasn't before.

'Hey, Tansy,' he says. 'You all right?'

'Yeah. Kind of. You?' I look at Amber, and back to Sam. 'So, you're not married or anything?'

Amber and Delphine laugh. Delphine is bouncing on the balls of her feet, probably planning her next move. She went and found Sam's village after she woke one morning and decided 'it was what I must do'.

'Of course I'm not married,' says Sam, chuckling. 'Fifteen-year-olds are not quite my thing. And anyway, I was already spoken for.' He and Amber look at each other and grin. 'And it's quite exciting to be out of Poosarippatti, actually, isn't it, Ambs? You know, you never quite appreciate the joys of the city until you've been somewhere else.'

'Yes,' I agree. 'Yes, I know exactly what you mean.'

'So,' says Amber. 'Everything's worked out? I have no idea how. You'll have to tell us everything.'

'What about you?' I demand. 'You have to tell me everything, too.'

'Oh, that's easy,' she says at once. 'I told the police I knew nothing. They believed me but asked me to stick around. I snuck off, which wasn't hard because at that point they discovered all the other children had gone. Showed all my cash to a taxi driver and negotiated a ride to Poosarippatti. It was the only place I could think of. I got there and felt a bit stupid getting out of the cab. I told him to wait until I'd found Sam. A couple of boys saw me and the next thing I knew, they'd run off and fetched him. And you know, it was so weird to see him in his village, surrounded by his family, who all look like him. And here's the thing I hadn't expected: they were absolutely truly lovely. They were all smiles, and all welcome, and I just succumbed completely. They fed me wonderful food and one of Sam's cousins gave me her bed, and they tried to speak English. I had the time of my life. Who would have thought it?'

I hug her, again. I cannot help it. She looks so much happier than she has ever looked before.

'And you?' I ask, looking at Sam.

'I did it,' he says happily. 'It feels weird that that should have been my life. But they're great. I mean, I was at home, straight away. And I'm going back there in a while. We're going to postpone Nepal for a while and go back and stay a bit longer. But nothing would have stopped Amber and me nipping back here to see you before you go home. We rode on the farmer's cart to the bus stop, you know.'

'And,' says Amber, 'you cannot imagine how much Sam's family love Delphine. They want to keep her for ever.'

I smile at Delphine. 'We all want to keep Delphine for ever,' I say.

'I thought you knew about the CC,' Delphine says suddenly. 'Is so clear. It is too plush, you know? They sell those children. I think you know that. I think everyone knows that.'

I wince. 'I didn't. I think I'm the only one who didn't work it out. Because I wanted everything Elly said to be true. I wanted it so much.'

We start walking towards the end of the road, and the sea. I hang back to talk to Sam.

'And you and Amber?' I ask.

He smiles. I can hear the waves crashing on the stony shore. 'Yeah, I know what you're saying. Amirtha was very sweet. Her mother will never speak to me again. When Amber turned up, it was like I had the old Amber back. She'd changed back to her real self. We're good. I mean, who knows? But for the moment things feel pretty solid. I think all the drama made her stop the fretting. She was really worried about you, but I told her you'd look after yourself. Anyway, where's your husband? I thought we were meeting him.'

I try to look unconcerned. 'He went to the botanical gardens. We're going home in a couple of days.'

I see Sam looking at me, and I look away. I try to look like someone who is going home to domestic stability and happiness. The main problem is, I don't know what that person would look like, and I am doing a fairly shoddy job of imitating her.

The four of us sit on the edge of the rough beach, and I wonder whether we look like real backpackers. Amber passes a water bottle along the line. She is holding her limbs out, optimistically, to the dark black clouds. The sea is high up the shore, and the air is so heavy you could puncture it with a pin and be drenched.

Suddenly I stand up. I cannot stay still right now.

'Hey, you guys,' I tell them. 'Come on. There's going to be a storm and we shouldn't be sitting on tsunami fucking beach.'

They look at me and stand up, like obedient children. I am not surprised: my humour and any personableness I have ever possessed has deserted me all of a sudden. I feel bleaker than I have for years. Max knows everything, and he marched off by himself to look at the flowers. I told him all about Jim, and he barely reacted. Everything is at stake, and his shutters are down.

I lead them to the café across the road, the place where I first met Brian.

'So,' says Amber as we dodge a couple of rickshaws to cross the road. 'When's Max going to be back? I want to meet him.

Otherwise we won't completely believe he exists. Although you spoke about him so much that I *feel* like I know him.'

I look at her. 'Did I?'

'Of course you did. And you slept with a photo of him under your pillow. I know you've had your problems lately, but you know they're trivial. I hope I end up with something like that, one day.' I see Sam looking at her, half amused. She smiles and looks down, coy.

'Really? Really really? You want to be like me and Max?'

She laughs. 'Yes.'

Sam speaks at the same time. 'Tansy, of course we bloody do, you idiot.'

chapter forty-nine

That afternoon, we are walking in Pondicherry, side by side, not going anywhere in particular. Max is telling me a long story about Joe and the lions at Longleat.

'And he said, Mr Lion – RAAAARGH!' he finishes. I smile and, as ever, try not to think about Joe. It tears me apart: Joe is the one who needs a mummy, and he has been soldiering on without me for too long. Toby has never had a proper mother. They seem like imaginary children now, like Elly's orphans, vanished into the ether. I cannot possibly have children who are actually mine, and be five thousand miles from them.

I look sideways at Max.

'What?' he says, with a little smile.

'You seem a little more friendly.'

He turns and looks at me, and this feels like the first eye contact we have had since we talked about Jim. The first honest eye contact. Something in me collapses in relief, and I bite my lip.

'I am a little more friendly,' he says. 'I'm sorry. I've been being a twat.'

'Don't be stupid. Are you permanently more friendly, or just because it makes life easier for now?'

Max clears his throat. We step out into the road to pass a group of people in robes. I notice a French school, over the road.

'Erm,' he says. 'You do realise that I'm not going to divorce you over one kiss, don't you?' I look down. I can feel the electric current of the pain it has taken him to say these words.

'I didn't realise that at all, no,' I say carefully. I think about it. 'But does that mean you're going to divorce me over something else?'

'I can see why you did it, in your own silly way. You know the most ridiculous thing of all? You were right. As soon as I got off the plane, I knew it.' He looks at me, and looks back at the pavement. I grab him by the arm, make him stop.

'Say that again,' I tell him. He looks down at me, and suddenly there is no one in the world but Max and me.

'I mean it,' he tells me, and he smiles with half his mouth. 'I'd made myself forget about the old backpacking life. I didn't really want to remember. I thought we'd made a good life in London and we should stick with it because, well, you know the reason. Even though the evidence that you were confined and miserable with it was staring me in the face. Even when I was plotting to get you over here and make you happy, I didn't remember just how amazing it is, what a privilege, to be able to get on the road.'

'Seriously?'

'And anyway, I've been struggling with something. It's not fair of me to let you tell me all the Jim stuff and not share this.'

'Do I want to know?'

'I don't think you do. But I have to tell you.'

'Do you completely have to?' I do not want to hear this, because I have an inkling that I know what it is going to be.

'Your thing with Jim,' he says. We are still standing, close together, on the pavement. People are walking around us and I hardly even notice. 'That knocked me for six. It happened under my nose and I didn't even notice. One evening, I was with you at home – I don't know what day it was, but I was – and you'd kissed another man. I know it would have been written all over your face, and I didn't even bloody notice. That showed me that if I didn't pay a little more attention to what you needed, then I would lose you. Maybe this is a male thing, but after I'd got past wanting to smash his fucking smug twattish face in, I could see that, well, another man finding my wife so irresistible that he'll attempt a classroom seduction, that means we need to look again at our marriage and it meant I should look at trying to hang on to what I've got, rather than let some smarmy git tease her away from under my nose. And, you know. I haven't been completely fair. Because I've been no angel either, in all honesty.'

I am tight with dread. 'Oh.' I listen to the sound of the waves crashing, in the distance. I want to put my fingers in my ears and shout something random so I don't have to hear. 'It's Sarah,' I say instead.

'Nothing actually happened. But yes. It was Sarah. I guess you noticed from my emails. Which were slightly written to make you jealous, in a childish sort of way. The moment you were gone, we did everything together, with the kids.'

'I noticed that. It was the last set of photos that meant I knew for sure.'

'And when Gav went away, then, more so. I leaned on her completely because it was actually a lot harder, dealing with the boys day in, day out, than I thought it was going to be. Doing all the things you've always done. Much more fun when there's another adult to talk to.'

I smile, in spite of myself. 'Isn't it just?'

'I was scared about her drinking, as well. I told myself I needed to keep an eye. And I suppose we got a bit closer than . . .'

'And . . . ?'

We both start walking on. I think it is going to be easier to hear this if we are doing something, moving, looking ahead. I don't want to be watching his face at this moment.

'I guess we started flirting with each other,' he says, in a strained voice. 'One moment it was harmless – we kept laughing about how wherever we went, people assumed we were married with four kids – and then it wasn't any more. We started getting these moments, where we'd look at each other, and the seconds would tick by. We started talking to each other, sharing everything. Sorry, I know how much you don't want to hear this. One evening in particular, we came very close to . . .' He stops. 'Well, very close. Very close indeed.'

'But you didn't?'

'We nearly did. We talked about it. I'm sorry.'

Much as I don't want to, I can imagine this conversation: the flirty regrets, the 'if there weren't other people involved', the conspiratorial smiles. I have read about this happening; I even know its name.

'You had an "emotional affair",' I tell him. My voice is flat, carefully expressionless. 'It would almost have been better if you had, actually, let something happen and then hated each other and never spoken again.'

'Almost. But actually, I think not.' He pauses. 'But yes, I do see it. It is in no way better than your thing with Jim. Not worse. Not better. A mistake. And Tansy, I have no idea what I was thinking of. There's never been anyone for me but you. Never.'

'Oh, Christ,' I tell him. 'And Max, for me, too. No one. No one in the world could ever . . .' I can't finish my sentence. He knows what I mean.

The first drops of rain begin to fall. 'I know where we can go,' says Max, and he takes my arm and leads me down a side road.

I don't care about getting wet. I walk slowly, savouring the way my clothes stick to me.

'A minute ago,' I say, 'you said that I knew why you wanted to stay in London and forget that there were any other options,' I tell him. He slows down and looks at me.

'Yes.'

'But I don't.' The rain is falling down my nose. I don't care.

He raises his voice, so I can hear him above the rain. 'Don't you? Really?'

'No.'

He smiles. His hair is plastered to his forehead, and he looks very different. He looks like he did when I first met him.

'I thought you did,' he shouts. 'I thought that was understood. It was to keep you safe. That was all. To make sure nothing could ever happen to you again, after all the bad things that have happened in your life. It only occurred to me very recently that a life where nothing ever happens to you is not, perhaps, all that great.' He takes my hand and pulls me across the road. I run next to him, savouring the water all over my body, my sticky clothes, my slick skin.

'Look, we're here. The Ganesh Temple.'

A live elephant stands outside the temple. I recognise it at once as the elephant from Elly's postcard, the one that I used to stare at, back in London. It is decorated with bright lines and patterns painted on to it. There is a garland of flowers around its gargantuan neck. The flowers are dropping and the painted decorations are beginning to run in the rain. Its trunk is waving around, seeking out something to touch.

'Stand in front of it,' Max says, and he takes out his camera. As soon as I am in range, the elephant touches me on the head with its trunk. A man walks past, putting up a black umbrella.

'Touched by Elephant!' he says. 'Very good luck.'

chapter fifty

The sun comes out, and dazzles me as it reflects off the rain that has pooled on the balcony. Amber and Sam have just caught a train south, to Madurai. I hope their train is safe now. The torrents could wash it off its very tracks. It is still raining, though less violently, and I poke my head out for long enough to look for a rainbow.

Delphine just wandered off. 'I wait for a place to pull me,' she said. 'While I wait, I stay by the beach.'

Our backpacks are packed. I was touched when I discovered that Max, the City man, had brought a backpack on his rescue mission, rather than an expensive suitcase. When I said so, he smiled.

'You do realise,' he said, 'that it wasn't a rescue mission?'

'What do you mean? Of course it was. I was desperate, and then you were there.'

'It wasn't. What would have happened if I hadn't turned up when and where I did? You had already got yourself from the forest, to the bus, to the homeless guy, which was a stroke of brilliance if I may say so, to the hotel. You sorted things out by looking at the paper, while I was attempting to formulate a brilliant plan, scared shitless that the boys wouldn't see you for twenty years. You would have been completely fine. I didn't charge in and pluck you from disaster, Tans. Don't rewrite it in your head to make yourself less capable.'

I thought about it. 'Oh,' I said. 'Yeah. Maybe.'

* * *

Through the drips and drops, I can see a figure running down the street. He has a plastic bag, uselessly, on top of his head, and his clothes are drenched. He reaches the hotel, and a few seconds later he appears, in his very own puddle, in our room.

'Hey,' he says, wiping his face uselessly with a thin towel. 'Um, our taxi's booked. And I'm wet.'

I let him hug me. I don't care about the wet. I pull him closer.

'Better get you out of these wet things, then,' I tell him. 'Hadn't we?'

Nobody ever told me this would happen. Lola was full of talk about not neglecting my husband's needs, about looking after myself. Neither she nor anyone else ever told me that it was possible to fall in love all over again, and to know that, this time, it is real, grown-up, and based on more than infatuation.

We are going back to London, to our jobs (or lack thereof) and our flat and our lives. I hope that things are going to be different. Max has promised that, in a year or two, he will ask for a sabbatical, and the four of us will spend six months somewhere new, doing something. We have talked endlessly about what it might be. I still want to come back to India. Max is, surprisingly, open to the idea.

'Do you really promise?' I asked him, sceptical. 'You won't get back into office life, and shut off from it all again?'

'I really promise,' he said. 'Going away does you good and we're unbelievably fortunate to be able to do it. Anyway, maybe I'll be made redundant by then. It's quite likely. We can set up home somewhere cheap.'

'We should stop flying, really. Greenhouse gases and all.'

'So we'll go overland. Ten times the adventure.'

I grinned. 'Deal.'

In return, I have promised to keep my alcohol consumption down to no more than two drinks per night, except on special occasions. I am going to earmark two days a week as dry days. I hope I can do it. Right now, I can hardly think of drinking at all, but I know that this will change when I'm back in the flat again, when my life is once again marked out by school runs, and when I find myself jobless, disinclined to go back to my own business, and wondering what to do. I wish I could get involved with children like the girls in the orphanage. Perhaps, in some way, I can. I need to keep the perspective it gave me.

I am not sure what it will be like, going home and picking up and starting again. In a way it feels braver than anything else I have done, and certainly it is more frightening than coming to India ever was.

As we get into the jeep that will take us to the airport, I look at Max's profile. He is watching the rain coursing down the glass. I look at the colonial mansions, soaked by the rain, retreating behind us. As we pass along the seafront, I watch the immense waves swelling up, almost reaching the promenade. I look at the few people who are out, hurrying along, holding covers over their heads.

'Home,' I tell him.

He looks at me. 'Home,' he agrees.

'But there's one thing,' I tell him, 'that I need to do on the way.'

Ethan is in his usual place, shaking and jolting around, holding conversations with people no one else can see. He is apparently oblivious to the rain, which is dripping off the end of his nose, washing some of his grime away. He twitches and twists, laughing and grimacing.

'Morning,' I say. He sees me and smiles, indicating the pavement with his head. I sit down without hesitation.

Ethan turns to me and whispers, in a loud stage whisper. 'Who is that? You know there's a man standing there?'

'This is Max,' I tell him. 'My husband.'

'The husband came?'

Max nods. 'The husband came,' he agrees. 'Look, thanks for bailing her out. We appreciate it.'

'Here,' I tell him. 'You said it was the parable of the fucking talents. So here, your money's grown.'

I hand him a bundle of notes. He doesn't look at it, just secretes it somewhere with a lightning movement, as if we are likely to change our minds.

'Yeah,' he says. 'No problem.'

Max crouches down, obviously unwilling to sit on the pavement. 'Look,' he says. 'Far be it from me to tell you what to do, but if you want we could help you. You could come with us now and have a shower, get cleaned up, cut your hair, get some clothes. There's plenty of money there for new clothes and stuff. Get back on your feet. Up to you.'

Ethan looks away. He twists his neck so he is looking as far away as he possibly can.

''S all right,' he says.

I see Max about to push the point, and I know Ethan will not respond well, so I try to change the subject.

'We're going now, Ethan,' I tell him. 'Back to London. So I won't be seeing you again, but I'll be thinking of you. My Chennai buddy.'

He grins. 'Yeah. I'll be thinking of you too, darlin'. I might even miss having you drop by.'

'You can change this, you know.'

'Yeah.'

I look at Max. He inclines his head. I hold my breath, kiss Ethan's cheek, and jump up. The taxi is waiting.

chapter fifty-one

Alexia's thoughts.

Back home.

Well, all I can say is, it's time to wind up the blog. This is the last entry I will make – although according to Rajiv, my lawyer, it did help get us out when he used it as evidence for our good intentions.

I cannot in fact talk about what happened in India. I can't think about that little girl. But she comes to me in my dreams. She looks over her shoulder at that woman, and then she reaches up and takes my hand. That is what happened, once. She put her hand in mine, and I had my daughter. It lasted for a few seconds. And the police ran out of the trees, and my life as I know it ended.

I see that Dee did a good job of updating the blog while I was unable to. I haven't read her entries yet, though, because I don't want to think about it. Both Duncan and I are uncomfortable with the fact that she was, in spite of our horrible time, pretty much taken with India. Mom said she's thinking of going back there, for a vacation. Duncan says it's George that she's taken with, and he could be right. I don't want to know.

We couldn't go back there if we wanted to. No great loss.

I have started to make inquiries about adopting from

China. No short cuts this time. We will stay on the waiting list as long as it takes, do all the paperwork it takes. I am not in a hurry this time. I am terrified that our experience in India will count against us.

But for the moment, we are pretending not to be local celebrities. We don't think about everyone looking at us and talking about us. They all think we were so stupid.

I don't think about that little girl. I spend every moment of every day not thinking about her.

Signing off for ever now.

Alexia

Comments disabled.

chapter fifty-two

I run to the flat, while Max is paying the cab, and press the door-bell five times. When Lola answers, I push past her, run past the wedding photos, and around the corner into the flat. The boys are sitting on the floor, making Lego castles.

'It's Mummy!' Joe yells.

'Hi, Mum,' says Toby, and he stands up and looks at me, shyly pleased. I walk straight up to him and pick him up. He is taller than he was, and heavier, and so lanky that it is hard to lift him, but I hoist him to my waist anyway.

'Toby,' I say. I bury my face in his hair, nuzzle his cheek and his neck. I smell his smell. It is a drug. 'Sweetheart. I've missed you so much. I will never, ever go away like that again, unless you come too.'

He submits to my hugs and kisses for a while.

'You weren't away for *that* long,' he says, when he pulls away and wriggles down.

'Toby!' Max interjects, from the door.

'But we did miss you,' he adds. 'Of course we did, because you're our mum.'

I am trying not to cry, but failing. Max puts a hand on my shoulder.

'I realised while I was away,' I manage to say, 'that I am the luckiest mummy in the world. There are so many people out there . . . and so many children . . . Well. Just that we should all love each other and appreciate each other and be nice to each other because we're unbelievably lucky.'

'Did you get me a present?' Toby asks.

Joe is standing back, gazing at me in wonder.

'Mummy,' he says, and when I open my arms, he launches himself at me like a bullet. I just have time to crouch down before he smacks into me. I cuddle him closely, smell him, and pull him tighter. I look at Toby over his head. Toby is looking through my handbag, searching for goodies.

'Home,' I say to Max. Everything about it feels right.

'There's no I in team,' he says, smiling. 'But there is an "us" in marriage.'

'No there's not,' Toby objects.

'Metaphorically speaking, Tobes,' Max says, 'metaphorically speaking.' He hands him a giant Toblerone.

Joe pulls away from me, and races for the chocolate. In their lives, this has been a blip, a tiny interlude.

I have been back home for nearly a week, when I notice something.

I have a large family, and I have friends. Sarah, almost inconceivably, is still my friend. It is hard, at first, but I tell myself that Max has had to get over my misdemeanour and give his blessing to the fact that I am delivering Toby into the care of Mr Trelawney each day, and so I must get over his, too. I make an effort, and find that I can do it: I can forgive them both. Sarah is terrified of me, at first. I see her at the school gates, and she shuffles away and avoids my eyes.

'Sarah,' I say. 'It's all right. Honestly, it is.'

She eyes me warily. 'It's not really, though,' she says. 'Is it?'

She's moving to Singapore in six months. This makes it easier. I convince her that we can still be friends, and eventually she believes me. Things are different from the way they used to be, but they had to change anyway. I am surprised at how magnanimous I am able to be. She agrees to go to yoga with me on Tuesday evenings, until they move. We have allocated Friday nights for drinking, if we feel like it. Other than that, we will do our best to develop a joint tea habit. I cannot slip back into solitary drinking: there is too much at stake.

On my first day taking Toby to school, I was so tense that I barely registered how surprising it was when a skinny woman with bad hair stopped me outside the gates and said, 'How was India?' I murmured some platitudes, and she said, 'I've always longed to go. I think we all had a few pangs of envy about that one.'

I was so surprised that I had to talk to her.

'I don't even know your name,' I admitted. 'So please tell me, Olivia's Mum, who you really are.'

She laughed. 'Hannah. And I know you're Tansy, but I didn't until recently.'

We walked in together, and so I had the most unlikely moral support possible when I came face to face with Jim.

'Good morning,' he said, and he smiled, but I thought it was a nice smile, not a lecherous one.

'Hello, Mr Trelawney,' I said firmly, and I kissed Toby goodbye.

'Did you hear?' Jim said. 'I've resigned. Come the summer, I'll be out of here and on the first plane to some waves.'

'Oh, how lovely,' I said politely, and turned and left the room.

Hannah was still with me.

'That's over with, at least,' she said, and winked, and walked off.

I spend time with my siblings, and Lola and my father. All of them, I notice, are good company. In fact, I almost have as good a support network as the one Sam's family have in Poosarippatti. Dad and Lola would love to be included in everything we do. Briony, Jake and Archie still live at home and would happily spend time with me and the boys. When I look around now, I see people everywhere. Even the flat is spacious and airy. It is nothing like the prison I built it into in my mind. It is our home, and it is perfectly big enough for four. I start to think about the little garden, which I always ignored. I could plant things, put chairs out there, make a barbecue.

On Sunday morning, I hold both the boys' hands as we head

to a café for a celebratory breakfast. Max grins at me over their heads. I know this is a honeymoon of some sort, that it will not be this easy for ever, but I am going to give it my best shot.

'Don't go to India again, Mum,' says Toby, when we are halfway across the road. A car comes round the corner, and we walk quickly to the other side.

'I'd like to, actually,' I tell him. 'One day.'

'But we will go with you, to Injia,' suggests Joe.

Toby looks at me, waiting for the answer. So does Max.

'Yes,' I tell them. 'Next time, you will.'

chapter fifty-three

Alexia's thoughts

I stopped this blog, but now I am reopening it again just to say that we are planning to travel to China in the fall, to meet a little girl by the name of Mei-li. It means 'pretty' and we are not going to change it although we might Americanize the spelling.

I will not keep a record of it as this reminds me too much of what happened to us in India. But I want to share the news.

I am terrified. Duncan pretends he isn't affected by our experiences in Chennai, and we rarely talk about them. I will not rest until we are back on home turf.

Wish us luck.

Alexia

Comments: 1

Alexia, please take this in the spirit in which it is intended: an apology. You know something of what happened, but you don't know why. Trust me that the other children are safe, well, housed in loving homes. You did humanity a service and we are happy beyond belief that you will at last get your little girl. You have no idea what a great thing you did for the other children.

I don't think you ever saw the orphanage in Mamallapuram where Sasika was living. I know (and I regret) that you saw the Indian prison system. Think of the worst aspects of that, multiply it tenfold, and apply it to children. That's where they live, with no prospect of escape if that orphanage is not on the Cara list for adoption.

Because of you and Duncan, fifteen children are out of places like that. That is fifteen children you have gifted a future to. The place where Sasika lives now is far more tolerable, and we have every hope that she will end up with a loving family – that may be underway already.

Truly, everything else pales into insignificance. I have no regrets about any of it. Sure, we used people, we burned a lot of bridges of our own, but we did it for a reason. I hope you will come to appreciate this.

Thank you. Remember, earthly laws count for nothing. Don't try to find us, but one day the two of us will contact you again.